The Rise of

Synne

LP O'Bryan

Copyright © 2024 LP O'Bryan

All rights reserved. No part of this publication may be reproduced, distributed, or transmitted in any form or by any means, including photocopying, recording, or other electronic or mechanical methods, without the prior written permission of the publisher. For permission requests, write to the publisher at the address below.

Ardua Publishing
Argus House, Malpas Street
Dublin 8,
Ireland
http://arduapublishing.com

Ordering Information: Contact the publisher.

This novel is a work of fiction.
The role played by real historical figures in this narrative is entirely fictional.
The imagined characters, however, abide by the generally known facts about the period in which the novel is set.

"I'll tell the loveliest dreams, stained with the foulest sins."

The Prophecies of Gytha.

Historical Background

This story is set in 1066, in England, in the period leading up to and following the defeat of the English forces at the Battle of Hastings.

That battle, which lasted an entire day, changed the course of English history. A Norman duke, William, later called the Conqueror, defeated an English army under King Harold and killed him on the battlefield. This story is mainly about what happens next.

1

At our evening meals, Mother made us hold hands while she whispered the prayer. I loved the feathery way she spoke and how she smelled, and my sisters and my brother too, and the way we all lived. I'd close my eyes as she recited, the veil of her love wrapping around us.

"One of you'll see the future. One will heal with hands, and one will marry the son of a king and become a queen." Mother always said that after the prayer, in her hushed tone, as if that made it more real. Then she'd look around and listen. That part disturbed me, but I got used to it and her predictions, and as I grew, I knew not one of them applied to me. When I reached my twentieth summer, they were all far beyond reach.

"Keep one ear open tonight," she said the day they came, the day she died, the day our lives shattered and my brother and I fled into the night, never to return, for fear that they might take us too.

2

Three Months Later

The Retreat from the Battle

"I do not care if I die." I bit my lip to stop me whispering the words again, in case my brother heard them. Stefan's eyebrow was twitching already. He was fidgeting too, his hand moving oddly, clutching at his cloak, then lifting his hand axe, then slipping it back into the loop on his belt, then clutching at his cloak again. Stefan is the best brother anyone could have. He shares his food and holds me tight when I want to give up and when we're cold we dance and laugh, despite all that has happened.

I'd been wondering when he'd start to blame me. "If you had real powers like Mother, you'd have seen all this coming," he said, his tone icy.

"I never said I had her powers," I hissed. Luck falling the right way, surviving something by a hair's breadth, these are things I could lay claim to.

The Rise of Synne

"Our last chance is gone," he said, despair twisting at his words. He'd leaned so close to me as he spoke, I could smell fear in his sweat.

"We are lucky to be alive," I replied. He grunted his disdain. I repeated the words as we walked along that moonlit forest path, all of us up to our ankles in churned mud from the spitting rain and the passage of the others who'd fled before us. Above our heads, giant beech, elms, and oaks creaked in the icy October wind.

But where were the Normans? That was the question that kept me moving, despite the bone tiredness, the aches and pains from stitching and scorching wounds, until I'd fallen to my knees, hands trembling, while the roars and whimpers of the injured and dying echoed like a chorus from hell.

"We are lucky to be alive."

"It feels good to be this lucky," he said with a snort.

My hands were fists. I forced them to loosen. They became fists again, out of my control. I pushed away the longing to turn, to look around, to check again for the Normans coming for us with their axes raised.

It came back to me then how I used to race to our mother, crying from the teasing of my older sisters, my hands in fists, like they are now. She'd soothed me every time with a promise that I'd been gifted as her youngest daughter.

And it was true; one of her gifts kept both Stefan and me alive. Healing, which I'd learned at her knee, gave us both hope, and had brought us here, bound to our fate.

Stefan staggered as he walked beside me. I pushed at his shoulder. He must not fall.

The stupid song we'd sung on the way to battle came back to me. The one they'd said would be sung on every street corner in London after our easy victory. It rhymed about a mighty eagle defending its young from foreign hawks.

But the hawks had won. They'd have to write a different song now.

A low growl made me turn. The stream of men behind us were grey-faced, staring, exhausted. Behind them, the moonlit path curved back to our pursuers, who would, no doubt, be coming soon.

"I thought we'd all be dead by now." Stefan's tone was sprightly.

"There's too many of us for them to kill us quick," I said. "It's hard work, killing. They'll need a rest after today." I touched the head of my hand axe, moved it to a more comfortable position on my belt. It had been knocking against my knee through my long tunic. I was proud of my skill with the hand axe. I especially liked how useful it was at keeping dull-witted men at bay.

A shout made us turn.

The Rise of Synne

"Let's stand to the side a while." I kept my voice low.

"We have to keep going," said Stefan.

I poked at him. "We need to see who's coming. Be quiet," I hissed in his ear.

We stood under a thick oak whose branches reached almost across the path and stared at the line of broken men as they trudged past. I waved at a man I knew and at others, too. "The healer is with us," one man called out. He raised a hand, palm towards me. Some men thought I could heal by touch, and I knew not to deny it. Faith can cure the worst afflictions.

The smell of damp leaves and rotting branches was all around us here. Stefan nudged me. "Who are you waiting for?" he asked.

I shook my head. We needed help to find our sisters, but I wasn't going to talk about that now.

"You did well, Stefan. Mother would have been proud of you."

A clamour of distant barking came. Fighting hounds, most likely. Let it be our men.

I went up on my toes, squinted back along the path. One of King Harold's thegns was riding towards us, his chain mail glistening liquid in the moonlight, hounds barking beside him, looking around eagerly as they ran, as if they might rip apart the next thing they saw. The thegn was a raven-haired man I'd seen sharpening blades the day before, for King Harold's sons.

I breathed in deep, put my hands up. I had to stop him. His hounds skirted around me. Two turned about, sniffing, slobbering, reaching up to me with their wet noses, their long white teeth. I said the animal calming charm, kept my head up. The growling diminished as the thegn stopped, his horse blowing hot breath into my face.

"Are you with King Harold's liege men?" I asked.

"Who are you to stop me?" He looked pale, drawn, worn out.

"A healer from your camp followers."

He shook his head and without replying, kicked his horse to walk on. I walked beside it. The stink of horse sweat enveloped me. He'd been riding hard. Stefan followed us.

"Did the king's sons or his brothers survive?" I leaned up, asked again when he didn't reply, louder this time. Our fate would hang on who'd survived the battle.

When the thegn looked down at me, it was as if he was staring at me from a hilltop. His words came slow.

"The king's dead. His brothers are dead. Is that not enough?"

The words sent shivers through me. "Did any of the king's sons survive?" I said loudly, going up on my toes. We had to know if there was anyone left who could help

The Rise of Synne

us find Tate and Gytha. It was why we'd joined their army, for help.

"They did," he said. He gestured behind with his thumb. "Two sons follow close enough, thank God." He pressed his fist to his chest in thanks.

A wave of relief rose inside me, as if a long-worked weaving had been completed with his words.

As he rode on, picking up speed, clods of earth flew. I stepped off the path.

"You really think the king's sons will help us?" asked Stefan.

"Have you a better idea?"

"Did you foresee all this?" He sounded peeved. He often sounds peeved with me, as if our predicament was my fault. There are benefits to being an older sister, but getting a younger brother to do the right thing is not one of them. "Is this the curse again?"

Stefan thinks our mother being a seer, as well as a healer, is the curse that brought ruin on us all.

"We're not cursed, Stefan." My words came out shrill, perhaps from fear that he was right, though I would never admit it.

He must not think we're cursed. Men who feel cursed throw their lives away in any skirmish.

His face glowed like snow in the moonlight. He was still my younger brother, but we were far from the woods we used to play in. I got an urge to hug him. To my regret, I did not.

"We're good Christians from a good Christian family." My tone was firm. "There is no curse. We do what the priests tell us. We can do no more."

Something was moving behind him. I squinted into the gloom, went up on my toes. Was this how it would end for us, with bickering?

Riders were coming. Men in mail shirts.

Our men, thank God. Some had bloody swords by their sides, others held axes, and every one of them was stained with blood from head to booted toe.

My chest tightened. Magnus, one of dead King Harold's sons, was in the middle of the group, his mail shirt loose, fresh blood streaking from his bare shoulder. But he was alive and staring ahead and soon he'd be past us.

Magnus was about my age, younger than many of the fighting men, and he needed someone to bind his wound. I did not care what people said about him, how arrogant he was. I did not dream of king's sons, like others did. Such dreams are foolish for an orphan and worse, forbidden, likely only to lead to shame and laughter.

But he could help us.

"Lord Magnus," I shouted as I stepped into the path. He looked down at me with blank eyes. My greeting had come out wrong, too cheerful for this desperate moment. I felt deeply stupid, but I shouted the words again, louder, as if some spirit had taken control of me. "Lord Magnus."

He looked at me. I bowed. You could never be sure how a lord will react to being called on.

He slowed his horse to allow me to walk alongside him. A bloody bruise marred his cheek. The skin around it was purple already, and his hands were blood-stained claws.

"Your wound must be covered, my lord. I'm a healer. I can help you."

He kept going, as if he hadn't heard me.

"We need you to survive, my lord." I raised my hand and smiled.

The briefest smile flickered on his lips.

"Perhaps you're right, healer," he said. He pulled his horse up and slid down to me, rocking forward as he reached the ground.

I put my hand out, held him, stopped him from falling. His blood felt warm and sticky on my fingers. I could smell his blood and sweat mixed together.

His horse pawed loudly at the mud at our feet, snorting, as if it wanted to keep going. Grunts and neighing echoed all around us. The other horsemen had stopped and were dismounting. Only one other had gold trim on his tunic under his mail shirt like Magnus. He had long wheaten hair, as pale as mine, and his moustache was thicker than Magnus's, and his face lined with deep grooves. This was Edmund, Magnus's older brother. Everyone knew who they were, Edmund and Magnus, sons of the late King Harold, two of the most powerful young men in the land. I bowed again as Edmund approached.

"You have to stop?" he shouted.

"Yes," said Magnus. "Ride on, if you want."

Edmund glanced back along the path and wrapped his mail-clad arms around his chest.

Magnus grunted, pointed at a nearby tree. "This is a good spot," he said. "Be quick, healer."

He stumbled, swiped me away as I went to help him, then sat under the oak and with a groan, pushed his mail shirt further away from the wound on his shoulder.

I could taste blood on my lips as I peered closer. Thankfully, the wound was not deep, and only a hand's breadth long. It did not need to be burnt and I still had catgut, a needle, and a slick of honey and willow bark salve in a pot at the bottom of my bag. I took the pot, opened it, threaded my needle, and quickly put three stitches across his wound, then rubbed a little salve on, gently. He groaned, stared at me, his eyes searching. Most people see my hair, in strings in the old mourning style, with its horrible new almost-white streaks – they came so fast after our misfortune – and wonder if they should stay away from me in case what had happened to me was catching.

"You trained as a physic, yes?"

I raised my hands. "No, I'm no physic. I'm a village healer. I know how to stitch wounds and apply salves. Healers were only asked to follow the King's army because there was a lack of physics after the march from the north." I gave him my best respectful nod and didn't add that only men can dare call themselves physics, but I can stitch and cure with herbs and bark as good as any of them and can say the same prayers they do too and other powerful ones as well.

A monk appeared beside us. I shied back. Monks were not always appreciative of healers.

This monk held his hand out and put his finger to the lip of my salve pot when I held it out to him. He scraped a little from it. I pulled the pot away. I would not allow him to waste any of it.

"Is this made with the old craft?" asked the monk as he sniffed at his fingers. "Are you a sorceress?"

"I'm a follower of Christ," I said, spitting the words out. There could be no mistake on that issue. I made a sign of the cross. "Everything I use and do has been blessed by a priest. Is that good enough?"

He sneered, as if he suspected I was lying.

"Who are you?" he asked, his eyes roaming over my rough, ankle-length, blood-stained tunic.

"Synne, from York," I said. "One of the king's healers."

"Well, Synne from York, your rightful punishment, if Lord Magnus dies tonight, will be to have your tongue cut out and fed to the birds."

My heart quickened, but I'd heard this type of thing before. Threats from people who thought harsh words would improve my healing skills, and I should be used to them, but every time I heard them, my gut tightened. I know what men can do.

"Lord Magnus will not die tonight. His wound is not deep." I said it with a scoff, sounding more confident than I felt. I hadn't even checked him for other wounds. I bent closer. "Anyone got a wineskin?" I shouted. Healers, I'd discovered, were among the only women who could demand things. I went too far with this, Stefan often told me, but I knew he was just jealous, either that or afraid.

Someone handed me a skin. I poured a little wine over the wound. Magnus grunted deep in his throat. The wine was yellow. It had honey in it. Good. I moved closer to look at my stitches. He was lucky, they were holding. A sigh went up behind me. Others had also seen the wound and my stitches. I rubbed a little more salve on his skin around the wound. He winced. I ripped a strip from the last

The Rise of Synne

of my linen, wrapped it around his shoulder, and pulled it tight. He sniffed and stared at me, his eyes blazing. I smiled, whispered a healing prayer, then a protective charm I'd learned long ago, and finally I touched his forehead and said a Hail Mary, loudly.

He grunted his thanks, his gaze flickering over me. For a moment I imagined I saw a flicker of longing there, but I shook my head. Do not be a fool.

"Can he ride, healer?" said an irritated voice behind me. His brother Edmund was standing over us.

"He can, but if it pleases my lord, give him a moment for my prayers to take hold." I kept my head up, a smile on my face. Lords do not like to be denied, but perhaps the brother would ride on and leave us.

"He must ride now. He cannot be taken alive," said Edmund. He put a wineskin to his mouth. Blood smeared around his lips as if he'd bitten someone's face off. Nothing would surprise me after what I'd seen. Stefan was standing behind Edmund watching all this, an astonished look on his face. He thinks I should hold my tongue tighter and bow more.

"Are you that healer who advised my father to rush to battle?" asked Edmund, leaning down towards me. A tingle of fear licked across my gut like the edge of a cold knife. I'd said to one man-at-arms on the way to battle that it was a good thing the king's army marched so fast. Was that what Edmund meant? Lords are good at finding people to blame.

"I never met the great King Harold, my lord," I said firmly.

Edmund's mouth twisted. "If my father had listened to me, and not the words of people like you, he'd be alive and in London, and my uncles would all be alive and with us too." He spoke fast, his nostrils flaring. One hand was near his axe head, at his belt. His fingers were twitching.

"I swear it, I never advised the king."

Magnus raised his hand. "Perhaps if you were more persuasive, brother, our father would still be alive."

His words sent a chill into the air. Edmund shook his head, turned away.

A rumble in the earth made us all look towards the path. No pursuing horsemen were visible in the moonlight stretching towards darkness and trees, though many of the men around us had their blood-smeared axes up already.

Stefan had his small axe in his hand. He was on the far side of the path now, grinning. I knew what that meant. He thought this was the moment he'd prove himself in front of these lords. He didn't realise that the only reason he'd been allowed to stay with this army was that I'd said he'd have no one if they sent him away.

And I'd have no one if he left me.

Thank Christ, the older healer who'd allowed me to join the army had a heart. I pulled my small axe from my belt. I'd heard too many dying screams to think violent death would be painless, but I would face it with all the strength I could muster. I could not run away with my brother this time.

Be iron-strong, was one of my mother's sayings. *There is no place for weakness in this world.*

Magnus had stumbled to his feet near me, his large axe up high now. "Get behind me," he said.

Normans on horseback, in their dark mail shirts with their swords up, shouting in their crude language, were charging towards us, their horses sending mud flying.

Thirty paces.

Twenty.

I raised my axe, put it to my shoulder, ready to swing or throw, knowing it was puny against what was coming. Cold sweat sprang across my brow. It slid down my back and chest, tickling me. My leg trembled. I firmed them. I could not let fear win. The rumble of the charging horses shook the ground under us.

"Hold fast," came a shouted command.

I could do nothing else. My chest had frozen. I would have to throw my axe or slash with it soon. Could I do it?

I'd not come face to face with Normans all that day. I'd spent it tending wounds, listening to the clash of weapons and roars, until it seemed normal to be terrified and not care about it and I'd started joking.

Now I could see the whites of their mount's eyes.

And the Normans in their iron helmets. Their blood-slicked mail shirts, each costing enough to buy a youngish slave, reaching down below their waists.

"Kill them all," hissed the monk. I had at one time expected a little more "thou shalt not kill," from Christ's followers, but I could not fault him, as the prospect of having our heads chopped off was mouth-wateringly near.

Roars echoed all around. The lead Norman glared contemptuously; his broken yellow teeth visible now as his lips curled.

He was almost on us.

I steadied my hand, hurled my axe, stepped to the side. I did not want it to strike his horse. I wanted it to strike the rider in his fat belly, but the blade bit into the horse's shoulder and shuddered as blood spurted. The horse reared. I went back a step. The rider struggled to regain control, grabbing wildly with one hand for the horse's neck. Two other Normans on horseback had gone around him; one had a black spear.

"Stefan," I screamed instinctively. I ran in front of the injured Norman horse, my head scrunched down to avoid its swinging head.

The Rise of Synne

I crossed the muddy path. Stefan had already thrown his axe. He was standing stiff and upright with his dagger in his other hand. I knew what he was going to do – rush inside with his knife. If he brought a Norman rider down, he could live off that for many moons.

I was almost on him. My hands came up to push him back.

But a black spear appeared in his chest, buried deep, as if it had always been there, though a moment before it had not. My neck strained. "No!" He had no mail shirt, nothing to protect him.

His hands came up to hold the spear. Then he smiled at me and crumpled.

And exploding stars appeared.

3

The fog came in so fast they were lucky to find the stony beach. It had been gleaming in the moonlight since the sun went down, but the fog had made it disappear until they were a spear throw away from the shore. They were lucky when they beached their ship that the tide pushed them high. The slippery stones slid under them like wet grass as they dragged the ship up the beach, helped by each icy wave.

The three men, the passengers on the longship, headed up the thin winding path towards the ancient stone circle, the light from the bonfire beckoning and soon near enough to see the stony path clearly, even when the moon went behind clouds.

Steady drumming and the wail of a pipe told them the ceremony was still in its early stages. They would be welcome.

It had been a long journey to find the man who'd sent them on their mission, first stopping at one port, then finding a ship that would take them to where he was

The Rise of Synne

raiding with his men, and then to here, to the bone festival on the far north islands.

On the other side of the circle, a group of warriors stood around the man they'd come to see. He wore a stag skull headdress, and his face was ash-white with black smears around his eyes and mouth.

When the jarl saw them approaching, he raised a hand and called them forward. The drumming stopped as they came close to him. The visitors stood in front of Jarl Erlend, then each of them went down on one knee.

"Did you do what I asked?" said the jarl.

The man kneeling a little in front of the others looked up. "Two daughters we sold into slavery. The mother died fighting for their honour."

The jarl nodded. "The youngest daughter, what about her, was she sold? And what of the son?"

"Both are dead a long time, the sisters told us."

The jarl shook his head. "You are a fool. They were alive in the springtime when we discovered where they'd been hiding."

He stepped forward and, as if from nowhere, a heavy black axe appeared in his hand. With a quick swing, he took the head off the man who'd answered his questions. Blood spurted high and onto his thick seal-skin boots.

He bent down to the other men and shouted.

"Go back. Find the youngest daughter. She too must be sold into slavery. They must never come together again. They are devil spawn. Do not come back until it is done."

4

Something wet fell onto my forehead. My head pounded horribly, as if a busy blacksmith had found his way inside. I opened my eyes.

"Stefan?" I asked, remembering what had happened and struggling to get up.

The monk kneeling beside me pushed me back down. He was holding a wet cloth to my forehead. Men were standing in a half circle around us. I was propped up against a tree. Bodies lay beyond. *Please, Stefan must be alive.* Churning cold grew inside me.

The monk made the sign of the cross over me. "You must recite your prayers every day," he said.

Hope rose inside me. "Stefan is alive?"

The monk stared down at me, his eyes narrowing, as if assessing whether to tell me something.

"You will live, healer. That is the miracle. The boy you were foolishly rushing to help is with our Lord and in a better place than this. What was he to you?" His tone was cold, tired. He'd seen too much death.

I could not answer him.

It was not true.

He'd made a mistake.

I tried to lean up again. A hollow opened inside me as I wondered if the monk was telling the truth. My chin quivered. I had to control it.

"Rest," said the monk, pushing me back. "You will see his body later. Was he your husband?"

I stared at the monk, hoping he would stop talking, just go away. This was all a bad dream. That moment the Normans had appeared and Stefan had been alive was so near, so close; could I not go back to it?

"The Normans?" I asked.

"We killed a few of them. The rest rode off. They're a scouting party. They'll report soon, no doubt bragging about how many of us they cut down."

An aching tiredness pulled at me, starting in my legs, working its way up through me.

"Stefan cannot be dead," I whispered. The monk was playing some game with me. Did he want me to pray for Stefan? Why would he lie to me?

The monk sighed loudly, pointed off to one side. "The dead are all there," he said matter-of-factly. "My novice died too. May they all rest in peace." He sounded resigned to death.

The Rise of Synne

I could not accept it so easily. I dug my fingers deep into the earth, into the slime. I had to wake from this dream. A damp, musty smell filled my nostrils.

The monk was reciting a prayer over me.

I should be the one dead. My thoughts jumbled on top of each other. How would I tell such news to my sisters? My throat tightened. I blinked. Stefan appeared in my mind, laughing. Then I saw our mother scolding him but smiling. Then a voice called to me. Mother?

"You've been saved for a reason, Synne," her voice whispered.

What an idea. Could it be true? If only. But if it was true, what was I being saved for?

I whispered a prayer. The monk made the sign of the cross again, stood, helped me to my feet.

Three bodies had been lined up beneath an old oak tree. One of them was wearing something that looked like Stefan's thick winter tunic. The pale face was half turned towards me. Panic threatened.

It was Stefan.

My chin quivered again. My breathing turned fast, and a flush of warmth rolled through me. I had to force this weakness away. I bit my lower lip as my face scrunched.

Magnus appeared beside the monk. "We have to go, Ulf."

I wrapped my arms around myself.

"I'll put her in front of me on my horse," said the monk.

"Do it," said Magnus. "We must move. There will be more of them coming."

I could not leave Stefan here, exposed like this to the snuffling animals.

"I will stay and bury my brother," I said loudly. He deserved to be buried. I would do it myself if I had to. I put both fists to my chest.

"The Normans are coming," said Magnus, steel in his voice. "They will be here any moment."

"I must bury my brother," I said louder. "He will not lie here for the wolves and the boars."

The monk Ulf gripped my shoulder, warning me not to argue with my betters. I shrugged my shoulder. I did not care what happened to me.

"If you're lucky, they'll just cut your throat," said Ulf.

"I will hide in the woods when they come. I know how to do that. They'll not find me. That is my brother's body." I pointed angrily towards Stefan, my hand shaking out of my control.

"I left my father's and my uncles' bodies on the field of battle. You will leave your brother." Magnus's words came hot and slow. His face had twisted. It looked as if he was having trouble holding himself from striking me.

The Rise of Synne

He nodded towards the monk. "Tie her across your horse; she cannot stay," he said. He put his blood-stained face close to mine. "My brother saw you helping our men today. He says you're a good healer. Lock your grief away." He raised his fist.

My fists tightened. "My brother died for you."

Magnus shook his head. "You want vengeance?" he said. His eyes were rock-hard.

I nodded.

"You must live to find it."

Memories of Stefan and my mother and sisters were flickering through my mind, a procession of faces.

"The village near here will bury the bodies," he said. He turned away. "They will know what to do."

I stared at his back. His arrogance was a wall. Stefan had told me that King Harold's sons were hated. I could understand why now.

"I need to get something from my brother's body," I said, all that had happened bearing down on me like a heavy weight.

"Do it fast," said the monk, his expression gloomy.

I bent over Stefan, closed his eyes, folded his arms across his body, unfastened the pendant on the leather thong around his neck, and hung it around mine with my own, pushing it inside my tunic. The bloody hole in the middle of his chest was still weeping blood. A long terrible shiver passed through me from head to foot as I put my hand to Stefan's cheek. It was still warm. Why was he not alive? My tears flowed hot then, streaming unstoppable down my face and I rocked back and forth, overwhelmed, sick to my core, so empty, so alone.

I sensed the monk standing beside me. My face was wet and hot. I touched Stefan's matted hair. How could I leave him? No, I could not.

I let this happen. This was my fault. I should have watched him closely. He was my younger brother. My only brother. I was responsible.

Hands pulled at me. I resisted them, twisting away. I needed more time. The monk and another man jerked me to my feet. I struggled against them. My hands were bound, my feet too. And I was thrown over a horse, still struggling, gasping to get free.

I would not have left Stefan any other way.

After a while, when it became clear that my shouts and my squirming would not free me, I quietened, a pain deep in my chest, as the great oak Stefan rested under disappeared into the gloom. Ulf, behind me on the horse, did not speak as I sobbed lightly. Around us, men rode in silence.

5

The darkest part of the night had passed, and the moon had slipped away when we finally stopped, our horses whinnying and snickering at the prospect of an end to them not seeing properly where they were placing their hooves.

My grief and despair had curdled inside me and turned into fierce determination. I cursed the Normans many times, loudly, to cheers. And then I cursed them quietly, wishing the pox on them all and that their eyes would spin in their heads.

What gave me strength was the memory of my mother's voice, which I'd heard when the monk told me what had happened. I was being saved for a reason. I did not know what it was, but there was a reason I'd survived. To save my sisters, I hoped. I whispered to my mother's voice, hoping that more guidance would come, but got no response.

The monk cut the rope around my feet before he pulled me down from the horse, then asked me, his hand gripping my arm tight, "Will you run if I set your hands free?"

"No." I hated him for taking me away from Stefan, but I would not get far if I ran.

"You made the right decision," said the monk as he cut the rope around my wrists. "Many things are about to change in this kingdom. Your skills will be needed."

"Why do you care, monk?" I asked. I had that light-headed feeling you get in dreams, when you don't know where you are, but your mind is clear, as if a storm has passed over.

He sniffed, pointed at the trees around us. "We stopped for some to relieve themselves. Do you need to go?"

I nodded.

"Do not go far," he said, his head to one side. His eyes were bloodshot. I wondered what he'd seen in the last few days. "Do you swear to Christ not to run away?"

I nodded.

I went a lot further into the trees than the few men who were relieving themselves, made sure no one could see me, then went a bit further. The moonlight was poor now as clouds raced across the web of stars.

When I went back to Ulf, the riders had all mounted up. Ulf patted the place in front of him on his horse, then pulled me up. I'd thought about running and hiding, and I

The Rise of Synne

was torn inside wanting to go back to Stefan, but what good would I be then for my sisters? Who else did they have? As we rode on, Ulf asked me about my family. I told him what had happened, about my sisters being captured by slavers, my mother being murdered in front of us. He said she would want me to live.

6

I hated the endless ride to London. Many times, I got a fierce urge to go back on my word, slip away, run into the woods, go back to find Stefan, to bury him, lie on his grave, and find a Norman to kill to get revenge. But I had to think of Gytha and Tate. They were likely alive. And I was free, and I could help them.

We hadn't heard any news about our sisters since they'd been kidnapped by those evil raiders. Stefan and I had tried to track them, but we were on foot, and it appeared as if they'd either disappeared into the air or skilfully avoided every village where we asked after them.

Stefan had annoyed me often those days with his stupid questions about what I assumed now were our mother's stupid prophecies, but I would happily hear him ramble about them again.

It took us ten days to reach the south bank of the river to see the great wooden piers of London Bridge ahead. We slept in villages, in a long hall one night, and in a crowded

The Rise of Synne

rush-strewn stable another, Ulf always near me, always caring, even when I didn't want him to be.

One night I walked outside and around the hut we had laid down in and among frosty moonlit trees until I came upon a man and woman humping violently, grunting loudly like wolves in mating season, their desire filling the night. I watched for a moment, then headed back.

The path shone icy bright in the moonlight that night, like a fine silver belt. I took my time, reminded of the moment I'd caught Stefan with a village girl. She had a silver belt buckle. I grinned for the first time in days. Stefan would not have wanted me to wallow in grief. He would have wanted me to find our sisters and find hope that even one of Mother's prophecies would come true. I'd not escaped the dread weight Stefan's death had placed on me, adding to the grief already there, but I would not let that break me. I must not.

Our progress to London had been slower than it should have been too, because of the wounded among us. I helped all I could with them, keeping myself busy. Ulf rambled a lot when we spoke, about how he expected the remaining family of King Harold to still defeat the Normans, and that we were all blessed to have survived the great battle, and that the coming victory would be aided by the holy trinity, and that all this had been predicted because of a turning away from Christ, and that a message from Christ promising to protect England would come. Soon.

He believes all this with a great passion.

I was not so sure that Christ was on our side, but I listened to Ulf, nodded, said nothing. I'd heard monks proclaiming their visions of darkness and fire and punishments and the end of the world for all, due to there being so many sinners. I'd also heard whispered stories about monks and abbots and bishops sinning in many remarkable ways. Stefan used to say that it was guilt that made them so fiery in their sermons.

Within days of leaving the scene of the great battle, it was obvious the Normans were not intent on pursuing us, so we took horses and carts from the villages we passed through, and those who were suffering with us, the walking wounded who'd been straggling our line out far behind us, were placed into them.

Someone said that the sons of our dead king argued about all this, and that one wanted to leave the wounded behind. Whether that was true or not I do not know. In any case, as we came near London, we had become an ox cart procession.

Two of the other healers were still with us. All the others, and the physicians, had all dispersed. The healers who remained were the younger ones. We spoke a little. I was still an outsider recruited late to the king's army, but we did our best tending the wounded, at dusk usually, rebinding wounds, helping men face pain and the possibility of being ruined by their injuries. During the day, as we passed through the forest, I watched for herbs to gather. I found Autumn Charm by the side of the road twice and boiled it with old bandages at night to apply the next day.

Our line of able-bodied people had diminished. Many had taken side roads, often heading west, others headed upriver or towards the sea. Some of our wounded we'd left behind in villages, as it became clear that further travel would kill them.

When I was asked what would become of us all, by a badly wounded man, I replied that we would defeat the Normans and wipe them out of all England soon. And that it could not be true that one battle would lose all of England.

When we reached London Bridge, I was near the head of a line of perhaps two hundred people, the final core of loyal thegns, fyrd men, and the village militia recruited for the battle, along with carts piled with wounded as well as a few dozen men from the personal entourage of the Godwins – the King's family. I saw no other members of his family aside from Magnus and Edmund in all that time.

For anyone watching from the stone river walls of London, topped by a wooden palisade in many places, along the north side of the river, we must have been a dispiriting sight if they'd watched our king's vast army heading south to fight the Norman Duke only a few weeks before.

We were fortunate about one thing though. The autumn weather held fine. That was a mercy.

I hadn't spoken to Magnus since the day Stefan had died. But I thought about him many times, about his annoying arrogant coldness. I knew that every young woman he met probably ended up lovesick for him, but I would not be like them. Just because he was forbidden to anyone but a lord's daughter, did not mean I would swoon for him, even for a moment.

Our line contracted further as we neared the city, and I spotted a woman riding by Magnus's side. She was close to him as we went through the marshes south of the river.

"Who is that with Magnus?" I asked Ulf, as we moved slowly along the muddy road, made worse by a rain that had recently passed over, showering us in a cold drizzle.

Ulf laughed. "Keep your thoughts well away from Lord Magnus, young woman," he said. "He is not for the likes of you, understood?"

The distant cries of street sellers carried across the river from the city.

"Does he bring his wife to battle?"

Ulf laughed in reply.

The Rise of Synne

I was confused by the woman. A brown wimple covered her hair, and flecks of beautiful golden locks peeked out. Her quilted red tunic went to her boots, and she looked at ease, riding at Magnus's side. Had she ridden out from London when word had arrived that remnants of the king's army were on their way? Was she his wife?

Ulf had his arms around me as he held the reins. We were still on one horse.

"Did your mother see the future? They called her a seer, you said, so are you able to do that trick too?"

"No, I cannot," I said firmly. "I can reassure people, tell them all will be well. That is all I can do. If that's reading the future, so be it, many are guilty."

Ulf laughed. People often ask healers about their future, their recovery, but if a monk or priest was nearby, I always suggested prayer is the best way to secure the future. Men of the church needed people to pray to Christ for their recovery and to thank him in coin when they did.

Not all monks and priests made trouble if they found out you'd been making predictions, but it was better to deny any knowledge of such things. Healers had to follow this path. I knew there were still some who likely claimed such powers, but I'd never met another with the powers and the belief in them my mother had. She'd spoken of her sadness that such skills were dying out, that seer-healers would soon become just healers as the old ways disappeared.

"What would you say to Magnus if he asked you about his future?" asked Ulf.

"I told you. I'm not able to predict the future, monk. I help people recover. I'm a healer." I said it firmly.

My mother's predictions were famous, no, infamous. They may have got her killed. I did not want to go down that road.

I made my face stiff. "And I swear," I said. "I do not care what woman is with Magnus."

"And you are able to cure love sickness too, yes?"

"I have no interest in such things," I said sharply.

Ulf laughed. "Good, Synne the healer, so I will tell you who your rival is. Elva is her name. She is the daughter of a thegn, a relative of his mother's. No doubt sent here by her to keep an eye on us all."

"She's his wife?" It was a bold question, but I could not stop myself. I knew only a little about the king's family when we'd joined with them on the march south to Hastings. The only news our family received in the north before that was about the king and his campaigns and occasionally who was trying to depose him. My mother did not allow us into the local towns where we might have heard tavern gossip. And the young healers I'd walked to the battle with spoke mostly about their home villages.

The Rise of Synne

"No. Who he marries was to be decided next year, by his father."

"He stood with his father in the battle?"

"He wasn't in the shield wall. Not quite old enough. But his father gave him a place in his personal guard, and he nearly died trying to save him."

"That's how he was injured?" I asked.

"He and his brother attacked the Normans who'd surrounded his father. He received a glancing blow. Edmund pulled him away. We are blessed they survived. No more questions."

We passed small houses with patched wattle walls and thin ribbons of smoke streaming from their roofs, and pigs and goats in pens by the side of most of them. Some pens had men and women around them, buying and selling from rough tables to anyone who passed.

Children ran alongside us, smiling and pointing. They laughed as if nothing bad had happened, no battle had been lost. It was good to hear them. One young girl walked behind the others. She'd seen maybe seven or eight summers and looked up at me with sad eyes and a swollen hand.

"Stop," I said to Ulf. "Perhaps I can help this one."

He swore but pulled our horse up. I got down, called the girl to me. She didn't come, fear in her eyes. So, I went to her, pulled some Autumn Charm from my bag, gave it to her and told her to boil it and use it with a bandage, which she would change every two days. The girl held the herb to her chest with her good hand and ran off, her eyes wide, before turning and mouthing her thanks. I did not know if it would save her from the wound sickness spreading in her, but at least she had a chance now.

The clearing where we stopped lay by the southern part of the only bridge into the city. The whole area was muddy and chaotic. Men and carts jostled for space, with shouts and the sound of horses and carts creaking creating a cacophony of noise. I'd passed this way coming south, hurrying to join the king's army, full of hope and expectations of a speedy victory and a share of the spoils. To the left of the bridge stood a wide pool of dark water. The whole area stank of dung. Two horsemen with Godwin wolf banners flapping rode ahead to the guards at the start of the bridge. All the people nearby stared at us as our procession of carts, horses, and the final remnants of a once-great army waited.

"Why don't we go across?" I asked Ulf.

"We have to get the bridge cleared and get permission to bring so many warriors into the city," he said.

I shook my legs out. My thighs were sore. Sitting on the horse day after day had given me pains that lasted through the night and stinging calf burns. My brother and I never travelled on horseback. We walked from village to village. If only I could go back to those days, Stefan by my side, someone to talk to, laugh with. I missed him terribly. It felt as if my arm had been cut off and where it had been, memories throbbed.

Ulf fed our horse a handful of oats from one of his leather saddlebags. I spotted Magnus looking in our direction.

My spirits lifted, but I tamped them down. Need brought on by grief is hard to dislodge. I looked away. *He is not for you.* I repeated the words under my breath. Magnus would never want someone like me, except for a night's sport. I would not be used like that. Lords marry ladies. My sisters had been right. You can pine for a lord, but you'll be better off looking away. But perhaps he or his brother could help me. I had to risk it.

"I will ask Magnus how his wound is," I said softly, as if it was no big thing.

"He has all the help he needs," said Ulf. He gave me a serious look.

"You can't stop me asking," I said loudly.

Ulf sighed. "He looks angry these days, healer. I would not go near him if I were you."

I didn't care. I was past caring. "I'll just ask if his wound is ailing him." My tone was soft again.

I slid from our horse before he could say anything else. Some men nearby had turned to stare at me as if I was an outlaw in their midst.

"Be quick about it," said Ulf, leaning down to me. "I'm a bit soft towards you 'cause of all you've been through. But he won't be. Don't say you weren't warned."

I walked forward, slowly, my head up. I was doing nothing wrong. When I got closer, I saw that someone had bound Magnus's shoulder wound again, though he still wore the same torn mail shirt, and his hair was still matted. Edmund was right beside him, his hand resting on the pommel of his sword.

I bowed a little as I came close, but not too low. Words flew around in my mind. I had no real idea about how to get his help, but I had to take this chance. When we crossed the river, I might never see them again.

"How is your wound, my lord?" I spoke brightly. My voice seemed shrill.

This was not going well. Any moment now, he'd wave me away. I looked at his brother.

"My only hope is your victory," I said. My hand went to my throat as a memory of Stefan and I swearing our oath to their father came to me. I bowed. Sucking up to lords is what they love, was what my mother had taught us. "If I can assist in any way, my lords, please tell me what to do." It was a dangerous offer, and my skin crawled at how they

The Rise of Synne

might take it, and my hand shook at my throat, but I had to speak out.

"We will see that victory," said Edmund, his tone was angry. "Perhaps first you can tell us why we've had no message from the Bishop of London or any ealdorman of the city and why we wait here like merchants." His mouth twisted into a sneer.

There was danger in this encounter. I could feel it. My mouth opened, but I had no idea how to respond.

"Brother, they cannot decide the fate of the crown without us," said Magnus. He waved dismissively in my direction, as if he wanted me to go. His beard was long and pale like wheat. "Do not ask this grizzled whelp what she cannot know."

I kept my head up but inside I burned with hatred for him. Grizzled whelp! I had to press my lips together tight not to say what I thought of him. A beating would be the least of my worries if I did.

Edmund had a smile on his face, but his gaze moved down my body. I was still thinking of a reply.

"I'm sure you have plenty of allies in the city, my lords."

Magnus nodded, as if to himself. "My brother claims the bishops must have heard we've got a seer with us. They claim that is why we lost the battle, because we were under the protection of the old gods." They both stared at me.

They were trying to shift blame for the battle.

I shook my head fast. "Because I'm a healer does not mean I'm a seer or worship the old gods. I'm a Christian. I pray every day." Each word spoken with conviction, ending with the sign of the cross. I'd heard about a healer being blamed for a failed crop in a village. This was the same sort of stupid thinking.

"Prove it. Get on your knees and pray to Christ," said Edmund, baring his teeth at me.

It was Magnus's turn to look me up and down. I was tempted to curse him. I made fists of both my hands and went down on my knees in the mud, not bothering to pull my tunic up. But I kept my head straight and prayed out loud and clear, spitting the words towards them.

O Lord, O King, Christ resplendent in the citadel of heaven, all hail and pray. Give clemency for thy people, and your mercy.

I repeated the prayer.

"Is that the only prayer you know, the Saxon prayer for forgiveness?" asked Edmund, interrupting me. "You probably heard the monk whisper that on the road after he'd been rutting you."

Ulf's voice came from behind me, high-pitched, annoyed. "My lord. She did not learn this prayer from me. I resent those charges. The Bishop of London will be the cause of the delay, whispering seditious words in every

The Rise of Synne

ear, telling people to be open to his countrymen, the Normans, our enemies. Let us not fight amongst ourselves."

"Did she seduce you, monk?" asked Edmund. He came towards me, grabbed my chin, pushed my head up to look down at me, the way they appraise slaves, then leaned close and said, "I know what you want."

Every muscle tightened. I wanted to push him away, badly, but thoughts of my sisters came to me, reminding me I must survive.

"She did not seduce me," said Ulf.

Edmund released my chin. I kept it up. I'd been handled like this a few times in villages after being caught stealing apples from an orchard or mushrooms from a field or water from a well that someone claimed they owned. I always kept my chin up. It annoyed people that I wasn't more scared, but having nothing means you have nothing to lose.

A crowd had gathered. They were waiting for a punishment to be meted out.

"Stand up," said Magnus. "We may find a use for you yet."

What did he mean? I did not like the look on his face.

"No," shouted Edmund. "She will remain on her knees until I give her permission to stand." He looked off to the side and smiled. He'd overruled Magnus. Was this his way of showing who really led us?

I followed his gaze. Elva was there on her horse, staring down at us, a pleased smile on her face. On catching my eye, she tilted her head to one side, as if enjoying my predicament. What had I done to annoy her?

I closed my eyes, began reciting the prayer for forgiveness out loud. It did not look like I'd be able to persuade either of these brothers to help me. But whatever came, I would endure. Stefan and I had tried, without help or gold. We'd come to London twice in the last year, visited the slave traders at the Dane market, and had been disappointed each time. No one remembered my sisters, or they wouldn't remember anything without coin, which we had barely enough to pay for our food.

"Get up," said Edmund. "My brother has a task for you."

"What task, my lords?" I came to my feet, brushing the mud off my tunic with fast, angry strokes. I was not about to lose my head, but I still did not know what lay ahead.

"You will go to the camp of the earls Edwin and Morcar and see if you can find out their plans." Magnus spoke fast, glanced towards Elva. She had come closer, her horse's breath visible in the air.

The Rise of Synne

The northern earls, Edwin and Morcar, had not even joined the battle against the Normans at Hastings. Some said their army had a good excuse for not appearing. They were recovering from a previous battle. Others just shook their heads that England had not been united, and that was why we had lost.

Either way, it would not be easy finding out the plans of the northern earls. It was a fool's task.

Edmund put his hand up. "You think she can do this?" He looked me up and down.

"A healer is ideal for this task. Few have seen her with us, and she comes from the north. And she looks the part." Magnus sounded very sure of himself.

"But she's not trained as a spy," said Edmund. He glanced towards the bridge. A horseman was approaching.

I opened my mouth, then closed it. This was all confusing. And I'd brought it all on myself. But more importantly, what was this talk of me becoming a spy?

"It is a simple task." Magnus waved a hand in the air. He didn't care what happened to me. "We do not need a trained spy. And she looks harmless. There are no spies available, anyway. Let her go to their camp and see what she can find out, brother. We need to know what they're up to." He looked pleased with himself.

"It's her right to say no," said Edmund.

I stared at him, my heart thumping hard. He was right, but he didn't have to say it. "I must find my sisters."

"Healer." Edmund's tone was low. "Do this for us and you will be well rewarded. Coin will help you find your sisters, yes?"

I nodded. "What about my brother's body?" I hesitated; my words had brought my sadness back up again. "I should go back and see he's buried first." I spoke quickly.

"Healer," said Edmund, with a sigh and a shake of his head. "You cannot go back now. The Norman army is not far behind. It will be your certain death. You cannot find your sisters when you're dead. Wait until the Normans are defeated, then seek your brother's resting place. I sent word the night he died to the nearest village to bury all our dead. If you want to find out where he lies, do as I say." He spoke fast and in a way that made me think he was used to forcing people to do things, binding them to his will.

I looked towards the river. I was torn as I wanted to go back and find Stefan's resting place, but I also needed to find my sisters.

I pressed my fist into my stomach, sniffed in hard, made my decision, and nodded. "I will do as you wish," I said.

"Good," said Edmund.

The Rise of Synne

I wondered at once if I'd made a stupid decision. I had no idea what this task would bring. But hopefully I could get it over quickly. "I'll find out what I can," I said. I pursed my lips. "But I will not cut throats for anyone."

"We do not expect you to be an assassin," said Edmund, sharply.

"And there'll be a reward when this is done?"

"Yes," said Edmund, with a crooked smile that made me wonder how often he broke his promises. "All we need is to know what they plan to do. Will they stay near London or return north? And anything else you can pick up. Any talk in their camp. We are not their enemies. The risk is slight."

He was right, the earls had been allies of his father. Their armies could still help defeat the Normans.

Edmund waved dismissively in my direction. "Go to it, healer. Make your way at once to find the earls. Do it quick and come back soon with news. Ulf will explain how to find them. And…" He raised both his hands, as if holding something. "All you have to do is to listen and come back. This is not a complicated task." He turned to Ulf. "Make sure she has enough coin to get through the city," he said.

"Come," said Ulf in my ear.

I backed up, relieved to be away from them. They made me nervous. Edmund was the type of lord who'd skewer you with his sword if you disrespected him. Magnus was as arrogant and annoying as any man could be. My head was spinning as I followed Ulf away. Even if I was only tasked with listening, I could sense danger on this path I'd made for myself.

When we reached his horse, Ulf handed me half a piece of hard bread, all he had left, and his water skin. I had a few things in the battered leather bag strapped tight to my side: my spare tunic, a bone comb, which I rarely used, and, more importantly, the last of my salves and herbs. I put the chunk of bread in my bag and slung the water skin over my other shoulder. If this offer had happened when Stefan was alive, he'd have urged me to take it, but I was uneasy. Something about the way the two brothers had dealt with me was wrong. What was going on that I did not know about?

While all this was going through my head, Ulf was trying to convince me that listening was a common task, which many people did when lords needed to know about allies as well as enemies, trying to reassure me. It only half worked and that was because I had come to trust him. Not many men got physically close to me, riding together almost skin to skin, without them trying to touch me whenever they wanted.

I pressed my lips together as a dark thought came to me. If the earls' men discovered I was listening for the

The Rise of Synne

Godwins, they would call it spying, and my life might end in some cruel way. But how would they know I was a spy? Who would tell them?

I decided then that I would find the earls, offer my services as a healer, and come back as quickly as I could with any simple gossip from their camp. Anything that might be enough for Edmund.

Let this be all over with quick.

"What would you have done if King Harold won the battle?" asked Ulf, as I tied my bag tight to my side. He passed me my small axe, which had been taken from me when they put me over the horse.

"We expected war spoils. That we'd get a share of it and—"

"You would have been at the end of a long line looking for spoils," he said, butting in.

"But we would have had something."

"You would have, maybe." It looked as if he was remembering something. He put his hand to his purse. "I will give you coin to last a few days, that is all," he said.

We'd spent every coin we had before we joined Harold's army on its journey south from his previous great victory. Everyone had said the king could not be beaten. That he would pay well, too. Our hopes had been high, Stefan's more than mine. He said if he had any experience fighting alongside King Harold, he'd be taken in by any lord to be a squire.

"Take this," said Ulf, after digging in his leather purse. He held his hand out. Five small silver coins lay in his palm, enough to find a place to sleep for five nights as well as food for each morning and evening. It could last longer too, if I found the lowest cost places to sleep. They were not hard to find.

Before I could say anything in reply, he pushed my shoulder with his finger. "Go fast across the bridge. It'll be dark before any part of our army crosses. The brother earls will be camped beyond Ealdredesgate, on the far side of the city. They camped there before. I expect they'll be in the same place, surrounded by their own men."

"How will this help them?" I nodded towards Magnus and Edmund. "Is this some stupid fool's errand?"

Ulf pointed at his head. "Think, girl. It's still not clear who will succeed King Harold and send the Normans back into the sea. If you can find out anything about what the earls are planning, and what they're talking about, that will be enough. Just come back with something."

"And if I can't find out anything?"

"Don't come back." He gripped my arm. "And consider yourself an outlaw and bring me my coin back, too."

I was trapped. "Where will you all be?"

The Rise of Synne

"Some of us will still be here or nearby. We need to hold this bridge. But don't take too long." He sounded frustrated. "Find out what their men are talking about. It won't be difficult for you. Do not disappoint Edmund and Magnus." He glanced over his shoulder. "They hate to be disappointed."

I followed his gaze. A young man was shouting at Edmund. We watched the altercation, as did a lot of the men around us. I caught only a little of what was said. The man was complaining that his brothers were all dead, and insulting King Harold, Edmund's dead father, as he did so, calling him a fool for going to battle so quickly. The man stepped forward, close to Edmund. Edmund did not reply. He pulled his sword out, raising it high. I thought it was a warning. Then a soft thud sounded as the blade struck fast into the man's throat, almost taking his head off. Blood spurted.

Edmund kicked at the man to push him off the road, rolling his quivering body. He raised his sword high then and turned to the men watching. A cheer went up. Edmund shrugged. Some of his men came forward and carried the dead man from the road and dumped his body near the river.

The whole thing made me shudder. When would all this stupid killing stop?

I looked across the river towards the city. Smoke was drifting up from holes in a multitude of roofs. Crosses poked from the tops of churches and high wooden towers. Grey clouds moved above it all. Would spying bring me closer to finding my sisters or would I end up like that man, a dead body for the scavengers to pick at?

I would have to harden myself to my task, to make sure that did not happen. If I failed, there would be no one to help my sisters. I had to survive. Seagulls rose together from the mud further down the river and passed upriver in a great squawking cloud. It felt like a sign.

7

I'd crossed the bridge fast and had walked almost completely through the city by the time darkness fell. I'd asked a few people about where the northern earls were, but no one knew anything, so I followed Ulf's directions to the northern gate. Many people looked angry, their expressions dark, as if a shadow had fallen over them. Men and women glanced about with fear in their eyes, as if expecting the Normans to appear around any corner.

News of the Norman success at the great battle had changed many things here. Most obviously, the city seemed to be full, bursting at the seams. Every house had people coming and going and more chamber pots than ever were being emptied from overhanging balconies with the barest shouted warnings. Riders and carts moved more slowly along the rutted streets because of the crowds, with shouts and curses and children's cries echoing all around. I passed a few small fields with dark leather tents set up in them, but most of the muddy streets were lined with merchants with shouts coming from shop fronts or from stalls in front of high-walled villas, hovels, and alehouses all pressed up against each other.

Peasants and vagabonds made up most of the population now. Slaves carried their burdens and men at arms moved quickly through the crowds while thin children darted about, and enticing smells wafted from bakeries and pie shops and cries of buy this or that filled the air.

It was time to find refuge for the night. I'd walked through London at night before, with Stefan, with only the occasional light spilling from an alehouse door or a burning torch at some crossroads to light our way. Between these pools of light, when the moon wasn't out, lay skin-crawling blackness.

If the moon did come out, it would be far less risky, but on a cloudy night like this, a lone woman would be easy pickings.

A prosperous-looking alehouse beckoned as the sun went down. And a welcoming glow from its door showed a view of a rush-covered floor inside as someone came out. A guard with a long-handled axe on his belt gave some comfort that the place would be less rowdy than some I'd passed. I bowed to him and asked, "Is there a sleeping place here for a lone woman?"

He looked me up and down.

The Rise of Synne

"I 'ave t' warn ya," he said with a shake of his head. "We don't allow women to sell 'emselves in this 'ere alehouse." He puffed his chest out. "If 'at's your business, be gone."

An equal-armed cross hung from his neck.

"I'm a healer," I said. "I do not sell my body."

"How do I know you ain't lying?"

I peered close at his face. "You have a boil under your eye. You must clean it daily with hot water or you will lose that eye for sure by Christ Mass."

His hand went to the boil. His dirty finger touched it.

"I said clean it, not make it dirtier," I said sharply.

He pulled his hand away, looked at it with a worried expression. "You can go inside."

The alehouse had newly changed rushes on the floor, a hearth in the centre with a welcoming fire burning bright, and long tables down each side. There were only a few men at each table and a feeling of watchfulness in the air, with none of the shouting and the laughter of whores I'd heard from other alehouses in London when we'd passed them with Stefan's eyes wide. The only women here were serving girls in long dark tunics to their ankles and, at the far end of the room, at a long table with barrels under it, sat an older woman looking at me.

The room went quiet as I walked to the smouldering hearth in the centre and put my hands out. I was used to the cold, but when I came near a fire, the warmth was hard to resist. I stood near the heat, my hands out, waiting for someone to ask my business. It was good to be inside, to be at a fire, to have stopped walking, searching, but as I warmed up, thoughts of Stefan came to me. If we'd been together, he'd have had jokes and gripes about the day and the task ahead.

So much had been lost with him. Too much.

I'd seen a man earlier on the street who looked like Stefan from behind and I'd almost gone to him, but that would have been stupid. I held a hand to my chest as a rising emptiness and longing came over me. If only he'd survived.

Since we'd come down from the north, I'd had many moments of stark fear imagining those same slave traders who'd murdered my mother coming upon us, but as time went by, I'd stopped worrying, and had begun to assume whoever had been looking for us at our home had given up. That was our hope, anyway.

If only I really had my mother's powers. She'd never feared anyone or anything. She'd heard voices sometimes telling her what to do – she said it was one of the powers of a woken seer – but what about me hearing her voice, telling me I was being saved for something? Did it mean I'd inherited her powers, or was I fooling myself?

At that moment, the woman from the back of the room came and took my arm in a hard grip.

"No whores in here," she said in a growl. "How did you get past my man? I'll have him flogged if you fooled him or paid him with whatever you have to offer." She looked me up and down.

I looked her in the eye. "I'm a healer," I said firmly. "I told your guard how to get rid of the boil near his eye before he goes blind from it. Perhaps you don't care?"

She laughed, released her grip. "Did you charge him?" Her eyes narrowed.

"No, I don't always charge. And as for being a whore, I'm looking for a place to sleep where I won't have men groping me and worse. Is it safe here for a woman?"

"Try the nunnery, back toward the river. They help strays," she replied, jerking her head towards the door.

"I can pay well for a safe place to sleep and for food." I pulled my thin purse from where it was tucked away.

"You can pay?" Her expression softened. She didn't smile, but it didn't look as if she would grab my arm and run me out anymore.

I nodded.

"Follow me."

She led me to the back of the hall, opened a slit in a patched leather curtain that acted as a wall, creating two parts to the alehouse. She went through to the back. I hesitated. Was this a trap? Would I be jumped on and my purse robbed? She turned to me, held the leather slit open.

"You'll not be robbed here," she said, shaking her head, as if sad that she had to say it. "Some alehouses in London have a reputation for getting men drunk and extracting every coin from them one way or another, but that's not us."

I believed her. The fact that there was no man on the other side of the opening helped. A narrow area between the leather curtain and the back wattle wall had a thick layer of rushes on its floor and wool blankets in piles at the back. I took a deep breath and went through. She pointed at a thick pile of rushes in the far corner. "You'll sleep over there, if you pay. No men are allowed back here. If anyone tries, we tell them they'll have something cut off if they force themselves on any woman here." She laughed.

I held a silver coin out. "How many nights for this, and food for the mornings and evenings?"

"One, in safety."

"Can I eat now?" I was hungry. Her price was high, but it was late. And seeing people eat had made my mouth water.

She nodded, put her hand out, her arm stiff. I gave her the coin. She led me back into the main area and to an empty end of a table not far from the fire. She motioned one of the serving girls to us.

The Rise of Synne

"Bring stew and a cup of ale," she said to the girl, who ran off with a smile and a nod.

"What's your name?" I asked the older woman.

"Mae," she replied. "And eat up quick and then sleep, girl. You look like you need it. There's a hole in a plank in a corner of the back room when you need. Do not piss on the floor like some of the forest women do."

"I'm no savage."

She turned and went to a nearby table where an older man sat. I was glad she didn't question me further. I was tired and my feet ached. I needed to eat and rest. The first part of my mission, getting through the city, had gone well, but the hardest part was ahead.

I ate the stew quickly when it came. It had grizzled meat in it mixed with hot seasoned oatmeal, leeks, and onions. It tasted good. The wooden bowl had a low rim, so the amount of stew served was small. I finished it quickly, ate the chunk of horsebread that came with it, drank the ale, and motioned the girl who'd brought it for more. When you pay good coin, you should get good eating.

The girl leaned down to me as she brought the refilled bowl. "Are you really a healer?" she asked, wide-eyed.

I nodded, smiled. I knew what was coming. Many people need help with things they'd never tell you about if they didn't know what you did. And healers must help everyone, even if you're about to curl up and sleep. She went and got a jug of ale. "I need a healer," she whispered. Her gaze roved around the room.

"What ails you?" I ate some of the stew.

"Not me. 'Tis my father," said the girl. "We live outside the walls."

"What ails him?"

"The stupid flux. I do not know what to do. He gets worse each day."

I reached toward her, took her wrist, pulled her close. "Do what I say, and he may yet live. No hard food. Salted buttermilk each day until he spends less time clutching his gut over the shitter. And only ale to drink."

"Thank you," said the girl. Her eyes sparkled. "Are you a follower of the old ways? The priest I asked told me to pray to Christ for my father; that prayers alone would heal him."

"Yes, pray. Pray to Christ but do what I told you, too. God the All Father provides foods to help us heal as well as for nourishment."

She nodded her thanks. I lowered my voice.

"Have you seen the earls Morcar or Edwin pass by here or heard talk of them or their men?" I asked.

The girl stared at me, then looked over my head. I turned. Mae was standing behind me.

She motioned for the serving girl to move away. "You must be tired," she said, looking down at me. "If you want

The Rise of Synne

to find the earls, I suggest you head north out of the city tomorrow, early." She studied me. It felt as if she was peeling away layers. "If you must join with them that is your decision, but you should know that the Normans have won a great battle and may be here in days." She sniffed. "At every table that is what the talk is about, and many are afraid." She put a hand flat on the table, leaned down to me. "I pray the king's sons will rally the kingdom before it's too late." Fear was visible in her eyes. She made a sign of the cross.

"You know more than me," I said, as I pushed the empty bowl away. I could not say I was at Hastings. Everyone would crowd around for news of it. I'd seen men followed for news of battles before. They were pressed to tell their stories endlessly.

She gave me an insincere smile. "There is good coin in healing these days?" she asked.

"Enough." I finished the last of the extra stew and upended the ale cup.

"I'm sure it's tiring work. Come."

She led the way to the back room and handed me a blanket.

"Will you join with the earls, healer?" she asked, with that same smile, which did not reach her eyes.

"Perhaps, if they'll have me. They are neighbours from the north," I said.

"I hope they do the right thing, healer," she said.

"What right thing?"

"I told you, the Normans could be at the gates of the city soon." She looked at me with her head to the side, as if I must be stupid. "Someone must stand against them. We hear they suck the blood from babies." Her hand pressed to her stomach, as if she was going to be ill.

I took the blanket, wrapped myself in it, and lay down on the thickest part of the rushes.

8

Rats scurried all around all that night, but there were not too many, and only one crawled over my blanket. I shifted fast as it woke me and swiped at it. It didn't come back. After that, I slept fitfully. I saw my mother's face again in a dream that night, pale, staring bravely up at the man devil who'd murdered her. I heard her voice again that night too, the same words she'd spoken before, reminding me that there was a task for me.

I dreamt about my sisters, too. Gytha stood in the doorway of an alehouse, saying Tate was waiting for me inside. I could feel their presence and I gasped with a pleasure I'd not felt in a long time. I opened my eyes to a rustle as one of the girls went to relieve herself.

I held my hands tight together, pressed them into my chest, praying I would find my sisters. They would likely be waiting, praying, for one of us to help them. Stefan and I had talked about it endlessly. Now would it come true?

Early morning shouts echoed soon after. Mae calling the serving girls to help her.

"Quick, we need to open up," she shouted. A deep gloom filled the alehouse, broken only by a small window, high up on the end wall, where grey light came in through a piece of oiled cloth nailed tight.

I watched from beneath my blanket as three serving girls fixed their tunics and pulled on their thin boots. When they were done, I waited awhile, then pushed off my blanket and went to the opening in the leather wall.

In the main part of the alehouse, near the front door, men were sitting at a table. They looked like bears hunched over in their dark cloaks.

Mae appeared, walking towards me fast, her eyes squinting.

"No gruel yet," she said. "I'll call you when it's ready."

I went back to my blanket. Why was she so concerned about what I was seeing?

The thought of going to the earls' camp was daunting now, a task I did not want to do and less with each moment. I wondered why I'd been sent on this mission. Was I part of some game Edmund and his brother were playing?

I felt trapped, like a deer that had fallen into a hole.

But my sisters would be in a worse predicament. I had to keep going. I had to be strong.

After a while, one of the girls came for me. The gruel was ready. I ate the warm oats at a table near the hearth where a fire was blazing. There was no honey for it, but there was a little goat's milk. The men I'd seen earlier were gone. The door guard was eating gruel at the other end of my table. When I finished my bowl, I shifted towards him.

"Did you wash it?" I asked him.

He stared at me with a blank expression. I turned to one of the serving girls who was passing. "Bring him a small bowl of hot water and a clean cloth and do this every day so he can wash that boil on his face," I said.

The guard had a sceptical look, but the girl nodded.

I went to leave the alehouse after helping him clean his face. Mae wished me luck with the earls. She patted my arm, leaned close. "Did you hear the prophecy that a woman will be the one to take revenge on the Normans? They'll have to watch out."

I nodded.

"You'll be safe with the earls. They're good men," she said. "They'll need healers."

I hoped she was right.

***

I reached the old city wall curving around the north of the city quickly. A muddy rutted street ran beside the high stone wall. The street was cluttered with stalls and handcarts. The wall looming above it was patched with many different-sized stones. The bottom parts looked ancient. Wooden stairs ran up the wall at intervals to a walkway where guards with shiny helmets looked down on everyone.

The gate I came to was only wide enough for two carts to pass each other. When I reached the gate, a cart laden high with sacks and barrels, pulled by oxen, was coming in and a string of packhorses was being led out. Men and women carrying wicker baskets were following the horses, picking their way in the deep ruts. Children ran about without a care.

Two guards with helmets and red tunics had stopped the cart coming in. They didn't seem interested in the horses and people leaving. As I went through the gate, I pulled my cloak tight. A cold wind was blowing hard from the north. Dark clouds were moving towards the city, heavy with the promise of rain.

I'd put my own neck in a noose, and I was about to hand the end of the rope to people I did not know who could pull that noose tight, just for fun.

Do not think like that, I told myself. There is a reason you dream about your mother and your sisters, a reason you hear her words.

I went through the gate. The road beyond had low, wattle-walled shacks on each side with closed doors. There were no alehouses here, but there were traders standing around tables with baskets of wrinkled apples,

The Rise of Synne

onions, and old-looking cabbages. Some of the traders were grey-haired and bent over, beaten down by life. I kept walking. The road passed by a stream. Women were washing clothes and hanging them on thin bushes nearby. I went down to them and asked the first one I met, "Do the earls of Mercia and Northumbria have their camp nearby? Have you heard where they are?"

She stared at me with wary eyes. "I know nothing about any of that," she said stiffly. She looked me up and down, then turned to another woman. "This one's looking for them earls from the north," she said. I had my excuse ready about being a healer, but she didn't ask me any questions.

The other woman was much older. She had a high forehead and fast-moving eyes. She pointed straight out of the city.

"Keep going, girl, you'll find what you're looking for. Turn left at the crossroads after the stone bridge. Can't help you more than that." She went back to her work, hanging a tunic.

I returned to the road and kept walking. Rows of long, thin fields appeared on each side, with lots of bare trees bent by the wind and patches of barren, thin grass. I pulled my cloak tight. There were fewer people on the road now and only an occasional ox-drawn cart. I kept walking, my head down, the icy wind cutting into me so much I began dreaming of the warm hearth in Mae's alehouse. I almost turned back a few times as the wind hammered into me.

Many riders, some of them men in mail shirts, passed me by. One of the men shouted something at me. His words were half lost in the wind, but I guessed what he was saying, offering me his attentions. I kept looking ahead, pretending I didn't hear. There was worse that could happen.

I found the crossroads and turned left. This road was quieter, with almost no other travellers.

On coming up a gentle rise in the land, with thin grass all around swaying in the wind and an earthy rain-smell in the air, a group of men waited beside the road ahead. They wore short mail shirts and had axes on their belts. As I approached, one of them stepped into the road and put his hands on his hips.

I tried a smile. This was a moment of danger. There were occasional roadblocks like this when you travelled around in times of trouble, but I'd always been with Stefan when I'd passed through the few we'd met. Most men do not like the idea of single women travelling around without a good reason. You could be a nun going to a convent or a widow going back to her family or a serving girl on an errand, but you had to have a good reason to be travelling.

The Rise of Synne

I bowed to the first man and then to the two other men observing me.

"What brings you this way, girl?" said the man, his thick-gloved hand out wide, stopping my progress.

"I'm a healer, offering my services." I smiled. "Does anything ail you?" It was one way of getting past people like him.

"You a spy?" the man asked gruffly.

"No, lord, I'm a healer," I said, my voice as loud as his. Was that a mistake? Should I be meek? No, stop it. Weakness in a woman made some men worse. That was what my mother always said.

The other men loped toward us.

"We're looking for spies," said the first man. "You look like one to me. Women don't go about on their own on this road unless they're looking for something." As he spoke, he motioned for the men to go around behind me to cut off my escape.

An unwelcome tingle of fear rose up my spine. I kept my smile rigid.

He squinted. "We're expecting Norman spies. You're working with the invaders, yes? Just say it."

The thudding of my heart was loud. I wondered for a moment could he hear it. I shook my head. Did he know something?

"I'm a healer, lord. I swear it. I travel from village to village, healing. Since my brother died, I must do this on my own. Healing is not a sin. It is allowed by every lord. Many find they need me." I tried to be firm in my response. I may have overdone it.

"How did your brother die?" He squinted at me.

A rustling behind my back told me I was surrounded. I did not turn. I would not show them I was afraid. I pushed rising panic away.

"It was an accident, a bad fall," I said. "He sickened and died after it."

The man nodded, his gaze flickering over my shoulder.

Hands grabbed at me.

My fear turned at once to calm now that what I'd dreaded had happened. A memory of my mother came to me – those men handling her, tears on her face, all the noises coming from the men, not her. I would follow her path. I could almost see her face, smiling, in front of me.

Then she disappeared, and I was looking at his angry face.

They forced me to my knees in the mud. I turned one way then the other, looking for help, but no other travellers could be seen, so I looked up at him, defiant, then beyond him. The road was empty, with not even a farmhouse or village visible, just trees and scrub grass.

"I have powerful friends," I said quickly. "Take care how you handle me. They will make anyone pay who causes me harm." I smiled, oozing a confidence I did not feel.

"What friends?" the man scoffed. "Who are they?" His tone was mocking, as if a woman like me could not ever have powerful friends.

"Take me to your lord. I will tell him, not you." These men had to be guards checking people coming from London heading for the earls' camp. They would not be allowed to kill or injure people heading that way. This was all a bluff. They wanted me to confess to something, anything probably. I kept my head high.

The man laughed. He pushed his battered leather helmet back a little off his forehead. "You're ready with an answer for everything, girl, aren't you." He took a step towards me.

"If I'm harmed, it will go bad for you," I said. I looked back the way I'd come. "There will be others on this road soon enough to give witness."

One of the men hooted in laughter.

I kept my expression stiff. Maybe I'd made a mistake leaving the city alone, but it was done now.

The older man came closer, leaned into me.

"I've a daughter 'bout your age. She needs a regular beating. I reckon you do too."

"If you value your life," I said, spitting the words into his face. "You will release me and let me pass."

He laughed. "You're a brazen thing. We'll bring you to our camp. You'll wish then that you'd told me the truth already." He grabbed my arm. One of the other men tied a rope to my hands. That man mounted one of the horses with the other end of the rope in his hands.

He rode slowly, thankfully. I followed him as the rope jerked me forward. We headed across the heath with me half running at times to keep up. Another man rode behind us to watch me. I'd made a mistake assuming I could just walk into their camp, as we'd done when we joined King Harold's army heading south to battle. These guards and their fear of spies all spoke of a big change since Harold had been defeated and killed.

After a while, the man in front stopped and handed me a waterskin with stale honeyed water in it. I drank some.

It started to rain. Giant, icy drops. I was used to walking in the rain, but not with my hands bound and being half dragged. We'd sometimes seen slaves bound like this, following a rider or a cart. The sight always made my heart sink. I imagined my sisters bound and dragged. But some slaves always put a brave face on such treatment, so I would too.

The Rise of Synne

I could hear my mother's words echoing inside me. Never ever, ever, give up.

They led me to a crowd of tents spread out by the side of a muddy path on the heathland. The tents looked bedraggled, but there were enough of them to sleep maybe a hundred men, a large personal guard, though not enough men to change the course of a war. The rain had stopped. Men were drilling with spears in an open area. Others were practising moving together as a section of shield wall. A few large, dark brown leather tents in the centre of the camp had red pennants fluttering wildly from them. We headed towards them. A line of spears rested against a wooden beam outside the one we were approaching. One of the spears made me shudder. It was black, just like the one that had killed Stefan.

The guards outside the tent stopped us as we got near. Two men, they looked like merchants, were sitting on low benches nearby. They had fur hats and fur-trimmed cloaks. Another man had long blond hair, a thick off-blond beard, and a red wool cloak.

We sat at the end of the bench. One of the men who'd brought me here stayed with me. The other one went off to talk to some guards nearby. It started to rain again. The man talking with the guards waved us to him.

"We'll go inside the earls' tent. You'll be on your knees begging soon enough," he said to me with a grin.

For some reason, I was hopeful. They had no proof I was a spy. And I had a good explanation for why I was here. I could prove I was a healer. I couldn't believe the earls would harm a healer without evidence. They'd have healers or a physician in their camp already, not many, but enough to make sure that injuries and simple ailments did not take men's lives.

The leather flap of the tent opened. I was pushed in as heat and the smell of ale rushed out. Two long tables with men sitting at them filled the nearest part of the giant tent. At the far end sat a long table facing the room. It had more men behind it, men in finer outfits, thickly quilted tunics. The walls of the tent sagged in. It looked as if someone had stupidly tried to recreate a great hall inside a tent but had failed. Two banners with gold embroidery stood behind the top table. The tent was warmed by braziers and lit by thick yellow candles on the tables. A buzz of conversation filled my ears like the sound of swarming bees. It was mid-afternoon. I thought about Stefan. He would have loved to see this.

Servants, many of them likely slaves, hurried around with baskets of bread and pots of ale and platters with cuts of meat. I became thirsty immediately at the sight of the ale pots and stomach-achingly hungry from the wonderful smell of all the food, though all that was tempered by the uncertainty of my situation.

The Rise of Synne

The men I'd come with patted me down, looking for a hidden knife. My axe had already been taken. They checked inside the thin bag strapped to my side, then released me from the ropes that had bound me. One of them pushed me forward up the centre of the room. Some of the men at the tables pointed at me and made comments and laughed. I did not understand some of them in the thick burble of noise, but I understood enough.

A few men gave me sympathetic glances. I kept my head up. I was a freeborn healer. I helped people. I could prove it.

Two guards, one on either side, sitting on stools, rose as I came near the top table. They each had a hand on the daggers hanging from their leather belts. No doubt they could have my heart cut out in moments. I kept my gaze ahead now with one hand pressed into my stomach to stop it rumbling. The men at the top table looked jubilant, as if celebrating something.

My jaw tightened. Surely, they couldn't be celebrating the defeat of King Harold. Why would they? These men might lose their positions and their lives under Duke William if he became king. His plan to take the crown of England was the reason for the Norman invasion. And then another thought came to me. Could the Northern earls be looking for spies because they hadn't picked a side yet in the contest for the throne of England?

The two men at the centre of the top table both had thick beards. It looked as if they were competing for beard growth. One of them had a rugged face with multiple scars, one of which looked livid and recent. The other had his hair tied back in the Mercian style. They were arm-wrestling as we approached. I was pushed forward to stand on my own in front of the top table.

The smell of ale, candles, and warm bodies was stronger here. Tense as a pulled bow, I licked my lips. They'd dried hard. I could taste ale and peaty smoke on them. Show no fear, I repeated to myself. I'd met village headmen many times. I knew what to say to appease most men. Village leaders were usually men puffed up with their importance, my mother said, and if a woman wanted to be a leader, all she had to do was tell endless stories about her great deeds, like men do, making half of them up.

The Mercian, Earl Edwin most likely, pointed at me and jerked his wrestling hand against the other man's, most likely his brother, Morcar, the Earl of Northumbria. Their names were well known, even in the village I'd come from.

"Morcar," he shouted. "The soothsayer was right, little brother. A new woman approaches you."

Morcar didn't look at me. He growled and pushed at Edwin's hand, leaning into the arm-wrestling match as men hooted and shouted ugly comments from other tables.

The Rise of Synne

Edwin's hand went back and down.

"I was distracted," he shouted. "Someone brought a woman in front of us in the middle of a contest." He stuck his tongue out at me. "What brings you here, girl? Are you here to be sold?"

I snorted; shook my head. "No, my lord," I said loudly. "I'm a free woman. A healer. I came to offer my services to either you or your brother, but I was stopped by your guards."

Morcar had a quizzical look on his face. "Do I know you?" he asked.

"No, my lord." I shook my head. "We've never met, but my family is from near York, so perhaps I look familiar." I bowed. Lords liked plenty of bowing and scraping. When I looked up, Morcar was still staring at me.

"What village are you from?"

"Stamford." We hadn't lived there since our family had been split apart and my mother murdered, but he didn't need to know that or about the curse some in our village said my mother had brought on us with her talk of prophecies. It crossed my mind with a jolt that if a man from Stamford was in this tent, he might say more about all that than I wanted to tell.

"Your people suffered these past few seasons," said Morcar.

I nodded. "I came south looking for work as a healer."

"We're on the lookout for spies," said Edwin. "You'd make a good spy, able to worm yourself under the enemies' blankets."

"I am not a spy." I glared at Edwin. "Send me away if you don't want my services."

"Why did my guards tie you up?" asked Morcar.

I turned to the men who'd brought me here. "I do not know, lord, perhaps because I wouldn't rut with them."

"What road was she on?" asked Morcar.

"The road from London," said the guard who'd brought me here. "And we did not try to rut her."

"How long were you in London?" asked Morcar, his eyes narrowing on me.

"Not long. I looked for work but had no luck." It was mostly true.

"You've worked with battle wounded?" asked Edwin. A slave was pouring ale into the gold goblet in front of him.

"Yes." I nodded.

"After which battle?"

"I helped outside York with my mother before it was captured, then we fled." That was true.

Edwin lifted his goblet and drank. I looked straight at Morcar.

The Rise of Synne

"If it comes out you're a spy, your head will be on a spike outside," said Edwin, gesturing at the walls. "Be afraid, if you are one."

The lightest of tremors ran through me. I hoped no one would notice and kept my hand pressed tight into my stomach. I knew what would likely happen if I was found out, though his words made it all the more real. But I would not let them see fear, not for a single moment. Fear would betray me, make what I feared come true.

I laughed. It was a fake laugh, I knew, but it changed the mood in the tent. "I cannot fear what will not happen," I said loudly. Cheers echoed.

"Quiet," roared Morcar, the Earl of Northumbria. The chattering stopped. The only sound now was the wind rustling against the sides of the giant tent and a faint hiss from the braziers.

"I heard healers are also seers where you come from," he said. "Are you a seer?" His head went to the side. It looked like he was trying to remember something.

Did he know something about my mother or our family?

"I do not see the future, my lord," I said. I made a sad face, shook my head.

Edwin jerked his thumb at his brother. "He wants to see his future. He wants to know what everyone wants to know, healer. Who'll be the next king of England?"

I shook my head. "I do not know, my lords. We healers know simple things – about people getting better from a sickness or if a horse needs rest or it may die. Healers know nothing about kings." My mother had warned me that talk of kings was a danger to us all.

Morcar was staring at me. "There are good men from Stamford who fought with us."

Fear tightened inside my chest. Would someone tell them about my family? Our village was small enough for anyone from there to know what had happened to us and why. My mother's prophecies were the cause of much talk. Some people hate anyone who claims to see things.

Morcar banged his fist on the table, once, then again. My skin crawled up my throat and down my back at the thought of what he could order. A chatter rose in the tent, then died. When quiet came again, he shouted, "Does anyone here know this healer?" He pointed at me. "Turn around," he shouted at me.

I turned, slowly, wondering if anyone would speak against me.

Seemingly endless moments passed. I held my breath. But no one shouted that they knew me, and eventually I had to suppress a grin. It was not the right moment to smile. My sisters often made fun of me for doing that.

"Take her away and make sure she cannot escape," said Morcar. He waved his hand to dismiss me. The men

The Rise of Synne

who'd brought me here took me by the arms and pulled me from the tent. As I went, stumbling, I was overcome by a strange premonition, a sense that there was blood on my hands, blood that I had spilled. I looked at my hands and was relieved. There was no blood on them.

They took me to a small tent with four guards standing around it and pushed me inside. One of the men tied a rope around my hands and the other end to a stake pushed into the earth in the centre of the tent. One other captive was in the tent, a giant blond Dane, lying on the packed earth on the far side, curled up, groaning.

"That Dane will not bother you," said one of the men. "He's had a finger cut off. It will be a week before his pain goes."

"I need something to drink," I said. My mouth was as dry as sun-bleached wool. And my mind was spinning from all that had happened.

"You'll get some in the morning, if you're lucky," said the man. Then they left us.

I sat opposite the Dane, folded my arms, lowered my head, and rocked back and forth, slowly, whispering prayers and charms to myself that I would survive, get away from this place, find my sisters. I pressed my fingers into the dry earth beneath me and prayed to the Queen of Heaven, and to our Earth Mother to save me. No clear reply came, but I took comfort in a strange sense I had that

I would survive. Perhaps Mother's powers were coming to me.

I certainly needed any help I could get.

A little later, one of the guards pushed his head in the tent flap, looked at me, passed me a small waterskin, then retreated. I drank from it with relish, despite my hands being tied. The water tasted like a sweet victory. Someone was listening.

I scrambled forward and passed the waterskin to the Dane.

He groaned, took it, drank from it until it was finished, threw it away, then moved his left hand in the air, waving it, as if trying to reduce his pain. The stump of his finger was weeping yellow pus. Someone had burnt the wound, but it was still weeping. He could die if the blood sickness took hold.

I'd sworn, when my mother started teaching me the healing arts, that I would help all who needed it. And I was not to be afraid of anyone in pain. People lash out in their pain and fear, but once you showed you wanted to help, most become docile, like children.

"Does your head hurt?" I whispered, gesturing to my head. The Dane nodded.

Someone in a village had laughed and described my willingness to help anyone as madness. And perhaps he was right, but that would not stop me.

The Rise of Synne

The Dane looked at me. Blue runes ran across his brow. The colour matched the blue streaks my father used to wear. They were one of the few things I remembered about him. This Dane's long blond hair was matted with blood, I could see now, as if it had sprayed there from his finger. I moved nearer to him and turned so he could reach inside my bag with his uninjured hand. He wasn't tied with both hands together like me. He was tied around the waist.

"Take the pot from my bag," I said softly.

The Dane glared at me as if he didn't trust me.

"I can help you," I said. "Take the pot."

He got the message, put his uninjured hand inside the bag, and rummaged around. He looked disappointed when he pulled out the salve pot and pushed the old wooden lid off with his thumb.

"You need that on your wound," I said. The pot held the healing salve I used on everyone for wounds and on myself, too. It was a buttery reduction of willow bark, onion, garlic, and strong wine. It worked usually, though not always. Sometimes the evil that comes from a wound spreads too quickly to be stopped.

The Dane shook his head, put the pot down, turned away. He didn't trust me.

"I swear on my life and to all the gods that I'm a healer sworn to help those who are ill. If you do not do what I suggest, you could die from the poison sickness."

He looked at me for a long time, his eyes boring into me, as if he was weighing up my soul. Then he put a finger into the pot and spread some of the salve carefully on the stump of his middle finger, wincing, twisting, and groaning, not loudly, but with great restraint. It was clear he was in real pain.

"Spread this again in the morning and pray hard to your god, and if you're lucky, you will see your wife and children again."

His face softened. Then he turned away to face the tent wall, groaning.

I slept strangely. First my sisters appeared in my dreams, asking me questions, then Stefan. He was talking fast, warning me about something. I woke with the dream still clear in my mind, but what he'd been warning me about was mostly gone. It was something to do with the prophecy. I was distracted then by pains all over my body from the way I'd slept, and the sound of horns blaring across the camp. The tent flap opened soon after and a guard pointed at me as another looked into the tent.

Were they going to release me? I pushed myself to my feet.

He spoke in a growl. "They know you're a spy, healer. It will be better for you if you confess." He looked sad.

"I have nothing to confess," I said equally loudly as dread filled me.

The Rise of Synne

He came nearer. "Whatever happens, you've been warned to tell all now while you still can. They know you're hiding something." He nodded his head as if he was sure of his words.

The Dane at the other side of the tent stared at me.

Had someone betrayed me? I kept my face straight as an urge to blurt out the truth and plead for my life rose inside me.

I pushed it away. "That is all lies."

"No," the man shouted. "You've had your chance." He slapped the back of his hand across my face, then stormed off.

I gasped, my body shaking, stinging pain spreading like a flame around my head. I'd been slapped before, so I knew the pain would go, but I also knew the feeling of vulnerability would last longer. It was a feeling I resented and was determined to resist. I would not crumple because of a slap. I straightened my face.

The other guard looked in the tent flap and laughed at me. "Looks like you've been discovered. You'll need the luck of all the gods now," he said in a rough Pictish accent. Then he left.

"I have that luck," I shouted after him, then I rocked back and forth.

"Be still, brave woman," said the Dane. He was cradling his mutilated hand.

I stopped rocking, took a long breath to calm myself, then cast my mind back to my sisters, how both Gytha and Tate used to hug me whenever I got into trouble because of my mouth, and how Stefan often joined us in the hug, until we were all locked together, inseparable. I could almost feel their arms around me. Stefan's message in the dream – was it about this?

Stefan used to ask me why I didn't use the powers I'd inherited from our mother to get us out of trouble by knowing what was coming for us. I'd laughed every time and explained that prophecies don't work that way. He'd always looked at me as if he knew I was hiding something. That made me laugh too. Not now.

Soon after, a twig-thin woman with her head covering pushed forward and wearing an old blood-stained tunic came into the tent. She poured watered-down ale into our mouths – first the Dane's, then mine. She also gave each of us a chunk of horsebread and a pitying look. As she handed the chunk of bread to me, I reached forward and gripped her hand.

"Do the earls treat all healers who come to help them like this?" I hissed.

She stared at me, her eyes wide, her gaze roaming over my face and body. She glanced at the flap in the tent wall, shook her head, hurried away.

"What were you two whispering about?" asked the Dane.

"Nothing. What did you do to deserve losing a finger?"

"Nothing." He spat the word out, turned away.

"What do they claim you did?"

After a long wait, he answered, "That I rutted a slave girl I'd not paid for."

"You paid a high price for that." I wondered was there more to it than rutting. I knew masters could expect compensation for someone taking advantage of one of their slaves, but I'd not heard of mutilation as a punishment.

"I'm still strong. They injured me, but I use my other hand for sword fighting. I'm good at that," he said. He grimaced, then went on. "Will you tell them what they want to know?"

"There's nothing to tell." I touched my face. It felt tender, as if I'd been kicked by a horse.

I held my hand at my face to ease the burning sensation.

"You were brought up to survive anything, like us, yes?" said the Dane.

"Yes," I said. My mother had taught us many things after my father had gone away. Never give up. Help people. Do whatever is needed. They were her rules.

"What happened to your family?"

"Dead or taken into slavery," I said. The throbbing in my face was getting better.

The Dane shrugged. Most people lived their lives in their villages without losing their whole families. But for some, their father went to war, and died, and the family went on. Not mine.

I was rocking again, back and forth, listening to the camp sounds, waiting. Would that evil man come again?

Later, someone else came instead. An older man in a fine brown tunic with red embroidery around its edges. He pointed at me.

"Freeborn healers do not get beaten in this camp while I'm still quartermaster," he said. "I've changed your guard."

He turned to the Dane. "You've been fed?" he asked.

The Dane nodded. The quartermaster left without looking at me. For the first time that day, I relaxed. They were not all evil here. The outcome of all of this was still not certain.

9

That evening, other guards came for me. "The earl Edwin wants you," one said. I'd eaten no more than a little bread all day and I was weak, but I'd been weak with hunger many times with Stefan.

I stood in the same spot in the earls' tent as before. There were fewer men at the tables this time and the air of jubilation had been replaced by a quiet soberness, like what you get in a hall the night after a feast.

Only one of the earls was at the top table. Edwin, the Earl of Mercia. A woman with red hair was sitting beside him, holding his arm, as if possessing him. She gave me a long, questioning stare, then looked away.

"You've been fighting," said Edwin, scowling at me.

The rope around my hands had been removed. I held my arms wrapped across my chest as I replied.

"I called someone a liar. Is that not allowed?" I threw my hands up.

No answer came.

"I am not a spy, my lord. When will I be released?" I spoke sharply, my voice nearly cracking, but strong enough. I would brazen this out.

Edwin stared into my eyes, probably expecting I'd flinch from his gaze. I didn't. "If I made you an offer to join our healers? Would you take it?" he asked.

"What healing needs doing?" I asked, my head up high, blinking in relief that my worst fears were just that, fears. If he was asking for help, that meant he believed me. I'd won. My hands pressed into my sides.

"Men from Mercia who fought with Harold have found their way to our camp. Many are wounded, some badly," he said.

"I will heal all where it is possible, my lord." The tightness in my chest was going.

He pointed at me. "You will do more than that. You will swear on your life to do all you can for our men. Do you swear it?"

The woman beside him gave me the slightest of nods, encouraging me to agree.

I waited a moment, watching his face.

"Yes, Earl Edwin. I swear it."

"Good, the lady Catheryn, here, has asked for your services. You will go with her and do whatever she tells you. That means everything she asks." His eyes widened.

The Rise of Synne

I nodded my acceptance. I had no idea what the woman would ask me to do, but I was not going to turn this down. The woman sitting beside Edwin stood. Her gown had rich gold and green embroidery lightly threaded down the front. She was taller than most women and as she came to me, she pulled her cloak around herself and put the hood up so that her hair was obscured.

"Follow me," she said as she passed by.

I followed her out of the tent, as if walking on air, and along a wide muddy track towards the back of the camp and into another large tent. My breathing had calmed. This was a tent for those in need of healing. My skill as a healer had become important again, and my mother had been proved right. Being a healer can save your life.

As we passed through the tent, the sickly sweet odour of rotting flesh came to me. This would not be an easy task.

Men lay on the ground on bloody blankets on dirty rushes. Many were curled up in pain. Some had weeping wounds. Others had a dazed, blank look.

Thick candles on wax-smeared iron holders lit the tent with a dim light.

Lady Catheryn turned to me. Her tone was sharp. "We have two other healers. That is all. We lost two physicians in battle. They are sorely missed. Our healers are exhausted. You must work through the night to help all you can, while our healers sleep."

My tone was brisk in reply. "I'll need food, any stew you have, and someone to boil water."

"You'll get it all."

I suppressed a smile. I hadn't imagined she'd cooperate so easily. She hurried away, as if wanting out of the tent and its grisly occupants as quickly as possible.

I found the two other healers at the back, both sitting on the ground with their heads between their hands, their eyes closed, and their hair uncovered the way healers wear it. I tapped the grey-haired woman's shoulder.

"I'm a healer too, go and rest," I said. "The two of you. I will see to the wounded tonight." It was a confident statement, but the right thing to do. More men would die tomorrow if these healers did not get rest.

The woman looked up. Her skin was pale, her eyes bloodshot. She put her hand out, held mine tight, her knuckles white. "Some will go across to the other side this night. We did all we could. I swear to Christ, and all the angels and the saints."

"Are there poultices and salves?" I asked. I'd been tasked with looking after sick people a few times during our travels looking for our sisters. Getting what you needed quickly was important.

The old healer pointed further along the back of the tent. "Go there," she said. Then she peered into my face. "I'll put something on that bruise. How did you get that?"

The Rise of Synne

"I called a man a liar."

She laughed, shook her head.

After applying a thick salve, she and the other healer, who I learned was her daughter, went off to rest. I walked up and down the ranks of the wounded, sizing up the task. I looked into each face, examined each wound. There is a feeling you get when someone is near death. A cold shiver in your heart. I got it several times as I moved around.

A cauldron of cold water appeared, carried by two young slave boys. "Take this to a fire and boil it," I said. "One of you stay with the fire, watching it. The other is to bring bowls of water to me when it boils. No one else is to take the water or use it." I said it firmly and glowered at them.

They went. Waterskins appeared after that and a thick stew, carried in a smaller black cauldron by other slaves. I took a small bowl of it myself; I needed to keep my strength up. Thankfully, there were chunks of meat in it. I chewed at them with the pleasure of the truly hungry. Then I went to work, moving from one man to the next with a light touch, a word, a poultice, some stew. The smiles and tears in return told me what I was doing worked.

The sky was getting light, and glimmers were filtering through cracks in the tent walls by the time I was finished dealing with each man. I must have cleaned and bound a dozen wounds and patted more heads and listened to stories, and told each of them all would be good, even though it wasn't true. Better to die with hope in your heart than despair. I would lie to anyone for that any day and any night. I whispered to myself, too. My mother's words kept coming back to me. *I was being saved for a reason.* But what reason? Was I meant to find my sisters or perhaps another of her prophecies would come true too? So much had changed after years of everything being the same, anything was possible. These thoughts sustained me, even as my body ached with exhaustion.

The slaves who came and went did good work. I assumed that meant they were well treated here. I found all the pots of salves, sniffed them, worked out which to use and put them on wounds, despite the cries of some of the men I touched.

Some men didn't cry out, for whatever reason. Some had their eyes wide open, and their faces twitched in pain, but they said nothing.

Pain, like fear, affects some differently.

It grew cold during the night. I sent off for cloaks and more blankets and for another brazier to be brought. Two smaller braziers arrived, carried by men with poles. Someone important would be losing their warmth that night.

I stepped outside for fresh air only once. The stars were bright, shining beacons in the upperworld. Rushing

The Rise of Synne

clouds gave notice that the weather was changing. Anything could come tomorrow.

The death of one young man made my head dip. He'd tried to grip my hand near the end, but his strength faded. Not long ago he would have been handsome, a young girl's dream, but now he had a festering wound on his face where his cheek had been hacked open and you could see his teeth. Someone had tried to burn the wound, badly. It hadn't helped. How he'd made it to this place, I could only guess. His wound would have been covered by a poultice bandage when they came here, and by hope.

It was the tears welling in his eyes, as he knew he was going, that set me off. His mouth moved, but no words came out. I held his hand tight, kissed it, muttered the Lord's Prayer over him as my tears fell on our clasped hands. I noticed a blue rune on his cheek and muttered a prayer to the old gods too, that they would know he had passed in combat.

As the light grew the next morning, I had the dead taken away. I'd heard a pit had been opened. I stood by the entrance of the tent, held my pendants where they lay on my chest, and prayed for those on their last journey. Exhaustion pulled at me, and my head thumped. I heard voices, too, mixed with the babbling from the wounded in the tent. Stefan's came to me clearly, asking why I had not saved him. I pushed away bitter tears. I'd failed him. I begged for my mother's voice after that, whispering her name and her mother's name before her to help me become a better healer.

Soon after, the two other healers returned. The old woman pulled me up from where I'd ended up sitting. She kissed both my cheeks. I could not even move my lips to kiss her back. I was so tired. And I'd seen and heard too many things.

"'Tis grand work you did last night," said the old woman. "You're from the north, too. I can tell by your accent. I thank you for your healing work, from my heart and that of my daughter and all here." Her daughter nodded, put a hand out. I swayed into darkness. It swallowed me.

10

It was late that day when I woke on a blanket with another thicker one over me. I was in a small tent. Other blankets and leather bags filled the back wall. I guessed it was the tent of the healers, but I didn't remember being carried there. My head was thumping, and my body ached in many places. I closed my eyes again, but it was no good. I opened them, found a waterskin nearby and drank deeply. Part of a loaf of horsebread had been left beside the waterskin. I devoured the bread. My hopes were high that all the accusations against me had been forgotten, and that my work healing their men would allow me to find out things and finish the job I'd been sent here for.

I went back to the tent of the wounded. There was a guard outside it now. He let me pass. Inside, the two healers were hurrying about. I asked what I could do to help and soon I was changing poultices and feeding men and whispering comfort to any man who looked at me with eyes that held fear.

I worked with only a short break to eat some stew. In the late afternoon, Catheryn appeared.

"Sleep again now, Synne," she said. "You'll be woken in the middle of the night to take over the healing and the watch."

Her gaze flickered around the tent. I expected the smell of festering wounds and imminent death was not to her liking. But it is the way of every thing.

I went back to the healer's tent and slept fitfully until I was called in the middle of the night. I took up the same duties as the night before. Two more men died that night. One claimed he was freezing, though he was beside a brazier. He grabbed my hand and babbled about the Normans at the end. Something about their giant horses. Just before he died, he swore an oath against the Godwins sneering at how stupid they'd been to not wait for reinforcements before taking to the battlefield, and how the northern earls must head back north and stay out of the fight for the crown of England.

***

The next morning, early, still tired, I was summoned to Catheryn and Edwin's tent. Two guards with spears blocked my way at the entrance to their tent. They called inside that I'd arrived. Catheryn cried out for me to be let in. The inside of this tent was more lavish than anything

I'd ever seen. A thickly embroidered russet-red carpet lay on the ground and a wide, bright tapestry with a hunting scene in gold thread hung on a rack at the back. The earl's sleeping area was most likely behind it.

Catheryn was sitting on a bench, leaning forward, her hair in wild disarray around her. She pointed at another bench near her on the other side of a carved wooden tray sitting on the carpet. On the tray, there were earthen cups and a bowl of crinkly green apples.

"We have honey water for you, Synne, and please, take an apple," she said. Her tone was soft and sweet. She smiled at me. It seemed forced, as if she was troubled by something but hiding it.

I sat opposite her, took an apple and bit into it. It was sweet, so good. I ate it fast as I glanced around to see who might be listening or watching us. The earl was not in the tent, nor were there any slaves or guards. I relaxed a little.

"I hear good things about you," said Catheryn after a few moments. "You saved lives that our healers thought lost. I give thanks to you from all these men and from their families." She raised her earthen cup towards me.

I bowed. Her praise felt good. "I did what I could. It is God's will if I succeeded." I glanced around again. "There is no monk in your service to hold prayers for the wounded or dead. It will help them." I'd seen how a priest or monk could relieve fear with a prayer, as if performing miracles.

Catheryn shook her head. "The earl sent them all away after the last battle up north. He lost all faith in prayers."

"Perhaps we can ask for a monk or a priest in London to do it?"

Catheryn raised a finger. "You are here for something else," she said. She sipped from her cup, her eyes searching me, trying to look inside me, looking for what, I did not know. She did not speak again for a while. Weighing her words, most likely.

I wondered what she wanted. Did she think I could have saved more of their men?

She leant towards me. "I want you to come with me to the Hallows Eve feast in London tomorrow in the woolmen's hall. You will sit near our table." She looked down at a part-finished embroidery in front of her. She was not asking me to come with her. She was telling me.

My mouth opened. I wasn't sure how to reply.

There had to be a reason for this invitation. A reason she wasn't telling me. There was something strange about this. It felt wrong. I'd never been invited to such a ceremony, ever. Since we'd left our village, all we'd managed to do was sneak in at the back of an occasional feast in a village hall. My mother had stopped us taking up

The Rise of Synne

village invitations in the years before she was murdered, after my father went to war and never returned. It was one of the reasons we weren't married young. No one ever saw us. It had felt as if my mother was hiding us, always promising there was a reason we could not marry any young man who called for us, never explaining exactly what that reason was. We sisters feared we would never get offers because of this. It had all made me feel like an outcast, different, even before she died.

"I do not have a good tunic," I said.

"I'll find you one." She pointed at the table, a smile on her face, making me think she wanted something. "Take that comb and use the water bucket behind the tent to clean your face and hair. And put that wristband on."

Beside the comb was a wide leather wristband with an owl head shape cut into it. A small ivory comb lay beside it. "The owl is from my mother's banner," she said forcefully. "Keep the band on." She would not be denied. "Do not join the healers tonight. Come back here when you have slept." She waved dismissively in my direction.

I took the comb and put the wristband on. It was a tight fit but looked good on my wrist. I left her, found the healer's tent, and slept for a while. Questions circled inside me. Why was I going to this feast? What did Catheryn want? I prayed I'd hear my mother's voice again with some advice. I held my amulet tight, but I did not hear her.

I dreamt of the men who'd killed my mother. They were looking for me.

***

I woke to find a tunic beside my blanket. My cheek still hurt, but only a little, from where I'd been slapped. I slipped the new tunic on. It was fox brown and made of soft, thick wool with an embroidered blue ridge along all the edges. When I put it on, a tingle of guilty pleasure ran through me. It was a fine tunic, the best I'd ever worn. It brushed softly on my skin. Who would I see tonight, I wondered? Unbidden, I thought about Magnus. I imagined him seeing me in this tunic, smiling. My mind works in ways it has no right to work. My body tightened at the thought of him. I shook my head to dispel these stupid thoughts.

I decided not to eat the hunk of bread that had been left by someone near the tunic. I said a prayer instead for the one thing I needed to come from all this, that I would find my sisters, and nothing would distract me. Then I went to find Catheryn in her tent. I had my old cloak over the new tunic when I arrived in front of her.

"Take that dirty thing off," she said loud and sharply, pointing at my cloak. "We'll throw it in the fire. Wear this one." She nodded toward a fine black cloak lying on the

The Rise of Synne

bench near her. It was beautiful, precious, too good for me. I hesitated, but under her glare, I took mine off.

"Take that and burn it," she said to the two slaves hovering in the shadows.

I put on the new cloak slowly, fumbling at its smoothness. I tightened my lips not to show pleasure. This was all a trick. It had to be. She would have it taken from me and laugh at my presumption. The cloak was as soft as the skin of a new baby. She nodded after I put it on.

"What do you want me to do at the feast?" I asked softly.

"Enjoy yourself," she said, then she put her head to one side, and smiled again in that strange way that felt as if she was seeking a way inside me. "And keep the wristband on display. If someone gives you a message for me, say it only to me, understood?"

I nodded. "Yes." Was this why she was trusting me? Did she fear her own slaves would report anything they heard to someone else? I'd heard before of outsiders being used for tasks for this reason.

"Be aware, Synne. All the woolmen go crazy at Hallows Eve." She said it with a smirk. "I've never seen so many ram's horns out than at their feasts. Do not be lured with promises, do you understand?"

"I'm not easy led," I replied firmly. I had good reason, too. I'd been fooled before. I'd given myself to a smooth-talking village boy, only to listen to his bright laughter and feel his disdain the following day.

Catheryn pointed at the golden bowl. "Hold this," she said. "You will swear loyalty to me with blood now." She paused, her eyes on me. Had my face given away my shock? "Are you willing to do this?" She put her head to one side, her eyes widening, daring me to say no.

Could I refuse her? Who knew what she would do if I turned her down? All I could hear was my heart beating and the hiss from the brazier.

"I'm willing." I said it loud.

She stared at me for a long moment, measuring me it seemed, then motioned me to come near her with a crooked finger. She looked like a cat about to pounce on its prey. "Do you fear me, healer?"

I kept my voice as low as hers when I replied. "No, I do not, Lady Catheryn. I'm just cautious, my lady." I pressed my lips together. I'd said too much already. A simple no was all she probably wanted.

"Trust me, Synne," she whispered, looking over my shoulder as if checking who could hear us. "I will tell you something you can use against me." She leaned close enough for me to smell the rose oil she used on her skin. "My mother owns a whorehouse. The best in London." She gave me a half-smile, as if only half convinced that what she said was true. Then her words came in a flood.

The Rise of Synne

"My own beauty was saved for someone of high standing, a prince or an earl. Because of that, she gave this to me." She waved her hand through the air. "Did I not do well?" She smiled wider.

"You did." I nodded. An earl was someone usually far beyond the daughter of a whorehouse owner, but Catheryn's beauty was obvious, and many men are weak for beauty.

"Tell me about your mother," she said. Her smile was smaller now, but real, as if confiding in me had brought her pleasure.

I opened my mouth, closed it, opened it again, unsure of what to say. I hadn't spoken about my mother in a long time. But it felt right to do so now, as if the words wanted to be said, to lift a burden from me.

"Trust me," she whispered. Her tone was silky. "No one else is here."

"My mother, she…" I began, my words tumbling over each other, "was a famous healer and a seer. People came to our village for help all the time. Me and my sisters wanted for nothing. After my father left to go to war, she died, trying to protect us." I stopped. Was that enough for her? I took a long, deep breath.

"What happened to your father?"

"He never came back. That's all I know." A tightness filled my neck. I blinked, pressed my feelings down.

"He's dead?"

"I do not know."

"What happened to your mother, Synne? How did she die?"

It took a few moments for me to tell her the story. "Raiders came to our house. They… they cut her throat and took my sisters." I spoke fast. "My brother and I searched half the country for them this past year. And now he's dead too, so it's just me searching." I was trembling, unsure if I was right to say it all.

"Men are such devils." Catheryn opened her arms to hug me.

I hugged her, hard, felt her compassion. Would she help me?

An urge to say more rose up inside me. My tongue had loosened.

"The elders in our village banished us. They were afraid the raiders would come back for us. They didn't want to help us." That memory still angered me.

"Such men deserve to lose everything," she said, her tone sympathetic.

I nodded. She was right.

She shuddered, as if my story had affected her. "I know you proper now, Synne. And I have tasks you can help me with, but first, you must swear the bond of loyalty between us will not be broken, as long as you live." She pulled a thin, gold-handled fruit knife from a sheath on her embroidered belt and put it to the pad of skin below her thumb, pressing it lightly in.

"Will you swear loyalty in blood to me, Synne the Healer?"

I replied, "I will." There could be no hesitation. I knew that.

Catheryn cut a little into her skin until blood oozed in a red ball. She let a drop fall into the bowl, then held the knife out for me. The wind had picked up outside, pushing at the leather tent walls as if a giant was pressing in on them. Without further thought, I took the knife, cut myself as she had done, and dripped blood into the bowl she held out until it mixed with hers.

"We are blood sisters now," said Catheryn. She took the bowl, wiped some of the blood on her lips, and passed it back to me. I did the same and tasted iron and salt on my tongue. She put her hand out, gripped mine tight. I felt the bond between us and a sliver of hope too that she would help me, though I knew it was too early to tell.

She shouted for her slaves, and for good bread and stew to be brought and a bowl of water. She seemed happy, glowing. Being blood sisters meant that someone was on your side. It was the first time I'd sworn this way to anyone. But I still wondered what Catheryn's purpose was in doing this with a lowly healer.

Then the stew came.

To my surprise, she admired my eyes and said I looked beautiful despite. I laughed. I knew I wasn't beautiful, even if some men had claimed it before. Such talk always seems a ploy.

She gave me short boots to wear and a blue brooch. I was wary where all this was going, but I kept quiet.

When we'd eaten, I asked, "When do we go to London?"

She rubbed her hands together. "Soon. There are horses and guards waiting. You can ride, I assume?" She blinked, concern evident on her face.

Some low-born people never went on a horse, but my father had insisted we all knew how to ride.

"Yes." My wariness was dimming. It pleased me she was bringing me with her, that she'd gone through all this with me. At the very least, my chances of finding out something useful would be better now. I wouldn't have to go skulking around their camp or try to extract information from dying men.

She stood. "Wait here," she said.

I breathed deep and slow, stared at the glowing brazier that stood behind where she'd been sitting.

I was her blood sister.

I didn't know what she wanted, but I had a chance to get what I wanted. The only problem with going to London was who was going to see me.

11

Catheryn gripped me through the upper arm of my tunic. I hadn't heard her come back. "There is something you should know." Her face came close to mine. Her blue eyes blazed angrily beneath her black hair. "The guard who hit you." She paused, leaned close.

"What about him?" A memory of his angry face when I'd called him a liar came back to me.

"It was Morcar who sent him to break you." She was whispering. I could barely hear her. "That's why it was so easy for him to get past the tent guard." She laughed lightly. "But you didn't break. That's a good sign."

For a long stupid moment, I thought she would kiss me, our faces were that close. Instead, she pulled back and examined me. I could hear her breathing, snorting almost.

Where was this all going?

She stood back, called for her slave, who helped dress her in a green gown with a ribbon of gold embroidery across the front and more along its top edge. When she was finished adjusting and examining herself in a small

The Rise of Synne

polished silver mirror, the size of the palm of her hand, which she got me to hold for her and move about, she said, "We are all here for a reason, Synne. Mine is connected to my mother, as yours is, I am sure."

She turned her head one last time, looking at herself, preening.

But she was right. My mother had gifted me everything that made me who I am. I was here because of her. We were connected still and always will be.

Outside the tent, men and women were waiting around in small groups. The slaves must have spread the word that Catheryn was heading to London in her finery. They'd expect her to be a sight. But they didn't expect me to be going with her. I was a healer and not one they knew. Some of the expressions on the faces around us were crooked when we left the tent, as if people were wondering what I was doing with Catheryn at all. Or were the expressions to do with her?

As I waited for my horse to be led forward, and after Catheryn was up in her saddle, the older healer woman I'd worked with appeared at my side. She pulled at my sleeve and whispered to me as I turned to her.

"She's not the earl's wife, beware," she said, all soft, like a cat purring.

I was shocked and went still for a moment. I'd assumed Catheryn was his wife, even though I knew it wasn't unknown for lords to enjoy other women while at war. This news also meant Catheryn's position was not as strong as I'd thought. I nodded my thanks.

My horse was a smaller mare than Catheryn's and it snickered a lot, but when I nudged it forward, it went up beside hers as we left the camp, with a line of mostly men watching us, talking to one another. I heard laughter in the distance as we left the camp behind, but the four men at arms with us had their grim faces on and were looking straight ahead as we set off in the middle of the afternoon towards London.

"You did not want to arrive by cart?" I asked her. Two of the men guarding us were in front and two behind.

"And take another day to reach London? No. We are needed there tonight." She picked up the pace and soon we were trotting steadily. We passed many carts coming from London empty and a few heading into the city, as well as some other riders who stared at us as we passed. The air was icy and still, with a distant fog on the horizon. It felt as if the world was waiting for something to happen. The occasional twitter of bloodwings and the groan of oxen could be heard at times, otherwise the clatter of hooves filled my ears and questions filled my mind about what I'd gotten myself into.

Catheryn had two leather bags behind her on her horse. I had no idea how long we would stay in the city, but from her limited baggage, it didn't appear as if we'd be there more than a night or two. The oldest of the guards accompanying us spoke to her many times as we rode, as if they knew each other well.

I was surprised that no other servants went with her, but when we reached London, I understood. Before going to the woolmen's hall for the feast, we stopped at a large hall inside the city wall. It had a high-walled garden and its own gatehouse and a wicker gate with sharp spikes on top protecting it. We went through the gate, which opened as we came near, as if we were expected.

Inside, Catheryn was greeted by servants and slaves as a mistress. The house had two levels at the front, and smoke drifted from the light, newly thatched roof. Smaller wattle and mud houses lined the outer walls of the square area inside the gate. Men at arms took our horses and led them to a water trough as Catheryn and I went into the main house. It was as well apportioned inside as the best village hall I'd ever been in. Drying game birds hung thick from a rafter at the back and a long loom stood to one side with a dark blue cloth on it with a pattern in pale blue thread.

A fire blazed in the centre of the room and a haze of smoke hung in the air above us. An older woman was sitting at a square table with loaves of bread and wooden beakers for ale in front of her. She wore a grey tunic with a pale blue embroidered border.

"This is a healer from the north, Mother," said Catheryn, using her thumb to point at me.

"What's the name?" asked Catheryn's mother, without looking at me directly as we approached. There was a hard tone to her voice.

"Synne," I replied.

Catheryn's mother coughed. It turned into a fit of coughing. I offered to help, but she waved me away.

"I've 'ad every healer in London give me potions," she said, between spasms of coughing. Finally, she looked at me with watery eyes. "But you're welcome in our house, healer. Where did you practise the healing arts?"

I wanted to mention I'd been with Harold's army, but I caught myself in time. "Up north," I said. "I travelled around after my mother died, healing people using all she'd taught me."

"Good, healers are needed in this city," she said.

"Have things got worse?" asked Catheryn.

Her mother nodded, coughed, put her hand to her mouth, and when her coughing stopped, she spoke. "They 'ad a Witan last night. Not one thegn or bishop would let Harold's sons speak. Their claim on the throne is weak. The Witan favours a boy, that youngling Edgar. Can you believe it? They say his Wessex royal blood gives him

The Rise of Synne

more claim to the throne than anyone else. But they might as well send William an invitation to come and take the city. Someone's sold the Godwins out." She shook her head, groaned. "Again, we are divided. It is England's curse." She took a deep, rattling breath. "What news from Edwin?"

"I'll see him at the woolmen's feast tonight, Mother. Synne will come with me." Catheryn sat down at the table opposite her mother. She patted the place beside her for me to sit.

"What do you make of all the men vying for the kingship, Synne?" Catheryn asked. She smiled at me as if we were friends.

I wondered again what she wanted. I wished that my mother would speak to me. I needed her guidance, to know if I should trust Catheryn.

"That's all men's business," I said. Best not to show any interest in such things.

Catheryn laughed. "You know a lot of things will change if the Normans get to rule over us." She pointed at her mother. "Did you hear about their new taxes?"

Her mother shook her head. "No, but I do know a lot of good people will die if this city defies the Normans." She broke a piece from the loaf of dark bread in front of her and handed it to me. "All that's good about England will be gone soon enough." She coughed again.

"Perhaps I can help you with a new potion?" I asked her with a smile.

She shook her head.

"We've no time for you to work your way into our hearts, sweet healer Synne. We must prepare," said Catheryn. She grabbed the bread from in front of her mother and pulled a chunk off to eat.

"Who will be there?" asked her mother, turning to her daughter.

"King Harold's sons, probably. The earls too. And a hundred stinking woolmen. Edgar, our supposed boy king, may be there. I expect he'll want to suck up to the woolmen like they all do."

Her mother laughed. "You'll be at the top table?" she asked.

"Nothing less," said Catheryn. "And Synne will sit near me." She put her hand out, grabbed my wrist, pressed some bread into my palm. I had no choice but to eat and smile, but the whole thing left me with a strange feeling. There were things going on between them I knew nothing about. Catheryn's mother was rocking back and forward, her eyes looking off towards something only she could see.

Then she turned and glared at me. "Will this be your first time at a big feast, Synne?"

"I've been to village feasts," I said.

The Rise of Synne

"So, it is your first time," said her mother, nodding to herself. "Well, if you want to please my daughter, stay in your proper mind. No ale." She swished her finger back and forth, then pointed at her daughter. "Has he done what I told you, daughter?"

"He will, tonight," said Catheryn. She pushed her cloak off her shoulder. Pale-bare skin, with a thick twisted-gold chain around her neck, came into view. The orbs of her breasts were almost fully visible when she leaned forward.

Her mother nodded, smiled. "What about you, Synne? I bet you're promised to some eager young man."

I shook my head. "No man'll marry me. I have no land, and I'm in mourning, and worse, I have no family to help in the bad times, so I travel around, rootless."

Catheryn's mother slapped the table, sending breadcrumbs flying. "No, Synne. Any young man would be lucky to get you, someone to heal him and be straight with him, as I sense you are." She reached a hand toward me and patted the air near my head, as if feeling my hair without touching me.

"But before you give yourself, ask the man who wants you, if he has won the spoils of war, or fame and position, for only then can he ask you for all you can give." Her hands curled in the air, intertwining.

It sounded like a practised speech, but it cheered me. When I'd been travelling with Stefan, I'd few hopes of finding any man I wanted to marry, someone I admired, wanted, but perhaps she was right, perhaps I might find someone who'd think they were lucky to get me. I allowed myself a smile. I'd kept my longings buried deep. But she was right, there was still hope. I might have a chance for someone. That was a good thought. Was that what I'd been saved for?

We departed for the feast as the sky darkened. The moon flitted between clouds while the flicker of torches lit the courtyard. Excited shouts could be heard in the distance as revellers enjoyed All Hallows' Eve, racing from house to house no doubt, demanding food or ale, with crowds of young men and women masked as wolves or bears or deer with parts of skulls on their heads and with their faces smeared in ash.

This was the night when the dead came back.

This All Hallows would be different. I'd heard my mother speaking to me from the other side, the veil between the underworld and ours opening. It might also mean the powers she'd had were waking in me. Perhaps it took death and grief to birth them in me, but so be it. I had changed. Something was different in me. Did it mean I'd be able to glimpse the future, what fate had in store for us,

The Rise of Synne

as she'd been able to? Would this All Hallows mark even more of her powers coming to me?

As we rode on, the crowds at the street corners seemed intent on devilry in a way I'd not seen before. This was a sign, surely, of the change people knew was coming after the death of King Harold and with the duke approaching the city. I felt it too. A swirling, excited, everything-is-changing feeling in the air, as if a storm was brewing. The world I'd known would not be the same. I would not be the same.

We passed open ground with a bonfire crackling and hissing loud, smoke billowing and a smell of burning wood and ale stinking the air. Crowds swirled around the fire, too, swigging from ale cups and wineskins. Many people were dancing or roaring into the air as a ring of men and women holding each other tight in the middle danced around the bonfire. One young man rushed into the fire, grabbed a stake burning at one end, and raced off into the night with two young women running screeching behind him. Laughter followed them.

When we reached the giant hulk of Woolman's Hall with its ram's skulls all along the roof edge, and a crowd around it, a cart was depositing people at a giant door, where golden light streamed out onto expectant faces. We waited at the back for those people to go in. I had picked up the excitement as the sound of revelry leaked from the wide doors.

In the shadows, at the side of the building, beggars waited, leaning against the walls of the hall. They knew there'd be leftover scraps for them. Our guards dismounted, held our horses, and stood on each side of us as Catheryn and I dismounted. She waited for me before going inside but went in a step ahead of me. The doors were held open for us and a doorman bowed low as we passed. A wave of heat and noise hit me as I went in. It made me blink.

Inside was the biggest crowd and the brightest hall I'd ever been in. My mouth opened. A thick smell of roast meat made my mouth water. It seemed to me that we'd joined a royal feast. What miracle had sent a lowly healer to accompany the mistress of the Earl of Mercia to a feast like this? I could not deny it. Catheryn was right, change was coming.

She turned to me. "Take my cloak," she said brightly. "Keep it with you and let no one take it from you." She gripped my arm, tight. "Keep your wristband on view. Now walk with me to the top table." As we set off, she kept talking. "Find a place at a table near the top of the room with some of the older women at it. You're my healer, if anyone asks."

The Rise of Synne

Within moments, I knew why she needed me to walk with her. The tables were lined up facing each other with a line of three facing towards us at the top. The passage between the rows of tables was narrow. Men were reaching across and passing ale and knives to each other. They were also grabbing at serving girls. They did it to raucous shouts of encouragement from other men at the tables.

The harassed serving girls slipped away from the men in a practised manner. Walking near Catheryn, who was a little ahead of me, meant I could slap aside any hand reaching for her. If Earl Edwin, visible now at the top table, and waving drunkenly at her, saw a man take hold of Catheryn, a fight would most likely start and perhaps blood be spilled.

She would not want her entrance to be marred that way.

As I watched, a space was made for Catheryn at the top table beside Edwin. He rocked drunkenly as he moved himself and his brother, Morcar, stared in my direction. No woman sat beside him.

After she'd sat down, I went to a table, two back from the top, where a group of older women, all in fine yellow woollen dresses, were sitting. One side of the bench at the side of their table was less crowded. I stood by the woman at the end. She turned to me and said, "Who are you, girl?"

"I'm a healer with the Earl of Mercia."

She budged up. "The earl and his partner are to be welcomed. That is what my husband tells me, so you are too. Sit, girl. Would you like wine or ale?"

"Ale, a small pot."

Ale and bread were passed to me. I sipped a little and exchanged a few words with the woman opposite, while keeping one eye on the top table, in case I was called.

The sweet smell of roasting meat was strong here. It filled my nostrils as a troop of servants brought still-smoking roasted whole sheep on spits through the hall. The spits were lined up along the side wall near us and servants cut hunks of meat off them and brought them to the tables on wooden platers accompanied by creamy leeks and braised onions in giant bowls. I waited impatiently and was finally served. I'd never tasted anything better. I enjoyed every mouthful. This night was turning out better than I'd hoped.

Catheryn was clearly enjoying herself too, swinging from side to side, talking to everyone around her with one of her shoulders bare and the top of a breast visible. Men openly stared at her. She was certainly different to any other woman at the top table; more lively, animated.

Drummers came into the hall in a line then, followed by flute players, their flutes held high. They all circled the hall, raising a fast, blood-stirring beat, as if an army was approaching. More wineskins appeared. I was offered

The Rise of Synne

more ale, but like most of the women at my table, I refused. Many of the women disappeared from time to time. I saw one talking to a man at a nearby table, remonstrating with him, her finger waving. Presumably, she was keeping her husband in check.

I was asked, twice, if I'd heard how many men had died at the great battle, and if I knew anyone who'd been lost. I shook my head each time, though it did not feel right to deny what had happened to Stefan. But I could not speak my denial, as I knew more lies might be demanded from me and feared how lies grow once one is out of your mouth. One woman looked fearful and on the edge of tears as she asked the question. I found out that her son had gone with Harold's army and had not been heard from since. I wished her good fortune but sensed a darkness around her and in her hollow eyes, which made me think she was right in believing he was dead.

She leaned over to me and whispered, "Some say them Normans will kill us all. They say they'll come in the night like wolves and cut all our throats." Her words came slowly as she blinked, wide-eyed.

I put my hand on her arm. "They'll not kill us all." I smiled, held her tight. There was something about her that made me think she would not survive all this.

She looked away, tears flowing, wiping at them fast.

"They are followers of Christ," I said. "They can't kill everyone. I hope you find your son. We must all be brave. Like wolves." I growled. She smiled, nodded her thanks. I kept my hand on her arm until she was distracted by the woman on the other side of her.

I went to find the necessary room. I discovered a line of men and women waiting outside the back of the hall. An icy wind bit at us all and bright stars above and a single flickering torch lit the small room with a hole in a bench where we could go.

When I was on my way back, a woman put her hand on my shoulder.

"Where did you get that wristband?" she asked angrily, looking at my arm.

"My lady gave it to me."

"What name?"

"Catheryn."

"You go tell your lady to come to the back of the hall at once. At once, you hear?"

I nodded, took note of her face, and went to the top table. A thought came to me as I went. This was why I was here. I was a messenger.

I waited for the right moment, then whispered the message in Catheryn's ear.

She leaned to Edwin, spoke quietly, rose, and came with me. The drummers were finishing up as we passed

The Rise of Synne

them. As we reached the end of the hall, I saw the monk Ulf at a table. My heart sank. Would he reveal he knew me by speaking to me? Many would know he was with the Godwins. Perhaps Catheryn would too. My stomach tightened.

I looked away from Ulf, but I knew he'd spotted me. Then I saw her, the woman who'd given me the message. She was sitting at the last table on the other side.

I led Catheryn to her, fast, and tapped the woman's arm. She turned and reached for Catheryn, who bent down and whispered something to her. The woman shook her head. Catheryn stood out among the revellers at the back of the hall, her clothes brighter, more provocative, but there was such a show going on, with jugglers now cavorting and the drums still beating; some eyes would be distracted.

"Where are you staying?" Catheryn asked the woman, as she stood back from her. They had exchanged other words, which I did not hear.

"The black dog," replied the woman. "Is this your slave?"

"No, no, we're blood sisters. She is my healer," said Catheryn. She put her hand on my arm. It was a possessive but friendly gesture, and it felt good, made me feel part of something. I got an urge to tell her things. To trust her.

My shoulders twitched. Someone's gaze was on me. I glanced around and stiffened. Ulf.

"Let us go, sweet Synne," said Catheryn with a sly smile, as if she knew everything I was thinking. She pulled me away with her. We walked around the hall until we'd returned to the top table. She waved at a few people as she passed but did not stop at any other table. I felt exposed walking with her, with many eyes on us.

Edwin opened his arms to her as she sat. She fell into them, entwined herself around him. He appeared not to care that there were men at nearby tables all looking hungrily at her.

I went back to my seat. I wanted to leave this place, having eaten my fill, and seen enough. I did not want to watch her anymore. A storyteller would probably arrive soon, telling endless tales of woolmen fighting some wolf or three, telling endless riddles about how brave the woolmen are. Men love such tales, don't they?

I took to staring at Catheryn and Edwin, willing them to leave. But they looked happy, him sharing morsels with her and her refilling his gold cup while she clung to him as if he was a mast in a raging storm. I knew I shouldn't think like this, but their good fortune seemed a goad, sent to show me how little I had. Resentment grew inside me. Why should she have everything?

The Rise of Synne

My plan, until the fall of King Harold, had been simple: earn coin and save enough to search for and find my sisters.

But seeing the power Catheryn had over this earl, it made me wonder. Was there more I could aspire to? A better life after finding my sisters. A powerful man I could bend to my will. I glanced down the hall, wondering if Ulf would spoil everything, but as each moment passed, it became obvious that he'd not be rushing to me, and slowly I felt more secure.

He'd seen me, for sure, and he knew now I was involved with the Earl of Mercia in some way. But he must know I'd return and tell them what I'd achieved when I had something good to tell.

But when would that be? I'd found out almost nothing so far and it seemed I was more likely to be sucked into Catheryn's plans than her into mine.

"Synne," a voice called from behind.

I jumped inside my skin and turned. It was Ulf. I wanted to scream at him to go away.

"What happened to your eye, Synne?" he asked.

"It's nothing. It'll heal soon. Go away," I hissed.

"You've done well to be here," he said with a slight smile, looking over my new tunic and washed hair. He made a sign of the cross over me. "I pray you do not fall into evil, my girl. Do you have news? We need news." He leaned closer. His friendly expression changed as he came nearer. The urgency in his tone concerned me. What had been happening with Magnus and Edmund since I'd been away?

I glanced beyond Ulf's shoulder. Had Catheryn seen me talking with him? Hopefully, she'd think he was just a monk who'd taken to me. I let out a sigh as I saw her laughing with Edwin and not looking in my direction at all.

"Go away, Ulf, you'll give me away," I said softly, but with force. "I have nothing useful yet. I'll come as soon as I can." I kept my face stiff, so Catheryn would not see anything was wrong, but I gripped the edge of the table. *Go. Please go.* I thought the words as I stared at him.

"Find out something, Synne. Magnus asks about you every day."

I stared into his wide, pale eyes. Was it good Magnus was asking for me? Probably not.

He made a sign of the cross over me and disappeared. I let my breath out, sat back, glanced again at Catheryn. She was staring at me. Not good. Beside her stood one of the doormen in his woollen outfit. He was leaning down, telling her something. Her expression changed. She grabbed Edwin's arm, whispered to him. They both stood immediately. Was this to do with me? I bit my lip. Should I run? How far would I get? No, I had to brazen it out. I

The Rise of Synne

stared at them as they came around the top table. I felt transfixed, as if by a flurry of arrows.

Edwin signalled to a man at one of the other tables as they came near. I expected hands to grab me. But they didn't, though a hubbub of noise rose all around us. Then Catheryn motioned with her head for me to join them. I grabbed our cloaks and followed, damp sweat trickled down my back. Stay strong. Iron-strong.

At the entrance to the hall, a haggard man was waiting. I'd seen him at Catheryn's mother's house. His face was blood-smeared and his expression wide-eyed and desperate. I knew at once, with a guilty tingle of relief, that this hurried departure was nothing to do with me. There was about something else, something dangerous, going on.

Edwin was already putting his cloak on, handed to him by a slave. He didn't have a long sword with him, but he did have a short sword on his belt. My small axe was somewhere back at the earls' camp. I missed it. Catheryn took her cloak as I offered it.

"How many men are with you?" she asked Edwin.

"Six," he replied.

"I have four. We have enough," said Catheryn.

Our horses were waiting in a stable yard at the side of the hall. I felt the suck of dread pulling at me. What had happened? The line of horses snickered and whinnied as we approached, looking forward to moving again. Each of us put on our own thin saddle to speed our departure, even Edwin, though the yard hands helped Catheryn. It wasn't long before we were riding through the streets as fast as we could in the poor light from two of our horsemen ahead with torches held wide in a hand, their other hand gripping their reins in a dangerous way I'd only ever seen once before, also here in London. The merriment of the night meant that many alehouses had torches outside their doors and there were blazing braziers at some crossroads. A glow in the sky ahead mesmerised me. I hoped it was nothing to do with us.

We passed drunken men and women. Some were rutting in any corner, while others walked around dazed or lay in the street, forcing us to ride around them.

As we turned into the street near the city wall, where Catheryn's mother had her house, I gasped, stood up in my stirrups to see better. In the distance, her building was burning fiercely. That was the glow lighting the sky. And I could smell the burning thatch and timbers. My mouth was dry as ash. We rode faster, the glow lighting our way. Her gate stood broken and open. We slowed as we approached. Was I dreaming? Could this be the secure compound we'd been in earlier? The dread that gripped me was sickening.

"Stay behind us, women," shouted Edwin, as he pulled his short sword free and held it at his side.

I ignored him, kicked my mount to move faster. People might need help. Her mother might need help. Catheryn followed me. We entered through the broken gate, just behind one of Edwin's guards. That man had an axe high in the air. He emitted a shout as we entered the courtyard.

No reply came. My breath was coming fast. I could feel the heat on my face too, and my thighs were tight.

Two bodies lay on the ground near the side wall. I could not see who they were, but Catheryn rode straight to them and screamed in fury as she leaned down to see their faces.

We all dismounted.

One of the men took our horses. Catheryn went down on one knee by the bodies. She pulled a battered-looking sword from under one of them. I went to the other body, a young man. His skin was still warm, but he was not breathing. He appeared to be a stable hand surprised by unexpected violence.

Edwin stood near the door of the main house, peering in. Smoke billowed from the roof as flames brightened the yard. Hissing, fizzing sparks fell around us. I dodged two as they fell. Edwin put his arms out wide to stop Catheryn going in.

"The roof will fall any moment. You will not go in," he shouted, looking first at Catheryn and then at me.

But I'd made my mind up already. I ran far to his left to avoid his grasping fingers while twisting my body out of his reach. Edwin groaned, clutching at empty air, as he realised he couldn't stop me going into the burning building. Catheryn followed my move, but on his other side.

As soon as I went in the door, throat-clawing sooty smoke hit me in the face. I went down on my knees coughing, spluttering, my eyes stinging, streaming.

But I could see down here, and I could breathe.

"Down," I shouted. Someone was coughing violently just behind me. Creaks and the hissing of burning wood drowned out my voice. Straight ahead, a body lay unmoving in the middle of the room. A gush of fear rose inside me as the heat on my face grew. It pulsed as if it was alive. I had to move fast.

"Come out," shouted voices.

I crabbed forward. Through the smoke and the glow, I saw it was Catheryn's mother on the floor. I had to help her. She might still be alive. I could not go back. The heat from the burning floor and roof prickled at my back and my face. The idea of burning to death pushed me forward fast. The more I went, the more it seemed I'd entered a bread oven.

The Rise of Synne

I coughed and spluttered from the hot air, a strong temptation to go back nagging at me, telling me to save myself, fool, get out of here.

Smoke swirled into my face. I went down.

A tremendous creak came from above. Then a shower of sparks fell all around me. Tears streamed down my face. One giant spark bounced onto me, burning into the back of my hand like a hot poker. "Aaaah," I screamed.

I knew then how painful death by fire would be.

I scrambled forward again and reached the body on the floor.

It was Catheryn's mother.

Her face was bone-pale, her eyes open, reflecting the glow of the fire. It was not the fire that had killed her. Blood lay all around her and a bloody gash in the front of her tunic showed where she'd been stabbed. I looked back. Had anyone followed me?

Edwin was scuttling across the floor towards me. He waved at me frantically to come away. In answer, I pulled at the body. Catheryn had to see how her mother had died. She had to have her mother's body to prove what had happened. This was no accident.

Edwin came beside me, pulled at my arm, while coughing violently. His face was close to mine. I gripped an arm of the dead woman tight, as if I'd not release it this side of hell. They'd often called me stubborn-Synne when

I was young. They were right. I'd rescued a boy from the river once, when none of the other children wanted to even wade out towards him. That had changed me. I knew I could do what others could not.

Coughing and shaking his head, anger visible in his eyes, Edwin took her other arm and we both pulled Catheryn's mother towards the door. As we came near it, one of his guards and Catheryn helped us, but as we approached the door, a burning beam fell near us. The guard was struck in the back by a piece of it that broke off as the flaming beam splintered onto the floor. He screamed in agony.

Edwin pulled him through the door as Catheryn and I dragged her mother's body the last few steps.

"What have you done?" Edwin yelled at me, as he slapped the face of his man, his guard, trying to rouse him.

My voice shook as I replied, "I had to go in. She might have been alive." My tone was defiant.

His expression hardened as he looked at me, as if he blamed me for what had happened. That made me angry. Was he that stupid?

A large part of the roof collapsed then, and a cloud of smoke and yellow dust poured out of the front door, sending us reeling back further, all coughing and with dust all over us. A woman with a bucket of water came to us and helped us wash our eyes and mouths out and finally, with the help of some of the other guards, we moved the body to near the gate. People there were peering in, staring with owlish expressions.

"Good riddance," someone shouted.

I was sure Catheryn would scream back, but she didn't. She cradled her mother's head and whimpered over it, repeating something over and over that I couldn't make out. I was sick from the dread of the fire and the shadow of death hanging over us.

Edwin was kneeling not far away, coughing still.

"We must go," he said firmly. "It's not safe here. Find a place for the bodies and I'll send men in the morning to put the gate back up and prepare the burials."

"I'm staying with my mother," shouted Catheryn. "You leave if you want. I will not!"

He looked at me. "Make her come." He was angry. "If whoever did this is nearby, and they don't see her leave, they'll think they can come back to kill Catheryn, too. I'll send men tomorrow to bury her mother." He held his fist towards me, as if this was all my fault.

I went to Catheryn.

"Edwin will send men tomorrow to bury your mother. Whoever killed her might be waiting outside to attack again," I said softly.

Catheryn stared at me as if I was dead too, then finally nodded. Her face was white and rigid with grief.

I went to Edwin. "Give her time to say prayers. Her mother has died." I spoke sharply. He should know to bend for grief.

He stared at me, then nodded. "Agreed," he said. He was not happy.

The rain had stopped before Catheryn suggested we go. We'd whispered every prayer over her mother's body, and she'd kissed her forehead many times and had lain across her mother for a while, weeping, inconsolable, in the stable near the gate. The horses we'd arrived on were inside it now.

Edwin, meanwhile, paced about after interrogating some beggars who'd been hanging around outside, probably looking to sift through the remains of the building for valuables.

I found honey in one of the other outbuildings, which Catheryn directed me to, and I made the guard, Catheryn said he was a thegn, as comfortable as possible, smearing the honey lightly on his injury and saying prayers and charms over him. I put some on the back of my hand too.

We headed back to the earls' camp soon after. People from nearby houses watched us go. Edwin had been right. Jubilant shouts accompanied our departure and there were men further back who stared at us with angry faces. What Catheryn and her mother had done to deserve all the hatred I did not know. I was tempted to ask, but her eyes were on the horizon, and her face was pale and stiff with grief, so I didn't. We rode on with our memories circling around us and the smell of the fire still in our nostrils.

12

When we arrived back at the camp, Edwin hurried to meet his brother. I went with Catheryn to their tent, then on my own to the healer's tent. That's where I found out about her mother.

"She got what she deserved," said the older healer. She was lying on her blanket, exhausted from a night spent watching the wounded. She leaned up on one elbow.

"I see the bruise around your eye is nearly gone," she said. "You heal quick. Did you use some charm?"

"No." I was irritated by the healer's question. She'd probably heard I was the daughter of a seer. This was the reason I didn't tell everyone about my mother being a seer. Some people would assume I had to be able to regrow limbs.

"What did her mother do to deserve it?" I asked. Memories of the smoke and me dragging the body came back to me. I coughed. The ashy taste of smoke was still in my throat.

The Rise of Synne

The woman grunted. "No point in telling you," she said. She held a small, rough wooden cross on a leather string around her neck.

"I'm a Christian, have no fear of that," I said. I sat hard on some blankets near the healer and pulled one tight around myself. I was exhausted. We'd barely slept, but I needed to understand why all this had happened.

"You will swear not to tell anyone all this, if I tell you," said the healer, leaning towards me so I could smell her oniony breath. "'Cause if you do, I'll deny every word."

"I swear it." I nodded, put my hand out, and smiled. The healer clutched it. Her words came in a torrent then.

"That old woman, the temptress Catheryn's mother, she took far too many daughters from many good families. She showed them how to make coin from selling themselves – piles of silver coins. She ruined many families. Fathers were unable to see their daughters married and raising grandchildren, and mothers lost helping hands in their kitchens. Be careful with that one… she's been taught the dark arts, tricks, and magics. Her mother deserved what she got."

Fluttering filled my belly. Was Catheryn as bad as this woman claimed?

The woman tapped her nose. "I'll say no more." She moved back.

I lay down, pulled my blanket tight, and went to sleep.

Hunger and thirst woke me later. I headed for the feasting tent where I found bread and ale on the tables and some of the night guards eating. They looked at me warily but did not engage me as I did not stay long enough for any of them to be friendly.

I was still wearing the tunic Catheryn had given me when I arrived back at her tent. I had to know how she was, and if I could help her. The guards leaning on their axes near her tent flap waved me forward. I stood still for a long moment before pushing through the flap. Catheryn would be grieving, and I should do my best to comfort her, but I also had to think about myself. An urge to run away had entered my head. But had I found out anything useful for Ulf and Magnus? Could I run now?

No.

Not yet.

I took a deep breath and stepped inside.

At the other end of the tent, sitting at the table, Catheryn and Edwin were deep in conversation. I went in front of them and bowed. To my surprise, they were laughing, softly. She had recovered quickly from her grief. She waved me forward.

"My healers tell me you have the healing touch," she said as I stood in front of her.

The Rise of Synne

"I do what I can," I said, then bowed a little in thanks for her praise.

"That may be, but you did not fix my thegn, girl," said Edwin, anger sharp in his voice.

I did not answer. Best to let his anger blow out. I hoped that Catheryn might take my side, say something about me pulling her mother from the fire. But when she spoke, it was about something else, something that shocked me so much I blinked rapidly.

"We've had an offer for your hand, Synne," she said sweetly. "I am minded to accept it."

Our eyes locked. "I'm free born." I spoke fast. "I cannot be given away in marriage by anyone." I had to make my status clear.

"You came to us as a prisoner, Synne. And in your own words, you have no family to protect you and therefore no hope of a dowry, so the earl has kindly taken the responsibility of deciding your future. It is a generous offer for your hand, before you say anything more." Catheryn's tone had iron in it. She would not be crossed. Her true shape was clearer to me now.

"Who asked for my hand?" I felt light-headed, as if I'd drunk way too much strong ale. Anger rose inside me, too. This was going too far.

"Morcar, the Earl of Northumbria, Edwin's brother," said Catheryn. "I'm sure you are pleased at so fine a catch.

You are fortunate indeed, blessed, indeed." Her smile looked genuine, as if she really thought I might be pleased.

"The Earl of Northumbria?" It was a ridiculous notion. He'd looked at me with pure contempt at the feast.

"Does he not have a wife?" It felt as if a noose was tightening around my neck.

"My dear Synne, you'll be his campaign wife. Of course, he has a wife of his own waiting for him up north." Catheryn laughed mockingly, as if the idea of me being his real wife was absurd. The sting of her derision filled the air.

My thoughts were befuddled by anger. My mouth opened, then closed. I was to be his concubine! I wanted to laugh at the idea. I gasped loudly instead.

"No need to thank me, Synne," said Catheryn. Her smile was thin, as if she was surprised at my reluctance.

"When is this to happen?" I asked. Would I have a chance to escape?

"You will go to him tonight."

I blinked, stared. "But I'm still bruised and not recovered from the fire." I put my hands up high. A tightness squeezed into my chest. They would not inflict this on me. Of that, I was determined.

"You look good enough for Morcar the way you are," said Edwin. "My brother likes a woman willing to speak her mind, as you are, and one who is tough-natured, as you are too."

Catheryn looked at him, blinking and smiling as if pleased with his words.

"You told him what Synne did in the fire?" she asked him. She put her hand out towards him.

Edwin nodded. "He thinks I must be bedding you both. I denied it and agreed to his proposal to prove him wrong. This will please you in the end, Synne, I am sure. You will see."

I kept my lips pressed tight. Arguing with them would not be profitable.

"He always runs rings around you," Catheryn said to Edwin. She waved her hand in his direction. "Go back to your brother. Tell him Synne will be with him after he has feasted."

Edwin stood and headed out of the tent, pulling his cloak around him as he went.

I had words forming and was about to speak, throw them at Catheryn, but she put a finger to her lips.

"He blames you for what happened to his thegn, Synne. That man saved his life in battle, twice. You will benefit greatly from this," she said. "Do not fight it."

I hissed my reply. "I will not benefit. If I am to be thrown to Morcar, I shall get him drunk and use one of his blades to cut my own neck." I trembled with my rage. Perhaps I could cut his neck too.

"Stop that talk. There is no need for any of that," she said. "You will use this moment to your advantage, Synne, and to mine, remember you are my blood sister. Above all, I did this for you." She raised a hand towards me, made a circling sign in the air as if casting a spell over me.

I shivered. Had she powers I didn't know of? Or was she just pretending and full of tricks, as my mother said witches are? I pressed my lips together.

"Morcar enjoys women who are bruised fruit, Synne. Women close to breaking. If you knew what he did at one of my mother's houses, you would desire only to listen to me to find out how to survive this night." She raised a hand. "This will not be for long. They are heading back north soon." She spat those final words out, pointing at me, clearly sensing my resistance to her plan.

"I cannot," I said. I surprised myself at the anger in my tone. I could feel the cords in my neck standing out. The only good news was that she'd told me the brothers were going back north. That meant they would not be supporting the Godwins.

"But you will, Synne." She nodded her head. "And here is why. You will be with him, one way or another, reluctant or willing."

The Rise of Synne

"What do you mean?" I did not want to know. But I had to.

She put both her hands towards me, as if to grasp me. "If you resist, I am to send you bound you to him. He enjoys that, seeing eyes bulge with fear. Do you want this?"

I stepped back, a memory of Morcar's angry face filling my mind. I needed time to think. Was this the reason she'd made a sister of me? That I would be an offering to him? Betrayal and fear licked at my gut.

"You do have to fear him, Synne," Catheryn whispered. "I have a way to protect you. I will show you what to do."

I kept my mouth firmly shut. There would be no persuading her. She clapped for her servants and ordered a red tunic brought for me.

I was wondering when I could make a run for it. It was dark. But I had news at last. That was good. And at night I would not be found easily once I got out of the camp. But could I get away? Would they set hunting dogs on my trail? Then I knew I didn't care. I had to be free of these people.

Whatever the consequences.

When the tunic arrived, Catheryn ordered the servants to leave, then for me to slip on the tunic. It was tight, but she looked pleased with the effect. I was waiting for my moment.

"This will be an opportunity for you, Synne," she said. She was watching me closely.

"How?" I said softly. I had to play this carefully.

"Do you believe in magic?" she asked, her eyes widening.

"What magic? I believe in charms and the prayers we say for a short winter and a good harvest and a quick recovery like everyone in every village I pass through does. I believe in all of that. Is that the magic you mean?" But I knew that was not the magic she was talking about.

From her belt, she undid a silver brooch the size of her thumb. Curling silver animal tails decorated its surface. She held it flat on her palm and put her nail under the top edge. A tail folded open. Inside it lay a yellow powder, like milled flour.

"If you wish to survive this night, tell him at the start you are his to command, and keep his cup of mead filled, and when he goes to take a piss, in readiness for his games with you, spill this into his mead." She snapped the lid shut, held the brooch out to me.

"Poison him?" I shook my head. "His servants will see me. They will call me a murderer." I did not want to touch her brooch, never mind use it.

The Rise of Synne

She gripped my arm, her hand tight like a talon, pulled my hand forward. "This cannot kill him." She laughed. "It will quicken his pleasure. I give it to help you. Use it and he will fall asleep soon after he drinks it. I'm trying to help you, Synne. My mother did this for the girls who worked for her, to make their clients sleep, and think that the strong ale had done for them and that they'd got what they wanted. Tell him he did it in the morning and he was as strong as a bear. Be smart, do what I say, Synne, take it." Her nails dug into my skin.

I took the brooch, nodded, as if convinced. She talked more after that, as if to keep me busy until I was ready for Morcar's tent.

I barely remember what she talked about. I was so distracted by what I was facing. But after a while, I began to listen. She talked about her mother, on and on, tears flowing eventually, as if a stopper had been pulled from a barrel and every drop had to come out.

She'd wanted to work in her mother's house, she said, as she was friendly with many of the women, but her mother forbade it and beat her about the face so hard one Yule, she had to stay inside until that winter was over, to recover her beauty. She'd hated her mother then, she said, but she understood her now, why she was the way she was.

All these stories jumbled in my mind. I began thinking of escape, while nodding and smiling and praying

I'd be allowed to walk alone to Morcar's tent. Escape would be an option if I were. There were things I could have told her, but I did not say any of them; her eyes were so fierce, as if she'd found something after a long search. She thought I would be like her, doing whatever any man wanted for a sliver of what they had to give.

One of her slaves came to tell her that Morcar and Edwin had gone to the tent of one of the other thegns, where there was a riddle contest and ale being drunk. Catheryn said I should have food brought from the feasting tent, but I was not hungry. Neither was she.

Finally, one of Morcar's servants came to summon me.

To my dismay, Catheryn escorted me with two of her servants all the way to his tent, all the while telling me how beautiful I looked, as if trying to encourage me. I thanked her. But I was not encouraged. I felt despair. I was not ready for what was coming. How would I escape now?

When we reached his tent, I wanted her to go on telling her tales. But she stopped and pinned the brooch she'd shown me on my tunic, at my shoulder. I was sure he would spot it immediately and would know what it meant and accuse me of planning to poison him. Maybe she had lied to me about what was in it.

Would she be that devious? Perhaps.

It had crossed my mind that she might want Morcar dead, that I would be the instrument of his destruction.

The grizzled guard at his tent flap opened it wide for me with a grin. I hesitated, but Catheryn pushed me in with a sharp shove in the back. The inside of the tent was as cold as the air outside. No braziers had been warming it all day like in Edwin and Catheryn's tent. It was dark, too. The only light was from three thick yellowing beeswax candles at the far end on an iron stand. You could have held only a small feast in this tent, if you liked rough benches and old muddy rushes underfoot.

I could not see him. But as I listened, I heard a sliding noise, the gentle whoosh of someone sharpening a blade. I whispered, "I am here." My mouth was dry, my breath thrumming lightly in my chest. Perhaps he wasn't here. Perhaps I could go. Perhaps that was his servant I was hearing.

I should go.

The gentle whoosh continued. I coughed. The whoosh stopped. Morcar, dressed in a loose black tunic, strode into the centre of the tent. He had a sword and a whetstone in his hands, and a bitter look on his face, as if something had been stolen from him long ago and he'd never recovered from it.

"Kneel," he said as a greeting.

Every muscle in me said this was the moment to run. But I would not get far. Catheryn might be beyond the tent flap, waiting for such a move. I decided to put him to sleep as quickly as possible, to do what she bid me do.

I walked to where he stood and knelt before him. I kept my eyes open and did not bow. I would not show total deference.

He reached a giant, dirty hand towards me. It felt as if I was watching myself, separated, distant from my body. I did not flinch.

He took my chin and jerked my face from side to side, as far as it would go, until the bones and muscle in my jaw ached for him to stop. It was the type of thing you do to a slave or a horse before you paid good coin, testing it for defiance.

I did not whimper.

I imagined shoving a dagger straight up under his jaw.

He squeezed at my chin, pulled my mouth down, and pressed at my teeth on both sides with thick, slimy fingers.

My stomach flipped.

"You look too soft to have come to murder me," he said.

I stifled a gasp. Did he know something?

He released my face, pushed me away. "Naah, you are a healer. You save people. So, are you a seer too, one of

The Rise of Synne

those with the old magic?" He moved his fingers in the air, as if feeling something.

"I'm a Christian," I said firmly, relieved that he wasn't sure I was out to murder him. I wiped at my mouth with my sleeve to take away the taste of him.

He put a hand on my shoulder and tried to pull me around. I pushed back, resisting him, following Catheryn's advice.

He laughed. "I was told you would bend to my will," he said.

"I'm not that easy." Closed my eyes and tensed, waiting for a blow. I said a prayer in my mind, ending with. *Come now and help me.*

"You think I'll strike you?" said Morcar with a laugh.

I opened my eyes, looked in his. "You might." I'd been beaten a few times, by village watchmen sent to get us out of a tumbledown house on one occasion and another time after sleeping in an orchard. Each time it got harder, as you knew what was likely to come.

Morcar laughed. The sound filled the tent. "I was warned you could be an assassin, not a spy." He slapped his hands together gleefully.

Had someone told him about the brooch? My hand went across my chest to hold my tunic, but I stopped it going to my shoulder. That would give everything away.

"Come, spit it out. Were you sent to murder me?"

"I swear to God and on the bones of St. George, I have no plan to murder you." I could not tell him about the brooch. I'd have to explain what I was expected to do. And Catheryn could deny it all. But my guilt would be proven.

"Did you murder Catheryn's mother? Someone said you found her alive and stabbed her under cover of the fire."

I shook my head firmly and fast. "No, that is not true." I could barely get the words out, I was so stunned by the accusation. "Who's spreading this vile talk?"

He pointed at a bench by the table. "Come, sit with me. Tell me your side of it." It felt as if I was sliding into a trap as I made my way to the table. Catheryn had also said Morcar might seem reasonable, as almost every man could.

He sat on the other side of the table. For a moment, I wondered if he feared getting close to me.

"You will serve me now and do what I say. That part was explained to you, yes?" he asked.

"Yes." I still hadn't taken my cloak off. He had a thick tunic on.

"You know what it means?"

"I'm to be your campaign wife," I said. "Though I must warn you, I have little experience with such things."

He slapped both hands down on the table. A folded parchment letter on it jumped, revealing the seal that had

The Rise of Synne

closed it with a man on horseback at its centre. "No matter. You will taste my food, and warm my bed, and perform other tasks from time to time. Understood?"

"Yes." Maybe this would be easier than I thought. Had Catheryn lied?

"Now, tell me, Synne the seer's daughter, what is your side to what happened?"

I coughed, then spoke. "Catheryn's mother was dead when I reached her, I swear it." I raised my hands, appealing to him to believe me.

Morcar shrugged. "I accept your explanation."

I smiled my thanks. "Will I be able to practise my healing arts?"

"Yes, yes." He brushed crumbs from the table. "And you will be set to heal some of a troop of boy slaves, who I will be sending north."

I'd treated slaves before. Some sickened as if they wanted to die, the badly treated ones. Others, the well-cared-for ones usually, seemed eager to get better and to go back to their lives of slavery.

"We will be leaving this windy place?" I asked. I tried not to sound too interested. Whatever he replied, I still had news to report.

He snorted. "Stay out of the affairs of men, Synne. Did your family not teach you this?" He shook his head, sure in his conviction that such subjects were beyond me.

I persisted. "Shall I go with you, that is all I wish to know?" I leaned forward.

He stared at me. "Yes, you will come with me if you serve me well tonight. I will say no more than that." He raised his wine cup high, as if he'd won something.

I bowed. As my face went down, I allowed myself a half-smile. I had found out something useful. I kept my face down. But could I get away from him?

As if he'd heard my thoughts, he growled, then shouted, "It's time to lift your tunic, girl."

I looked up at him with a weak smile. "I thought you'd never ask." I lifted my tunic, revealing most of my legs.

"Perhaps you would like two of us tonight to warm your bed?" I said excitedly, teasingly. I winked at him.

He grinned widely, his expression changing to eager. "Who is the other one?" he asked.

"Another young healer is waiting for my call to join us." I smiled even wider, pulled my skirt up a little more. "We are good together. We will both be wrapped around you." I stuck my tongue out and flicked it up and down as I'd seen a dancer do at an alehouse.

His eyes widened even more. The room had become warm. Had I gone too far? No. No. Keep going.

"You will do this?" He looked shocked and pleased.

I put my hand out. "We will." I moved towards him, cupped my hand to his groin and squeezed, hard. He was big already. I stuck my tongue out again, licked upwards. His eyes bulged.

"Shall I go and get her, lord? She's waiting for my call."

He hesitated, then nodded. He was almost drooling.

I bowed low, walked to the tent opening, and slipped outside. It was dark and it was raining. Good. Better still, Catheryn wasn't there. That had been my big fear.

I walked fast to the healer's tent, relief and fear pushing my legs on. I'd done it. I was out of his tent. The trick had worked. But for how long?

One healer was there.

She was sleeping. I found my bag, grabbed it, and slipped out of the tent at the back by sliding under the bottom edge. I walked through the rain, sliding sometimes, heading towards the woods in the opposite direction of the road to London. My heart was fully in my throat and I was soaked through.

How long would he wait before looking for me? He'd probably send a servant to the healer's tent. I had a little time. But not much. His imagination and his hopes for what was to come had given it to me. If I got far enough away by dawn, I'd be free. I had my chance.

The rain was pelting down, icy, horrible, flowing down my face.

Murmurs of voices came from some tents as I went past them. Some showed flickering light from a candle, but most were dark. I'd heard hounds barking in the camp at night, but tonight the rain was keeping them quiet. I walked fast. I did not run. Running would be suspicious.

Every sense was heightened. I could smell the mud and the grass underfoot and hear the creaking of the trees not far away and taste the sweet rain of freedom on my lips. Every step I made was open defiance. They could inflict a cruel death on me if they caught me, but I'd done everything I could to be free. I would die proud. I would not be a tool for their evil wishes.

I made my hands into fists. If someone tried to stop me, I would fight, no matter what the cost.

"Hey, you, where you going?" came a shout, as I passed the last tent. It had to be a guard on the camp's edge, hiding from the rain.

"I go to do a necessary in the woods," I shouted, keeping going at a purposeful pace.

"There are shit holes back the way you came," was the reply. The voice seemed near.

I didn't turn. I kept moving, but I shouted back. "Too many men there. I need clean grass and to do it without everyone watching," I said forcefully.

The Rise of Synne

No reply came, but I could feel eyes on me. Please, believe me. If he did, he might not even tell his commander he'd seen me when asked in the morning, in case he'd be blamed for letting me get away.

I stumbled onto a mound of dirt, almost ended up face down in it, but my hands came out just in time. A distant, rain-muffled shout echoed. Was that Morcar's voice? I stumbled on.

The rain was falling like an icy waterfall as I reached the trees. Fear and cold gripped me, making my hands tremble, my feet squelch and slip. The leather boots Catheryn had given me were not suitable for this weather, but they shouldn't fall apart in one night. I glanced back. The camp lay like a dark thick blanket with tiny glows of light here and there from lamps or candles inside tents. Some of the lights were moving.

They were looking for me.

I kept going, my breathing quickening. Go faster!

I glanced around constantly as I went through the trees, my heart beating loud and fast now. I expected to hear the shout of my doom at any moment and figures running at me with no chance of escape.

I prayed and muttered and chanted over and over for protection as the rain got worse. Then I laughed. The rain would protect me.

I pushed through undergrowth, climbed over fallen trees, scratched myself, all the while looking for a hunting or droving path. But my eyes were deceiving me; all was black and deeper black around me. I almost twisted my ankle, and then my feet fell away, and I tumbled onto my side, knocking the wind out of myself as I slid down into icy water with my heart almost stopping. I stumbled upright, feeling myself for injuries, water pouring from my cloak, scratches on my hands and arm. I'd lost my bag, but I had to keep going.

I screwed my face up. Tears I'd held back until I was away from people asking and staring at me and pushing me and hitting me, flowed.

I remembered Gytha and Tate struggling as they were dragged away by the slavers.

At least I was free.

That thought made me wipe my face, stop my snivelling, and walk on, ignoring all pains, all cold, all losses, as I wrapped my hands tight around myself to stop my body shivering. I was not chained. I would not give up. I would never give up. Never, ever.

I remembered my mother saying that you can get used to anything, that this was the reason bad kings kill everyone in a village – to eliminate all future opposition from the people who'd survive anything to exact their revenge.

The Rise of Synne

This was why she'd taught us what you could eat in the forest, at any time of year, especially when acorns were plentiful and all you had to do was boil them or soak them in a pool, wrapped in cloth, until the brown juice inside was all gone.

All these things Mother had taught us, was why we'd survived. I blinked fast, stumbled in the rain, kept going, though something was rustling in the trees.

A boar most likely. Bears didn't come this far south anymore. I kept moving. The boar would not attack me unless it felt threatened. I found another stream, walked down it following the flow of the water, heading away from London, I hoped. They'd expect me to go to London, where runaways could hide.

I had to avoid all human contact.

I stumbled again and fell again and crawled all that night, sometimes in the stream to put off their hunting dogs, and twice after that heading into the woods when the stars came out and retracing my steps back to the stream, until my mind was beyond bone weary, and my thoughts slipped round and round as if I was in some dread game at the entrance to the underworld.

Eventually, after I'd prayed and recited all the charms I knew for finding rest, anything, an empty hunting lodge, an abandoned farmer's hut, a woodsman's lean-to, and I'd found nothing, a strange elation came over me as I realised there were no sounds of pursuit either.

I'd gotten away.

I'd escaped. I had.

The rain eased as dawn approached. It was only a drizzle as the sun came up. The stream was wide now, too. I could not jump across it. And a rocky hill loomed on one side. I looked for a crevice or a cave to sleep in.

What I found was an overhang of thick bushes by a rock wall. I suspected there'd be dry ground near the rock under the thickest part, and I was right. I crept in and tried to sleep, while shaking from the cold. I prayed long and hard before I slept, hoping that my dreams of warmth would come true.

***

I woke late, the sun high behind broken white clouds. Again, in my dream, my mother had spoken to me, talking about her prophecies, how one of her daughters would see the future, one would heal with hands, and one would marry the son of a king. It all seemed so far away.

The sounds of the forest were all around that morning, birds cooing, a light wind rustling the branches and best of all, no distant hounds barking. I listened for a long time.

No hounds.

I let my breath out. I was safe, for now.

Thirst was my next concern. I crawled out from my hideaway and drank icy water from the stream.

I needed shelter, not another night in the open coming into winter. I had a lot of experience checking farmsteads for empty cow biers or any building abandoned by the many families destroyed by the recent wars, so I did not despair. Every village had such places.

I stood and walked towards the rising sun and gathered acorns as I went. I had a plan. I'd return to London the long way round. And I'd find the Godwin brothers.

I had information for them.

13

It took ten days to get to Bishopsgate, the gate into London far to the east of where the earls had their camp. A gatekeeper looked me up and down with narrowed eyes as I went in, as if I was something dragged from the forest, but he let me through when I smiled at him. I'd grown thin, I knew that from looking at my arms, and I could not claim to be a healer without any salves, but hopefully, I could use the Godwins' name inside the city to get water and beg bread from someone who still supported the old king.

I'd survived on acorns and milk I'd taken from cows before their milking, and scraps from kitchen waste and half-burnt breadcrumbs I'd found behind a baker's house, ready to be fed to his pigs. I'd slept in byres, broken houses, and abandoned hunters' huts, and I'd travelled mostly at night. The true winter had not come yet. We'd been lucky with no early snow.

London had far more people swarming through its streets than I ever remembered. Streams of beggars passed me by, their eyes glazed, expressions sullen. Most were

The Rise of Synne

men who looked as if they'd been in our defeated army. Some had patched up head wounds or arms in slings. I asked every baker I saw, but no one would give me even their crumbs free. Finally, after walking halfway to the Thames, I saw a healer's sign, a snake curled around a staff, painted on the wall of a house. I offered my services to the woman there in exchange for a meal. She groaned but relented after asking me what I would use to make a healing salve for a burn, and I answered correctly.

"One meal, a half day's work. Then on your way," she said.

I agreed. I found out from her, healers always have news, that the Godwins still had a small camp of followers on the south bank of the river. Someone there would know where Magnus and his brother were.

I walked across the city, feeling hopeful, and over the groaning wooden London Bridge as night approached. The small camp of the old king's followers was still on the cleared ground near the pool beyond the bridge. Refugees from towns the Norman army were burning and pillaging had camped with them. It took me a while to find out that neither Magnus nor Edmund was there, but Brother Ulf might be, if I could only find him. I looked and looked, but I didn't see him and as it grew dark, I found a place to sleep in a cook's tent. The man remembered me from being with the army on our way to battle.

***

The following morning dawned grey and drizzly. I'd begun to pity Catheryn. She thought I would jump at the chance to be Morcar's concubine. But I was not her. I could never be her. She'd become one of her mother's whores. Her fate was a stream that follows the way it must, the easiest way to the sea.

I searched the camp after I woke, taking one section of tents at a time, peering inside each, asking if anyone had seen a monk recently. I was shouted at, witnessed arguments and humping, saw people packing up to leave and others arriving to take their place. The cook had given me a small hunk of bread to take with me, which I was grateful for. But he didn't know where any of the Godwin family were and he looked at me warily when I asked after them, as if he didn't trust me. It seemed things had changed since I'd gone on my mission to find the earls.

It was almost noon before I found a monk who even knew Ulf.

"No, he's not here. Ulf went with the defeated king's sons into the city," he said, stopping to look me up and down.

"Where in the city?"

"Go out to Billingsgate, look for a large hall with a wolf's skull outside. That's where they'll be."

The Rise of Synne

I must have looked blank-faced, as he added, "Go downriver, after you cross the bridge. You can't miss it."

I thanked him, set off, followed his directions. Eventually, I came upon a wooden dock with a high palisade wall behind it. A ship was unloading at the dock. Another waited, bobbing in the river. The tied-up ship had a high, green-tinged seahorse prow. A line of roped-together slaves, a few looking around, most with their faces down, were being led to the moored ship from a large ancient-looking hall with stone walls and a thatched roof.

Before I reached that building, I saw the hall with the wolf's skull on the far side of the muddy road, facing towards the river. Smoke streamed from its dark, ancient-looking thatched roof. I imagined a fire roaring inside and a boar being turned on a spike. My mouth watered at that thought. I'd not eaten well in a week. Outside the hall, men were milling around. But its doors were shut and a line of men at arms stood with their hands at their axes, ready to cut off hands or heads if they had to.

A giant gatekeeper stood at the door, his head to the side, listening to a man with a fur collar exhorting him. It was only when I reached the crowd and pressed in – it was three deep – did I hear what the man was saying.

"I'm owed, sir, for supplies King Harold took with him south. His sons must pay his debts," the man said, his tone wheedling. Another voice called out, "I'm owed for horses taken north early this year." Another shouted, "When will the sons raise their banner and strike back at the Normans harrying us merchants?" This was unsettling news. It meant that the Godwins were being pressed, not supported. But I had found them. And I'd done what they'd asked. I had news.

The gatekeeper appeared unmoved by these pleas. "You'll all be paid and in good time," he shouted. "I have the list of payments and they'll all be made, for sure."

"When?" came angry shouts.

"Not today. You waste your time here today. Come back in a week."

"We cannot wait a week," came multiple replies.

"You will have to. I have nothing for you today. And if you press further, your claims will be denied." He turned, knocked twice on the wooden door, and slipped inside when it opened. Some of the men around me, there were a few women too, departed, grumbling loudly, but a small group stayed. They looked the more desperate of the people who'd been waiting.

"Are you owed coin too?" asked a thin, bent-over man, after nudging my side.

"I'm looking for a monk," I replied. I didn't want to say more. Edwin and Morcar might have spies here.

"Those Godwin monks are a strange lot," he said.

"What do you mean?"

The Rise of Synne

"You know the Godwins are slave traders, don't you?" he asked.

Most lords had slaves and traded in them, some more than others.

"You young people. You know so little beyond what you hear at your mother's knee."

"And you know what?" I asked, angry at the old man's sneering attitude.

"Where do you think their gold comes from?" he asked, shaking his head slowly. "The sky?"

"I never heard of them selling slaves."

"They don't. But they charge slave traders ten times the tax other merchants pay." He leaned toward me, his voice shaking with indignation.

"What is this to you?" I asked.

He blinked. "I seek my freedom. I am a slave. I belonged to a thegn who died at Hastings. I have his sword to prove it." He had his hand across his chest. He pulled it away. The pommel of a sword became visible under his cloak.

"I was with him to the end," he said proudly. "I fought at his side. How many slaves do that? His dying wish was that I would be freed. I want my manumission recorded in the church records at Bristol, where we are from. I need the Godwins' permission for that. They cannot deny me."

The crowd around us had thinned some more. There were only five or six of us still waiting for entry. This slave seeking his freedom, still had his attention on the door. When it opened a little for one of the guards to slip inside, he stepped forward.

"I beg you," he called out, both his hands up high. "Please, I'm here over seven days. You said that would be all I have to wait." He held his hands up higher. His tone was a wail as he continued. "Please, my lords, I was promised an audience. I will die at your door if I am not seen."

His pleas made me squirm. The door was open a crack. The nearby guards looked at each other. One put his mouth near the door opening, said something to someone inside. Gulls cawed and shouts echoed from the river.

The door creaked open some more and a voice called out harshly, "Show yourself."

The old man stood forward. I took my chance, went behind him. A guard's mailed hand and arm reached out and pointed at the old man.

"Come," a voice said. The guards ahead parted. The old man stepped forward. His knees seemed to give way. I took his arm. He held my hand tight. We both slipped inside. I suppressed a smile. I was in.

The smell of boar cooking hit me, and I swallowed hard, my mouth watering fast. The gloomy hall had men

The Rise of Synne

lounging at long tables on both sides and a spit over a flaming hearth with a giant boar on it in the centre. Beyond it lay a table half in darkness. That would be where the brothers, Edmund and Magnus, and Elva probably too, and hopefully, Ulf, might be. I licked my lips. A fluttery, empty feeling filled me. I bit my lip as I walked slowly with the old man up the centre of the hall, steadying him with my arm on his. The men at arms at the tables around us did not pay us any attention. They had their heads together in little groups, as if they were all plotting revenge.

Smoke from the spit stung my eyes as we got near the central hearth. The old man pushed me back with a soft word in my ear. "Thank you. I hope they grant you your wish, too."

I said nothing, just hung back as he went towards the top table. Neither Magnus nor Edmund nor Elva nor Ulf were at it, but a thegn I'd seen with them was sitting in the centre of the table with another younger thegn beside him and pale-yellow goblets in their hands.

The old man bowed low to them. I chanted a charm for him, whispering it in a low voice.

Listen to this plea, Queen of Heaven. I beg you. Listen to this plea. Listen, I beg you. Listen.

"Come forward, old man," said the thegn. Guards lounged at either end of the table, but they did not come into the centre of the hall, presumably because the old man did not seem to offer any threat. But when he straightened his back and threw his cloak over his shoulder and his sword was revealed, the guards came forward, fast. I felt a lightness in my chest and hoped he would not be punished for showing a sword.

"I bring you the sword of my master," shouted the old man. He undid the wide leather belt holding the sword and handed everything to one of the guards. The guard laid the sword on the top table. The old man knelt in front of it, slowly. He was barely able to stop himself from falling over.

I took a step forward to go to him, but one of the guards growled at me and put his hand out to block me. I went to go around him, but the guard moved fast and grabbed my shoulder with a tight grip.

The thegn had a smile on his face as he watched all this.

"Old man, go eat something. You look weak. We'll hear your story later. I want to speak with this woman who came with you. Come forward, orphan healer." His eyes were on me. They widened as I pushed the guard who held me away.

I didn't remember speaking with this thegn, but I had seen him with Edmund before the big battle. Had someone told this man about me or about my mission? I was pleased but also scared by this thought. How many people knew I was a spy?

I bowed briefly.

"You have been through lean times, I see," said the thegn.

"I wish to speak with the monk, Ulf," I replied, my chin up. Better not to tell anyone I had a message for the Godwin brothers.

"He's not here," said the thegn. He pointed at the tables one by one. "Anyone here need a healer?" he shouted.

No answer came but a muffled laugh.

He waved dismissively in my direction. "You can go."

I stood my ground. "When will the Godwins return?" I asked.

"Tonight," a voice behind me shouted.

"You've got your answer," said the thegn.

"There is a feast here tonight?" I asked.

"Good guess," shouted someone behind me. "For a scrawny healer."

I raised a fist high, shook it, in answer to his insult. Someone laughed, mockingly. I shook my fist again, stuck my tongue out as I turned to face the tables.

I walked down the hall. "Sit with me, healer," came a call as I passed a table. It was the old slave who was looking for his freedom. I went and sat with him. He put his arm around me.

"You must eat," he said. "You need your strength. Bread is coming. You can have half mine."

I shook my head. "I cannot take what you need." My fist was still tight.

"I had some already, and you can pay me back later, healer, yes?" His grin was half toothless. "By not letting any man stop your mouth."

"I won't." I raised my fist. This was not the welcome I'd dreamed about.

He raised his fist to mine. I laughed. A slave arrived with a hunk of horsebread and some hard cheese. It smelt like the best cheese I'd ever even had. The old man pointed at me. I nodded gratefully when the slave passed the bread and cheese to me.

"What's your story?" asked the old man with a smile.

I told him all about being a healer with Harold's army and how I'd lost my brother to the Normans. I knew I could trust him.

"What about before that?" he asked as he slurped his ale.

I told him about Stefan and travelling the country healing people.

"Will you stay in this city, if Duke William comes to London seeking to burn us or slay us all, if we don't bend the knee to him?" he asked.

"When will he be here?" An image of Normans fighting in the city came to me, like a memory, or was it from a nightmare?

"They ravage all in their path and will reach London Bridge soon, they say. If they cross into the city, there will be a great slaughter. They kill everyone who defies 'em, children and all." He shook his head. "My master gave his life to stop 'em."

I chewed at the bread. "Can't they be stopped from crossing into the city?"

"Maybe, but they will not give up easy. London is a ripe fruit ready to be plucked."

The men at the other end of our table appeared listless, as if they were waiting for a battle they knew they would lose.

"But fear not, healer," continued the old man, his tone lifting. "There'll be a big feast here tonight. I heard prattle about it outside. The Godwins' allies will all be coming together to pledge their loyalty. Perhaps if everyone bands together, they can defeat the Normans." He patted my arm, pinched my cheek.

I hated people doing that, but this time I didn't care. I stuffed the last of the bread in my mouth, drank my ale, and went to relieve myself. A riddle contest had started when I returned. The old man had found another jug of ale. I listened to some stupid riddles. One was about Duke William. I did not realise it until someone shouted his name.

After that, a storyteller began singing a long and painful lament for King Harold. It ended with a promise that his sons would take vengeance on Duke William, whose headless body would be tossed into the sea at Dover and his head placed on a spike at London Bridge, as a warning to all who would invade this great kingdom ever again.

That received a rousing cheer. I liked it too.

As I looked at the men stamping their feet in approval, I spotted Ulf. He was at a table near the door talking to two older, prosperous-looking merchants with fur-collared cloaks. My heart lifted.

"I'll be back," I said to the old man.

I almost ran to Ulf, who cried out as he saw me, "Synne, thanks be to God, you've returned. You have news." He hugged me warmly. I hugged him back.

"Have you eaten? You look famished," he asked. "I hope the rascals who run this hall are not as tight-fisted as I heard."

I pointed to the old man. "An old slave shared his bread and cheese with me," I said.

The Rise of Synne

Ulf held my arm, pulled me, and led me through a door at the back to a long skinning hut leaning up against the side of the hall. Its earth floor was muddy and red from blood. A table at the back had young women eating thick brown broth at it. One wore an iron neck collar, signifying she was a slave who'd run away more than once.

Ulf gestured for the slave at the end of the table to make room for me.

"I ate bread and cheese already," I said.

"You've not seen yourself," said Ulf. "You look as if you've been eating grass since I last saw you. Sit, eat," he ordered.

I stood beside the table. The slave was forcing broth into her mouth fast, as if afraid it would be taken from her in the next moment. Her hair hung in dirty streaks from her head. A weal on her cheek and another on her arm marked some recent altercation. I thought of my sisters and what they may be going through and inside I shook. Were they even alive? I smiled a little at the girl. She grimaced, untrusting, looked away.

"Finish up quick, slave, make space, and pass your bowl to the healer," said Ulf.

The slave turned to me, her eyes wide in wonder that I had someone to speak for me.

"I cannot take food meant for slaves," I said as I pushed past Ulf.

He grabbed at my cloak. I slipped through his fingers.

"You're as stubborn as ever," he said loudly, coming after me.

"Those slaves need to eat." I turned on him.

He shook his head, as if he thought me stupid. Then he continued with a sigh. "I'll not force you to eat."

He led the way to the front of the hall where men at arms I remembered from the battle at Hastings were sitting at a table. We sat at the end of that table, where there was room. "Tell me everything," he said, putting his head near mine.

I told him almost everything. I left out the part about me telling Catheryn all about my family, and her making us blood sisters. Ulf laughed so much he coughed when he heard how Morcar had wanted me and how I'd escaped.

"He didn't like you going first into that fire, showing him up," said Ulf. "That's his problem." He shook his head. "You're lucky you got away. He has a bad reputation."

"You might have warned me."

He snorted. "I didn't want to tell you anything you might blurt out."

"Thanks, I was trying to help Catheryn's mother. Was that wrong?"

"No, you did good," he said, slapping the table. He gazed into the distance, a smile on his face, then crossed

The Rise of Synne

his arms, hugging himself. "I'd have loved to have seen his face when he realised you weren't coming back. What a fool!" He rocked back and forward on the bench.

I didn't know whether all this meant good news or bad. Had I done enough?

"You will give an account of all this," said Ulf. "I expect they'll want to question you. Stay by me until Magnus and Edmund arrive."

"I was promised a reward," I said quickly. Asking Ulf would be easier than asking the Godwins. I was determined their promise would not be forgotten.

Ulf breathed deep, took his time before replying. "We must defend London against the Normans first, healer. You'll be needed for that. Be patient for your reward. You will get it for all you have done."

I'd imagined Magnus thanking me, smiling at me. I stared up the hall. Was I being foolish? Perhaps. My mother had told me about wishing things and how sometimes if dreams happened, they would be different from what you'd expected. I clutched at my pendants through the front of my tunic, as I did often, when I thought about Magnus. I did not pull them out from inside my tunic with a monk beside me.

"Was that Dane you met interested in who you were?" Ulf asked, a curious expression on his face.

"No. Not much."

Ulf gave me a strange smile, as if he was hiding something from me.

The old slave from earlier walked past behind Ulf. I realised he was trying to work out if I was being held or assaulted by Ulf. I gave him a smile and he returned it.

Someone had come to speak to Ulf. I could not hear their words. I looked up the hall. The boar on the spit would barely feed this growing crowd. This was not a proper feast with endless meat like the one at the woolmen's hall. Then I noticed the chains hanging from one wall, tied up, but ready for use. My mouth opened as the truth dawned on me.

"This is a slavers hall," I said, pulling at Ulf's sleeve when the man departed.

"Yes, yes. Slavers are the richest traders in this city, though not that popular anymore." He put his head near mine, lowered his voice. "Which is a good thing. Many people say we monks should support the slaver traders, as that is their way of life, and slaves are property that cannot be taken away, but it is a disgusting trade. Many blame the Danes for it, but many profit from it too."

My mind was turning fast.

"Are there many slave markets still open in London?" I asked.

"This is the only one still open," said Ulf.

"My sisters may have come through here," I said softly. A tingle passed through me. Had the fates arranged for me to come here, to find my sisters' trail? I felt elated, the feeling you get when you discover the trail of a family of boars or deer deep in the forest. Something prized and elusive. To find one is enough to make you want to follow it, wherever it leads.

He shook his head. "There's no way anyone can be sure about individual slaves," he said. "Once they come to market, they've no names but whatever their new master gives them."

I knew I might not be able to use Gytha and Tate's names to find them. But they were healer's daughters and would likely use their talents to stop the worst things happening to them.

I'd thought a lot about what it would be like to find them. Sometimes I held my pendants so tight when such thoughts came at night, they cut into my skin and my palms bled.

Shouts from the entrance made everyone at the tables turn. Hunting dogs were barking wildly outside. The doors were flung open. With the shimmering grey of the river behind them, Edmund and Magnus, with Elva between them, came striding into the hall, dark cloaks swishing. They must have been using the dogs to keep the rabble away.

My eyes widened and I smiled. I could not stop myself.

Everyone in the hall went silent. A mighty cheer went up, as if the men in the hall hadn't been sure the sons of Harold would be coming at all. Most began pounding on tables and stamping their feet as the brothers came up the hall, their fists high in greeting. Edmund looked around with a grin on his pale face, lapping up the adulation. Magnus and Elva had more serious expressions. I wanted to go to them with my news. It felt as if was being dragged by a rope. But I stood my ground. This was not the moment to do that.

They headed for the top table and took up places on the left side. The seats at the centre and on the right were still empty. Edmund shouted greetings to some of the men near them, and both he and Magnus waved for the cheers to die down.

They had their swords collected by servants, who took them away and placed them on a long table at the side of the hall, which had other swords and axes leaning against it or laid out on top.

Elva had seen me as she passed. She whispered something to Edmund as they sat. He looked down the room in my direction. He whispered something to Magnus, who also looked in my direction. Our eyes met. He smiled.

The Rise of Synne

The urge to go to him grew. My feet started moving. I put my hands on my thighs to stop myself.

Was he interested in me? Or was I just being stupid? Stupid, most likely.

He looked away. What a stupid fantasy to think he might like me. Totally stupid.

How had I ended up like this, daydreaming about a powerful man and getting stupid ideas? That's what you get for being on your own and half-starved with no one to help you. Stupid. I shook my head as I could throw off all thoughts of him.

My life had been so much easier before we'd joined King Harold's cause. Stefan had been with me. I wished him with me now. He'd laugh at my stupidity, hug me. I missed him, someone to chatter to, but more importantly, someone to trust.

Many who follow a king end up dead, my mother had said. How right she'd been. We'd risked all, and Stefan had lost all following a king. I gripped my pendants through my tunic again, not caring if Ulf saw me. Something good had to come from Stefan's death, please.

Ulf nudged me as another cheer rang out. I looked down the hall towards the open door. It was gloomy outside. Torches had been lit at the door and the sweet smell of burning rushes soaked in pig fat drifted into us. A tall wiry man in a blood-red cloak with bushy ginger hair and a wild beard had come in through the door. He was surveying the room, looking at each table. He moved forward, pounding backs and slapping shoulders as he came.

Behind him were three women, all in thin red tunics, which stuck to their bodies. A hollow opened inside me, a premonition, though I did not know why yet. All three women had long black hair tied back in ponytails. Each had a hand-wide beaten-gold collar around their neck. Each had stony expressions that gave no indication of their thoughts.

The hollowness grew.

"The Dublin slave master is here," whispered Ulf, glaring at the man and his entourage as they came up the room.

"Why is…" My next word ended stuck in my throat. One of the women looked like my sister. I squinted. Could it be?

No.

But maybe. No. No. It couldn't be her.

Time stopped the way you can make it in dreams. I stared.

"Gytha," I said as she came near, but she passed by with her gaze straight ahead, unblinking.

My hand reached towards her. Ulf caught my arm, pulled it down, held it tight.

The Rise of Synne

Cheers echoed from the men all around us.

A deep shudder passed through me and right into my hands. It felt as if a blade had swung so close to me, I could feel its burn. I struggled to get free of Ulf.

I had to go to her.

"That's my sister," I hissed at him.

He gripped me tighter, with two hands now. "You will not go to her," he hissed back at me. We were swaying. People were looking at us. "You must do nothing to enrage that man in front of all these people. Slave masters like him cut throats the way we cut bread. And that one is the worst for it. If she is your sister, and you want to help her, 'tis better he doesn't know who you are." He flung his arms around me and laughed, pulling me to sit down.

I stopped struggling, watched their backs, wondering if my mind was playing evil tricks. Was that really Gytha, my eldest sister, the one who'd made me honey cakes when I was little and brushed my hair when I was sad? Missing her, since she'd been taken, was an ache that never ended, an injury you could ignore sometimes, but never for long.

Perhaps I was going mad, like Stefan said sometimes if I rambled about my dreams. The woman who looked like Gytha had followed the slave master without turning. Gytha would have turned when she saw me. The slave master sat at the main table at the top of the room, very near the centre.

His entourage did not sit. They stood behind him. I squinted in the gloom and the smoke rising from the big central hearth. Each of the women had a knife in a leather holder on their belt. And with a rising sense of elation, I was sure.

It was Gytha.

She looked at me. Our eyes locked.

Everyone else in the room disappeared. Her mouth opened, but slightly. She stepped back, but only a half step, as if in shock. She'd seen me. The slave master turned towards her. He was quick. She shook her head slightly, narrowed her eyes, then looked down at him. She'd sent me a message to stay where I was.

I looked away as the slave master scanned the room. He'd seen something or felt something.

"That is my sister," I said softly. I could not believe my words. After all this time, after all this praying, I'd found her. I had a desperate urge to run to her, to hug her, to not care what happened.

Ulf still held my arm again, tight. He spoke slowly. "You must wait for the right moment to speak to her, Synne," he whispered. "And if it doesn't come tonight, you will accept it. That slave master tortures his property in ways I cannot even tell you. He does it to show other slaves what will happen if they defy him. If your sister is his slave, which it appears she is, you must buy her freedom and never show him how much you want her. Her price will only double or more if he knows someone is desperate to release her. That's who he is."

I didn't like what he was saying. "We were all free until she was taken." I was barely controlling myself, looking around the room, wondering if my other sister, Tate, was also here. But I couldn't see her, though I examined every face at every table, twice.

"Be still," hissed Ulf. "Once a slave has been sold to a man like him, he'll not care for words or pleas from you or me or anyone but a king. He'll claim slave owner rights and laugh at you."

How was this right?

Who knew what evils my sister faced with this man? I had to find a way to free her. I'd been gifted with finding her, my prayers had been answered, which must mean I'd be gifted with a way to free her.

I watched as she poured ale for the slave master and stood behind him, her expression firm, her gaze straight forward, not looking at me.

Perhaps she'd give me a sign?

Please, give me a sign.

I felt drawn towards her, ready to go to her, even when I looked away.

A cheer rang out, even bigger than the last, louder than any before. I turned. Who was it? Another slave master?

No.

The earls Morcar and his brother Edwin, and Catheryn, were coming up the centre of the hall. My mouth opened wide. The fur collars on their cloaks bounced as they walked, with stomping and the banging of tables following them, and with three men at arms behind them in light chain mail, all of them with swords, axes, and daggers, as if they were expecting to go to battle.

I closed my mouth and turned away to avoid being seen. I felt sure, with real certainty, that there were eyes on me, that Catheryn had seen me, that she would send someone to grab me and make up some excuse to bundle me away and punish me with spite. And who would oppose her?

Ulf? No! Magnus? No! The Godwins would want the earls' men fighting for them when the Normans arrived at the gates of London.

"Do you think they'll want to punish you?" asked Ulf softly. He'd come off his bench and was leaning over me, between them and me.

"They can claim I'm an escaped prisoner." How could I argue with them? And what sort of revenge would Catheryn want?

The Rise of Synne

"The Godwins might protect you." He flicked his hand in the direction of the top table.

I laughed.

Now that I'd told Ulf what I'd found out, I might easily be discarded. I kept my face turned away from the top table. I was expecting my name to be called at any moment, a hand on my shoulder. Finally, as the cheering died, I dared to glance up the room. I could not resist it any longer.

To my eye-blinking relief, Catheryn was not even looking in my direction. She was leaning over Elva and talking to her, animatedly. I glanced along the top table.

Gytha, my sister, was staring at me.

My mouth opened a little, but I didn't dare smile.

Her left eyebrow was slightly raised, as if she'd been waiting impatiently for me to look at her. I nodded, slightly. She glanced towards the main door and then back at me.

She wanted me to meet her there.

This was it. We could slip away together. Everything I'd dreamed about would come true. But we had to be quick.

I turned my back to the main table, stood slowly, picked up an empty ale cup as if I was going to fill it.

"Where are you going?" asked Ulf, his hand reaching for my arm.

I shook his hand away. I was a little too far away already from him to grasp it tight. "I'm going to the back of the hall. They'll not see me there."

He let me go.

I was sure I stood out like a stag on a beach as I walked down the side aisle of the hall. At every step, I expected my name to be shouted from the top table and a summons I could not resist following.

I even thought I heard my name in a jumble of shouts.

I stopped and almost turned to the front at that point, but no summons followed, so I kept going, daring myself with each step, and moments later I was deep in the busy gloom at the end of the hall, servants and slaves all milling about, mostly getting in each other's way.

Stifling my excitement, I looked from behind a wall of men and women at the end of the hall, all lined up, all observing their masters. I checked around the room quickly for Tate, and for one exciting moment I thought I saw her, but when the woman turned her head, a sinking feeling came over me as I realised she wasn't Tate.

Catheryn was still sitting like a queen bee between Morcar and Edwin, lavishing her attention on Morcar, who was engaged in an arm-wrestling contest with Magnus, who was sitting on the far side of them. The two men were rocking back and forth, laughing, champions testing each other's strength.

The Rise of Synne

I looked for Gytha. She wasn't at the top table. I glanced around the room. She wasn't anywhere to be seen. Had I got her message wrong?

Ulf appeared beside me. "Do not run away," he said. His eyes were almost popping, his head moving up and down as if by doing so he might convince me to agree.

My words came out haltingly. "If Catheryn comes to take me, I cannot be sure what I will do." I'd seen knives on some tables as I came down the room.

"If you see her coming for me, pray my hand will be steady when I strike her. Better to die quick than be dragged back to their camp for some evil punishment they'll devise." I meant it too.

He stepped closer. "Stop. You will do no such thing," he said. "This feast is for stitching an alliance against the Normans. We need luck and skill to make it work. The fate of England depends on us. If you see her, disappear." He spoke sharply, then walked back towards the top table.

I guessed where he was going. He had to find out from Magnus or Edmund what to do with me.

A warning voice inside me shouted that I must get as far away as possible from Catheryn and Morcar and all of them. But I could not run away without speaking to Gytha. I was fixed to the spot as if a trap had caught my feet.

I tried to calm my breathing as my mother had taught us. I counted to seven, slowly, then started again. Then again, whispering the words over and over until a woman near me noticed and stared at me. I stopped saying the words out loud. She moved away.

Something sharp poked into my back.

A voice whispered, "Do not turn."

Gytha. I knew her voice. It felt like a warm embrace. I smiled and the noise in the room grew quiet as I listened for what she would say.

"Good to see you, sister." Her words were soft, sweet. "I thought you were lost. Is Stefan here?"

"Stefan is…" I couldn't say it.

"Is what?"

A long moment passed as I pressed my lips together, fighting an urge to wail at our loss. Then it came out. "Dead."

"*Ughhhhh*, no." Her words were a groan.

"We were looking for you," I said without turning, pressing my lips tight at the end as tears prickled my eyes, threatening to overflow. It was all I could do not to turn and hug her.

"Be careful," she whispered harshly. "If my master sees us talking, he'll assume I'm plotting. I must go back to him. We leave as the tide turns in the morning."

"Is Tate with you?"

"On the ship."

I let out a strangled gasp. Tate was alive; my worst fears were just that, fears. "Can I help you?" I asked, desperation in my tone.

"Find gold. The slave master would sell his own mother for a bag of it."

I hesitated for only a moment. Finding gold would not be easy, but there were ways.

"I will," I said. My mind raced. What I needed was the powers my mother had, to heal, protect, and shape the future.

"Tate will be happy I spoke to you."

"Why is she not here?"

"She answers him back." Gytha sighed. "We talk about our mother's prophecy about us sisters all the time. It keeps us strong."

"Me too."

"I must go."

"Where's he taking you?"

"The slave markets at Dublin."

I knew, with an icy pain near my heart, that there was little I could do for my sisters that night. But I would not give up. I was grateful I knew where they were going and who they were with. This meant there was real hope.

A warm finger touched my side for a moment through my tunic, sending a throb through me, and then she was gone, leaving me alone again.

Bending forward, I breathed in fast, unable to hold myself. Memories flooded me: Gytha's laughter, the nights we all slept together when it was cold, Gytha and Tate feeding me when I was ill. I groaned as the pain of the memories pulled like a band around my head. I shook. People nearby moved a little away from me, the way you do when someone falls ill in a market. I straightened, saw Gytha up the room. At the top table, her master's eyes were on her. Had he seen her with me? I was scared. For her. Not for me. My face went stiff, expressionless. I would be iron-strong. If I displayed any emotion, they might guess who I was in a heartbeat.

I forced myself to look at Elva. She was deep in conversation with Edwin. Morcar was nowhere to be seen. Where was he?

A hand gripped my upper arm, tight. I spun around.

"Leave at once," whispered Ulf, not bending down. "Find the alehouse behind this hall. Wait there. Tell the owner you are with the Godwins."

My breath shuddered out of me.

Ulf was not behind me when I turned. He was gone.

Stopping an urge to run, I walked at a normal pace to the doors. One was open just enough to let people pass in and out, one by one. Two burly men were in front of me, leaving and complaining as they did so, asking what the doormen were so afraid of they had to almost bar the

The Rise of Synne

doors. I went close behind them, pulled the hood of my cloak up around the back of my head, glad I'd not taken it off. As I reached the door, a shout sounded.

"Stop her." Morcar's voice, but distant.

I didn't turn. That would reveal me.

My heart leapt into my throat. I slipped past one of the men in front of me, who was still arguing, and went through the door in a moment. I was running along the side of the building a moment later. The echoes of Morcar's shout hadn't died in my mind. But then another shout came, angrier. "Out of my way!"

I leapt over a sleeping hound and over a beggar, too. I almost slipped. The corner of the building seemed impossibly far away.

Could I get there before he came out?

I lengthened my stride, reached the corner, went fast around the building, slipping as I did, and ending up half falling against a wicker fence with sharp pieces that stuck into me. The light was darkest grey now, almost black. The torches at the front of the building were no help. The sky was cloudy too. Everything was grey with only distant flickers of yellow light far in the distance. I ran my hands along the wicker, high and low, looking for a break. There were often breaks in wicker fences meant to keep animals in place. Another shout came. "Which way did she go?"

I didn't have much time.

I crouched, shaking, ran my hand along the bottom of the fence. If it was old, animals may have already pushed a way under it. Please, fates, let it be old. The skin on my fingers was rough now, nicked, perhaps bleeding, but I could not see them, and I did not care. The sound of thumping boots filled my ears.

I was going to be caught.

He would drag me away.

Then I found it. Thank the Gods.

A small gap between the bottom of the wicker and the muddy earth. Large enough for a big fox. I yanked my cloak off, pushed it through the gap and slithered after it on my face, my shoulders scratching wicker on each side and all down my back. My face was in my cloak, smothering me as I slithered and shuffled from side to side until I found myself deep in brambles on the other side of the fence. I pulled my feet through behind me, rested, then stifled my breathing and hugged my knees. I had to be quiet.

Something hit the wicker fence further along, shaking it. The blow was so hard, I thought the fence would fall over on top of me, but it didn't. It went back up.

"I'll catch you, little healer. Come out now and I'll let you live. I won't hand you to those Danes looking for you. Make me wait, and I'll give you to them." These shouts, from back along the fence, were so confident and so near,

The Rise of Synne

I imagined him smashing through the wicker easily and plucking me out of the darkness. I made myself smaller.

And what did he mean about Danes looking for me?

Did he mean the people who'd murdered my mother? Why would they be still looking for me? Perhaps. But why? I shook my head. It was all too strange, like one of those riddles you can never guess the answer to.

But there was no possibility I'd submit.

Grunting followed. Morcar moved like an animal, sniffing and snorting on the other side of the fence.

The noise continued, first getting weaker, then stronger again. I held my breath each time he came near and prayed silently.

Banging on the wicker started, moving closer and into the distance. Would he try to break through, climb over? I slid a little away, pushing into the painful spikes of hard brambles. If he had a sword with him, he could slide it through the wicker. I prayed the ale he'd drunk would lead him to give up soon. He could not know I was so close. In the darkness, he could not know if a pit or a midden waited for him beyond the fence if he pushed through it.

I felt around me with both hands in cold, wet mud. There were more scratchy, hard brambles on each side and more ahead. I'd assumed this land belonged to the alehouse Ulf had mentioned, but I could be wrong. Above, purple-black clouds moved towards a black ridge in the distance, a rooftop perhaps, some way ahead. The moon, low down, gave only little light even when it half appeared through clouds. Was that the alehouse ahead?

The banging on the wicker came again, then fell away. I was barely breathing, still wondering what to do.

If I moved, would he hear me?

If I stayed, would he find me?

"Look, I see someone skulking by the riverside," came a shout from the other side of the fence.

"Is that who you're looking for?"

The banging on the wicker stopped. The distant thud of running feet followed, then disappeared.

I prayed. More shouts came, but all far off. This was my chance. I felt my way forward on my hands and knees, and then half crouching, I pushed through a break in the brambles. A snuffling noise made me stop. That was when the smell hit me, and I knew where I was.

A hog pen.

I had to get out.

Hungry hogs, fully grown, can overpower even big children and the weak, and working together, they can keep an adult down as they eat you. If no one comes quickly enough to rescue you, you can die in unbelievable pain as hogs fill their stomachs. Some of them are used to eating human flesh too. Dead slaves get fed to them.

The snuffling was close.

One or more hogs were coming my way. Perhaps they'd heard me or sensed me. I moved, half crouching, toward the roofline I'd seen. I brushed against something large, round, slick and warm. Another came on the other side. I was stuck between them. I wanted to scream.

The snuffling changed to eager grunting.

I flailed my hands, slapping and punching to get through the hogs. My best chance was to keep moving. Not fall. Not ever fall.

There were more ahead, swells of dark-grey-like waves, and more grunts from hungry hogs woken from their slumbers.

Then, like the dawn after you'd prayed forever for it, a square of light appeared ahead and a woman leaned over a half door, calling out, "Who goes there?"

"Shhh, the Godwins sent me," I replied half-whispering, fearing the hogs and Morcar too.

"Get over here quick," hissed the woman. "Or the beasties will get their breakfast early this day."

I pushed past warm pigs, felt biting nicks on my legs. Shuddering, I kept going, but faster, pushing, sliding past a press of slick warm backs.

I made it to the doorway, gasping. The round-faced woman opened the lower part of the door. I stumbled in, fell to the rush-strewn floor, crying out in shock, "Close the door."

"'Tis closed already, girl. What are you thinking, coming in through the pen like a thief?"

"Close the top door," I said, each word desperate.

She closed it. "Someone coming after you, is that it, my girl?" She crossed her arms.

I rolled into a sitting ball, hugged my knees, rocked back and forth. That had been too close. Please, fates, never again, not like that. I could not speak. Every word might bring more danger down on me.

"Is it a man?" she asked, her voice softening.

I nodded. My rocking came faster.

"No man will force you from here," said the woman gently. She put a hand on my shoulder.

"Just you wait and see if he comes to our door." She put her head near the door and listened. I noticed a short, blackened cudgel in her hand. It looked dangerous. We waited, listening, together.

Slowly my breathing came back to normal, but still I shivered. Not from the cold. From all I'd been through, from how close Morcar had come to catching me and the feel of the hogs and how they might have eaten me.

I remembered Gytha. That I'd found her at last and knew where she and Tate were going. That filled me with hope. I'd longed to find her. And at last, I had. The fates had smiled on me. The mother of heaven had listened.

We waited some more.

No sounds came from beyond the door except the occasional grunt of a hog. I noticed the pungent odour of smoke for the first time. This house was used for smoking a lot of meat.

"We must clean you up," said the woman. "I'll give you something to wear too, but first let's wash the mud off you."

Relief filled me, a sense that this woman would protect me. That she might be able to. She was as tall as Morcar and looked well capable of wielding a war axe and cutting off the head of any man, as if it were a summer flower waiting to be taken.

For a moment, I thought maybe I should be afraid of her, standing by the door, listening, giant hog legs hanging, curing, from the roof above her, and a large, blackened pot dangling over a smouldering fire in a cavity in the end wall. Then I saw them, the plump faces of two golden-haired children peeking out from under oily furs on a bed set into the back wall and I knew I could trust her.

I sat on the rush-strewn floor as she heated a large pot of water over the fire. I let my eyes close as the events of the night played over inside me. It's a blessing we can't see what our fate will be. If we knew the things coming for us, we'd probably never go on.

When she told me the water was ready, I stood, slid out of my cloak and tunic. She gave me a pot of water to dip my head in and wash much of the mud off myself with my hands, all the while the children making shocked noises at the splashing water. She also gave me a small piece of tallow soap fragranced with thyme. I held it as if it was a charm, sniffing at the sharp fragrance, then moved it slowly across my hands and skin, enjoying its feel.

My bare skin was warmed by the glowing embers of the fire when she changed my water, brushing the dregs of it out through the bottom of the back door and taking fresh, cold water from a barrel in the corner.

"Use as much soap as you need," she said. "We get it almost free from a soap maker who likes our ale, our bones, and our banners."

"And you," the small boy shouted.

The woman smiled.

I took the thick woollen cloth she held out for drying.

"You run the alehouse?" I asked.

She shook her head. "No, not me, love, but I work there. It's next door. We pay rent at harvest time to the Godwins. We are fortunate to have them as our lords."

"You've heard the Normans are coming?"

She nodded, got another drying cloth, and handed it to me. "If they take over, one thing's sure. They'll confiscate all this Godwin property, and we may be out on the road by Mid-summer's Day, if they raise the rents the way many claim they will."

The Rise of Synne

I looked around for any sign of a man. "You lost your husband?" I said.

"I did, yes, bad luck. I blame the fates. He went to war when he was called up, before the young one was born, and never came back."

She said it matter-of-factly, as if she'd got over his death a long time ago. When a husband is called to fight for a lord, there is a good chance their families will never see them again, except in heaven, as the priests claim.

I finished drying myself in front of the fire.

"My brother died for the Godwins," I said after a while. I wasn't sure why I said it, but I wanted to.

"God rest his soul."

"If the Normans take London, what will you do?"

"There are plenty who want to keep them out of our city, by axe and sword and fire if needed." She said firmly, "If London holds, England can too."

She was checking the dryness of thick brown tunics hanging in a corner and passed one to me.

"Harold's sons will surely fight the duke," I said.

"I hope they cut all their evil Norman heads off."

"You know Duke William played a trick on Harold's army at Hastings?"

"How do you know this? Were you there?" She wasn't someone who'd be easily fooled.

I nodded. "The duke got his men to feign defeat to break our line, so there'd be gaps in our shield wall for his horsemen to break through."

She shook her head. "I heard his wife is behind his trick. The great Matilda." She said the name with a sneer.

"Well, it worked. We would have won the battle otherwise." So much had happened since that day it seemed like an age ago. I took a slow breath.

"Take this here tunic," she said. "The past is woven in. It cannot be undone." She passed me a rough tunic. "It ain't as fine as some, but I'll give you a thick cloak, too."

"I cannot pay you," I said.

"No need, girl. I'll wash your garments and take them in exchange. 'Tis no robbery. Let's sleep on it."

She handed me a bowl of vegetable pottage stiff with soft onions and garlic and showed me a rush-thick corner of the room where I could sleep and gave me a wool blanket that smelled of hogs. The room was warm, but I shivered through the night and woke many times to muffled hog grunts and dreams of my mother coming to me again, her voice icy-clear as if she was right beside me, warning me, pleading with me. But what she was warning me about, I did not know. It had to be about Morcar.

Morcar might still be looking for me. I had to be ready. I held my arms tight around myself and listened to the low breathing of the woman and her children. Deep inside, I was choking with frustration. My sisters were leaving the city and there was nothing I could do.

14

I woke with a start as a hand shook my shoulder. "They're here for you," said the woman.

Panicking, I pushed myself up on my elbow. Had the Dane slavers found me or was it Morcar? I was still in the tunic she'd given me. I had no shoes on, but I could run in my bare feet.

She held my shoulder. "Calm, these are friends. They fight for the Godwins. I went to the alehouse early to see what men were there and found many Godwin men."

Relief rose fast inside me. I stood, shakily, as if I'd been supping ale all night. She held out a thick woollen cloak and my boots, which had been cleaned. I put everything on and went to the door on the other side of the room. It led into a smaller smoke-filled room with hogs' heads, legs, and bellies hanging from the roof and smoky embers burning softly at its centre. I coughed and headed for the door in the far wall.

A rush of daylight blinded me as I pulled it open.

The Rise of Synne

Two men with gleaming axes on their belts, with leather helmets pushed back, were waiting outside. I'd seen one of them before, during our retreat from Hastings. He was smiling now, unlike back then.

"It is you," he said. He held his fist up in a salute. "It's a good sign for us to see you, healer, on this auspicious day." He looked over my shoulder. "She's as good as new, Mother," he said to the hog farmer. He waved at me to follow him. "Come, we don't have much time."

The road was a muddy lane. Another farm lay on the far side with wicker-walled pens. Further along, a large alehouse had a crowd of men stomping their feet outside in the crisp November air, some of them sharpening swords or axes and others shouting greetings or insults at each other. I could smell them all as we approached, the familiar smell of stale sweat. There must have been about a hundred of them waiting there. That meant there were more inside the alehouse. Something was happening.

For a long dread moment, I thought this all might have to do with me slipping away from Morcar's grasp the night before, that he'd turned on the Godwins perhaps, but I rebuked myself. There was a lot more going on than I knew about.

And then I saw him, and a light-headed feeling came over me.

Ulf was standing in the doorway of the alehouse stopping people going in. Two men at arms were being turned away by him as we came near. On seeing me, he raised both his fists in triumph.

"You made it. I prayed half the night to the Queen of Heaven that you'd get away. My prayers have been answered," he said, his smile beaming.

"Was that you who told Morcar to look down by the river for me?" I asked as I stopped in front of him.

"Would I misdirect an ally?" he said, a comical frown on his face.

"The earls are our allies?"

He sniffed. "They were invited by the Norman duke to his new council, but they turned it down. So, they are with us, for now." He reached his hand out, touched my cloak. "Fine cloth. You are a lucky one," he said. "I hope you'll come with us today and bring your luck with you."

"Where are we going?"

"Come inside. You'll find out soon enough."

I followed him. All the tables in the alehouse were packed full of men. More were leaning against the walls. Shouts and chatter filled my ears as soon as we entered.

The top table was empty, but in a far corner, Magnus and Edmund stood talking with two of the thegns who'd survived Hastings. They were engrossed in conversation, but Magnus spotted me and for a moment, our eyes met. I

The Rise of Synne

felt a surge of heady anticipation and then dread. Would they believe what I'd found out?

They had to. I walked fast up the room. My news about the earl's heading back north was important. If they followed through, it would impact the Godwins' chance of beating back the Normans.

One of the thegns spotted me, nodded in my direction. All four men turned towards me. The noise in the room seemed to grow louder. For a moment I thought I might not be able to speak my mouth had dried so much.

If I played this right, they would be in my debt. You can be meek or strong, rabbit or wolf, my mother used to say, no matter where you find yourself or how you feel inside. You decide your own fate.

"You came back," said Edmund with a sneer. "What did you find out, what they eat for breakfast?"

I forced my words out slowly. They seemed to be coming from someone else. Someone sure of herself.

"You don't need the earls to defeat the Normans," I said loudly, in a tone that matched his sneer. It was a bold statement, but there'd be no respect here for defeatism.

Grunts of approval came from the thegns.

"What is your news?" said Edmund. Magnus had his head to one side and a curious look on his face.

"I saw a letter from Duke William to Morcar. He plans to go north soon. He wanted to take me."

Edmund pressed his fist into his other hand. "I guessed it," he said. "They sell themselves to the highest bidder."

"Anything else?" asked Magnus.

I shook my head.

"Go back to their camp and find out more," said Edmund.

My mouth opened. It felt as if a hole had opened under me. I could not go back.

Ulf spoke up. "The Earl Morcar was in a rage when he was looking for Synne last night at the feast. From what I heard, after she managed to slip his grasp, he will do something wicked to her if she goes to him."

Edmund made an exasperated sound. "Your usefulness is over for spying then," he said.

"I am still useful as a healer," I said, matching his tone. "It was what your father let me in your camp for."

"She is right. We need healers more than ever. We've lost too many. We must keep her with us," said Ulf, equally firmly.

Magnus nudged Edmund. "You promised to tell her where her brother's buried and to pay her. Keep your word, Edmund," he said.

Edmund let out a loud, dismissive groan. "I'll keep my word, brother. But she cannot take the road south now. The Normans are strung out all along it, in every village. I will not send her to her death." He gripped the pommel of his sword. "She stays with us, and when we have Duke William's head on a spike, she'll be told where to go to pray over her brother's body and be paid."

He pointed at me. "Go, keep our injured men alive and we will protect you from Morcar's thrusts." He raised his fist high, pushed it forward, and laughed.

Magnus shook his head, kept his mouth shut, his lips pressed tight together.

Ulf nudged me in the back, but I was already turning. I walked down the centre of the alehouse with many eyes on me. But I was hopeful. I was still in the entourage of the Godwins. I could expect protection and sustenance and more. It felt as if I was floating down the hall, my feet barely touching the ground.

The Godwins would surely rally enough men to their banner to defeat the Normans. And with even a small share of any spoils, I could search for my sisters. A weight came slipping from my back. I had hope. What stopped it sliding off completely was the thought that there were other people still looking for me, the Danes. But I had a good chance against them, with the Godwins' protection. Perhaps Magnus could be my protector. I sighed. Don't be stupid.

"Sit with me a while," said Ulf, coming up behind me. He grabbed my arm. "And listen to me." He squeezed tighter. "Do not get between those brothers."

"What? I didn't!" What was he on about?

"Do not even think about either of them. They've been arguing, Synne, and can turn on you in a moment."

"Why would they turn on me?" I said, slapping his hand away.

He groaned loudly. "Have you ever tried to separate two young bulls?"

I shook my head.

"That's what I thought. Just stay away from them. That's what any farmer will tell you with bulls."

"Don't worry, I don't plan to get trampled," I said.

He laughed. We found a table with a little free space and sat. I took bread from a passing serving girl carrying a basket of loaves.

Some of the men at our table were rubbing whetstones against blades or checking pommels were secure. Others were deep in conversation, probably making pacts as to what their comrades should do if they fell in battle. I'd seen a lot of that happening before the great battle at Hastings.

"What are all these preparations for?" I asked.

Ulf put his hands together, as if in prayer. "The bastard Normans forced the men of Middlesex back to

The Rise of Synne

London Bridge yesterday," he said softly. "We're expecting them to try to take the bridge today. We must defend it at all costs."

"I'll come and help," I said. Find a way to be useful, my mother had beaten into us. "I can bind wounds and save lives."

Ulf pointed to the other side of the room. "Go get salves and bandages from the old healer there. You know her, don't you?"

It was the same healer woman who'd been with the Godwins at Hastings. I looked for the younger woman who used to help her. I couldn't see her.

"What happened to her helper?" I asked.

"Ran away, I expect. You can be her helper today," said Ulf. "But listen to me well. Do not get caught in the fighting. Stay back and wait for injured men to be carried out or crawl out before you help."

"I know when to go forward and when to stay back," I replied. "You don't have to teach me." I poked my finger into his chest.

His eyes widened. Women were not supposed to answer monks back. I didn't care. My mother's voice, her passion, the voice of truth, was speaking through me.

He leaned close. "I like you, Synne, but you push your luck like a Dane with an axe looking for a fight or…" He paused. "Someone who aspires to be martyred."

"I speak what I want." He was right. But any fears of what other people thought of me had been lost, perhaps back in the shit of the hog farm, and he was wrong. I did not want to die. I had things to do.

"I see that, Synne, but don't stir things up. This is your friendly warning. Shackle your tongue." He stuck his out at me.

I stuck mine out at him in reply, then gestured as if trying to tie a knot in it, then I headed for the old woman, his laughter following me. My mind, like a dog on a scent, had gone back to thinking about Magnus. Had there been a smile on his face when he'd looked at me or was I being stupid thinking his arrogance meant interest? I looked around for him, could not see him. I was being stupid again.

The old healer greeted me with open arms.

"Thank the Christ. 'Tis a proper miracle to see you back with us," she said, hugging me tight. "Have you eaten yet, girl? You must eat quick before we move out." She didn't wait for my reply. She took an empty bowl from her table and handed it to me. "Take this to the alehouse woman." She pointed down the hall, one hand flapping in that direction. "She'll fill it for you." She grabbed me again, hugged me hard. "We'll see death today, but you and I will not die. We have good work to do saving men for their wives and children, especially the unborn ones." We held each other.

"You're as good as a saint," I whispered in her ear.

"Don't let the monks hear you say that," she whispered.

"I don't care who hears me," I said loudly.

She laughed nervously.

I ate a bowl of thick stew. It had chewy chunks of meat in it. I drank some watered-down ale. As I ate, a noisy clatter sounded around me as the men all began to rise and head for the door. It took a long time for them to pass outside. The alehouse owner stood near the old healer woman as the last men went out. He was wringing his hands.

"I ain't been paid even half yet," he grumbled, as I came near.

"We'll all be coming back tonight to sleep here," said the old healer. "You'll for sure be paid."

The alehouse owner shook his head. "If you're victorious, you mean, then you will come back and only half of you." He spat on the floor.

"We'll be victorious for sure," I said with a smile. "How can any army defeat them?" I pointed at the last of the men passing out, some of whom had shiny mail shirts and helmets on. "But say a prayer for us."

I'd seen the lines of men at Hastings, and I'd been sure there that King Harold could not be defeated, but Norman tricks had undone him. Harold's sons had to have a better chance against the wiles of the Normans. They knew the Norman tricks now.

Maybe this day might bring me close to Magnus. I closed my eyes, gripped my amulets through my tunic, and said a prayer.

Outside, the men were all marching away. There were other people at the rear of the line; some were women who needed to see what would happen to their men, and some of them had children with them. There were also a few merchants with small carts. Dogs yapped around all this, and onlookers who'd come out of their houses stared narrow-eyed.

Some people cheered as we passed, but not everyone, though it lifted my heart to know that many of the people of London were with us. A few held out a hand too, as if they thought we might have something to give them. All I had was a touch to give.

I touched one hand and the old man it belonged to smiled.

"They want the lucky touch of our victory to be on them too," said the old healer woman. She had a shoulder bag over each shoulder and looked strong enough to be

The Rise of Synne

able to drag a mail shirted man from beneath a shield wall all the way to safety.

Memories of Hastings came to me. I'd seen the Normans up close there. They would not be easily defeated. I sniffed the air. Was rain coming? The wind had shifted. Dark clouds were rolling in from the west, moving fast. I pulled my cloak tight as we walked after the men. When we got near the bridge, I saw that the clouds would pass to the south of the river. Hopefully, the rain would drench the Normans.

That would be good. A sign perhaps that the day would favour us.

The houses near the bridge were mostly shuttered and abandoned. A few had cudgel-wielding men standing outside, grim-faced. When the front line of our forces reached the bridge, we all stopped, stragglers and camp followers too.

The old healer woman, her name was Frida, went to sit on a low stone wall that overlooked the river. She called me over. The breeze was stronger, icy now. The cries of the gulls grew louder as if they'd sensed something was afoot.

"It'll be a while before they get themselves sorted," said Frida. A small wooden cross hung around her neck.

"You work with the monks?" I asked.

She shook her head. "Long ago, not these days." Up ahead, a war drum had begun its slow, insistent tune. She put a hand on my arm. "You know what happens in battle, girl. If you want no part of it this time, run away. I'll not tell. Days like this leave scars. If you get too many, they fair twist you up inside." She had a faraway look in her eyes.

"I'm twisted already," I said. I smiled. I would get my wish today. Revenge is good cold. I would see Normans dead today.

A rolling hush fell on the men up ahead of us. Someone was shouting a speech far off. We listened, as snatches of the words were relayed back by other men to ones behind and then back again, until eventually all we heard were a few words about an easy victory, that we'd win this day well, and show the Normans that England and its people would not lie back and wait to be ravished.

Cheers passed down the lines of men after that, but I had no idea what the final words were. They were lost in the tumult.

The men around us all moved forward again. We followed. Soon the bridge was directly ahead, about the length of two ships away, and I could see Magnus and Edmund directing men onto the bridge and slapping shoulders as men passed.

The Rise of Synne

The bridge looked different, too. Each wooden pier had a banner fluttering on top of it on both sides of the walkway. Some of the banners had black Godwin wolf heads on them. Others had a yellow cross or what looked like a bear's head. Others were too far away to make out.

The banners flapped wildly in the stiff cold breeze. Men at arms were arrayed on the bridge to almost halfway across already, far enough to be out of arrow reach from the far side. On the far side, the camp of our tents was gone. I spotted a few people bent over where the camp had been, picking through anything that had been left behind.

Smoke that had previously drifted up from houses across the river to the left and right rose no more, and no fishing boats were pulled up by the pool on the south bank near that end of the bridge.

Excited chatter came to me as we waited for something to happen. I caught a little of it on the wind. *The bridge will not easily be taken. Will we be able to hold it without burning it? And does William the bastard duke have some new trick for us today?*

The old woman went to a cart piled with bread. She came back with a small, hand-sized loaf for each of us. She pulled some hard cheese – it had a nice pungent smell – from the giant bag she carried over her shoulder and broke some off for me.

"We'll have to wait a time," she said with a sigh. "Best you tell me all about yourself. And I'll tell you how I ended up here."

We sat with our backs to the wattle and daub wall of a deserted house and told tales about our lives. I even told her about my sisters. She tutted and hummed at the ending to that story. She told me about a husband gutted in a fight and another lost to a shaking sickness. His death was why she'd become a healer. She missed being married but did not want her heart broken again. She asked me, "What about you; where is your husband?"

I shook my head. "Never married," I said.

"You should have been married already," she said with a sad shake of her head; words I'd heard often enough to know I was better off not replying to them. "But you have your eye on someone, yes?"

I smiled. It was a good way to deflect the endless questions about men thrown at you if people thought you weren't sworn to someone. I'd had offers from men as Stefan and I had travelled the county, but what they all wanted was a slave, a wife at the beck and call of their husband. I would not abandon the search for my sisters to be any man's slave. And luckily, being a healer meant I did not have to.

"Who is he, then?" asked Frida. "Is he up ahead with the men?"

The Rise of Synne

I stopped smiling. She was too good at guessing.

"Does he know you have your eye on him?"

I stared ahead.

"If he survives the battle, will you promise me something?"

"What?"

"You'll tell him what your heart is saying to you."

I nodded. Anything to stop the questions.

A baker came over and sat on his haunches in front of us. His skin was speckled with flour.

"I'm all sold out, ladies. I'll be off to get some more." He grinned while looking at me, displaying half-broken teeth. "Will you stay here for the fighting?" he asked.

"We're healers. We stay for the fighting. That's why we're here," said the old woman.

"Maybe your daughter would like to earn some easy coin by coming back with me and helping me." He grinned, jerked his head back toward his cart.

"Go away, quick," said Frida angrily.

"Huh, maybe your daughter needs to get away from you," he said. "You're putting her life in danger."

I rubbed my hands together as if thinking about his offer. Then I spoke, sweetly at first. "If I go with you," I said. "You'll have to watch me careful like, as I may pick up the first knife I see and ram it quick into your belly and twist it until you squeal like a stuck pig. And yes, I would like to hear you squeal like that, oink, oink." I grinned at him. It was the type of mad talk that saw most men disappear, fast.

He stumbled back, his eyes glittering with malice. "Christ in heaven protect me from a witch like you," he said. He spat on the ground between us, then walked back to his cart.

Frida laughed as he went. "There's not many would have the guts to do what you just did," she said. "Where did you learn to speak like that?"

"On the road, with my brother going from village to village. There's a lot of men like him who think they can do what they want, just 'cause you're poor."

"Look, he's cursing us," said Frida.

The baker was talking to some men near his cart and pointing at me, throwing his hands around. He wasn't used to being spoken to that way.

The old woman stood, pulled me up. "Come on, let's get up nearer the bridge," she said.

We moved between the lines of men. Shouts came from behind us, but I didn't look back and we were soon too far gone for them to do anything. Some of the men we passed knew the old woman, and some knew me, so we were greeted warmly as we went through the ranks. Most men knew we could be saving their skins by nightfall, and they made way for us, then went back to leaning on their

The Rise of Synne

war axes, if they had one, or talking with the men around them.

There is a strange, dark feeling that passes through men who know that death in battle may be near. The hurried breath of fear and the pride in strength and the sway of anger all mix into a heady, infectious brew.

We came quickly to an open area for carts to turn or wait before crossing the river. The bridge was directly in front of us. Groups of men at arms talked loudly here, bragging, stamping their feet, slapping each other's shoulders, laughing, some swinging their fists and cursing the Norman enemy with venom. Many were without mail shirts, only the lucky ones had them.

Many men didn't have iron helmets either, just leather or wool caps and jerkins. These were mostly fyrd men, freemen sent by a lord allied to the Godwins to do their sworn duty and die if necessary. Some may have fought with us before. Others may have been too late to get to Hastings in time. Stefan had told me about the different groups of fyrd men as they'd joined us on the march to Hastings. He'd hoped to start his fighting career as a fyrd man, if he could get a lord to agree to accept him. All those dreams, lost. I could still hear an echo of Stefan talking about them in my head. It left me with a fierce ache inside, a longing, like a long-buried desire, to avenge him.

I looked forward to seeing Normans dying. I know that's not what monks want us to want, death for others, and sometimes in a soft moment I'm tempted to forgive them Normans, but it still doesn't take away the deep ache for revenge.

Shouts echoed around us as we came near the bridge. Orders were being cried out and replies coming back.

Then a hush descended.

On the far side of the river, something was happening. I went up on my toes. Seagulls were crying out, dipping and diving in the wind, oblivious to all of us.

A rider on a giant white Norman warhorse, with the duke's personal banner, red with a yellow cross, and streamers flickering at the back, was walking his horse slowly towards the bridge on the far side.

Behind him came a line of Norman cavalry that stretched and blurred as far as the eye could see.

When the rider reached the south side of the bridge, he raised his banner high and a war horn blared, sending a single long note on the wind to us.

For a moment, the world stopped.

A mocking cheer went up on our side. Individual curses screamed out. Some of them must have carried on the wind to the Normans, but they did not cry out in reply. A tremor of defiance ran through me. I made a fist. They had to be defeated. Everything depended on it.

The Rise of Synne

Our ragged shouts turned into an organised chant. "Out, out, out." The old Saxon war cry. Every one of us joined in, even us two women, the only women I could see anywhere in the throng.

Our men were screaming pure outrage at the Normans daring to come here. Some of our men were waving their battle axes or their shields in the air. Frida beamed at me. I laughed. The shouting continued as I looked up and down the riverbank. As far as the eye could see, stood men with raised fists or weapons in the air, showing they were ready to defend London, to defend England.

Vibrations from the shouting ran deep inside me. I would never forget the power of those voices. They gave me hope and nailed the need for vengeance straight into my heart, that persistent urge I'd grappled with, the way temptation grapples with you.

I hadn't felt this way at Hastings. The shield wall there had formed up early in the morning and though the roars had been similar in nature, some were about the Holy Cross, there'd been a tiredness in our shouts back then, after our fast march south to battle.

Now our shouts were bold and fierce as the Norman warhorse stepped onto the south end of the bridge and walked slowly forward.

A stream of Norman foot soldiers came behind it. Archers and infantry men all following the lone rider.

The horseman rode to just outside arrow distance, about a quarter of the way across the bridge, and stopped. A mocking cheer went up from our side. I joined in, though it wasn't clear at all what was happening as the wooden piers, banners, and the ranks of men at arms on our side meant all I could see was the banner the lone horsemen held.

A hush descended.

Squinting, I could make out that the banner was still, flapping in the wind, and beyond that, Normans in helmets filling what had been an empty part of the bridge, only a little wider than two passing carts, meaning eight or ten men could stand shoulder-to-shoulder with their shields up. Our shield wall, blocking Norman progress at the centre of the bridge, followed a tight pattern – the first line of shields down at the ground and higher up, others overlapping, from the next line of men, and another line of shields interlocking above the heads of all the men in the first two rows. It was a tight shield wall.

Breaking such a wall would not be easy, while spears and swords poked out at anyone who dared to push or ram it.

Warning shouts echoed from the bridge and a testing shower of arrows from the Norman side arced high into the air and clattered down in front of our line. A few went further, hitting our shields.

The Rise of Synne

There may have been an exchange of words at the front line, before the arrows, but we didn't hear it.

I saw arrows arcing high from our side. I did not see what they struck.

Restlessness hung in the air. Some of our men took to banging their weapons or their shields on the ground. Rolling thuds echoed as others joined in. The desire to fight filled the air all around, like the whiff of strong ale. I wanted to be part of it. I wanted to see the Normans brought down, axe to axe, face to face, their men falling down.

A jarring cacophony of clashing weapons drifted to us in the wind from the middle of the bridge like a far-off storm. The Normans had pushed forward despite our arrows. The noise grew, the metallic clashing-battle-sounds mixed with screams so far off they seemed unimportant, though we knew what they meant.

It felt strange, stupid, that what was happening here would determine the fate of a kingdom. We had to win. We had to defeat them so our nightmare could be over.

"Let's move onto the bridge," said Frida softly. "There'll be men to heal soon."

She pushed through the lines of men at arms, stumbling at times over helmets on the ground or the head of an axe being rested, but the men let us through when she called out, "Make way for healers. Make way."

I followed her. From the reactions of the men we passed, it felt as if we were sacred, protected. I'd heard someone say that the reason men don't put us healers into their sagas is that they don't want reminding of what happens to flesh in war. For some of the men, those looking eagerly ahead to our shield wall, we were probably invisible, and if asked, they'd probably not even remember us slipping by them, so focused were they on the fight.

I'd gone close to our shield wall only twice at Hastings, to staunch bad wounds, and it had been the same there.

As we moved along the bridge, I saw Edmund. His helmet had a golden ridge on top. He was talking animatedly to thegns around him, all in their shining helmets. I looked for Magnus but didn't see him. Edmund looked at me as we passed but didn't acknowledge me. He just stared at me, iron-faced. I wondered what he and his brother had been arguing about.

The wooden planks were vibrating under me, as if an animal up ahead was stomping on them.

We kept going.

I'd seen Frida many times at Hastings, and she'd been the same there, calm, dealing with injured men fast. The high-pitched screams and blood-stirring curses and the crash of weapons filled my ears now.

The Rise of Synne

I could see up ahead a gap all across the centre of the bridge between the rows of grim-faced men around us and the shield wall ahead, a giant iron-bossed hog in the middle of the bridge. Norman arrows fell from the sky in waves, *thunking* and *whooshing* not far in front of us, almost non-stop. Most dropped in the gap between us and our shield wall.

Only a few flew from our side now.

From what I could tell, with the river flowing fast beneath the bridge and the riverbanks far away on either side, we'd not given up much of the bridge yet. It was hard to tell. We went forward some more, getting even closer to the fighting. Around us, men stared at us as if they were looking through us at something else, their past perhaps. I could see their breath coming out too as their chests heaved. And I could hear the leather straps of mail shirts creaking as men moved and I could smell their fear-filled sweat.

My skin felt tight all over and my hands had become fists, until I forced them to loosen, and then they became fists again, as the clash of weapons grew loud and louder with each step.

Our ranks were tight, but there was still a gap in the middle for us to get through and occasionally a young man in a mail shirt and leather helmet hurried past us, carrying news or some message one way or the other.

I saw my first wounded man of that day.

He was lying at the edge of the bridge, as if someone was planning to discard him over the waist-high wall with its old, blackened-wood rail above him.

Frida gripped my arm. She'd given me her second shoulder bag. It had a honey salve pot and lots of strips of linen in it. "Go, see if he can be saved before they tip him into the river," she said. "Be quick."

I pushed past men, they were just staring, and knelt beside the injured man. He'd been pulled back from where the arrows fell. I knew at once there was little I could do for him. He was breathing only faintly, and his wound was to his cheek, exposing his teeth and the sparkling white bone of half his jaw and blood was pumping from it fast. The wound was from an axe, most likely. He had another wound on his thigh. It, too, was bleeding heavily.

I took his hand in mine and whispered the Lord's Prayer over him, my head bent. I could feel his fingers tighten and his hand grip me as if in thanks. It went limp as I finished the prayer. I put his hands together, gently, closed his eyes and went back to Frida. Behind me, I heard a faint splash. I looked around. The wounded man was gone.

All I could see of the fighting now was an occasional spearhead or sword poking above the shields ahead and sometimes an iron helmet rising high, of the type the more

The Rise of Synne

experienced men at arms wore. Desperate grunts and the infamous Norman shouts of "Dex Aie," *God be with us*, came clear in the air, showing how close we'd come to the Norman spearhead.

Another injured man arrived.

He'd stumbled here himself. He appeared to be lightly injured. All he was doing was holding his head, but when I lifted his heavy iron helmet off, I saw blood all over the back of his neck. I wrapped a bandage around it to help stop the bleeding.

"Take him to the end of the bridge. He may live if he gets away from here," said Frida.

He stumbled into me as I put my arm around him. I held him tight, and we headed back. He was able to walk, thankfully, though slowly. The wind whistled through my cloak. It was even colder here, out on the river. The air had a salty taste too, which left my lips dry. And the wind was getting stronger. Was there a storm coming?

His blood dripped onto me as we walked. The smell of it filled my nostrils, the warm iron smell of battle. The nods of encouragement and grim smiles from men as we passed made the task easier.

As we went through a group of fyrd men at the end of the bridge, they stared at us as if we'd come from a nightmare. The shouts of battle were far in the distance now.

I helped the injured man to beyond all the fyrd men where the women and old men were waiting for news. We passed slowly along the line. I was hoping someone might know the injured man. A woman shrieked when she saw him. She was my age, perhaps younger, and she quickly took over my job, pushing me away with a sour face, as if she thought I was trying to steal him from her. She didn't realise how lucky she was that a healer had helped him and that she'd found him in all this chaos. I'd not seen a physician who could have helped him since we'd arrived at the bridge, though it was possible there was one or two around somewhere looking after thegns and lords.

The sun was going down as I walked back onto the bridge. A woman with her back to me had a brown wimple covering her hair, with flecks of golden locks visible at the side. It had to be Elva. Beyond her stood Edmund. She was leaning close to him and whispering in his ear. Something about how close they were together made me think that Magnus had been spurned, unless the two brothers shared her.

Was Elva who they'd been arguing about? I could believe that. I did not imagine either Magnus or Edmund as the type to share a woman. I expected each of them, as King Harold's sons, could have any woman they desired as theirs alone.

The Rise of Synne

A shout came from the centre of the bridge. We all peered ahead.

"'Tis the bastard's banner, look!" some man shouted. I went up on my toes but did not see it. On the far side of the river, I glimpsed massed cavalry, holding still, steam coming off them, waiting most likely for a chance to force their way across the bridge. There were many banners there. Shouts passed through the crowd around me, one person copying another, as if we were all one single animal, sensing our prey.

I slipped forward through the crowd until a shout went up right behind me. I turned, wondering if it was Elva or Edmund. But it was a torchbearer making his way up the bridge, his spluttering torch held high in the air. I waited for him, then followed in his wake. He was a young man wearing a polished leather jerkin. As he passed up one side of the walkway, he lit waist-high braziers. Each brazier had charcoal in it, and wood piled up beside it.

I knew what this meant. The Godwins would burn the bridge if they thought the Normans might force their way across.

I reached Frida. The young man with the torch turned and went back along the other side of the bridge, lighting braziers. I bent down beside Frida. She was on her knees, wiping blood from a wounded man's face.

"Hold his hand," she whispered, leaning to me. "He doesn't have long." I took his hand. It was cold. I could feel the suck of death, see the dark shadow of it on his face. He looked up at me, smiled a little. Then his grip loosened. His eyes went dim as if he was looking through me at something more important. I shivered, imagining his soul departing to the underworld.

Frida gripped my arm. "Did you see the duke?"

I shook my head, staring at her. She was splattered with blood.

Her eyes were wide. "What a sight. He dared to come onto the bridge! And his herald came close to the front line. He waved the banner. The one they say is the pope's. His herald shouted in that whiny Norman tongue that they will pay a gold coin, and welcome who sets down their arms."

I breathed in fast, anger rising inside me. "He's a cunning wolf."

"Aye, and there were threats, too. Claims that London will burn from end to end if we do not submit." She pointed at our shield wall. It seemed to have moved. I stared, trying to work out if it had.

"We drove forward as he spoke. The Normans must be sore afraid if they make so generous an offer." She ended with a half-crazed laugh.

I stared at the back of our shield wall. It looked like a metal and wood snake. The strength and persistence of our

The Rise of Synne

men was the result of practice, I knew, but on and on they held their shields up while waiting for the arrow or spear or sword thrust that slips between the shields to find them. They roared and cursed the enemy to keep their resolve up, I knew that, but it was the bond with their shield wall brothers that kept them going.

I listened to the shouts and grunts and cries of agony and then I had to blink once, twice.

"It's Stefan," I said. A strange sensation, as if I was floating in a dream, came over me.

A young man at the back of our wall, helping hold up a shield, stuck almost full of arrows, had glanced back toward us.

Stefan!

The shape of his face, his hair, everything. It was him. I stepped toward the killing ground. Frida grabbed my hand as I went past her.

"No," she shouted.

My feet were still moving. Something else was in control.

The last man between me and the open space where arrows littered the wood and more were falling held my arm tight as I tried to get past him.

"We wait to be called," the man said, without looking at me, as if he thought I was intending to take a place in the shield wall.

Frida was beside me. "You told me your brother Stefan's dead," she said angrily. "You cannot see him if he's dead." She shook my arm. "Come back," she said.

I pointed at the man I thought was Stefan in the last line of the shield wall. He'd turned away from us. His brown tunic was exactly what Stefan used to wear. I wanted so much to go to him, to tell him all that had happened, how much had changed, and about my hopes, too. My mouth opened, then closed, all dry. The wind slammed into my face, like the flap of a demon's wing, and the taste of blood and salt filled my mouth.

"Make way," a shout came from behind us with yells and cheers along with it too.

A passage had opened between our lines of men. Striding toward us came Magnus, his mail shirt glistening in tight waves of silvered mail, and beside him, Morcar.

Cheers followed them. Both had their helmets under their arms. They were demonstrating the alliance between the northern earls and the Godwins, and the men around them loved it.

Magnus had a giant war axe in his hand. Morcar had one too. Their faces were purposeful and grim.

My breathing stopped. Morcar and Magnus were rallying our shield wall together. I stood still, not that I had much room around me with men pressing back to make way for them. We were near the side of the bridge. I

The Rise of Synne

watched the two of them pass, my head up, almost daring them to notice me. But they didn't. Their gaze was fixed ahead. A cheer went up from every man around me, and weapons rose high. I stood on my toes then, a shiver of admiration rising inside me, and for a long moment I imagined Magnus putting his arms around me. I had to hit my fist into my chest to stop my senseless mooning over him.

Someone poked me in the back. I jumped. It was Frida. "Stop staring," she said. "Go, help the men I'll send back to the end of the bridge." Then she was gone.

As I passed back through the men at arms, I heard two of them talking about the Norman offer of gold, as if they were considering it. I laughed, then shouted, "Norman gold has blood on it," as I went past them. When I looked back, they were both staring at me as if they wanted me dead.

They'd have to get in line.

I waited at the end of the bridge until I spotted a man being half-carried towards me. I waved for him to be brought close. He was placed down on the hard, icy ground in front of me. I bound a light wound on his side and asked him if he could walk. He nodded. I told him to find his lord and tell him he could not fight again until next season. I did the same for another man, barely able to walk because of a leg wound.

A third man died as he was dropped at my feet. Two more men died at my feet, despite all I did. I stood up then, looked around. Night was falling fast with a clear, cold sky above, the stars bright. The moon was up. I'd barely noticed the day ending.

"What's all that?" I asked the men who'd carried the last dying man to me. Across the river, a yellow and red glow lit the horizon, upriver and down.

The younger of the two answered. "The bastard Normans set all the houses alight." The other man shook his head. "They take a place and then burns it. I'd hate to see London if they make their way across," he said.

We stared as the glow across the river grew, like a vision of hell. Soot sprinkles drifted in the air and a faint smell of burning came to us on the wind. I put my hand up. There weren't more than a few black specks, but others around us were doing the same and looking at their hands, too. I put that hand on my heart and said a silent prayer that the Normans would never take this city. Maybe this could be a good sign. It might deepen the resolve of our defenders.

On the bridge, someone was being carried towards me by four men. They came straight to me and put the man down at my feet.

It was Magnus.

My mouth opened. I gasped.

The Rise of Synne

His eyes were half-closed, but he smiled a little when he saw me.

"Morcar didn't make you run away then," he said.

I knelt beside him, glad he was still alive. "Save your strength," I said bluntly. His mail shirt was ripped at the shoulder. Blood was visible through the gap. The wound was close to his old wound. That was not good. His shoulder needed binding, fast.

"Take off his mail," I said loudly to the men who'd carried him. That took longer than it should have and was accompanied by muffled grunts of pain from Magnus, but when the metal shirt was off, I was able to smear honey gently on his wound to further groans, and then bind tight the finger-length of open bloody wound on his shoulder. I used a long strip of linen wound under his arm.

I leant down near him when I was finished. His skin was as pale as snow, with streaks of blood on his face and moustache. He might have been struck on the head too, as he looked dazed, his gaze still, which might have caused damage I couldn't see. I held my hand over his bound wound, pressing it to try to stop it bleeding. I waited, said a prayer. For a long, horrible moment, I feared I might lose him as his breathing slowed. Then his lips moved. I leant close to hear his words.

"The bastard retreated," he whispered.

I could smell sweat and blood. "Is it a trap?" I asked.

He nodded. "I warned Morcar not to follow 'em." His brief smile lasted only a moment. "But he wasn't at Hastings. If he had been…" His voice trailed into a low growl.

Looking down at him, a memory came back to me. Gytha, my sister, had almost drowned in the river near our home when we were young. I'd dragged her into the rushes. Her face had been the same pale shade as Magnus's now. Afterwards, she'd laughed about it, but I couldn't get what had happened out of my mind all that summer.

A rat ran past Magnus's head. Another jumped over his legs.

"The rats are running from the fires on the other side," someone shouted.

"I'll find your brother," I said, leaning down to Magnus. "He'll know where to take you. You need someone to watch that wound, bind it again." I was holding his wound, but blood was seeping through the linen.

Magnus reached his hand toward me, spoke softly. "These men will take me. But you must come and find me," he said. He paused. I wondered where I would find him. Then, as if he'd read my mind, he said, "Come to the hall of the wolf skull."

In his eyes, I saw a need I'd not seen before. I nodded. On his signal, his men lifted him away from me. I breathed

The Rise of Synne

in deep, looked around for the next man I could help. I did not want to wish anything for Magnus but a quick recovery.

I saved five men that night and watched four others die. There may have been more. I lost count and memory of all the faces. I was praised by some for the work I did. Others just stared through me. It was bloody work, enough to make my mind clench at the end and every good feeling slip away until I felt like a stone inside. And no more foolish thoughts of Magnus. The fire on the other side of the river had moved on and could be seen burning in the distance, when it was announced by a wave of shouts that we'd pushed the Norman forces totally off the bridge. Chants of "Morcar, Morcar," came to me on the wind, disturbing me. Please, don't let him be the hero of all this.

The old healer woman appeared beside me as I finished with one man, having bound his wound tight. She told me to come with her. She had a place for the night waiting for her in an alehouse, she said. My body ached all over. I'd seen too much death and been reminded too many times of my mother's end, and of Stefan's, and of the vengeance I'd wanted so much and what it meant in blood.

All my fears of earlier that day were gone. We'd held off the Normans. We could defeat them.

We shared blankets in a rush-strewn corner of the alehouse, after sharing cold stew, which had been kept for her. I told her it was hers, but she insisted on sharing.

"You deserve it, and more. The men you saved would want you to eat this night," she said.

"What about the ones who died under me?" Some of their faces were still in my mind, like a waking nightmare. It seemed to me that some of the deaths had been my fault.

"They'd want you to eat too," she said softly.

"I could have saved more." I rocked back and forth, while sitting in the rushes with a blanket over me, a few candles providing a dim light and a miserable heat.

"Stop it, do not doubt your work," said Frida. "If we save a few from the many that pass by, we do well, girl. Be proud. Your mother would be proud. You know it, don't you?"

I couldn't reply as a swell of tears forced its way up. This time I could not control them. I'd been remembering a handsome young man who did not want to die but did. And I'd remembered my stupidity, dreaming of Magnus while men died around me.

15

I listened to the occasional roars of celebration for our victory and prayed long into the night to the Queen of Heaven, and to all the gods, above and below. My mother had always told us, "Believe in all the gods, just in case."

I prayed for Magnus too and for a way, any way, to rescue my sisters. I'd been fortunate in finding out they were alive, and where they were going. But now I had to save them. And with our victory, there was hope.

Memories of our life before my mother had been murdered came back to me, in a strange clear way, that hadn't happened for a long time.

As sisters, we used to weave through the winters. Some in our village claimed our tunics were lucky, as they were made by three sisters, all daughters of a healer and a seer. Gytha and Tate used to claim that as the youngest, our mother's gift would be strongest in me, but I'd not had faith in Mother's powers passing to me. I'd been impatient when I was young. I'd tried to force things, to see the future, heal with ease, but everything had been such a struggle, and I'd stopped believing.

Frida nudged me awake. It was still dark. She was carrying a tiny stub of a candle. Its light barely showed her face.

"I have to go," she said. "I live outside the city and my children are waiting for me."

"What about the bridge?" I asked, rubbing my eyes. I was thinking the Normans would try to cross again.

"The bastard's army has moved on. I am duty-bound only to attend until a battle ends, no longer. There is no Norman army on the other side of the bridge, Synne. He moved his men away yesterday while we were still fighting."

"He's given up?" I asked hopefully. "He'll go back to France?"

She shook her head sadly. "No, he'll look for another way to cross the river."

"Where can he find that?"

"There's a ford. 'Tis a long way upriver, so he won't be coming to the city soon." She touched my hand. "But he's not giving up. They say he never gives up." She leaned closer. "Perhaps you'll come with me? I can take in a good healer."

I shook my head. I knew where I was going.

The Rise of Synne

"So be it, but be careful, girl," she said. "There are dangers in every corner of this city."

She pulled the hood of her cloak over her head as she left. I settled in the rushes with my cloak wrapped around me, listening to the scratching of mice and rats and the squawks of crows and the cries of seagulls outside.

I'd find Magnus. I'd tend to him. That look in his eye told me he needed me. Perhaps it was true. I hoped so.

At first light, the alehouse keeper brought in a cauldron of gruel and a stack of chipped red bowls to feed everyone sleeping in the room. All of the men lying in the rushes had been at the bridge the day before. We all got a bowl of warm gruel and ate, mostly in silence, at the trestle tables, which had been pushed to the walls before we slept. News of the Normans heading upriver to find another way across and into the city must have reached everyone by now, as the mood had turned. The men were quiet.

I found the midden, waited my turn, made sure the door was properly closed before I went, then washed my face in a half barrel of water. The sun was shining when I went outside. I headed downriver to the hall of the wolf skull. Seagulls swooped endlessly, and on the far bank of the river, thin spirals of black smoke rose high in the air, showing the destruction the Normans had brought with them.

When I reached the wolf skull hall, a small crowd had gathered outside. The slave ship was gone and there were no other trading ships in the river. I stared downriver, wondering how my sisters were. Some of the men outside the hall were men at arms who looked disgruntled. Others looked like traders. I slipped along the front wall of the hall, pushing past a few men until I could grab the arm of one of the door guards.

"Magnus told me to come," I said when he looked at me. "I am Synne, the healer. Tell him I am here."

He looked me up and down, disappeared without replying, and a while later, as I shivered in the wind wondering if I'd be allowed in, he came back and motioned me to go inside. A roar of disapproval from the crowd greeted this, but the door guards ignored it all and I slipped behind them and inside the hall as the door cracked open.

Men sat at every table. They were sharing bread. Empty gruel bowls waited in stacks on each table. The talk was all in muted voices. No one sat at the top table. A low fire in the hearth at the centre of the hall flickered and sent smoke to the roof. Behind the top table, a thick black wool curtain hung all the way across from one wall to the other. A guard leaned against the wall at one side of the curtain.

I walked up the side of the room and told the guard I'd been summoned by Magnus. He pointed to the other end of the curtain. I went there and pushed through at the edge, holding the rough wool for a moment, hesitating, full to the brim with anticipation. Would he still need me? How was he?

Three large yellow candles lit the area beyond. A small low brazier stood on the floor, glowing heat. An old woman was perched on a stool on the far side of a long wooden bed. A figure lay in the bed beneath layers of furs. The oak headboard had a wolf carved into it. A giant black wolf skin with small pale patches lay on the floor. The bed stood on a low wooden platform.

A young man was sitting on a stool in a corner of the room sharpening a dagger. He scowled, pointed his dagger at me, as if measuring the distance between us. I ignored him, went to the bed. Magnus was lying in it, his eyes closed. A twist of fear made me lean down to him.

The old woman stood. "What do you want?" she hissed.

"Magnus asked me to come," I said. "I am Synne, the healer."

"I know who you are. And I know Lord Magnus has no need for another healer. I'm here for him," she said. "You can go. And be quick about it, before I get the guard to throw you out on your ear."

I bent over Magnus and touched his cheek.

"Get away from him," the old woman said angrily. "We don't trust you. If you do anything to harm my lord, his page here will put a dagger in your heart before you take another breath. Move away from my lord Magnus." Her words all spat at me.

I looked at the page. His hand was back at his shoulder, with the knife tip in his fingers. I'd no doubt he could have the blade in me, close to my heart, in a moment. I moved back. Magnus slept on. I stepped back again. The page lowered his weapon. The old woman smiled at her victory. She pointed at the curtain for me to go back the way I came.

I stepped forward onto the platform and stamped my foot.

My boot cracked loudly on the wood. Nothing happened. The old woman glared at me, her eyes bulging, gesturing with both her arms for me to go. I stamped my foot again, harder.

"Magnus," I shouted.

"What?" said a low voice. Magnus pushed himself up on his elbow.

"It is nothing. Just lay back and rest, my lord," said the old woman.

"It is me, Synne," I said.

"At last," he whispered. He let himself fall back. I smiled wide at his words. A door had unlocked.

"Where have you been?" A pale hand appeared at the top of the blankets. "Everyone else out," he said. His hand waved briefly, then disappeared.

I breathed deep.

"But, my lord," said the old woman. "We need to watch you. Your brother gave us orders."

Magnus's voice came louder. "Do my bidding or I'll have my men remove you both," he said.

The old woman grunted in annoyance, but she and the page left me alone with Magnus. I went to him, stared down at his face, still pale, and examined the bandage I'd put on his shoulder. There was a little more blood on it, but the bleeding had long stopped.

I sat on the edge of his bed, pushed a lock of hair off his forehead, then touched his cheek the way my mother had taught me.

"They are right. You have the healing touch," whispered Magnus.

"Who was right?"

"I heard men talking about you, about how many you saved. Even Elva spoke about you."

I looked around in case Elva was hiding somewhere and I hadn't seen her. "She's not here?" I asked.

"Gone off with my brother," he replied. He smiled as if he was glad she wasn't here.

I brushed his hair from his forehead. I had to say this now, in case he got the wrong idea of what I wanted from him. A tremble passed through me. I'd been thinking about this moment all the way here. Would I say it right?

"I am…" I said. I stopped. A foreboding had taken my tongue. That was unusual for me, but he was the old king's son, someone who'd always been far out of reach for the likes of me.

"You are?" he said softly. His eyes were wide, questioning.

I leaned close to him. Something strange had tightened every muscle inside me.

"Synne, speak. I'll not blame you, whatever you have to say. Have you taken the bastard's gold, like some are doing? Will you go to him and serve in his army?"

I shook my head, fast. "No. I would not take coin from Normans."

"What then? You'll go north?"

"No."

He groaned. "Talk to me." He closed his eyes. "Do not fear me. I have no plans to force myself on you."

That was good, but I'd sensed he was not that type already. Something else was stopping me speak. The pull I'd felt towards him since we'd met was disturbing me. I wanted to tell him this, but I would not. He'd laugh at me, for sure. But still every part of him spoke to me. His stubbled chin, the sweaty smell of him, his blue eyes like the sky. I thrilled at his closeness, at our being alone together. But I had to set that aside.

"Is there some other reason you're here?" He looked me in the eye.

I was still trying to form the words. He was different now from the clamped-mouth man I'd admired from afar.

I'd seen changes in injured people, especially men who'd been hit on the head. Fever of the head unbalances the humors and causes confusion, confessions, and pleas to spill from men's lips, as if they've been freed from the bonds of duty and respect. I had to be careful not to believe all the words that might come out of his mouth.

Above all, I must not tell him how I felt about him.

"I have come to help with your healing, that is all," I said. I had to make that clear.

"I am grateful," he said. "I am sure my family will be too. Did you see them?" he looked towards the curtain.

I shook my head. He looked around, as if looking for ghosts.

"I'm sure they'll come to see you."

He looked wistful.

"I'm in your hands," he said. He lay back, winced.

I held his hand, which was outside the cover now. I could not resist. The warm feel of his skin sent a warm jolt up through my arm. I stiffened, pulled my hand away.

I stood. I should get to work. Healing requires more than words and kind touches. "I'll boil water, clean your wound, and put on a new bandage," I said briskly. "How does your head feel?"

He groaned from somewhere deep in reply.

I went to find the cooking area. There was no one at the main hearth, so I went out through a door at the back of the hall. Two women were in a small hut, leaning up against the hall. They were cutting apart a pig's leg. They had a fire going and a cauldron over it, with water in a large jug nearby. I explained who I was, found a bowl, took some of the water, and told them I was going back to help Magnus. The older woman gave me a clean linen undershirt after I answered some questions about who I was. She also gave me a small pot of their best honey.

Removing the blood-soaked bandage on Magnus's shoulder set him to suppressed screaming, even though I was as gentle as I could. But if I didn't change it, he risked a painful death. I felt around his head too and he winced away from me as I touched just above an ear. He needed plenty of rest.

He gripped my arm as I pulled away, so hard I had to force my nails into his skin to get him to release me. We were locked together for a moment with his eyes on me, blazing angrily.

He released me. His head fell back and soon after, he babbled as I bound his wound up. I applied a little honey to his head too. After a while, I understood some of what he was saying. Fear was driving his words.

"The bastard's cutting the city off, healer. Do you hear me? Do you? He has us in a noose of our own making. None of the fishermen can work. Not one. They're afraid of burning arrows if the wind takes them anywhere near the south bank. The carts full of produce from south of the river have stopped coming. They've all stopped." He shook his head. "There's too many mouths to feed in London."

"They cannot lay siege to London," I said softly. "It's far too big, surely?"

Magnus leaned up a little. "He doesn't have to lay a total siege. He just has to stop food coming in and there'll be riots soon after. The Earl of Mercia has received two bags of gold already, they say, and will get more. If he and his brother go north, we are lost."

"What about your brother? Edmund can match the bastard's offer, I am sure. Your father's treasury must hold more than enough to pay off a few earls."

He looked at me, then away. "They took Winchester where most of the treasury is." His eyes narrowed. "I talk too much. I'm not sure why, but I sense I can trust you." He straightened a little, stared at me. "If I talk about such private things with you, you must swear on your life that you'll never speak of what I tell you to another. Do you so swear? On your life."

A warm sensation came over me. I was being trusted with his secrets.

"Say it, healer. Swear it on the lives of your sisters."

"How do you know about them?" Should I fear him?

"The healer who you worked with yesterday. She came early this morning for coin before you arrived. She told me lots of things about you."

I had no choice. "My name is Synne, the healer." I looked him in the eye. "And I swear on the lives of my sisters, and on my own life that nothing you speak about to me will be repeated elsewhere, ever."

His hand reached for me. His grip was firm when I took it. It felt right as we held hands, upright like brothers do. I felt his warmth and his strength.

"Ulf told me things about you, too," he said, releasing me.

"Good things, I hope." What had Ulf told him?

"He said you are loyal, a good healer, and might help us defeat the invaders. He also said some Danes were looking for you. Who are they?" His eyes searched mine, trying to see inside me.

I thought about lying for a moment. "If they're who I think they are, they're the ones who murdered my mother

The Rise of Synne

and took my sisters. For some reason, they want to make me a slave as well, like my sisters."

"Why?" He looked as perplexed as I felt.

I hesitated. Should I tell him my fears? "I do not know."

"Something to do with your father?"

I shook my head. It was truly frustrating not knowing why I was being pursued.

"Who was your father?"

"A Dane."

"Just any Dane?"

"My mother told us almost nothing about him."

He lay his head back, looked off as if he was thinking about something. "We need people like you."

I wanted him to say *I need someone like you.* "I'll help any way I can."

He grunted. He sounded distracted. "The Normans sent my brother a message. They want us to submit." He looked at me with a bleak expression.

"Edmund will submit?"

"He told them if they went back to their lands in Normandy, we would let them keep them." He snorted with a wry laugh.

I straightened myself. I was sitting on the bed near him still. My mother used to talk about the plight of kings, how they always had to watch their back for knives, especially from within their own family. She'd claimed she had ancestors who'd helped found York, that we were descended from a great healer, but her family had lost all our possessions and were better for it.

"He's a wily old fox, that Norman duke," I said. "Everything he wins is by a trick. I need the midden."

I stood, went toward the curtain. His words came to me as I pushed through.

"We can be wily foxes too, Synne."

I didn't reply. I had a lot to think about. When I was finished with the midden, I walked around outside. I needed air. Magnus needed me. That felt good. He trusted me, too. But I would have to be careful. He could discard me in a moment.

A group of men were still hanging around near the door of the hall. Another group, some ten men in all, waited up the road outside a small, decrepit alehouse. These men had their backs to us, and axes hanging from their belts. It looked as if they were waiting for a fight.

When I pushed back through the curtain to reach Magnus, I found Elva sitting on his bed, stroking his brow. I hadn't seen her arrive. An urge came over me to step back and leave them, but I resisted. She was a powerful woman, but Magnus had confided many things in me, and he wanted me here. I had every right to be by his side.

The Rise of Synne

Elva turned, looked at me the way a raven looks at its prey, with hooded eyes and a blank expression.

"So, you survived," she said, looking me up and down. "Lord Magnus tells me you bound his wound again." She pointed at his shoulder.

I stepped closer, but not close enough for her to stab me. Her other hand was hidden in her cloak. It could easily be clutching a dagger.

"I did," I said. I looked straight at her. I would not fear her.

"You know it will be your life that will be forfeit if he passes into the underworld," she said. "All Godwin healers carry that burden. I hope for your sake he survives."

Her tone made it seem she might be pleased if he died, to give her an opportunity to take such a revenge on me.

I shook my head. "That is not what happens to healers where I come from. We do not get blamed for helping." I said it firmly. She expected me to be scared, but he would not die in my care.

"I don't expect you have much experience in dealing with the families of kings."

"Magnus will live," I said with force.

Elva stood. "Good. There is a Witan meeting at old King Edward's Hall on Thorney Island tomorrow. Edmund hopes his brother will be there." She sniffed, as if displeased to be a messenger between brothers.

I had to fight to suppress a smile. Edmund must be set on stirring things up between himself and his brother, sending the woman who'd once been his brother's concubine with the message, flaunting his own hold on her.

But I'd heard not one word from Magnus about Elva since I'd arrived. If he cared for her, her name would have come from his lips by now, surely. My sisters, if they were around, would have warned me of the dangers of displeasing someone like Elva, that I should bow and scrape for her. But I would not, I could not.

"We'll see how Lord Magnus is tomorrow," I said, moving around her, taking my place on his other side, my head high.

Magnus spoke in a low voice. "What is the question the Witan has to decide?"

Elva pouted, then replied. "There was much discussion into the night as to who would open the Witan and who would ask the question," she said. "But finally, it was agreed that your brother will do both. His question will not be unexpected."

We waited.

"He'll ask the nobles, bishops, and guild leaders of London if they'll prepare a defence for when Duke William tries to take the city again." She walked around the bed and leaned towards me, her hand out, reaching for

The Rise of Synne

my face. I did not flinch, but held my own hand loose, ready to swing at her. Expectation stilled the air, but all she did was stroke my cheek with a cold fingertip, then pull away.

"Edmund needs his brother by his side tomorrow. Make sure he gets there," she said to me, and then, with a swirl of her dark sable-collared cloak, she was gone.

Magnus looked at me. "You see why I need to be that wily fox you spoke about," he said.

"First the fox needs to eat," I said. "I will see if the pottage is ready." I went beyond the curtain, wondering if she'd really gone. When I saw the door at the front close after her, I finally relaxed.

A fire in the hearth in the main hall had been lit and a piglet was roasting over it. The enticingly juicy smell of it filled the hall. In the hut in the yard at the back, I found pottage bubbling. The smell of leeks, onions, and garlic made my mouth water.

I was told they would bring bowls of it as soon as it was ready. I dipped chunks of rye bread in the pottage and brought the bread to Magnus on a wooden board.

He sat up, groaned, ate some of the bread while swaying from side to side. He did not look like someone who'd be travelling to the other side of the city in the morning.

"How is your head?" I asked. There was one possibility. I knew that traders in London sold strong dwale – a mix of herbs, some from eastern lands, which could make a man smile while his limb was being cut off. A year before, I'd watched a healer give it to a man whose foot was festering so much it needed to be taken off and the end of his leg put to the fire. The man survived. Many who need such a treatment die as it's carried out, screaming in agony.

"Shall I ask the cook to buy strong eastern dwale for you?" I said.

He grimaced. "Something Norman traders sell?" he said. "Do I need it?"

"If you want to go to the Witan tomorrow without a bit between your teeth to bite the pain away, yes."

"Get it, Synne. I have to be there."

The steaming pottage arrived. I asked the old kitchen woman to fetch dwale if it could be found. She'd know the places to find it.

We ate in silence, with me sitting at the end of his bed. The old healer woman who'd been with him the day before came to see him. Magnus shooed her away. I was getting comfortable with being his healer.

I asked Magnus who'd be at the Witan.

"Local lords, reeves, elders, that weakling youth some idiots want to crown king, and all the biggest traders

The Rise of Synne

and any bishops in the city, of course. They'll all be there," he said. "And the northern earls too, I expect. Morcar and Edwin. Unless they've run off already."

I passed him some watered-down wine that had been brought to us.

"You'll come with me," he said. "Only noble ladies usually attend, but you can come as my healer."

I blinked, not sure if this was good news. Perhaps I'd see Morcar again there or the Danes looking for me. I shivered. I could not let that stop me. It would be an honour to go to a Witan with Magnus, the son of a king. Any orphan knew that. I had to go.

As if sensing my thoughts, Magnus said, "Morcar might ask me to sell you to him when I'm finished with you." He smiled.

My mouth opened.

"Who knows what he'll offer. Perhaps a purse of gold."

"Just one purse?" I was pushing my luck, but I could not stop.

"Are you worth more?"

"I'm a free woman. No one can sell me." I leaned close to him to say the words slowly and clearly.

He had a serious expression now.

"Good. I don't sell free women," he said.

This was good to hear. "Will you speak at the Witan to support your brother's question?" I asked.

"Perhaps. The wind is blowing against us. Some of the weak-hearted in this city bleat that they will all be eating rat stew if the Normans ford the river and cut off our supplies from the north and west. We are too divided to stop him, they say." He groaned, shook his head, as if he had lost his determination to fight on.

"Can they be stopped before they cross the river?"

He shook his head. "We cannot march west to stop him in force and defend the city as well."

"So, they will give him the kingdom out of fear of rat pottage?" I leaned back, rocked from side to side as anger came over me.

"You have a fire in you," he said. "What fuels it?" He put his head to the side, stared at me, a half-smile on his face.

I took the pottage bowls, and headed for the kitchen. I could sense his attitude towards me had changed. But as soon as he recovered, he might set me aside, quick. Better to keep my distance, no matter if I did feel like responding to him. I must not be used and discarded like an apple core after the juiciest parts are all swallowed.

When I returned, he was sleeping. I sat on the end of his bed, weighing everything up. I had a duty to my sisters, and I had to take every chance to help them, but I also had

The Rise of Synne

to be careful. I touched his leg through the wool blankets. His eyes opened.

"You asked about the fire in me. I'll tell you what it is. I fight for my sisters," I said. "That's what fuels me. I'm bound by fate to help them."

"Do you know where they are?" His voice had a growl in it, as if he was used to being asked for favours and could guess where this was going.

"They were taken by a slave trader to Dublin."

"Are they as good at healing as you?"

"No, but they're the only family I have left." A lump formed in my throat. I swallowed it. "They will not be slaves for ever. I must help them." I spat the words out with indignation.

Magnus nodded. "How do you know where they are?"

"I saw one with a slave trader who left by boat from here a few days ago."

"The Dublin slave trader?" He sounded sympathetic.

I nodded, waited, wanting him to say more, for him to offer to help me. He didn't. But he knew what I wanted. And I would not plead with him. A voice inside me told me to wait, be patient.

Barking from outside the hall echoed in to us. I remembered the people waiting outside. Magnus looked away, as if he was remembering something too.

"We need good fortune to turn this war and make all things right again," he said.

I needed more than nice words from him, but now was not the time to press my case.

"What would a fox do in our place?" His voice was low. "If you know the answer to that, they'll make a saga for you." He reached for his shoulder, as if to scratch his wound.

I pushed his hand away. "Do not scratch the wound or anywhere near it. If you do, your arm will likely go black, and you'll be dead in a week."

He let his hand drop. His eyes closed and his breathing slowed.

I went to the brazier, stoked it, moving the deeper glowing charcoal with the poker. I put in more charcoal from a pile against the end wall, then went to get honey-dipped bread for him and more thin wine, as he'd finished the skin by his bed. I was thinking about what he'd said. It felt good that he was asking for my advice.

The cook arrived back soon after and gave me a small red earthenware jar about the size and shape of a man's finger.

"This cost as much as a feast," she whispered. "I hope you know how to use it. The trader said this could kill a warhorse if taken all at once. A few drops are all that is needed." She stood close to me. "You're not planning to kill the lord, are you?" Her gaze burrowed into me.

I shook my head. "I'm no murderer. I'm a healer," I said.

"I know his mother will be grateful; if he lives," she said.

"You know her?"

She nodded.

"Where is the rest of his family?"

She shook her head, slowly. "Gone west, to their estates, to prevent them all being taken by the Normans. His mother will not come to London while Normans threaten it."

"Not even for her son?" That sounded strange.

"I hear tell grief for her husband has forced her to bed."

That explained why Magnus had so few supporters here.

She asked me about my sisters and when I told her I'd seen Gytha, she put her hand on mine.

"You'll find a way to help them, the Mother of God will be at your side," she said.

I bit my lip. "I will…" I stopped myself. I did not want to tell her about my hopes, but she must have guessed as she looked me in the eyes and smiled.

"Magnus trusts you, I see it," she whispered after glancing in his direction. "He's right to. Not only are you fair and have a good heart, you're a healer with two sisters and a mother a seer. There is something special about you, Synne. I can feel it. Others do too." She raised her hand as if feeling warmth around me.

I hugged her, took a deep breath, and then she was gone. She may have just been trying to cheer me, but I didn't care. Her words echoed things my mother had said when I was young, and it pleased me.

When some more weak wine came, I half-filled his cup and put three thick drops of the dwale in it and stirred it with my little finger, then tasted a little on my lip to see if it tasted good.

It tasted strange, as if rotten rosemary had been mixed in with it.

"There is dwale in this," I said as I passed him the cup. "I need to see if this much dulls your pain. Tell me if it works."

A while later, he was sleeping. I touched his leg. He did not wake, nor when I pressed it hard. I sat back and stared at him. What the kitchen woman had told me was still going around in my head, but it was far from clear if Magnus would think the same and help me find and release my sisters.

16

"How is your wound?" I asked a while later when he stirred.

"Good." He smiled in a strange way, his teeth showing. That was not like him.

"Will you be able to ride tomorrow?" I asked.

He nodded, his eyelids fluttering.

I smiled, though I was not sure if he'd be well enough.

It was getting dark. One of the kitchen slave girls brought in lit candles. I'd imagined more visitors would come to see him, because of who he was, but none did.

I went out to the guards at the front door and asked if anyone had come for him. A grizzled older guard laughed.

"Some people have come for Lord Magnus, but we were told not to let anyone pass." He bowed. "Except for his healer, that is."

The guards knew who I was. That gave me a slippery kind of happiness I knew could slide away in a moment. Now I had to test if they would do what I asked.

"We travel together upriver in the morning to Thorney Island. Lord Magnus will need guards and horses. Do you know what to do, what to prepare?"

"Of course, healer. Will he need a cart?" The guard's eyes narrowed. He was probably wondering how ill Magnus was.

"I've helped injured men get back to their village by riding beside them," I said. "I expect we can do that in the morning for him."

He nodded. "We should go at first light," he said. "I'll have the horses and men ready."

***

I woke early, my hand gripping the pendants. There was blood on my palms again. I pulled my cloak tight. The brooch Catheryn had given me was missing. My head felt heavy, stuffed up. Wondering what would happen the following day had made it difficult for me to sleep. Some nights since Stefan had died, my hands would shake like frightened slave's. Holding the pendants helped. Magnus being so close but so far away was unsettling, too. I'd ended up tossing and turning on a pile of wolf skins in a corner, my fitful sleep filled with dreams about fire and blood. Catheryn was in them, angry, as she wanted to kill me. A dog barking woke me up then, and the seagulls

The Rise of Synne

crying for food. The first grey light of dawn could be seen through a smoke hole in the roof.

I woke Magnus, gave him two more drops of dwale in a little wine. We got his red tunic on with lots of grunting and his lips tight with pain. The dwale was not working well yet.

We ate some of the leftover honeyed bread and drank wine he insisted we take before the journey. It was stronger than what I was used to, so I only took two mouthfuls. He took more.

The older guard came looking for us as the sun rose. Magnus motioned for me to stand away and not to help him as the man pushed through the curtain.

"Are the horses ready?" Magnus asked, firmness back in his voice.

"They are, my lord," came the reply from the old guard.

"Let's be off to the Witan," said Magnus.

"One thing you must know, my lord. Threats were made against you yesterday, from the men who'd been demanding to see you or your brother."

"Which men?"

"Followers of the Aetheling. They spent half the day yesterday demanding to see you. One of them threatened to kill you if you didn't come out. We ran him off."

"Idle threats," said Magnus. He snorted derisively. "They won't get paid if I'm dead."

"Shall I fetch your axe?" the guard asked.

"Strap it to my horse," said Magnus. "I have my dagger if anyone gets too close." He pointed at me. "My healer rides with me, so I can protect her."

The old man nodded, his face impassive. "Her horse is ready, too."

We went outside. I held my arm around Magnus and my body tight to his, as if we were betrothed and he was holding me, but in reality, I was helping steady him.

Outside, five men on horseback waited as the sun glistened downriver across mud flats in a golden ball as the screeches of the gulls echoed. A light breeze, heavy with salt, cleansed the air. No one was on the road. That felt unusual. In all the towns I'd been in on a river, traders would be wheeling carts at this time or ships would be arriving or leaving.

The old guard helped Magnus onto his horse with a push. We'd made a sling for Magnus's arm, which was under his cloak, but the arm couldn't be used for much. The other guards looked at each other and one rolled his eyes heavenward.

Magnus must have seen it, as he pointed at the man before we moved off.

"Yes, I'm wounded, but I'm not dying. I'll be fighting with you all again soon. I go today to support my brother at the Witan. Stay close if you value your lives."

The man bowed. So did the others. We moved off, two men ahead, the rest behind.

I rode beside Magnus. These horses were big, but they were not the giant warhorses the Normans used that had shocked me at Hastings. My horse kept snickering and nudging close to the mare Magnus rode. He didn't need holding up, thankfully. He settled in his saddle as if he'd been born there and leaned forward more as we went, as if we'd been riding all day already.

I poked his thigh with a finger as a light rain started. "Your hood," I whispered when he looked at me with sleepy eyes. He pulled his hood up as the rain fell, stronger suddenly, washing over us as we passed London Bridge. Some men at arms were still on the bridge and others were lined up in front of a large alehouse. Across the river, I glimpsed red Norman tents in a row. They'd staked their claim.

Magnus hummed for a while, the effects of the dwale most likely. As we came to a small church, I saw a group of men beyond it at the opening of a lane leading towards a warren of wattle and daub houses leaning into each other.

The men appeared to be waiting for something, work perhaps. Then I saw clubs in their hands. And a few had long-pole axes with small axe heads, ideal for bringing men down off horses.

Our guards in front had seen them, too. They stopped their horses. I poked Magnus's knee.

"My lord, trouble," I said.

"We'll race past them," he said, sitting up straighter. "Get on my inside as we pick up the pace."

He shouted a word I didn't know, but the guards seemed to know it, and the ones ahead pulled their axes from their belts and held them at their sides. In a few moments, we were all pushing our horses to a canter.

The men with clubs and axes were spreading out across the road.

I'd not galloped often and never with men with axes and clubs ahead. But my horse moved with its companions. It seemed to know what was happening. Its stride lengthened, urged on with shouts from all around me. I gripped the pommel of my saddle and released the reins a little so my horse could run. The end of the reins slapped against my hands. Mud in the road from Magnus's horse flew into my face as my heart thumped. Everything was a blur of colour and noise, and thigh tightening bouncing as shouts echoed from all around.

I leaned down low towards the horse's neck. He was grunting, his mane flying. Spittle and mud hit me. Getting past these men looked impossible. They were spread out

The Rise of Synne

ahead, blocking the road, axes and clubs up, waiting with smiles on great bearded faces and roars and curses coming from them.

I whispered a prayer.

Our old guardsman was in front.

He had an axe in his hand, holding it one-handed, the axe head pushed out wide to slam into anyone trying to reach him or unseat any of us. Magnus cried out something I did not understand. He had a dagger in his good hand, and his reins, too. Two guards' horses were directly ahead of him, riding wide in their position, allowing Magnus and me to ride behind and between them.

One man in the road tried to stop our flight, a giant with a head like a boar's, holding a two-headed axe up high. He stood straight in the road, turned sideways, crouching a little, getting ready to swing at us.

Magnus had spotted the man. His dagger was in his hand nearest the giant, but as he was holding the reins too, it didn't seem that it would be useful. Then he let go of the reins and held his dagger out.

My heart missed a beat. He was going to fall.

The giant had his axe up.

My vision became a tunnel. And then, from the left, the old guardsman's horse came across in front of Magnus and a moment later the giant's axe curved in the air like a scythe, cutting into the old guardsman so deep across his stomach I thought he'd been sliced in two.

Magnus roared, leaned forward, aimed his dagger at the giant as he closed on him from his other side. The dagger slashed the man's cheek as he artfully leaned away. Magnus passed, glanced back, rode on, grabbed for his reins, leaning forward awkwardly, almost falling off, then reined his horse to a stop. I was right beside him, ready to help, my ears full with the beat of my blood and the sound of our horses' hooves on the hard earth road.

The old guardsman was down in the mud, his horse rearing near him. Men were hacking at him with long-pole axes.

The road here was straight and empty of other people. The wattle and daub houses on each side showed only closed doors and shuttered windows. The butchery was happening only a stone's throw away. One man was pointing at us. We knew what would happen next.

One of our men said, "It was the way he wanted to go, in battle, protecting his lord."

"I'll go back for him," said Magnus. He was rocking in his saddle, clearly disturbed by what he was seeing. "We can charge them."

"We can, if you want us all to die," said the man. "Do not forget you have an injury, my lord."

The Rise of Synne

Magnus groaned in frustration. The butchers had finished their work and were coming towards us, axes swinging. There seemed to be more of them now, strung across the road from side to side. We could not go back. It was too late. We turned, rode on, moving at a fast canter through light spitting rain, looking back occasionally, my anger twisting at my gut.

The next part of the road was also empty. It felt as if everyone in the houses, pressed cheek to jowl on both sides, knew something was afoot. Smoke filtered from a few thatched roofs, but every door was closed. I glanced back again. No one was following us.

Soon after, we crossed a short wooden bridge over a muddy stream with wet cloaks hanging along one side. We were moving at a walk. The rain had stopped.

People were out on the following section of road and a few carts, too. Two young men bowed for Magnus, but most of the people we saw simply got on with what they were doing. One of the passing carts had bodies in it and was being trailed by a group of desolate-looking women and crying waifs.

Magnus rode beside me. "There'll be a lot more carts collecting the dead if the bastard gets into this city," he muttered. His eyes were half shut, but he had a firm grip on his reins.

"How's your wound?" I asked him.

"Better for the dwale," he said. "But I can feel it wearing off."

We crossed another sturdy-looking bridge over a wider, but equally muddy stream. We were close to the river now, which was wide and curving away to the left, visible through occasional gaps between the houses and animal pens or down narrow lanes. The buildings on both sides here were more prosperous, a few even had two floors. And the alehouses had multiple banners outside. A few also had a wooden walkway connecting them and iron torch holders in the walls. I hadn't been in this part of the city before. It felt different to the area near London Bridge. The people looked wealthy, and no one bowed to Magnus as we passed.

He scowled around him. These people were likely the ones who'd prefer peace to fighting and would bow to the Normans quickly, if they had half a chance for peace, so they might live the way they were used to.

A young man raised his fist as we passed an alehouse.

"Look, some still support us here," said Magnus. He looked relieved, but it was a poor straw to hold on to.

As we rode on, more carts appeared, going both ways. One we passed had bread in it. The smell was heartwarming and strong enough that I could almost taste the warm bread. I shifted again in my saddle. My thighs were sore. I wasn't used to the constant rubbing of a hard saddle.

We came at last to a gate in the city wall. Guards looked down on us from a wooden walkway at the top of the high stone wall. Other guards stood by the open gate. They bowed to Magnus. They knew him. People coming and going stood out of our way too.

Beyond the gate was a low bridge over a stream, whose muddy waters almost reached the level of the bridge. The road lay straight beyond. On one side there were pens for animals and on the left, marshy ground leading down to the river.

Up ahead, also to the left, a large wattle and daub hall loomed, close beside the river on a piece of slightly raised ground. Beyond it, to the right, stood a giant stone church with narrow pillars along its walls and two square stone towers at its entrance.

The hall, ahead on the left, had a wooden watchtower at either end. As we came close, I saw it had a palisade wall around it. The palisade looked old. A trickle of horsemen rode in front of us as we neared the gate in the palisade wall. Three monks in brown tunics prayed on the other side of the road, their hands together, their expressions fixed, their eyes darting.

"That was some ride," said Magnus, turning to me.

"We did well to stay alive," I said. It did feel as if we'd had a lucky escape. Perhaps my prayers had been answered.

"This is where we're going?" I asked.

He nodded.

The stink of horses, manure and sweat, filled my nostrils as we waited along the palisade wall for men up ahead in polished chain mail to go through the gate. As we got close, I spotted a line of horses jostling, all tethered along the wall of the giant hall, steam rising from some of them, the ones that had come a longer distance or at speed, most likely.

At the gate, men at arms waited, axes or swords dangling from their belts, helmets on and mail shirts shifting and clinking as they moved. The sight made me think that we'd made a mistake not getting Magnus to put on his chain mail. Was there a possibility of fighting at the Witan? I'd only ever heard of decisions being made at distant Witans.

The man letting people through the gate recognised Magnus and motioned for him to pass. Magnus pointed his thumb at me, while interested eyes watched.

"This is my healer. I need her with me." He pointed at the guard behind us who'd spoken up after the attack. "This liegeman will also come inside. He'll tend to our horses." He turned and addressed the other men further

The Rise of Synne

back. "Say prayers for our souls and for England over at the abbey. We will come for you."

We dismounted inside the gate. A crowd had gathered in front of the double-height doors of the hall. It had elaborate animal carvings and a giant carved cross at the top. People were being let in, slowly into the hall. Most of the men had weapons. I spotted only a few women. Two had their hair piled high with dark yellow veils draped over it. One had a light blue silk tunic on under her cloak. Another wore a wolf skin cloak with a white rabbit fur collar. She had raven black hair, with a white streak on each side. She was attended by a younger man who also had long raven black hair.

I felt itchy and self-conscious. My long red cloak and equally long dark brown tunic marked me out as a servant here.

But even to be here was a miracle. Penniless orphans didn't ever attend Witans as far as I knew. An urge came over me to tell someone how far I'd risen, but I had no one to tell. Where were my sisters?

I pulled my cloak tight at the neck and clamped my mouth shut in case I might make a fool of myself by my accent, or indeed, by anything I said.

Magnus was beside me. He didn't look at me, but many of the people around stared at the two of us. I could feel questions in their eyes, especially about me. I kept my chin up. We reached the top of the line. Magnus handed his dagger over to a man who was placing weapons against the wall.

"Watch where they put my dagger, I may ask you to get it back for me," he whispered to me.

I nodded. A guard put Magnus's dagger beside a row of small axes.

The hall had two side aisles separated by thin stone pillars from a wide central aisle, where benches were lined up facing each other. Candles in a row of elaborate iron holders lit the hall. The end window, in the shape of a rose, had pieces of thick coloured glass in it.

"My lord Magnus," a man's voice called out.

I stayed behind as two men slapped Magnus on the back. I saw him wince, but only for a moment. He turned to me and twisted his mouth. I knew what that meant. I was to give him some dwale.

I walked along the side passage and away from the crowd near the door. There had to be beer or mead here to mix the dwale with. People couldn't make decisions without something to drink. I looked around as I went. The hall was the biggest I'd ever been in. It had a raised floor of dark wooden planks. I passed a tapestry on the wall with a vivid hunting scene embroidered on it with horsemen engaged in a deer hunt. Another tapestry on the far wall showed a swordsman and a red dragon. I'd never seen

The Rise of Synne

anything like these tapestries. The images lingered in my mind, even when I looked away.

Up ahead, there was a long table with women around it. Barrels were stacked behind the table. Horns and drinking goblets and cups were lined up on top of it.

I put my hand on a thick glass goblet. One of the women put her hand on mine as I went to lift it.

"All serving girls work for me," she said. "Who let you in?"

"Lord Magnus," I said. "I'm his healer." I stared back at her, daring her to go further.

She lifted her hand, waved it in the air dismissively. A shout echoed from down the hall. We all looked towards the main door. I went up on my toes to get a better look. An axe had been raised high just inside the door we'd come in through, as if it was about to be used. Many hands reached toward it. A growl, then a flutter of movement passed through the people near the door. Another shout rang out, but from a different voice.

"Hand it over or leave."

The axe came down, slowly. As the crowd around the door shifted, I got a glimpse of the man who'd been holding the axe up. My mouth fell open. It was the Dane I'd been imprisoned with. His yellow hair and the faded runes across his forehead were unmistakable.

I poured mead from a flagon on the table into the goblet I was holding. I pulled the bottle of dwale out and put a drop into the mead.

"What are you doing?" came a voice accusingly. I spun around. It was Elva.

17

"It's to help Magnus," I said.

Elva's eyes narrowed. "You're poisoning him?"

"No," I said sharply. "This is to help him."

She stared at me. "Magnus makes bad choices. I hope he hasn't made another one keeping you around."

"He came here to help his brother, despite his injury. Is that a bad choice?" I pushed my face towards her.

"Edmund doesn't need Magnus's help," she said with a laugh. She flicked hair from her forehead and was gone. I watched her as she swept into the centre section of the hall.

Was she right? With the Norman Duke harrying all before him, and making his way upriver to encircle London, surely Edmund needed all the help he could get for any plan he might have to defend the city? Or was something going on that I didn't know about? Had something happened since Magnus had been injured?

I watched Elva sit on a bench with her back to me. I went back to Magnus while holding the mead goblet and trying to see who Elva was with. Yes, it was Edmund, and beside him were two older men I didn't recognise.

The Dane I knew came striding up the hall. He headed straight for Edmund, who stood to greet him. They gripped both arms, as blood brothers do. The Dane whispered something in Edmund's ear.

"What took you so long?" said Magnus, poking me in the thigh when I got to him. He put his hand out. I gave him the goblet. He downed the contents in one gulp, then winced.

"I hope you put enough in," he said. His gaze went to where I'd been looking.

"My brother has new friends," he said in a cynical tone.

"That one is a Dane who was punished by Earl Morcar when I was at their camp."

Magnus nudged me again. "You make a good spy," he said.

"I do not."

"You will," he said. "Now follow me."

We went into the centre aisle of the hall. Men had taken up places on each side here, sitting on the benches. Three chairs with high carved backs stood facing down toward the benches. These chairs were empty. Edmund was sitting on a bench near the top of the hall with people all around him. There was a space on the bench behind him, meant for Magnus. In the aisle behind, stools were lined up. Elva was sitting on one of them. Other women and men were sitting on the others. Elva had a hand on the stool beside her. She waved at me. She was keeping a stool for me. I smiled, sat on the stool, but shifted it a little away from her. She looked up at Magnus, a friendly smile on her face.

"I hope she satisfies you," she said with a smirk.

"More than you ever did, Elva," said Magnus. "Healer." He put his leather boot near mine. "I will signal when I need you." He put his hand on Elva's shoulder. She smiled up at him, a vision of insincerity. "My healer is under my protection, is that understood?"

Elva nodded, still smiling, as if no bad thought had ever entered her mind.

As soon as Magnus was gone, she turned to me. "You've bewitched him, yes?" She laughed, waited for me to answer.

I let out a scoff, then looked away and watched the men in the room. Some had fine cloaks with embroidery that made them look like women, others had wolf skin cloaks or thick wool London cloaks, the type they said could repel rain.

I'd no idea who these men were, but they oozed status and power. On the far side of the hall, with a sharp surge of apprehension, I spied Edwin and Morcar. Elva must have spotted them too, as she leaned close to me and said, "Does the Earl Morcar want you, too? Did you bewitch him as well?"

I shook my head. The idea was ridiculous.

Three men were walking up the centre of the hall. The one in the middle had the top of his head shaved. He wore a heavy black cloak fringed with white fur.

"Bishop Stigand," whispered Elva. "He's with us, I think." She laughed.

The bishop sat, slammed the end of his staff into the wood beneath him, called for silence, waited, then shouted for the doors to be locked, and finally, as the chatter in the room slowly died, he recited a long prayer in Latin, I remembered part of it from a mass, though it seemed different, even longer. Then he asked us to pray in our hearts. A lot of mumbling followed. Finally, he waved for Edmund to speak.

The shouting started soon after. From what I could make out, there was a strong feeling in the hall that London should surrender.

Edmund and his supporters shouted back at all this, calling anyone who spoke in this way a coward. That led to a general uproar. One man crossed the aisle, his fists up. He was held back by two of the men sitting near Edmund, who went to him, then threw the man back to the other side.

The Rise of Synne

Edmund stood.

The bishop called for silence, thumping his staff on the wooden floor repeatedly. As the hubbub died away, he called on Edmund to speak. Edmund spoke slowly and deliberately, describing what would happen if William, a Norman duke, were to become King of England. His tone grew angrier with each word.

"He will seize your land, rape your daughters, and take your wives to do as he wishes," he said. "He wants everything."

"Not if we submit," came a shout from the other side. "It is your family that will bring all that on us by defying him."

The hall went quiet for a moment as breaths were sucked in. Then the shouts broke out again from both sides, but louder. Almost every man who'd been sitting on the benches was up, screaming or shaking his fist.

"I heard you are Catheryn's blood sister. What side do you take in all this?" asked Elva, wide-eyed, clearly enjoying putting me on the spot.

"I am on England's side," I said. She was far too well-informed. I had to assume everything I'd spoken with Catheryn had reached Elva's ears.

"Catheryn will surely expect her blood sister to be on her side," said Elva. She gave me a conceited smile, the type some people use who enjoy knowing more than you know about something important.

"What do you want from me?" I replied.

She gasped, then leaned closer and whispered, "I want you to be proper careful, Synne. Catheryn has some fierce reputation." Her eyes were wide, watching me for signs of fear most likely.

A memory of a strange dream came to me. Someone had been coming for me with a knife in their hand. Who was it? I couldn't remember. What use are visions of the future if you can't remember them?

"She doesn't scare me."

"She should," Elva whispered.

"I don't scare easy." I'd learned how to protect myself as we'd travelled from village to village. Outlaws would try to take everything from you if you couldn't run faster than them or fight the ones you thought you had a chance against. Catheryn, I'd definitely have a chance against.

Elva shook her head as if I was crazy, stood, walked towards the end of the hall, and disappeared into the crowd. A nudge against my boot made me look up. Magnus was beside me.

"We've wasted our time coming here," he said. "Most of the lords have made up their minds already." He grunted in frustration. "We don't have the heavy purses we need to pay them off anymore."

The Rise of Synne

"Your brother spoke well," I said.

He shook his head. "My father would have done it better. He'd have got their support when he spoke." There was a distant look on his face. "He'd have had the whole hall with him. Men believed in him."

He sat, put a hand on my thigh. I stiffened. I'd half-expected something like this at some point, but to do it here was a surprise. I was paralysed by conflicting emotions. His touch made my body feel alive, but he could not assume that he could just have me and discard me.

I opened my mouth to rebuke him, but Elva returned, and she had Catheryn with her. My jaw clenched. I had to stop myself standing up to confront her. What did this mean? Would she try to take me? I'd fight her if she did. The two of them stopped right in front of us. Magnus's hand released my thigh.

"Your brother's offer has been made, Lord Magnus," said Elva. "It was not accepted. You and your brother's estates in the south are what Morcar and Edwin want. For their support, you must give them up." She glanced at me. So, this was what was going on. Bargaining.

Catheryn nodded, then gave me a withering look, her eyebrows raised, which said, *I'm not finished with you.*

I stared back at her. She would not dare do anything to me here. If she did, she would regret it.

Magnus laughed, then shook his head, as if throwing off some cloud that had come down on him. "Might Earl Morcar keep his word this time?" he said. His words had a bitter edge. "What I remember was that Morcar made promises to my father he did not keep. We need more than promises this time."

I was witnessing their bargaining.

Catheryn smiled. "We agree, and we suggest an exchange of hostages." She looked at me. "Starting with your healer, who will go today, now to the Earl Morcar," she said. "I am to stay with you."

I gasped, coughed. All eyes turned to me. I glanced across the hall, saw Morcar staring at us, his eyes wide. The shouting in the hall was continuing. It grew louder by the moment, the voices drowning out my thoughts as if we were in battle.

I shook my head. "I'd rather be dead," I said.

Catheryn laughed as if that was their plan.

Magnus put his hand up. "Before we talk hostages, we heard the earls have been invited to the Norman Duke's council. Is it true?"

"It is, but they've not accepted," said Catheryn, still staring at me.

"Propose other hostages," said Magnus. "I have a different plan for my healer."

Elva let out a derisive snort. "What plan?" she said.

The Rise of Synne

"We have received word from the Normans; she will act as our messenger."

"What?" Catheryn's expression changed. She spat out the next words as if they hurt. "You'd trust this ignorant scheming healer as a messenger?" She swung her boot in the direction of my ankle.

I shifted my leg fast out of her reach. I was taking in what he'd said. Was this why I was here? I turned to Magnus.

He looked into my eyes, smiled in a strange, unreal way. "All my previous personal messengers were killed at Hastings. A replacement died at the battle on the bridge. My brother has sent all our other messengers out to raise men from every village within seven days' ride." His voice rose as he spoke, as if he was annoyed at having to explain himself. His good hand grasped the air in front of him, making a fist.

"Do not argue with me."

I was staring at him.

He put his hand out to me and said, "Duke William promises safe passage to our messengers."

Was this what he wanted me for? To be his messenger?

Elva looked displeased. She was standing beside Catheryn. "Someone must go with her." She spat out the words.

Magnus nodded. "My men will go with her."

Elva looked from Magnus to me, her head shaking. "But, but she…" she said, grasping for words. Catheryn's face was partly red.

I was pleased at their discomfort. Catheryn had been thwarted. I had become a protected messenger.

Magnus motioned with his head for me to follow him, then strode off.

I smiled at Elva and Catheryn. Catheryn put her out to grab at me. I stood back out of her reach.

"He will not be yours, Synne," she hissed. She had a smug look on her face. "Those Danes looking for you will find you soon. You cannot escape your fate."

I laughed. "Go back and tell the earl you failed him… again."

Her face filled with spite. I thought she might lunge at me.

"You think because those brothers fight over you that you'll get one of them?" It was Catheryn's turn to laugh.

I blinked. Did she mean the Godwin brothers had been fighting over me? No, Magnus would have told me. She was up to one of her tricks.

"Did you have trouble on the way here?" asked Elva. Her head was to one side.

They both glared at me as I stepped back. I walked away fast, turning back to watch them only once. They

The Rise of Synne

knew something about the attack on us on the road. Should I tell Magnus that I might have been the target?

Seeing Catheryn, a memory had come to me, from a dream with her in it, her face like how she looked now, all red and angry, but holding a knife.

Magnus was waiting at the main door. We collected his dagger and headed out of the hall and toward the abbey.

I reached for his arm as we pushed through the crowds.

"Elva knew about the attack on us on the way here," I said. I had to drive a wedge between him and Elva. She was as trustworthy as a snake.

"I told my brother what had happened. He must have told her," he replied.

I was going to ask him had he and his brother been fighting about me, but the words stilled on my tongue. If it was true, he was unlikely to admit. If it was a lie, he would laugh. Better to stay quiet.

A dense crowd had gathered between the hall and the abbey. Pennants fluttered above it all and traders pushed through with trays or baskets looking to sell their wares. Beggars and the crippled held their hands out and pleaded with everyone. Magnus pulled coins from a purse on his belt and distributed some as we went.

When we'd extracted ourselves from the throng, we walked fast over the muddy grass to the abbey. I was thinking about what Catheryn had said about the Danes looking for me. Would she help them find me? The abbey was not as busy outside as the hall we'd left behind, but there was a trickle of men and women coming and going to it.

We walked around the people in line at the main door. "We're not here for alms," said Magnus to two burly monks who were questioning people going in. "We're here to pray."

They let us pass. Inside it was gloomy, except for rows of candles on iron candlesticks at the front of the church and more spread out in the side aisles. We found Magnus's men sitting on a bench against the wall in the far aisle.

"Have you prayed enough?" asked Magnus as we approached his men.

One of them gave him a thumbs up.

"Two of you take the healer to the nearest ferry upriver, help her cross, and escort her on the other side. She'll be taking a message for me. It's vital that she get through to the Norman camp without being abducted or stopped." He looked from face to face. He didn't look at me. He assumed my going along with all this was a given.

That annoyed me. Perhaps that was what they'd been arguing about, how to use me.

The men looked at each other and then at me.

The Rise of Synne

I stiffened my face to give nothing away. I'd imagined that it would be a day at least before we set out, and that Magnus would want to tell me in detail what I was expected to do. To start quickly felt like being thrown in a river. My thoughts raced. I was going to the Norman camp, to the heart of the enemies' forces.

The guard who'd given the thumbs up asked, "Will we stay across the river for long, my lord?"

"Have no fear," said Magnus. "Your task is simply to escort a messenger. I expect you all to return in one piece, and with my healer in one piece, too."

The men's faces spoke for what I was feeling. Confused. Two of them had twisted smiles.

"The healer is your messenger?" said one man, wide-eyed disbelief on his face.

Magnus gave him a cold look.

The man bowed. The other guards did, too.

"Wait here," he said to them. "I need to speak with my healer."

He motioned for me to follow him, then went up the aisle to a quiet place beneath a tapestry of the Virgin Mary ascending to heaven.

He stopped, put a hand on my shoulder, looked around, checking if anyone was near enough to hear us.

His gloved hand was heavy. I straightened. He would despise weakness above all things.

"Your task is simple," he said. "I gave it to you, Synne, no one else, because I know you can do it. You carried out your last task with skill that surprised us all." That thought warmed me, but it also made clear why I was with him today. He wanted to use me.

He went on. "When you reach the Normans, ask for Odo, the duke's brother. Show him this to prove you came from me and to get his protection." He pulled a gold ring from his finger. It had small red stones embedded around it.

"This will also ensure you are protected from all Normans. Show it to any who need convincing. Tell them it's one of Odo's rings." He leaned close. I could smell wine on his breath. "Know that I trust you, Synne. That is why you've been chosen for this. We must know what their offer is if we submit." He winced, put his good hand out to lean against the wall.

"You need dwale?" I asked.

"No, no more of it. I cannot think straight with it."

I put my hand out, touched his arm. I was glad he'd responded that way. The dwale was almost finished. "You said, if we submit. Does this mean the end of resistance to the Normans?"

"No, it's not like that," he said. "We are testing the water, fishing." His eyes widened and he smiled as if trying to convince me.

The Rise of Synne

There was something wrong about all this. Something I was not being told.

"I've never done such a thing or anything like it," I said sharply. I stared at him.

"That does not matter," he said with a shrug. "You are not going to negotiate." He was angry. "We just want to know their terms. That is all. You will be safe." Each word at the end was separate.

"So, I must trust the Normans. That's my fate. What a good plan."

He laughed, shook his head. "Trust me, Synne." He leaned closer. "I have no one else to ask. You'll be treated well if you tell them you're a messenger. We treat theirs well. The duke will want an agreement. He cannot want to lay siege to London. Winter is closing in. Many of his men will want to go back to their homes." He smiled. "This is his chance to make concessions."

He'd nearly convinced me.

"You will be rewarded too, Synne." He said that part slowly. "We'll help you find your sisters." He raised his chin, smiled, convinced his words would win.

He leaned forward. "And you're protected. You're one of three sisters, a daughter of a seer." He leaned closer, his face animated. "My brother tells me there's a prophecy about a seer who will save our family. It could be you." He threw his hands in the air.

I stared at him. We stood still, listening to echoing voices and sighing from the wind outside. Was I that prophecy coming true? Or was he using it to get me to do what he wanted? I was tempted to go along. A part of me was drawn to him like an orphan to a feast.

And what choice did I have? Any prospect of the Godwins winning further battles against the Normans was poor now. London was divided. They'd lost so many men and Magnus was injured. His promise to help me was worth it. But I'd have to survive to fulfil it.

I nodded. "I'll do it," I said.

He gave me the briefest of smiles, then went back to his men. I was wondering what the Normans would make of me and where the Danes looking for me were.

The two men who were to guard me looked at me when I went up to them, as if they wondered what they'd done to deserve this mission.

18

It took four days for us to cross the river and catch up with the Norman army. Three times I thought we were all going to die, twice when Normans were left behind at village crossroads and once at a burning house where they stopped us and placed their weapons at our throats. But each time I showed them the ring Magnus had given me and told them I was a messenger. And each time they let us through with a lot of guttural talk in their language that I did not understand. Thankfully, they did understand the word messenger.

We passed through many empty villages and found places to sleep, though we ate little those days, mostly the horse bread my guards carried with them and shared with me. The Normans hadn't bothered to burn everything in their path, but there were enough smoking village ruins to know they weren't too far ahead as we came close to their army.

I prayed each night and every morning to Christ first, of course, then to the Queen of Heaven, then to all the other gods who would listen. I prayed for my sisters, that I would be able to help them and also for my dead brother, and my mother in heaven.

I used prayer those days to keep my mind still, reciting the ones my mother had taught us, as if they might save me. Perhaps they helped, but I still shivered with fear when I saw Normans up close. They were all wild-eyed and full to the brim with blood lust. That look men have after they've slaughtered and know they can do it again whenever they want. They seemed gleeful at the bloody destruction they'd brought to our land.

Some of these Normans looked at me and nudged their comrades as if they thought I was a gift for Odo when I mentioned his name. After it happened twice, I started thinking it might be true. I tried to put such thoughts aside. I would not believe them until I had proof.

My dreams darkened even further. They filled with shadows, pursuits, blood. I woke every morning clutching my amulets and had to push them back inside my tunic in case someone saw them. There would be questions if someone did; what did they stand for, why had I clutched them so tight my palms bled? Questions I did not want to think about.

Smoke appeared on the horizon the next day. We were close to the Norman army.

The Rise of Synne

Near midday, we came upon a cavalry rear guard moving slowly, and then wagons pulled by oxen and finally we reached the Norman army camp on an open heath, with rows of tents being raised and a palisade of stakes going up around it.

Our escort took us to a large faded-yellow tent near the centre of the camp. It had a golden cross on top of it. Guards outside spoke swiftly in their sing-song tongue with the ones with us, then motioned us to dismount, and took our daggers, the only weapons my guards and I had, as the men with me had left their axes behind in London.

We waited outside the tent, under the glare of Normans, as it began to rain. I pulled the hood of my cloak over my head. The men with me did the same, as did the Normans. Finally, a shout came from the tent, and I was ushered inside, my heart beating in my ears. This was all happening too easily. Was the worst to come? Each day on the way here, I'd imagined the Normans torturing me. I'd given myself a pain in the head wondering would that happen. I'd also begun berating myself for agreeing to do this. I should have demanded more. I'd not be able to help my sisters if I was dead. The time for truth had arrived, and I was glad.

Torture would either happen or not. Better to know your fate, than to have worries about it stabbing away in your head every moment, awake or dreaming.

A nose-clenching odour of incense hit me as I stepped inside the tent. A low wooden table with a thin yellow cloth on it stood at the far end with stools around it. The ground was mostly covered in rushes. The patter of raindrops hitting the leather tent filled my ears with an insistent drumming as my eyes got used to the gloom. A man was kneeling at the back of the tent, behind the table, facing the back wall.

His head was shaven at the back in the Norman style, and he was wearing a black tunic, the same as the tunics priests and bishops wore on our side. He had a gold chain around his neck. It was a thicker chain than I'd ever seen a man wearing. Who knew what such a chain could buy if it was sold?

I coughed lightly to indicate my presence. The drumming of the rain continued. The man did not respond. Two braziers glowed heat into the tent, but it was still cold where I waited near the tent flap. I heard a mumbled prayer, so I stood quietly, wondering what he would do with me, imagining the worst, until a pleasant voice in a foreign accent said, "You are both a healer and a messenger, yes?"

Even though I was expecting to be spoken to, I jumped in my skin as soon as he spoke. I felt a little ill too as if I'd already been told I was going to be tortured.

The Rise of Synne

"Yes, my lord," I said. I'd given my name as Synne the healer to the guard outside.

"Good, I am Bishop Odo, brother of Duke William, soon to be rightfully crowned King William, King of all England," he said. "Have you eaten today, healer?" He was tall and had one of those faces that gave nothing away. I did not like him claiming the English throne for his brother, but I knew Normans were like that, proud and full of themselves. I was determined not to show any weakness, no matter what I was feeling inside.

"A little, my lord." Very little, if the truth was told. I kept my head up.

He clapped his hands. From the gloom at the back of the tent, a servant came forward. Odo spoke to him in their language, then stood and walked towards me.

"Show me the ring," he said. He had a dagger with a jewelled handle on his belt. His hand lingered near it, as if he expected me to be an assassin ready to pounce.

I held out the ring.

He peered at it. "I did not think I would see this again," he said softly. "Come, healer, sit." He turned his back to me and walked slowly to the table. It felt as if he was opening himself up to being attacked. Was he really expecting me to try to stab him? I was glad that was not my mission. He was so obviously testing me. When he sat on a stool at the table, a man moved out of the shadows beyond. He had a bow in his hand, and an arrow nocked. If I'd been an assassin, he would have put that arrow through my heart before I'd reached Odo's back.

Bishop Odo said something to the man, which I did not understand, and the man left us. I sat on a stool on the other side of the table. Odo bent his head, mumbled a prayer. As he finished, two women arrived with rye bread and steaming stew in red bowls.

"Eat," said Bishop Odo. "We do not want to be accused of not showing hospitality to a messenger from a leading family of England." He smiled. It was the smile of a boar about to gobble its prey.

"Thank you," I said. I was grateful for the food, but wary. I ate a few spoonfuls. The stew was good. Then I remembered something. "Can my guards be fed?" I asked, my wooden spoon poised over the bowl.

"What if I plan to cut their throats, not stuff them with our food?"

I put my spoon down and looked at him, my face stiff. I would not give him the pleasure of showing any concern. I'd met men who promised violence before. Some of them would get to it quickly, as if to prove their words. Others liked to drag it out. Was that where we were going?

Laughter echoed. Bishop Odo rocked back and forth, his hands at his mouth, fingers wide as if he was demented. "What have you heard about us?" he asked, his voice filled with mirth, as if he enjoyed playing with people. "We do not abuse people, especially not messengers, without some good reason. I already gave orders for your men to be fed and placed in a tent out of the rain." He threw his hands wide.

"Good," I said. I picked up my spoon and ate some more.

The serving women reappeared. A pale-green goblet of wine was placed in front of me and bread of a thin yellow type I'd not seen before. I sipped a little of the wine and tasted the sickly sweet bread. The wine was strong and bitter.

"You are in mourning?" he asked.

My hair was still streaked with the pale strands of sorrow. I'd tied it in strings again too.

I nodded.

He did not ask me why. He ate quickly and drank eagerly.

"You're wondering why I eat alone?" he asked, looking across at me.

"No."

"I must pray tonight for our complete victory. That is why I do not sit in the main tent with my brothers and our men. I need peace when I eat and when I pray."

"Am I disturbing you?"

"No, you have come at a good time. My prayers are perhaps answered with you. I have prayed each night, you see, since we were beaten back at London Bridge that the city submits soon, so that lives can be spared."

He paused, smiled at me.

I finished the bread I'd been given and sipped a little more wine. I did not trust a word he said. He sounded like the type of man who'd say anything to achieve what he wanted.

"You pray a lot on campaign?" I asked. I tried not to sound impertinent, but I could not resist asking. It was strange to me that a bishop who followed the words of Christ was part of an invading army, killing wherever they went.

His voice was soft when he answered, as if he was talking to a child. "The pope, may he be praised by all in Christendom, commanded me to pray every day from the start of our campaign until our final victory is declared. I follow the pope's orders strictly. You know he prays for our victory too?"

He was goading me. I cleared my throat, took another sip of the wine. "Will I meet the duke?" I asked, though I was not looking forward to meeting him.

"You can tell me your message. I am the duke's closest adviser. All messengers who do not speak our tongue must give their messages to me."

The Rise of Synne

He stared at me. As the duke did not speak our tongue, I had little choice but to tell him. "I've been tasked to find out what you'd offer if the Godwins submit."

The bishop laughed. This time, it was not forced. He shook his head. His hands went out to both sides, high up, as if I'd handed him victory laurels. "Healer, you're not supposed to come to the matter at hand so quick." He reached a hand towards me. "Perhaps there is some other reason they sent you?" he asked. He put his head to the side. "Is there?"

"Not that I know." I held his gaze. He was quick-witted, asking a question I too held in my head.

"Perhaps you are here, Synne, because your masters sent all their ill-fated messengers out already, to round up men for their traitorous cause." He picked up a bone-handled knife and pointed it at me.

"You will tell your masters we found all their messengers, the ones they sent out despite our call for followers of the Godwins, the throne stealers, to lay down their arms." He raised his hands high again, this time his fingers clenched into claws. "That act alone, raising an army against a rightful king, is treason enough to have them all hung by their necks from trees with their tongues cut off and in a pile."

The temperature in the room had grown warmer. I wanted to wipe some sweat from my brow, but I resisted.

"Do you understand all this, messenger?"

"I do."

He pointed at me. "You are close to one of Harold's sons, yes? Very close, perhaps." With his other hand, he patted his chest at his heart, a smile on his face.

"Not that close."

"How is Lord Magnus these days?" he said, ignoring my denial.

"Well." I could not say anything about Magnus's weakness.

"He has fully recovered from his wounds?" Odo's eyebrows went up.

I stared at him. He had good spies.

"He is good," I said.

Odo flicked his knife up into the air. It twisted and twirled and fell on its point with a heavy thud. It was a trick he must have long practised.

"And all the Godwin boys want is to know our terms for their family to surrender?"

I nodded.

"Does that include the surrender of London and of all the Godwin lands and estates in England?"

"I have been tasked only to report your offer."

He pulled his knife from the table and examined the point.

The Rise of Synne

"Wait here," he said, after a moment of us listening to the rain patter on the tent walls. The smoke from the candles seemed sickly sweet to me now.

"I will speak with my brother about this," he said as he stood. "Finish your food and take more wine, but do not leave this tent. It is unfortunate that my men are a lot rougher than me with people who disobey my orders."

As if he'd arranged it for that exact moment, a distant scream came raggedly through the night air to us. It was far off, muffled, and it sounded as if someone was being tortured.

He didn't blink. He just headed for the flap at the front of the tent and exited without another word.

I sipped at my wine. Anything could happen now. My skin crawled along my arms and my back. But I sat still, as if I'd been nailed to the stool, listening for any sound that might indicate my fate, jumping inside at creaks and shouts. I breathed deep to slow my mind. One thing was sure, the Godwins were in a bad position. It was still possible that the Normans could be defeated, but it would require a fortunate turn of events. And as for Magnus? What would be his fate?

Could I help him survive? Would that be my fate? Was that how the prophecy would play out? My healing saving a king's son? Did that mean we'd be together, that we'd survive?

"Please, let my mother's powers be in me," I whispered to myself, my head leaning forward.

A little later, the servant women came in. I pushed my bowl away and refused more wine. She didn't stay long.

I went to the brazier and stood by it, warming my hands. Beyond, water was seeping into the tent along the bottom of the leather wall, making dark puddles. An occasional shout echoed from outside. I listened to them and to the rain and the beat of my heart. Some of the shouts sounded like men being tortured. Was that voice familiar? I listened carefully. Was that one of my guards being tortured?

I held my fist to my chest and paced along the tent wall slowly. I found a flap at the back, but when I opened it a little, I glimpsed the back of a mail shirt. A Norman guard was standing right beside the tent. Part of the roof went out beyond the wall, providing shelter to anyone close by. If I wanted to get past this guard, I'd have to slit his throat in a moment. As I let the flap go, a voice called out behind me.

"We meet again, healer, and in a similar fashion. Our fates are intertwined."

I spun around. It was the Dane who'd had his finger cut off. His cloak was dripping wet, and his hair slicked down to his face.

The Rise of Synne

I snorted with surprise, motioned him to come to the brazier.

"How is your hand, Dane?"

He held it out. He had a mailed glove on with one finger clearly short.

"I fight with two hands again," he said triumphantly.

"Why are you here?" I asked. He looked prosperous. A gold Thor's hammer hung from his neck and a new red cloak rested on his shoulders. I wondered if he knew that other Danes were looking for me. Best not to ask. If he did not know, I would be telling him. If he did know, what could I do?

"You first, healer. Why are you here?"

He'd been sent to find out things from me. "I'm here as a messenger for Lords Magnus and Edmund. You?"

"The same, but for the earls Morcar and Edwin."

"Even after they took your finger off?"

"You do not know the crime I committed." He laughed, shook his head. "I'm lucky that is all they took. In my country, I might have had my balls fed to me." He pointed down at himself. "I am very happy they are still there." He grinned at me as if he wanted me to be happy for that, too.

"You met with the duke?"

He nodded. "Will you meet him?" he asked.

"I don't know. I met his brother."

"The bishop?"

I nodded.

"He is a great man. Duke William was lucky he had Odo at his side at Hastings."

I moved my hands closer to the brazier, widened them to the heat. I thought about Stefan and all the other men who'd died because of the duke and his ambition.

"How many died there do you think?" I asked.

"They are still counting."

"Are you going back to London?" I asked.

"Soon; first I have my task to do."

"To find out things from me?"

He nodded. "You must tell me how injured Lord Magnus really is. Will he fight again this season do you think?"

"I'm no warrior," I said. "I cannot judge these things."

"What about his wounds? How bad are they?"

"A nick to his shoulder, that is all." I looked him in the eye. I was not going to betray Magnus.

"They've taken one of your guards and are questioning him," he said with a devious smile.

I held myself steady as an urge to press him about this came to me.

"Why?" I said it forcefully. I was pushing my luck, but I had to.

"The man was insolent."

The Rise of Synne

I looked at the Dane. He glared back.

"So, this is what we must expect it will be like under the Normans," I said. "Every one of us must lose an eye or a hand or our tongue or our lands for speaking out of place."

He nodded. "Yes, and it is a good thing," he said eagerly. "The people of this land need to learn who their rightful king is, and to be thankful for him, always."

I opened my mouth, ready to dispute his claim as to who was the rightful king, but a distant scream sent me up on my toes. Was that my guard? Were they doing this now so I could hear it all?

"What are they doing?" I said softly, but angrily.

"Whatever is necessary to break the man." He looked pleased.

"Is this the right way to treat messengers?"

"You are the messenger. He is your insolent guard."

"My guards must be treated as I am." I made my hands into fists.

"And I must know. How bad is Magnus's injury?" He spoke as if he was dealing with a child.

I waited before responding. I was wondering if there was any way I could get at his dagger and cut his throat and mine before their torture started.

"It is what I said, a nick."

"They know how bad Magnus is injured, healer, and that his brother thought he'd die, and told people that, so you are not telling Odo anything they do not know already. This is a test."

I went silent. There was a game going on here that I knew little about playing.

"Tell the truth, healer, and they will trust you. Think on it." He took his cloak from where he'd dropped it on a stool nearby and walked out. I was left with my fears, my defiance, and the rising patter of the rain.

I paced up and down. I was well trapped. I'd felt loyal to the Godwins, initially because they might have raised Stefan and I up, helped us to rescue our sisters, but now that I knew Magnus, I had my own reasons to be loyal to him and to fear for his fate. These included my dreams about us being together for more than a night or two, and for my mother's prophecy to come true.

"Come here," said a soft voice. I turned. Bishop Odo was back. Had he been waiting in the shadows for the Dane to leave?

"I've spoken with my brother. This is the message you will bring back with you, healer. On their surrender, the Godwins will be allowed to live, but they must all go into exile and not return to England, not once, ever, on pain of death." He waved his hand dismissively.

"That's it? Exile?"

The Rise of Synne

"They can take anything with them that they can personally carry." He pointed at the tent flap. "Go now. Find the tent near here with three guards outside. Your men are being held there. You will all leave at dawn. Guards will be sent with you back to the ferry you crossed the river on, and with God's will, you will make the sons of Harold understand that their cause is doomed, and that all they do by resisting us, is cause more unnecessary deaths."

Anger rose fast inside me. I had to ask him. "What about the guards who came with me? Are you done torturing them?"

"Neither of your guards were tortured. There was no need. We know everything we need to know." He gestured dismissively and went to the table he'd been praying at when I first saw him. He knelt behind it and bowed his head.

I took my chance and headed for the tent flap, and then into the pelting rain, looking for the tent he'd spoken about. I found it. He was right. My guards were there, sleeping on rushes. A candle in a strange slim holder lit the tent with a pale-yellow glow. There was a space beside them. They looked up as I lay down.

"Are we finished here?" one guard asked. "It's an abomination to be with these puffed-up pigs." His voice lowered as he said those words, but I know why he spoke that way. My guards looked scared.

"We go at first light," I said.

They both grunted in reply, then turned their backs to me. I felt safe with them. They had fumbling hands for each other at night, not for me. It was probably why they'd been picked to protect me. But still, it took me a long time to get to sleep that night. Everything that had happened with Odo and the Dane kept repeating in my mind. The significance of it all. Impossible though it would have seemed only a few months ago, I'd met the bastard duke's brother. I'd have laughed if someone had told me that would happen. And he'd given me a message. But what would the Godwins' reply be?

I expected them to dismiss the offer out of hand, and they might be right to. The Normans could still be beaten. If they were defeated at London Bridge, they could be defeated at its other gates. Magnus and Edmund had to stiffen the resolve of the city's leaders. They didn't need the earls.

What about Magnus and me? I'd wondered about him sending me on this mission, but he'd been right that I'd be safe as a messenger. And I was a survivor. My mother had often talked about surviving attacks after my father had married her. She'd claimed it was her power to sense the future, and to change it, which had helped her. She'd spoken a lot the summer before her murder about my time coming, how I'd see things I could never imagine and

The Rise of Synne

would learn how to influence fate too, to turn it to a new path. I hadn't believed her. But what had happened this day had made the first part of her prediction true. I was on the path to making her prophecy come true.

19

I woke with pains all over and a guard shouting something I did not understand into the tent, but I knew what he meant – we were leaving. The sun was coming up and the snorting of horses filled the air.

I stood, brushed myself down, glared at my guards, and we all went outside. Our daggers were given back to us. Three Norman guards were already saddled and ready to go with us. I looked around for Odo. I didn't see him, but a little bit away, observing us, was a tall man with yellow hair. His arms were folded over his chest and from his tunic, I knew he was one of their leaders.

As we mounted, our Norman guards rose in their saddles and bowed towards the man. That was when I knew. He was Duke William. I'd seen him. And he'd seen me. A shiver ran through me, as if I'd been touched by ten thousand ghosts; the talked-about alehouse count of the men whose deaths he'd caused, even before he came to England.

I looked back at him as we moved off. He was still watching us. It was dry that morning, but a low fog had risen from the damp ground, giving him a shroud-like background.

One of his men motioned for us to move faster. We did. It felt freeing to be getting away from that place. Their army was a stain on our land, a giant dragon devouring everything in its path. As we came out from their camp, a group of cattle were approaching, herded by Normans, no doubt the spoils of some overnight raid on farms in their path. They looked a peaceful group, but I knew each stolen cow belonged to a poor farmer and that each family most likely hated the Normans for the suffering they were inflicting.

On the road back to London, my guards told me about the questioning they'd been subjected to, and the goading insults about the Godwins they had to listen to.

The sullen Norman guards who came with us turned back at the same ferry stop we'd used to cross the river. We had to wait half a morning before the ferry reappeared. This time it was a smaller flat-bottom boat with high wicker sides capable of taking only one horse across at a time. The rowers on each side were different too, but the man at the steerboard was the same.

"Is there any chance the bastard will be sent back into the sea?" he asked with a grin, after our final horse came over.

I raised a fist. "Every chance," I said. "England is not done."

***

We rode fast to London. It was almost nightfall when we arrived. We were lucky to get in too, the gates were about to close. We passed through the city as fast as we could. Parts of it looked deserted, other parts had drunken men crowding around alehouses in numbers I'd not seen before. The city was partly hunkered down, holding its breath, and part abandoning all reason.

There was still a guard on London Bridge and still Norman tents on the other side with glowing fires near them, but the number of men on our side of the bridge had gone down to maybe a few dozen. A jumble of wooden staves and brushwood had been set up in the middle of the bridge, so the Normans knew we could set it alight at any moment if they dared to cross.

Magnus was eating with a few men in the wolf skull hall when we got there. No men waited outside clamouring to see him, and inside, the hall was mostly empty with candles burning only on the table Magnus and his men

The Rise of Synne

were eating at. He looked improved, and my heart gladdened.

But where had all the other men gone? As I walked up the hall, the eyes of the men at Magnus's table swivelled to me. One of the men at the table was Ulf. He opened his mouth and stood when he saw me. He let out a welcome shout, raised a fist.

"The healer has returned. I told you she would."

"Did you leave any food for us?" I replied. I was ravishing hungry and so were my guards.

Magnus pointed at a serving girl leaning against the side wall.

"More bowls, quick," he called out.

I ate as if I hadn't eaten for days, which was almost true. I noticed the stew was thinner and there were more onions and leeks in it than meat now. But I didn't care. All food tasted good when you were that hungry.

As I finished, Magnus asked me about the Normans, what their army was doing.

"They are consuming the land, eating everything up or burning it," I replied.

"You met the duke?"

"I saw him."

"Wait for me back there," he said. He pointed with his thumb toward the back of the hall. He did not want me telling everyone what had happened.

He pointed at the two guards who'd escorted me.

"You two, tell us what you saw. What is the size of the duke's army? Did you see any siege equipment in their baggage train?" He sounded eager for what they would tell him.

The guards who'd been with me started talking. I went slowly to the back. I heard them giving numbers for cavalry and archers and talking about the lack of Norman siege equipment.

When they started talking about me meeting Bishop Odo, I went behind the curtain into Magnus's sleeping area, took off my cloak, and paced up and down. How would Magnus react to the Norman offer? Exile was not a welcome thought.

One of the serving women came in, stoked the brazier, and gave me some weak ale. I asked her for a spare tunic. Mine was half-covered in mud that had been splattered up to my shoulder by our horses. She brought a thick, dark green tunic to me. It was coarse and scratchy, but I was well used to that. I changed into it, while listening to the wind bending the wattle walls, and the murmurs of men talking.

I was by the brazier, stoking it, when, at last, he came.

He stood beside me, his hands out to the heat.

His tone was different, softer. "Tell me everything that happened," he said. He put an arm around my waist.

The Rise of Synne

I spun away from him.

"I will, my lord," I said. "But do not assume I am easy for you." I said each word slow so he would not miss my meaning.

He put his hands up. "I never thought that," he said with a smile.

I rocked on my feet, balancing between being angry at his assumption that I would fall into his arms and a desire for him to hold me I had to push away.

"I am a healer," I said firmly. There was a little shake in my voice that annoyed me greatly. "I've done what you asked. If rutting is now required, I will go." I stepped back.

My body tingled. His skin was smooth gold, and his eyes had a curiosity and playfulness to them that annoyed me and called to me at the same time. A loud voice in my head said run away, quick. Another said stay, you must stay, see what happens.

I stayed and I watched him.

He was powerfully built, and he smelled good. I shook my head. Stop it. Healers are not whores. We do not rut those we heal. We would never be allowed to do healing in any village if the women of the village discovered we were whoring. Every door would be barred to us.

I would stay and resist him.

On his face I saw yearning, his eyes wide, his lips parted. That set off a yearning in me, but I resisted it.

A moment later, breaking the spell between us, a shout echoed, as if the fates had conspired to interrupt us.

"Magnus, where are you?" It was Edmund's voice. I stepped away from Magnus.

"Back here," he shouted. He shook his head, displeased.

The curtain flung wide, and Edmund came in, his axe handle slapping against his leg, a brown leather inner helmet pushed back, but still on his head. He saw us, laughed, pulled the helmet off, tossed it on the low table.

"I thought you'd be here, healer," he said. "A guard told me you rode through the city like a woman with a new babe looking for shelter. What news of the Normans, Synne the healer?" He had a sullen look, as if he hadn't expected me to return at all.

"My lord," I said. "Your brother's guards, who came with me, will tell you all about the size of the Norman army and all about their defences." I was being evasive, but he deserved it.

Edmund shook his head. "I want to know what happened with Odo," he said slowly. "Not what they talk about in every alehouse between here and Mercia."

He pulled his axe from his belt. For a moment, I thought he was going to threaten me, but he didn't. He laid

The Rise of Synne

it up against the wall, then went to the brazier, warmed his hands over it and called me to him with a nod of his head. I went a little closer, but not close enough for him to grab me. There was a strange feeling in the air, as there were unsaid things going on I wasn't aware of. Perhaps he and his brother had argued about me.

"I need ale," Edmund called out.

The serving woman arrived so fast she must have been listening from somewhere beyond the curtain. She brought a jug and more goblets, and when she filled mine, she gave me a quick smile and a wink. I smiled back at her, but only for half a moment.

"Tell us both what happened with Odo," said Magnus.

"I met with him," I said, standing my ground between them. "He's as wily as any man ever." The serving woman put the jug of ale on the low table near the brazier. Her eyes were filled with awe as she glanced at me.

"True," said Edmund. Magnus had gone quiet.

"Come then, what happened?" said Edmund, his voice raised. The serving woman disappeared with a final glance at me, that I read as her wishing me luck with these two.

I told the brothers almost everything. When I got to the part about what the bastard would offer, Edmund hushed me, looked around, and said, "Speak softly. These walls have big ears."

I told them what Odo had said. Silence followed, except for the hissing of the brazier. Magnus was the first to speak.

"Our lives, and just what we can carry. That's all we get! Another Norman insult. We should offer him his life after we crush his stinking army and send all his men to a bloody hell." He was angry.

Edmund didn't seem surprised. I expected the same reaction from him, but there was almost a smile on his face as he watched Magnus.

"Brother, we can use this," said Edmund. He stared at me. "But first, healer, if I ever find out that you spill what we talk about to anyone else." He shook his head slowly. "I will find you and I will split you open with my best dagger. Understood?"

I nodded. It sounded like he meant it, too. "I've sworn already to keep my lips sealed, my lord. I keep my word." The real danger, I'd realised as he spoke, was that one of them, at some point, might decide I'd broken my vow based on some rumour and cut me open just to keep me silent about everything. My path out of this lay through a thicket of danger.

"Are you rutting her yet?" Edmund asked Magnus, pointing his thumb at me.

"She is my healer, that is all," said Magnus. He almost looked unhappy with that.

The Rise of Synne

"You are still the same, Magnus," said Edmund. His gaze turned to me. "Synne, you will take a message back to Bishop Odo, saying we accept their terms."

"I did not agree," said Magnus angrily.

Edmund put his hands up. "Think, Magnus. Our spies tell me they are vulnerable at night across the river, with only a few guards posted."

Magnus looked perplexed.

Edmund looked at me. "What did you see on the road to his camp?"

"Men with horses at every crossroads," I said.

"Yes, he has strung his army out," said Edmund jubilantly. I was confused, too. If they were going to submit, why was he talking about the Normans being vulnerable?

Then it dawned on me. Edmund would not submit. It would be a trick.

"You want Synne to take a fake submission to Odo?" asked Magnus.

Edmund smiled.

My heart sank.

"No, the two of you must do it," he said. He waved in my direction. "The duke will not believe this if it just comes from a healer, and I cannot go. It must be you, brother."

Magnus's mouth opened. Nothing came out.

"You must go quickly, too," said Edmund. "I will muster our men." He grinned. There was something all wrong about this talk of trickery. Was he intending to put his brother in harm's way?

"You must not attack while we are at their camp," said Magnus.

"No, of course not, brother. You will be back here before we do anything." He smiled, but with his mouth only, as if he was thinking of something else.

"When do you want us to go?" asked Magnus, his face stiff.

He'd given in to his brother alarmingly quickly. This was a moment I needed my mother's powers to see our future, but all I could sense was trickery and danger.

"In the morning," said Edmund, with a wave of his hand, as if it was nothing he was asking us to do. It came to me that he'd worked all this out before. He'd planned this. He walked to me, poked a finger into my shoulder. "You will go back to Odo tomorrow." He said it in a way that made it clear I should not argue.

"And say you agree to their terms?"

Edmund nodded, looked me up and down, his eyes taking me all in. "My brother will go with you. You like that, yes?"

Magnus groaned.

The Rise of Synne

"I will sleep with the serving women tonight," I said, looking from one brother to the other. Magnus's lips pressed tight. He was holding himself back.

I headed for the curtain. I did not like the way this conversation was going. Magnus was very different on his own.

"Are you not one of those healers who can heal pricks?" shouted Edmund to my back. "I'm told you can make things rise from the dead." He laughed.

"You are mistaken," I said in reply. I went and slipped through the end of the curtain and headed for the hut at the back, glad to be away from him. It was dark, but a glimmer of light from the door drew me on. I found the three serving women, one I'd learned was a slave, asleep in a ring around the small hearth. It had embers still glowing and a giant pot hanging above it.

I sat on a stool, wondering if Edmund would try to force me back for his pleasure and how I would resist, and finally, when it appeared this would not happen, I lay down and slept fitfully on thick rushes mixed with old ashes with a blanket over me. My dreams were of Catheryn and of the Norman Duke, and more vivid than ever. There was blood on my hands, and men at arms were shouting and pointing at me. I had done something. But what?

My mother had taught us that dreams can show us what awaits us, because of our fears and our joys, but only if we are open to knowing what is coming or want to shape it. My vivid dreams came so often now I expected to see them all happening, but when, that was what I wanted to know?

***

In the morning, I ate with the serving women. The gruel was hot and filling and I found a little honey. I also got a small cup of warm, fresh goat's milk. The woman in charge of the kitchen patted my shoulder as I finished and wished me well. She said she would pray for me to Saint Lewina, who'd faced the devil many times. They all stared after me as I stood to go and see if Magnus was preparing to leave. One of them must have overheard the brothers talking the night before and told the rest of them what had happened.

"Tell no one where we're going," I said, looking at each of them in turn. They all nodded. What more could I do? Magnus and Edmund should be more careful of their loose tongues.

When I went into the main hall, Edmund had already departed. Magnus was about to put on his polished mail shirt. I helped him with it. His wounds had partly healed, but the movement in his left arm was still limited. He could not raise it far. It would be a long time before that arm could hold a shield.

The Rise of Synne

"I've ordered two guards to come with us," he said when he saw me. "Are you ready to go?"

I nodded. "You think this is a good plan, appearing to surrender?" I asked.

"My brother thinks so, and I've sworn to follow his lead."

Was I right in what I'd been thinking about during the night?

"The Dane you saw at the Witan, the one who was with your brother. He was at the Norman camp," I said.

"You didn't say that last night." He wasn't angry, just curious.

"I told you everything that had happened with Odo. That's what you asked about."

"What was the Dane doing there?"

"Negotiating, so he said. Perhaps for your brother." He had to be told.

Magnus stood straight, testing the weight of the mail shirt he was wearing. It was a light one. It would not stop an axe, but it looked the part and, with a split halfway up the centre, could be worn on a horse.

"Edmund will not negotiate behind my back," he said. "If he wanted me dead, why would he bring me this mail shirt?" he asked while pointing at it.

"It won't stop them killing you," I said.

"They won't do that; we are messengers."

"If your brother raids the Norman camps across the river while we're with them, they'll have good cause to break all rules."

For a moment I thought he might accept his brother might put him in danger, but he just stared ahead.

"Do you always do what your brother says?" I asked. It was a story I'd heard many times. Sorely injured men telling me they'd been fighting because of oaths they'd made. To break such oaths would mean losing everything – family, home, all respect, even their life. To be outcast, and marked as one, was a fate worse than death in most cases.

He put his finger to his lips. The serving women had come in with gruel for him. I went to the midden while he ate. When I got back, he was sitting on his bed with his boots in front of him.

"Where are your other guards?" I asked.

"Edmund ordered them to go to him." He looked at me as he pulled his boots on. "He says he needs them all. They could be attacked any time."

"He should have left you some. You could be attacked, too."

"Elva's pregnant."

That news about Elva made me wonder what her plan was. Did she want rid of Magnus? Was this all about what lands they'd retain if they did submit to the Normans? She

The Rise of Synne

and Edmund must know the risk of sending us to the Norman camp, where we'd then live or die on a whim.

"This smells like a trap," I said softly. It certainly felt as if everything was closing in around us, our choices becoming limited.

He held his hand towards me. "You're right. I've considered it, but I'll not run away from my duty, healer. I'll not become an outlaw and allow my brother to claim I deserted him in his need." His expression was grim, as if he knew his fate already and was planning to accept it.

I did not like it, but his stubbornness spoke to me. It had bravery in it.

"You do not have to come with me," he said quickly. "You can go, run away. No one will come looking for you the way they would for me."

I sat on his bed. Silence followed, except for the distant sound of cawing gulls. He had offered me a way out. Should I take it? He walked around, tightened his belt, fixed his dagger to it, then moved it back and forward, as if frustrated with it.

He was waiting for my answer. I could leave him, put my feelings for him aside, think about my life, but if I turned this down, what hope would I have?

I had to face the danger, for Gytha and Tate, and for the fate I could earn for myself and Magnus. As I looked at him, I realised how drawn I was to him. He'd not forced himself on me, or even forced me to go with him, and that was admirable. I blew air out in a long whoosh.

"I'll go with you," I said. "You'll need someone to watch your back."

It was the first time in a while that I'd seen him smile properly. Then he laughed and raised his fist. "You can watch my back," he said.

Horses were waiting outside in the grey morning light. Two light baggage horses carried sacks, horse meal, and other provisions. It was a better-equipped trip than my previous one.

We moved fast, riding through the city. A few people recognised Magnus and bowed. Most looked grim-faced and intent on their business. The Yule festival was weeks away, and there were still only a few pigs' heads and legs hanging in front of shops. The uncertainty and a sharp wind had emptied the streets. This would be unlike any Yule I'd ever known.

Would I see another?

We crossed the river by the same ferry. The ferryman claimed he was the only one still operating between London Bridge and Wallingford. When he saw Magnus, he tripled his price for crossing and gave a low, respectful bow. Magnus paid.

The Norman army had moved on from when I'd met them and was now camped near a dark wood with thick

The Rise of Synne

brambles all along its edge. The camp had a palisade wall of thin tree trunks around it. I doubted it would stop any determined enemy.

We'd picked up a Norman escort after crossing the river, which made our journey easier. I used the same ring as before to show them we were messengers.

The guards at the gate laughed when told who was with us. Two of them bowed low, almost curtseying at Magnus. It was an insult, but Magnus didn't appear to notice. He was looking into their camp.

He'd been quiet all the way from London. He did not make any advances on me. If he'd been the type to force himself on me, those nights would have been his opportunity. I heard him muttering prayers each night and I wondered if it was all the men around that stopped him reaching for me or if he had no desire for me.

We gave up our horses inside their camp gate. A ten-man escort of guards took us to Odo's tent. Perhaps they thought Magnus was some great warrior. He certainly looked like he could be. He walked with a swagger and his mail shirt was brighter, different from the mostly dark and battered ones the Norman guards wore. What they didn't know was that if he had to fight, he'd be found out soon enough. You don't get far in a fight with only one working arm.

Odo's tent was beside another larger tent this time. They both had pennants flapping in the air above them. The head of the guard unit escorting us ushered us inside the tent and left us. No one was there. Thankfully, there was a glowing brazier to warm us.

As we waited for Odo to return, Magnus went into every corner of the tent. He looked at the stitching on the leather tent walls and at the workmanship on the low table, distracting himself, I guess.

I paced up and down. The sounds of the camp, men shouting orders, horses neighing, distant banging, all came to me as if in a dream, in which I was trapped with no way out, waiting for something bad to happen. I held my arms tight around myself. It was warm by the brazier, but cold near the tent walls.

"Stop pacing!" Magnus shouted after a while. He seemed frustrated.

"My legs are aching after all the riding we've been doing," I said.

"Just sit," he said.

I paced one more time to annoy him, then sat on a low bench near the table. "What happens if they demand more?" I asked, leaning near him in case anyone was listening beyond the tent walls. It was a thought that had been troubling me since the previous night.

"We'll find out," he said. He leaned back and his eyes widened. I turned. Odo was standing there, quietly watching us. My heart thumped.

"Welcome, Lord Magnus Godwin," said Odo in a friendly manner, his Norman accent more pronounced than I remembered. He nodded at me.

Magnus gave him a short bow, then extended his hand.

Odo did not take it.

Magnus took his hand down. "Bishop Odo," was all he said in a tone that could only be described as dismissive.

"Forgive my rudeness," said Odo. "We hear there is a pestilence in London. We cannot be too careful. We have a lot of men with us now, as you know." He gestured wide with his hands.

Magnus was stony-faced.

Odo came to the table and sat on a stool at the end. He pointed at the bench on the other side of where I was.

"Join us, Lord Magnus. Wine is on the way. Are you hungry?"

Magnus shook his head, but he sat. Odo gestured toward me. "Your healer did well to get you here. Does she have many other talents?" He put his head to one side as looked at me.

"Our healers are not whores," said Magnus.

A warm feeling came to me. I guessed now why he'd not tried something with me. It would be easier to get him to bend to their will if I was his lover.

"Neither are ours," said Odo. "Forgive me; what I meant was, is she also a good seer? We heard healers in this county can be seers too and see the future."

The two of them looked at me. Did Odo know something about me? It was my turn to speak, but I wanted to be sure to get my answer right. I was used to talking with powerful men now, so I wasn't shaking like a twig in a storm, but it did take a few moments to decide my words. I spoke them as clearly as I could, probably too loud, if anything.

"Yes, my mother was a seer, my lord, born to generations of seers. But I do not claim her skills..." I stopped mid-sentence.

"Yet," said Odo, finishing my sentence and taunting me too.

"I did not say that." I said it firmly, with a shake of my head. He was a bishop and would despise anyone who claimed powers outside of what the church could do.

Two serving women arrived. They distributed green glass goblets and filled them with wine. I asked them to water mine down. They did.

"I am sure you have more skills than you tell," said Odo, glancing at Magnus. "Perhaps you daydream of a

The Rise of Synne

lord to keep your bed warm, healer?" Again, he put his head to the side.

I didn't reply. He turned to Magnus. "What about you, Lord Magnus? Do you dream of being king someday, if your turn comes?"

Magnus shook his head. "I don't dream any such thing, bishop. What about you; what dreams do you have if your brother falls?"

Odo spoke softly. "I dream only of spreading the work of Christ and our blessed pope, Christ's bishop here on earth. He has given me tasks for this land, and I shall carry them out." He pointed at Magnus. "You are a traitor to the true King of England and should beg for forgiveness," he said.

"I will not beg. My father was crowned king," said Magnus, spitting the words out.

Odo slammed his fist on the table, making the goblets shake. I grabbed mine to stop it tipping over.

"If your oathbreaker father had accepted my brother's legitimate claim to the throne of England, many, many people would still be alive, some of our best liege men." His face was red. "We lost the flower of our men at Hastings." His hands swept angrily through the air, then he put them down on the table, as if they were claws. "But we must draw a line under all that, and plan for peace in England, yes? That is why you are here, is it not?"

"It is," said Magnus, his words half-strangled as if he was fighting hard to control himself. "And we will submit. You have your victory."

Odo raised his hands, as if in joy. "Does this mean you and all your family will support my brother, the duke, in his rightful claim for the throne of all England?"

It was a big question. Could Magnus say that his family would all submit? He'd spoken about his mother to me on the road, and that there were other brothers who'd gone to her after Hastings, and how she was unlikely to ever submit to the duke.

"I speak for myself and my men," said Magnus.

Would it be enough for Odo?

Odo had a half-smile on his face, giving nothing away. "Soon there'll be a submission ceremony for you, Magnus. My brother has been taking submissions from all over this land, and almost every day someone new comes. It has slowed our progress as there are so many." Odo's smile was confident, gleeful. He put his hands together, his palms wide apart but fingertips touching. "I am so happy my prayers have been answered with you. Everyone can see which way the river is flowing in this land."

"Which way the wind blows you mean," said Magnus quickly. He was looking at me with a defiant expression. Odo replied instantly.

The Rise of Synne

"We Normans are the river, son of the oathbreaker. We wash away all that stands in our path. We are not the wind that blows one way, then another soon after." He was angry, his eyes bulging.

"You've a long way to go before you wash away all who stand against you," said Magnus, defiance in his tone.

Odo stared at him, his expression still, controlled now.

I enjoyed Magnus baiting Odo, but it did not help our cause. The way Magnus was staring at Odo it came to me that Magnus wanted his good name preserved, perhaps for his death to be a reason for the people of England to rally around his brother. Could he be that stupid?

I'd heard of young men going into battle with a death wish, because some woman or their family had spurned them. If Magnus wanted to avoid submitting to the Normans, he might wish to die or at least show he wasn't scared of death.

Odo took a sip of his wine.

"I will submit with my brother after we agree on the terms in full," said Magnus.

"The terms are what I told your healer. Nothing else." Odo said the words slowly.

Magnus's expression was cut stone.

"The healer will go back to your brother tomorrow," said Odo. "You will be our hostage, Lord Magnus, to stand for the good behaviour of the rest of your family."

Magnus did not look surprised. Perhaps this was why he was so gloomy on the way here. He'd expected this.

"When do I meet the duke?" he asked. His expression made clear that he thought negotiations had not finished.

Odo shook his head. "You will not meet the future king at this time." He reached a hand toward me but didn't touch me. "My brother wants to see the healer tonight."

All noise seemed to quieten. I stopped breathing.

Magnus's face twisted. He glared at me, as if it was my fault the duke had asked to see me. I breathed in, brought my hands together, one hand cupping the other as a fist, holding it tight. Fate was twisting in unexpected ways. Should I be concerned about the duke's fearsome reputation? He'd executed many prisoners, so the stories went.

Magnus let out a snort of indignation. "The healer cannot agree to anything without me," he said.

"This is not about you," said Odo with contempt.

A smile came, then disappeared fast from my face. Why did the duke want to see me?

"I will not submit if the duke forces himself on my healer," said Magnus bitterly, shaking his head.

He was trying to protect me, even though he had little power to do so here.

"Do not presume my brother's intentions," said Odo. He stood, stepped back from the table. "Let's go, healer."

I felt rooted to the spot. Magnus had a startled look on his face. Events were moving slippery fast. Odo was already at the tent flap.

"Do not force me to bring you to him trussed up," he shouted.

Magnus was shaking his head as if I had a choice.

"I will see what he wants," I said. I followed Odo.

Outside, it was cold and dark with distant pricks of light from torches visible at the main camp gate and a pale glow from some of the tents. The wind had picked up. I pulled my cloak tight against an icy blast. It seemed as if I was in a dream or a nightmare. I was going to meet the duke.

What did he want? I put my arms around myself. He must have many women among their camp followers who would eagerly do his bidding at any moment. It had to be something else, but what? Was he ill?

Odo was standing at the flap to the nearby larger tent. Four guards in mail shirts and with helmets on waited near the flap. Odo motioned me to him.

"My brother does not force women to do anything, healer. He does not have to. They come to him," he said with a wry smile.

"What does he want from me?" I kept my voice firm.

Odo laughed.

"You speak up like few Norman women do," he said. He put his palm up high, as if holding me back.

"Do I get an answer?"

He laughed louder. "They were right what they said about you. Here is your answer. A few days ago, we captured a woman. She claims to be the last seer in England." He paused, looked around, softened his tone. "You have the powers of a seer in your blood, so we need you for something." He did that thing again of putting his head to one side.

A memory came to me in a rush. My mother had helped at a ceremony when an old seer had visited our village. The woman had needed my mother to be there when she performed a rite that would allow her to glimpse the future.

"The seer needs a helper?" I asked.

Odo's eyebrows went up. "You're quick," he said. He shook a finger at me. "But I must warn you. Do not cross my brother. He executes the defiant in ways you do not want to hear about. And I have seen too much blood already to be entertained by it."

The Rise of Synne

All that made me feel dizzy for a moment. I straightened myself, brushed the front of my tunic with my hand. He looked at me as if he'd expected me to beg for his protection, but I would not. I do not know if it was seeing so many people dead already, or the torments of those left behind, but a voice inside me said I'd been saved before and would be saved again.

"What ceremony is the seeress preparing?"

"She claims she can see the future," he said.

"You allow this?" I said softly. "I'm surprised that a bishop will have any part in such a thing."

He crossed himself. "We test this woman, that is all."

He pushed through the tent flap and went inside. The bright yellow glare from a multitude of candles hurt my eyes as I followed him in. The inside of the tent must have had a hundred, perhaps more, candles of all sizes, all glowing. It was larger inside this tent than Odo's too and had a selection of mail shirts, axes and swords gleaming on racks near the entrance.

A stench of incense and wine hit me immediately, along with a murmur of voices. At the other end of the tent, a single long table had men at it. A small roast boar sat on a platter on a side table, half-carved. Normally the smell of boar would have made me hungry, but this one smelled too sweet, as if they'd poured some strange honey on it.

Three braziers stood in the tent, near the top table. Elaborate embroideries hung at the back and along the sides of the tent.

The three men at the table looked at us. One man at the centre with blond hair dominated the table – William, Duke of Normandy, the man I'd seen watching me depart the last time I'd been in their camp. His eyes were on me, examining me, like a bear eying its prey.

He had a long bone-handled knife in his hand. A chunk of dark meat hung on the knife point. He stopped it moving toward his mouth, put the knife down, and waved for us to come forward.

There was no sign of the seer. Pages, young boys in short tunics, moved swiftly around the tent. The duke shouted something in Norman. Two pages scurried faster.

Something poked into my side. "Go to him," said Odo.

Be proud, always, my father had taught us; keep your head up no matter what. I moved into the open area in front of the top table with my head high.

All the men at the table were staring at me, as if I was a dog that had snuck in. One of them, a man with a streak of white hair, slapped his hand on the duke's shoulder and let out a shout. I didn't understand what he said, but I got the gist. They thought I was an offering.

"Bow low," said Odo insistently from behind me.

The Rise of Synne

I bowed, but not as low as I am sure he wanted.

The duke shouted again. I knew he hadn't a word of our language. How could someone who wasn't even able to speak to us expect to take over all of England?

I was seething deep inside. This man was responsible for my brother's death. And many, many more. He deserved to die too, like they had, or worse. I stared at the tapestry behind him, sure that if I met his gaze, he would know at once that I wanted him dead more than I valued my life.

"Sit over there, girl," said Odo sharply. He pointed to a bench in the shadows along one wall. I went to it, my chin still high. When I reached it, I sat and held the bench with both hands, as if it was a flimsy craft in a storm-tossed sea.

Odo had disappeared. A servant arrived with a goblet for me and a wine jug in her other hand. She poured wine for me after I took the goblet. I sipped a little. I did not gulp it. Who knew what they would put in it for me? A nudge to my shoulder sent me jumping almost to my feet. It was Odo.

"She'll be here soon," he said. He leaned down to me. "You see the man with the white hair? That is the Lord of Longueville. He fought with great honour against the Saracens. He helped to stop their advance. Everyone in

England should be grateful to him. The Saracens would be here if he hadn't stopped them."

Odo was close enough now that I could smell the wine on his breath and garlic, too.

"The other man cut the hands from the usurper Harold." Odo grinned at me, as if he expected me to be shocked. But I'd seen men mutilated in battle. Such things are the price of war. Seeing them was the price of being a healer.

Odo nudged my boots. "He hacked Harold's feet off, too." He grinned. His eyes were wide with the pleasure of their victory.

I did not react. We knew King Harold's body would be mutilated. It was expected when a leader fell in battle. The same would have happened to the duke if he'd lost.

"She is here," said Odo softly.

I looked to the back of the tent. A shadow had appeared. As it moved forward, it became the hood of a dark grey wolf skin cloak, which was thrown back after a few steps to reveal a tall, thin woman with a long shield of black hair and a blue rune on her forehead. Her cloak came open as she strutted up the tent. It was lined inside with white cat fur and on her hands, she wore white cat-skin gloves. On her feet were black fur-trimmed boots that went almost to her knees and were laced with leather strips. I smiled in recognition. I'd seen a seer wear this type of boots before.

In her hand was a staff with brass circling its upper part and a small shiny brass knob on top. Her pale-green tunic under the cloak had a belt sparkling with amber beads and other stones. Her necklace was shards of glass and beads. It sparkled. She oozed power and the wind fluttered as she came up the tent, making the walls tremble.

She took in everything, searching with her gaze until she found me, then gave me the slightest nod.

"You know the divination chant, yes?" asked Odo in my ear.

"Yes." There was more than one, but one would be enough.

He straightened.

The last time I'd mouthed such a chant had been for my mother at a feast in our village. She didn't teach all of us sisters the same chants. We learned different ones. For most of my life, her chants and her readings and predictions had been childish games. Until she died.

The seer walked straight towards me. My heart quickened as she came. When she arrived in front of me, she stamped her staff in the dirt and bent down until she was directly in my face.

"I am seer Gudrid. Do you know the great chant?" she asked, her eyes narrow, a sharp tone in her voice.

"My mother taught me," I replied. A woman like Gudrid had gone from village to village when I was a child.

"I hope she taught right," she said. Her voice was deep.

"I am not a woken seer, not yet," I said looking into her eyes. Perhaps she might be willing to help me take the next step in becoming a woken seer. I'd not met another seer since my mother had been murdered.

She moved her face close to me. Odo was almost on top of us, listening.

"Did you learn the chants and recite them for your mother?"

"Yes."

"Did she teach you the curses?"

I nodded. My mother had taught me many of the old ways.

Gudrid put her head to one side, opened her eyes wide, as if she was trying to tell me something. She mouthed something then, as her gaze flickered towards the duke.

"What is your name?"

"Synne."

"If you believe you are ready, Synne, you are ready. But first, you will start my reading this night. Agreed?"

I nodded.

The Rise of Synne

"Come with me." She grabbed my hand and pulled me after her. We headed for the back of the tent. I stumbled as I went, but came to my feet, my heart beating fast inside my chest. What I'd believed might never happen, might now happen.

Odo followed us. A shout, and then another, came from the top table. The seer ignored them. When she reached the tent flap, she pulled me close and whispered in my ear.

"Our powers come by blood. You must believe in them. Then they will come to you."

My mother had said the same words. But words can seem hollow if you do not know what they mean.

The seer put her face next to mine, so close I could feel the heat from her cheek. "They know who you are," she hissed, as soft as a snake.

"What?"

She pulled at her hair, held out her hand. "Take it," she hissed angrily. "And curse him with all you've been taught when the time comes."

I took her hand and something hard came into mine. I knew what it was without looking – one of the amber beads tied into her hair. I pushed it into the little purse tied to my belt. As I did, I felt light-headed. This was what I'd need for a waking ceremony. A gift from a seer.

"Get his brother to ask him the question. I will be outside," she said. "A foul stink of blood and offal fills the air in here." She went out of the tent. A guard who'd been in the shadows went after her.

Odo was directly behind me. "What must I ask my brother?" he said. His gaze roved over me and stopped at my hand.

"A question," I said, hoping to distract him, with some of the seer's defiance in my tone. "Ask your brother what's in the dreams that haunt him."

"That's it?"

"It is enough."

He walked up the tent. When he reached the duke, he bent down to him, pointed back at me, said something. I was still near the tent flap, at the edge between the bright world of the victorious duke and the darkness of the night and the seer's world outside. I breathed in the remnants of strength the seer had filled the air around me with.

Odo motioned me up the room. I walked to them, my head high. If I was fated to die tonight, so be it. I had done all I could.

Odo stood in front of me, looking me up and down. "My brother has seen a boar running from him in his dreams. This has happened many times."

I bent forward, started the divination chant, slowly. The Varthlokur is the great chant in the old tongue. Each

The Rise of Synne

word takes longer than it should, all chanted to a slow rhythm.

I am the water,
I am the summit,
I am the vale,
I am the spearhead,
I am desire.
Who knows all secrets?
Who knows the will of the darkness?

The duke and the men around him were listening intently. Long ago, when my mother was alive, I'd sweated at a moment like this in front of people, my forehead soaking wet, but now I didn't care.

Odo raised his fist as my chant stopped. I blinked. The glow of the candles seemed to be growing, a golden light filling every part of the tent.

I held my hands tight to my chest.

The duke looked around, as if he had noticed the glow in the room changing. The wind had stopped too, as if it was listening.

From the back of the tent, a shout echoed. "Bring me his goblet!" The seer was back inside.

I shivered all the way from my shoulders to my toes, but I ignored it and walked forward with my hand out, pointing at the bastard's goblet. Odo said something to his brother, leaned over and picked up the goblet and brought it to me. I looked inside it. There was still some wine in it. I brought it to the seer. She grabbed at it, peered inside as I backed off, then flung the contents in the air and waved at the falling wine, making marks in the air with it.

She reared up, pointed at the bastard.

"Know this, Duke William," she roared. "You are cursed."

I held my breath. That was not a wise thing to say.

The duke pointed at her, his finger jabbing. He said something in their strange tongue.

Odo laughed, shouted.

Someone grabbed me. My chest tightened as if a belt had wrapped around it. I could barely breathe.

Guards were holding me on each side, crowding in on me. They pushed me, stumbling, to the back of the tent where the seer was. My alarm grew. Were they planning to slit both our throats for the seer's words?

A throbbing had started in my neck as if my blood knew what was coming.

A guard with a black cloak, its hood up obscuring his face, appeared in front of me. I'd not seen him earlier. He had a shiny dagger in his hand. I gasped almost soundlessly. I knew what this meant. Death. The seer was being held tightly near me. She struggled, spat too, her feet off the ground at times as she was being held up.

I did not struggle. A memory of a hall and a public reading like this had come back to me.

20

A hot slap of blood struck my face, making me turn my head. The stink of it, all slippery salt and iron, assaulted my senses. To my shame, I did not think of the seer. All I thought about was what it would be like when my blood drenched the rushes underfoot. I mouthed a prayer. *Save me, Queen of Heaven, save me in my hour of need.* A loud and desperate gurgle sounded from the seer. The guards released her. She fell forward onto her knees, blood spurting from her neck onto the earth, her eyes wide. My body felt cold, clammy. The seer's lips moved.

My body shook.

This would be me in a moment. My blood wetting the rushes.

The executioner stood in front of me, his knife back, steady. I whispered the prayer again, slower.

The knife glistened, curved back through the air.

But it did not come for me. He'd swung it to scare me.

The Rise of Synne

Glee filled his face as he watched my reaction, my frightened blinks. A hammer thumping in my head pushed deep into my skull.

Odo was beside the executioner. He said something to him I did not catch, then spoke to me.

"We do not permit agents of Satan, such as this seer, to spread their wicked ways in this land anymore. Now the last seer is dead, Christ can be restored to his rightful place in England. Do you not agree?" he said.

I'd heard the Normans had the support of the pope, who wanted to sweep away the way we did things in England. That meant our old ways, our mix of charms and prayers and healing and visions would be wiped away. But why would they kill the old seer unless they feared her powers? I tossed my head and stared back at him.

He laughed, held my arm tighter. "You have spirit, Synne, so do not fret, you will not die tonight. You will live because it suits us, remember that. You will return to London in the morning and tell Edmund if he wants his brother back, he'll come with all the bishops and all the other lords in London to submit to us at Berkhamsted a week from now." He pressed his nails into my arm, marking his will onto my body.

"Release me," I said, spitting the words out.

"You're as wilful as they come." His nails dug into me. "I should you hand you over to those looking for you."

I stared back at him. If he was going to hand me over to someone, he wouldn't be suggesting me as a messenger.

"Do you want Magnus to die in front of you?" His eyes glistened with malice. Had he guessed how I felt about Magnus?

I licked my lips. They had the slick of blood and the taste of death on them. I could not bear to have Magnus's blood on them too, but I would not show this.

"You will do as I say, and you will come with them to Berkhamsted, and tell us if Edmund and the others will be true to their word." He let go of my arm. "If you lie, and I can smell a lie, I will have my friend slice Lord Magnus's throat for you, the way the seer's throat was cut. And you will taste his blood, too."

He whispered those last words and then gestured with his hand, dismissing me. The guards grabbed me. At the other end of the tent, the duke was laughing with his men, not even paying attention to what his brother was doing.

I was pushed out of that tent and into Odo's. I stumbled into it and fell beside a stool, gripping it for something firm to hold on to.

"What happened?" asked Magnus, coming to me.

I could not speak. I was full up with rage and sadness and a fear that made me shudder as I remembered what I'd seen. Magnus waited, a comforting hand on my back.

The Rise of Synne

After a while, when my breathing slowed, and as I saw no guards had come to play some other tricks on me, I stood, went to the brazier to warm myself, trembling a little inside, but needing heat.

Magnus put his arm around me, held me. I did not stop him.

"I will go back to London in the morning with a message for your brother," I said.

"Whose blood is on you?" There was a hint of panic in his tone as he stood away from me to look me up and down.

"They cut a seer's throat in front of me. Is there water here?" I put my hands to my face, my fingers a claw on my skin.

"Yes," said Magnus. He fetched a jug of water, poured some into my cupped hands. I splashed water onto my face over and over until he told me the blood was gone. The blood stains on my hands were a light pink now. My tunic was stained with blood, too, but I didn't care. I was alive. Magnus was alive.

He put a hand on my arm. "What is the message for Edmund?" He had a curious look on his face, as if he'd half guessed there were things I wasn't saying.

I told him about Berkhamsted.

He raised his fists and bent his head. "We are undone," he said softly. "Tell my brother I am ready to meet our father. He does not have to go to Berkhamsted for me."

I shook my head, anger rising inside me. "No. You will not die. That is how we defy them." It was what he needed to hear. I would not taste his blood, too.

It was his turn to pace up and down. I pulled a blanket around me. He sat next to me. I was exhausted, as if the marrow had been sucked from my bones.

Later, I tried to sleep, the two of us close under a blanket. He held me tight to him and his body felt good, warm, strong, against mine. He had to survive this. He pulled me closer, but I pushed back. This would not be the way we came together, with Norman guards listening nearby. He did not press me further.

Memories of what the seer had said and done turned in my mind. I wondered what her prediction for the duke meant and about the gift she'd given me, and her words about how my powers would come and who I was. It all felt unreal. Could any of what she'd said help me, help us? In my half-sleep I saw my mother's face, up close, as if I was looking at her reflection in water. She had her hand out to me and was saying something.

Before I could make out her words, shouts woke me. A dim light seeped into the tent. It was dawn. Two guards had appeared.

"Healer," one of them shouted.

"Yes," I shouted back.

"Come."

I only had time to grip Magnus by the hand and hold him for a moment and then push him away, hard. We could not look weak in front of any Normans. Ever. It was enough that I had felt his heartbeat close and could see the abandoned look on his face now. Our difficulties were forging a bond between us. But how strong would it be and was I imagining it?

He held his hand up, his fingers wide in a parting gesture as I stepped back. I pressed my fist into my chest, then turned away, biting my lip. I could not look at him any longer.

***

Halfway back to London we came upon a line of prisoners, young English men stumbling, tied to each other by a heavy rope. They had their heads down. Many had blood on their tunics. Some had open wounds and were groaning with each step.

"Where do you come from?" I shouted, hoping one of the men would reply, wondering what this line of captives meant.

"London Bridge," came a shouted reply. One man looked at me, his expression bleak.

This was not good. It probably meant that Edmund had attacked across the bridge, and that he'd failed. I felt crushed inside. Odo would soon find out that Edmund had attacked while his brother was negotiating. They might cut Magnus's throat for that alone.

Was he lost? I could not think it.

The guards that Odo had sent with me crossed the river with me this time. They escorted me as far as the main London road, too, within sight of the city walls. Their audacity, coming so close to the city, was disturbing. It meant they didn't fear anyone on this side of the river anymore.

I reached the walls at about midday and headed through the city to the wolf skull hall for food and to change my tunic before going to see Edmund. I did not look forward to the meeting. It seemed likely he'd placed us in a trap. I was half-covered in mud and so exhausted I wasn't sure I'd be able to speak with Edmund without bemoaning his trickery if I met him like this.

When I reached the wolf skull hall, the guard outside took one look at my horse, and at me, shook his head, led the horse away, and pointed me to go in the door with his thumb.

Brother Ulf was inside. He left his bowl of pottage and came to hug me. He looked beyond me then. "Lord Magnus?" he asked.

"A Norman captive."

He stamped his foot, groaned loudly. "I warned Edmund this would happen," he shouted. He pointed at me. "Get some food in the kitchen and …" He looked at my mud-covered tunic. "Find something else to wear." His face was full of anger, as if it was my fault Magnus hadn't returned.

I should have stayed quiet then, but I couldn't.

"I've been with a devil and that's what you say, find something else to wear," I said, spitting the words out. I'd suppressed everything since the death of the seer, but I couldn't hold it anymore. I needed to fight with someone.

"Do not blame me," said Ulf, his hands going up.

"Who should I blame for all this." I pointed at him.

He didn't reply. I stalked toward the back of the hall and into the hut beyond. Ulf called my name, but I did not go back to him.

As I went through it, I hit the doorpost with the side of my fist so hard the wattle wall shook. The warmth of the hut beyond – they had a small fire going – wrapped around me as tears of frustration threatened. A deep feeling of loss enveloped me, making me groan and bend my head forward.

The older woman came to me, wrapped me in her arms. One of the other girls patted my back. There was no need for words. They knew the terrible things that could happen, the blows of men, the injuries and death dealt out under cover of one stupid excuse or another.

"Synne." Ulf was behind me. "Why did Odo send you back?"

I straightened. Be strong or die. "I have a message for Edmund."

"Tell me it. He's expecting me as soon as I get news."

"Outside," I said.

I hugged the old woman and her helper, asked them for any food they had to be brought out to me as well as any old tunic they had. I headed back into the hall with Ulf beside me. I told him about the meet at Berkhamsted, and that I was to go as well. He raised his eyebrows at that. I also told him about the prisoners I'd seen on the road back and my fears for Magnus.

He put his hand out to me. "People are talking about you," he said softly.

"What are they talking about?"

"Some people want to know why you went with Magnus. I heard Edmund tell someone you're a famous healer, that your touch can heal."

I shook my head and groaned. "That is the worst news. You know there are Danes looking for me?"

"Why?"

I shook my head. "I don't know!"

The Rise of Synne

He sighed, then went off to find Edmund. I didn't care that he was giving the message. I didn't want to see Edmund. He'd betrayed his brother. I despised him. All his bragging about how easy it would be to defeat the Normans was just that, words. If I went to see him, I might throw his words in his face. That would not be good for Magnus's cause or mine. Men like him expect nothing but deference and smiles from women.

After eating a bowl of thin pottage, I went to Magnus's sleeping area and took off my clothes. I put on a tunic the servant girl had brought for me and moved my belt and purse to it. Then I went to the hut at the back, asked them to wash my tunic and cloak, and told them I'd be sleeping in Magnus's bed. I wanted to be near his smell.

They said nothing, just bowed, even though I was no more than his healer. I wondered should I tell them Magnus was a captive.

I decided not to. I did not want the whole city deciding that the Godwins' cause was lost.

I drifted into a dark sleep soon after. London was burning. There was blood all over my hands. I woke in a sweat. It took a long time for me to sleep again.

***

I was roused by seagulls cawing as the dawn light filtered through the smoke hole in the roof. Memories of Magnus holding me taunted me.

I found the amber bead the seer had given me and held it up to my eye. A tiny dragon had been carved into it. The bead's ends had been squared off too. It felt warm and was heavy enough to blind an eye if you threw it right. The dawn light filled it when I held it up, as if it could hold the light inside it. It reminded me of something my mother had taught us, that one small thing can change everything.

I put it to my lips and said a prayer for Magnus to live. I didn't want him to live just for me. If he was free and we were together, he would help me find my sisters. I bent my head and said the prayer again. Come back to us.

I put the bead away and went to eat gruel in the kitchen. It was warm and filling, but there was no bread to go with it. Supplies of many things had stopped, the old woman said. She would go out later and search for any open bread shop, but she wasn't hopeful. She looked worried. She asked me what was going on. She'd heard rumours that the city would submit to the duke and that any who'd supported the Godwins would lose their property and their livelihoods.

"It's not over yet," I said. "Don't lose faith."

"Faith in what?" said a voice behind me.

It was Ulf. He looked tired.

"An English victory," I said.

"We pray for that every day," he said. He took a bowl of gruel and left the kitchen.

I followed him.

"What did Edmund say when you told him the message?" I asked as I sat down near him.

"Shuush," he said. "No one must hear any of this."

There was only one guard at the other end of the hall, so I wasn't sure what he was worried about, but I lowered my voice anyway.

"The merchants and the bishops of London will all sue for peace, I hear. They want to surrender the city. There is talk of a coronation for the duke at the Yule festival."

He groaned in disgust.

I gripped the bench under me. The tide had turned and was running fast in the Normans' favour. We'd won at London Bridge, but if we didn't have the support of the merchants and the bishops, it was all for nothing.

"What does Edmund say about all this?"

"He wants a better deal than what they offered."

"But he's going to submit?"

"I do not know." His voice rose.

"He put Magnus's life in danger. That's not right."

Ulf stared at me almost accusingly, then departed without another word.

I spent the rest of the day helping to prepare a stew that would last a few days to keep myself busy. I helped look for bread, too, all the way between the hall and London Bridge. There was none to be had.

That afternoon, I ate at the table with the kitchen girls. The stew was thin, but good.

I slept badly again that night and the night after, wondering about Magnus and what Ulf was doing, and if I'd ever get to see Magnus again.

***

I was eating a small bowl of gruel when Ulf returned. I was in the hall. There was only one old guard at the door. All the others had gone to Edmund long ago.

Ulf nodded and sat. "I have news," he said.

"What news?"

"Magnus is alive. He will be at the coronation. He's expected to swear allegiance to the new king then."

I shook my head slowly. "He's agreed to this?"

"We assume so."

At least he was alive.

"Am I going to Berkhamsted?" Perhaps, if I was at Berkhamsted, I'd see Magnus.

He coughed. "Edmund laughed when I said that."

"The duke wants me there."

"Edmund does not care."

The Rise of Synne

I was about to say more when he put his hand up.

"Why do you want to see Magnus? Tell me, I'm not stupid. I have eyes."

I put my hands wide on the table. "You tell me about the coronation," I said. I did not like where he was going with this talk about Magnus.

He laughed, then replied, "An English bishop, Aldred, will present the new king to us, but a Norman bishop, Geoffrey, will lead the ceremony in French. It will be on Christ Mass day." His eyes narrowed. "Duke William plans to have every English lord there. They will all swear allegiance and show everyone that has submitted to him, including the sons of Harold, who he has shown mercy to."

I was thinking about Magnus. The idea that he would be near, just across the city, but that I might not see him, set a burrowing anguish moving inside me. Then it came to me, what I could do.

"Can you get me into the abbey for the coronation?" I asked. I had to be there. Magnus would be there. I had to see him. I could not just sit here and wait for news. I did not care about any risk involved.

"Not a good idea," he said.

"I must be there, Ulf." I made my hands into fists. "Magnus will need my help if they've injured him."

"It will be mostly English lords and their ladies and a lot of Normans there, Synne."

"I'll go anyway, even if you don't help me." I shook my fist at him. "There must be a way I can get in." I stood, paced to the wall, then back. I am not sure why, but a voice inside me said I had to be at the coronation. "Ulf, he might need me." I put my fist out to him.

He looked shocked at my insistence, then, after a long sigh, he said, "Perhaps if we tie your hair back tight, I can get you in with the choir. They wear their hoods up most of the time and they're about your size."

I didn't hesitate. "Yes, yes, and I can sing too. I sang in church when I was young." I didn't tell him how little I had sung.

"I don't know how this will help," said Ulf.

I gripped his hand. "I will see him, see if he needs me. That is enough." I needed Ulf to help me. I'd been sitting waiting for too long. "This is what I am praying for."

He hummed. "You've changed, Synne the healer. It is good to hear you talking about prayer."

I opened my mouth. I wanted to tell him about the seer and about the bead she'd given me, and what it meant, but I decided not to. Monks mostly liked things that had crosses on them.

He stood. "I will find out if it's possible. Practice your chants. You know the Gloria I expect, yes?"

"Yes."

"Practice it."

21

I spent a lot of time helping in the hall, searching for bread each day, finding some occasionally, watching people in the city becoming more and more agitated as the days went on and winter deepened, everyone looking at each other as if we might all become enemies, everyone likely wondering what would happen to them as the Normans tightened their grip on the city.

My hopes of getting into the coronation ceremony, and the uncertainty about whether that would happen, felt like a stone inside me. Each night I became bitter, as thoughts of Magnus, perhaps dead already, pulled at me. Was I stupid thinking I might have helped him?

My amulets helped me. I held them each night and prayed for Magnus and my sisters, not for me, and that my mother's prophecies would all come true.

Yule and the Christ Mass festival were getting closer, though there was little to cheer and little prospect of anything to feast on this year.

The Rise of Synne

Soon, talk at the markets confirmed that the duke would be crowned in the abbey on Thorney Island. Some were happy that the fighting would end. Others said that Norman troops had already entered the city. One rumour, confirming my worst fears, pulled me further down.

That rumour claimed Magnus had been murdered by the Normans in revenge for the attack on their camp across the river. I refused to believe it. Then I did believe it. Then I prayed for it not to be true, rocking back and forth, calling to my mother and the Queen of Heaven, praying over and over, hoping that some of my mother's power to bend fate had come to me. Please, come to me.

Ulf's failure to return as the coronation drew closer made me increasingly agitated. I decided, twice, to go and look for him, but each time I changed my mind, in case I went one way, and he came from another, looking for me.

I thought about the seer and what she'd said about my powers coming to me through blood. I prayed it would not be through Magnus's blood.

No one else came to the hall during those days. We were being shunned. People living around us knew this was a Godwin hall. They knew the way the wind blew and the river flowed. The followers of dead leaders disappear fast, like the morning mist.

Even the last kitchen girl left us. Just the old kitchen woman remained and one old guard who slept a lot.

Finally, when I was sure he'd abandoned me, Ulf came back. It was the day before Christ Mass. I approached him slowly, wondering if he had bad news.

We hugged for a long time.

"What's happening?" I asked. "You've been gone so long I thought you'd abandoned me."

"Almost every lord and bishop from London went to meet the bastard at Berkhamsted. They all bowed low, every last one of them."

I let my breath out. "Magnus?"

"He's alive and will submit at the coronation with all the others."

"And I can go to the coronation and see him?" Relief at the news Magnus was alive made me shake inside. My prayers had worked.

"It could be dangerous for you."

I put my hand out, gripped his tight. "I do not care. I will go there even if you do not help me."

"What good will it do, you going there?" Ulf was angry. He raised his hands.

I stumbled on, the words and the plan coming out of me from where I do not know. "You know, there is a prophecy that says a woman will take our revenge on the Normans."

He looked unimpressed. I pressed on. This was my chance.

The Rise of Synne

"That woman can be me. The seer they murdered reminded me how I can curse their new king. His coronation is the right time to do it." Ulf might laugh at my talk of curses, and of a need to see Magnus, but there were monks I'd met who believed in the old ways, the powers we gained from the land and from our blood. Ulf might be one of them. I stared at him, my mouth half open, waiting for his reply.

He sighed, long and hard, then turned it into a grunt. "We have to go to the abbey now, before all their guards get there." He smiled. "I am here to say I'll get you in with the choir. I was with them earlier. That is why I came back for you."

I smiled, anticipation flowing already inside me. I didn't care Ulf had almost made me beg. Doing this was right. I would see Magnus and I would curse their new king.

"Is there a sharp knife here so I can cut your hair?"

I went to fetch one. Questions turned in my mind as I rubbed my finger against the knives, testing them for sharpness. Would I see Magnus? I whispered the binding chant for him, the chant that bound me and my sisters together with the pull of fate.

Ulf found me a winding cloth to bind my breasts tight, then started tying my hair up. That took less time than expected. My hair had not grown much this year.

A clean brown tunic with a thick hood emerged from his bag. He'd had that with him all along. I put it on, pulled up the hood and glimpsed myself in the small, polished disk I'd found at the back of the hall. I looked like a young monk. No woman would wear her hair like this. I told the old woman I was going to become a nun. She made a sad noise and raised her eyebrows as if she didn't believe me.

"You'll not make a good nun," she said.

I laughed.

We travelled fast. The streets were deserted, as if the city was holding its breath. We arrived at the abbey at compline, the time for night prayers. A multicoloured glow came from a few painted glass windows as the cathedral loomed high in the air above us like a stone cliff. This was not like any Christ Mass eve I'd ever known. Usually there was great excitement as everyone thought about the holiday and feasting ahead. But the few people around did not look excited. Every face was anxious, pinched.

Ulf told the monk at the entrance that I was a replacement for someone sick. The Norman guards let us through with a nod to Ulf. He whispered something to them. They laughed. We went inside, and after knocking lightly on a side door, we went below ground. I was allocated a rush mattress in the corner of the basement, being used as a dormitory. There was a line of such mattresses, all with sleeping figures on them covered in

The Rise of Synne

blankets. The sound of ragged snoring all around and my thoughts about the day to come kept me awake.

Would I see Magnus? How would he be after all this time as a captive? A single candle near the stairs provided the only light as the echo of snores filled the air and my thoughts went spinning round and round. Again, the amulets gave me strength. I held them so tight the pain from them cutting into me distracted me.

We were woken in the middle of the night for the first prayers. We recited them in the empty dark nave of the abbey, with only a few guards standing watch and one lit candle beside us. After prayers, we went in single file back to our rush mattresses for a little more sleep.

The basement was gloomy and cold. I'd mumbled my way through the prayers, hoping no one would notice me, almost forgetting to speak as my mind struggled against sleep. With my hood up, I was just another older choir boy. I kept my hood up even when sleeping. Others did too, though they were probably doing it because of the cold.

We were woken again by a handbell and given hard horse bread, harder cheese, and weak beer in a small hall at the side of the building. Afterwards, we were lined up and walked towards the main part of the abbey.

I remembered Ulf's final words before he left me.

"Keep your hood up all the time."

I did, but still the leader of the choir glared at me as I took my place with the rest of them standing in the far side aisle. Now that it was brighter, I'd been staring at the walls. I'd never seen anything like the painted pillars and walls glistening in the candlelight. Images of Jesus on the cross I recognised, but others I didn't. They were probably saints, as they had golden halos around their heads. It was like being wrapped inside a tapestry, though one of the walls and part of the roof had still not been painted. The choir leader came to me. I was fixed to the spot as he glared at me, unable to move, wondering if he'd reveal me.

"Cause no trouble," he hissed. "You are fortunate to be allowed here. Ulf's word will not help you if you cause problems." A moment later he waved, and the boys and young men around me began to chant. The sanctuary, a little further up the nave, was protected by an elaborately carved wooden screen with an opening in the centre through which I could see a high-backed golden chair in front of the altar. It sparkled in the light from the candles all around it illuminating the beaten gold that sheathed its back and arms to make it seem alive, almost breathing.

Only a few Normans, most in sparkling chain mail, stood in the abbey already. More were constantly arriving. They'd taken their helmets off, some held them under their arms, but they still had their swords and daggers with them. The air was heavy with anticipation and the smell of beeswax and rosemary candles. This was the smell of Normans. Their voices washed over me, rising and falling like waves.

Every row of men had someone with a banner at the end; some had gold embroidery hanging from an elaborate spear, others were of a plain type with stitched emblems, mostly animals but plants, too, and axes and crossed swords, of course. I saw gold embroidered cloaks and stared at the wearers as trumpets blared out, and wondered who they all were.

The young man beside me, he was the same height as me but looked younger, nudged me hard. "We spent five days preparing for this," he whispered. There was a bitter tone in his voice, as if he was angry that I'd joined the choir so late. "Follow my lead. You'd better be as good as we are."

I nodded. This was the moment to dread. Like most people, I knew some chants from church on a Sunday. If you didn't attend church, if you lived in a village like ours, it would quickly be noticed and remarked on. But what chants would they use today?

I was at the end of the second row of the choir with a giant candle in a holder blazing light not far from my shoulder.

Shouts echoed from the direction of the main abbey entrance. Most of the choir looked around. I didn't. I imagined it was a signal for the arrival of the duke, but the shouts died away and were replaced by muttering and the clatter of heavy boots on the wooden floor. I could not help it, I looked around. A figure in black passed up the centre aisle and went through the gate in the screen separating the sanctuary from where we and the rest of the audience stood. I saw a face then. It was Odo. He was following the figure in black. I couldn't breathe for a moment. Would he see me? I'd hoped he'd be in the sanctuary.

Behind him, two other black-clothed men followed. They were wearing thin yellow belts. All these men carried long staffs with either a wooden or a gold-swathed curl at the top, which made those staffs look like two elaborate shepherd's crooks.

I was glad to be in the second row of the choir. I hoped I was out of sight of where Odo had gone in the sanctuary, near the throne where Duke William would receive the crown of England.

The choir began a chant I did not know. I followed along, softly, matching the words of the boy beside me. He stared straight ahead. I realised I was chanting out of step, so I switched to mouthing the words, fearing my voice could be my undoing.

We began a new chant. Shuffling and clanking noises from the end of the abbey echoed. I did not look around.

The next chant, I remembered a few of the words. I sang along with the others and held my hands together in front of me like the rest of the choir. I knew then what they meant when they ask: have you the guts for something? Stopping your stomach twisting with fear is a useful skill.

I almost jumped from my skin when the blare of war horns set all heads turning. Shouts of joy followed. The duke must be here. My heart pounded as the shouts accumulated one on top of the next.

Some of the Normans standing in rows in the main aisle in front of me shuffled, others turned to watch, a few headed towards the entrance of the abbey.

"What's happening?" I asked the boy beside me.

He pointed at the screen. I could see the gold-covered throne and just one black-robed bishop, who was looking down the abbey, but not Odo. I looked around quickly. Was Magnus here? I stood up on my toes, staring over heads.

More shouts echoed from the end of the hall. The feared word *fire* came to me. I stood tall on my toes, looking for smoke. What was going on? Then, like a wave in the sea, most of the people in the abbey started heading for the main door.

Some shouted in panic for others to make way. There was still no smoke or fire visible, but there was a lot of shoving and pushing and shouting.

It appeared that everyone would be gone before any coronation would take place. I held my hands tight to my chest, one hand wrapped over the other fist. I'd spotted someone who might be Magnus.

I stepped back, put my hand on a wooden pillar, and leaned up to get a better view. Perhaps I should go to him?

And then I saw Odo talking to people, calming them, it seemed. A chill of premonition rose inside me. He would see me. There was almost no one between us, and sure enough, with his gaze roving around, he spotted me, and smiled thinly. I looked straight back at him.

He came towards me, his black habit streaming behind him. There would be no escaping. If I tried to run, he'd call out for me to be caught. I would not get far.

I waited for him, made my face into a smile, though I knew he'd be suspicious of how I was dressed.

His face was stiff as he came close, as if he had a lot of other important things on his mind.

"What are you doing here, Synne? And like this?" He looked me up and down, waved his hand at my tunic, then pulled my hood back.

"I'm here to be in the choir," I said innocently. It was true. I straightened, expecting a blow, or worse.

"You mean you came to disturb my brother's coronation, don't you?" His gaze flickered around, then

The Rise of Synne

stopped at someone behind me. He shouted something in Norman.

His fingers grabbed, then squeezed my arm. He shook me, his anger taking hold of him.

"What do you know about the fires that were started in the city this morning?" he asked.

I shook my head. I didn't know anything.

22

Odo shouted something in their tongue at the man he'd summoned. Hands grabbed for me. I twisted. "I know nothing about fires," I shouted, glaring at Odo.

"Stop your lies," he said, shaking his head. He spoke to the men behind me.

I was pushed through the last of the crowd moving out through the front entrance. Almost everyone in the abbey had gone already. I smiled. It was not the coronation they'd hoped for.

Someone had spoiled it.

Smoke was drifting high into the sky. The stench of burning wood hit me. Some houses between the abbey and the city walls were alight. Flames were leaping high. Crowds had gathered too, and a line of people were passing buckets of water from the river. I saw axes raised, their blades hacking into a house near the abbey.

I was unable to see more as I was pushed and then half-carried along the river path heading upstream, and then into a wide meadow beside the path. I feared for my life at that moment. And I hadn't even seen Magnus. I should have kept my head down. What were they planning for me?

The meadow was chock full of horses, all hobbled in long lines with men and boys moving between them, brushing horses down and talking to them as if they were children. In one corner of the field stood giant horses. It looked as if they could jump a river.

Near them, a brazier had been set up by a large, battered leather tent. As I was pushed inside it, a distant cheer made heads turn and even the horses look up. The tent was empty, except for a table at the back. The men with me raised fists in the air and looked at me as if I was dirt on their heels. They were all tall Normans, the backs of their heads shaved high. Some of them began talking fast to each other, and smiling, as if they were preparing for something. I guessed the duke had been crowned.

Two of the guards who'd half-carried me here pushed me towards the back of the tent.

"Why are you dressed like a brother?" one asked. I could smell garlic on his breath.

Another, louder cheer, rang out far in the distance.

"To be in the choir at the coronation." I flung the words at him. If they were going to kill me, let them get it over with.

He turned to the other man. They spoke fast in Norman.

A woman appeared grappling with a barrel. She placed it on a nearby table and opened a plug hole near the bottom after placing an earthen cup below the hole on the ground. She made cups of the ale for the men with me and then started making ale cups for a line of men who'd appeared.

"The celebrations begin," said my guard with a grin. He went to the woman handing out the cups and started talking to her. She spoke to another younger woman who'd arrived, then beckoned me to follow her. My guards followed us, ale cups in their hands. The woman led us along a muddy track behind the tent. It was filled with covered carts. Some were of a type I'd seen before, with wicker sides and a leather roof, others were large four-wheeled wagons of a type I'd never seen. Some were gaily painted in red and blue and had small pennants and little iron bells attached to each corner of the roof.

From inside one such large, covered cart, laughter emerged. The woman knocked on the side of the cart and shouted in Norman. A face appeared at the back of the cart in a gap between the leather sheets hanging from the curved roof. It was a dark-skinned woman's face with a sun emblem painted in gold on her forehead. I'd seen moors like her in the city before, but they were mostly men. The woman looked me up and down and laughed.

She beckoned me to her and when I came closer to speak with her, she pulled me into the cart, yanking me by my tunic with help from another woman behind her.

Inside the cart were three other women, sitting on thin benches at the sides. Some had small pots and brushes in their hands. Two of the women had their breasts out, which the others were painting. My mouth opened. What was Odo up to?

One of the women had her hair in long braids with red ribbons tied into them. Another had long, bone-white hair arrayed around her.

One of them pointed at me and laughed. The woman with the sun on her forehead lifted my tunic up a little at the bottom.

I swiped my hand towards her.

"Stop," she hissed. Her hand was up and in a fist. She had heavy rings on each finger. "The duke's brother has ordered you to be dressed up nice for their big feast tonight. Do not resist. If you do, we'll have to beat you until you whimper for us to stop. We are here for their entertainment. It seems you are to be their entertainment too, though I wasn't told what special tricks you can do." She raised her eyebrows, pinched my side in a swift motion. "What do you do, girl, dressed up like that? You like monks, do you?" She made a kissing motion.

"I am not a whore." I spoke each word slowly and with anger.

Another of the women grabbed the other side of my monk's tunic and started pulling it up. Then a third, larger woman stood in front of me and pushed her face towards mine. She opened her mouth. Her bottom teeth had been sharpened into points.

I let them take off the habit. A man's voice called from outside. The women shouted back, and one of them passed me a thin green tunic with gold embroidery in a swirling pattern of leaves down the front. I put it on quickly, my hands fumbling. It came only to my knees. I tried to pull it down further.

The women laughed. "It is the most modest thing we have," one said.

I stopped pulling at it. At least it had long sleeves and a high neck. Someone grabbed at my hair, tousled it, and rubbed something through it. I looked at her hands. They were oily.

One of the other women started rubbing oil on the legs of a red-headed woman with a stern look on her face. The woman beside me whispered, "There'll be many men wanting to be with her tonight." She ruffled my hair, smiled at me.

The Rise of Synne

"Cheer up, girl," she said. "You are going to the feast of a conqueror." She shouted something in Norman. A replied shout came from outside.

At all this news, a fluttery dread filled my stomach. What were they planning for me? How would I be their entertainment? A woman passed me a wineskin. I drank from it. Whatever was in it burnt sweetly in my throat.

The plucking of a lyre sent laughter through the cart and a moment later, the flap at the end opened and a black-haired musician with his hair pulled back and a pure white painted face – plastered in lily root no doubt – peered in. It was hard to tell if he was a man or a woman. He sang a song in some strange tongue then and gestured at us, and one by one we stepped down from the cart. I had to be pushed. Whistles broke out from some men standing around as we gathered outside.

A line of horses waited. My two guards stood near them. They both glared at me, as if I'd come directly from the lower world.

"Do not try to escape," said the woman behind me, nudging me hard. "They'll only drag you back if you run. There are way too many of their people around for you to escape. Enjoy this celebration, girl, while you still can."

I did not want to enjoy their celebration. This was a grotesque night following a shameful day and it could well mark my end, too. My only hope left was that I might see

Magnus before whatever they were planning for me happened.

The woman with the sun on her forehead pointed at the lead horse. "You take that one. I'll be right behind you." She looked me up and down, stuck her tongue out, licked her upper lip, slowly from side to side and said, with a curious look on her face, "What do they want you for?"

"I don't know. I'm a healer."

She shook her head, laughed. "A healer; that won't save you anyhows. We had a healer with us before. She was a strange one." She widened her eyes. "I hope I don't have to find a place to bury you, too. That would be a terrible waste." She stared at my body, looking me up and down.

Her words filled me with dread. The healer she was talking about had to be the seer who'd died in front of me.

Was that what they had in store for me? A blade?

If Odo wanted someone to blame for the fires that day, they'd have an excuse to do anything they wanted to me. They could blame me for anything.

I stood straight as I went to the horse. Two of the guards come forward to help me mount. I motioned fast for them to stand back. The women behind me hissed in support.

I went up on the horse without any help and kept my head up all the time. One of the women handed me a long, dark cloak. I pulled the cloak around me. It went down almost to my ankles. I still had my muddy boots on. When the cloak was settled, she pulled at one muddy boot, measured it with her hand, then came back a few moments later with soft black fur-lined boots that went halfway to my knees. I patted the horse's neck. His coat was thick, shiny, and clean.

Each of the women had similar long boots and cloaks when we departed. We looked like a troop of rich nuns or the daughters of earls. Each of the women had the hood of their cloak up and over their head. I did the same.

It was a good thing too. The road into the city was full of drunken Normans. They looked as if they'd all downed a barrel of ale each and far too quickly. Some were vomiting, others were laughing hysterically, and others arguing about things I could not make out.

A few men reached toward us, but we had guards on each side also on horses, and when they wielded their vicious-looking clubs, men stepped back. Our guards looked as if they were well used to using clubs to get compliance.

We passed into the city. A stench of burning hung in the air, though I could not see where it came from. The gate was still open with blazing torches above it, even though the sun had recently gone down. A press of Norman guards were checking everyone coming and going. We were allowed in with nods, without being stopped.

We went left up and along the city wall. More torches lit the road and a procession of people moved with us. Shouts echoed in the distance, and then a ragged cheer. We rode into an open square where a crowd was milling about. Excitement filled the air. You could smell it from the people and the lines of torches on poles, each with a helmeted guard by it. The torches ran straight through the centre of the square, allowing riders to move to a large hall on the far side and crowds to gather on each side without blocking the passage. The hall had a row of marble pillars, with blue paint visible on some of them. The tall building had red brick walls, and along its front torches blazed and flickered. It looked as if it had been patched together from something far older.

Some in the crowd turned to us and began shouting, *Long Live the King* and other words I did not understand, as if they thought our arrival heralded the new king. They kept these shouts up as we rode through the centre of the square. At the front of the hall, three steps led up to a polished, double-height oak door. Every time someone went up these steps, the crowd cheered. Some of the people in the square were Normans, men with that strange, distinct hairstyle, but there were others too, Saxons and

Danes. Some of these men pointed and made gestures at us women, but we did not react.

It made my heart sink to see the crowd celebrating. The love of a victor had won the loyalty of some here in London already.

A waning moon rode high above us all, the symbol of change. I wanted to vomit, though I had nothing to bring up.

We rode past the front of the hall. Norman guards stood shoulder-to-shoulder in rows there. They also blocked access to a lane at the side of the building where horses and carts were waiting.

A guard let us through into the lane. On one side, halfway along, a door opened into the hall. A Norman in a clean blue tunic stood at the door shouting orders. Barrels were being carried in as we approached. The woman with the gold sun on her forehead slid down from her horse, bowed to the man, touched his arm, and went inside. We all followed, passing our reins to boys who appeared, with more guards pressing in around us, staring, winking. When I arrived inside the hall, noise and excitement hit me like a slap in the face. I'd never heard such shouting and such jubilant roaring.

The glow from uncountable candles made it seem like we'd been transported to some heaven, a jubilant Valhalla, or some other hall of the gods.

We moved quickly down the side aisle. Servants were running about with plates and cups and piles of bread and platters of food and benches. The smell almost hit me. Roast boar has an unmistakable sweet scent. It made my stomach move.

This feast was different in many ways to the others I'd ever attended or even seen, from the lowest village hall feast to the Godwins' feast after we came back to London.

The men here were louder and a heady air of triumph filled this hall. The Normans were jumping about, dancing, and even hitting each other with their fists and sharing drinking horns and laughing and locking arms around each other.

There were women here too, but mostly as servants, as far as I could see. And there were types of people I'd not seen before – not just moors, but a group of giant redheads with their hair shaved at the back, Norman style, and another group of men with thin pale faces who all looked like brothers or cousins they were so similar to each other, and they all had their heads fully shaved.

There were monks and priests in clean tunics, too, with cropped hair and gold chains and decorated crosses hanging from them.

The celebrations were in full flow. This was their moment. A Norman duke had been crowned King of England. At the top of the hall, a wall of banners on new

The Rise of Synne

pale wood spears stood proudly behind a long, almost empty top table. Some of the banners had blood splatters on them.

We went through a gate in a dark wicker fence blocking access to the back of the hall, beyond the banners. Cooks and servants milled about there. Three hearths in the middle of the floor had boars roasting over them and more boars, already cooked, were standing on spits nearby. Platters of roast swans stood to one side, steaming, and wheels of yellow cheese had been stacked in a corner.

Any hunger in me had been twisted out of me at the thought of what this celebration meant for England, and the river of blood it had taken for them all to be here.

I was also wondering what they had planned for me. What entertainment would I provide?

A table nearby had wicks floating in small cressets providing dim light. The table had wooden bowls strewn about and a few servants were eating rapidly at it. The smell of tallow, boar and sweat prickled my nostrils. The table was commandeered by our guards. We were motioned to sit on the benches.

A moor appeared and spoke to one of our guards. The guard pointed at me, then turned on his heel and left. The moor came to me, glaring as if I'd insulted him. I did not flinch, but it was not easy to hide my expectation of immediate injury or worse.

"Do not try to escape, girl. We will call you when we're ready." The man leaned close to my face. "It will be much worse for you if you run."

I stuck my tongue out at him. I'd got the message.

He laughed, then went to a nearby table and took up his post, watching me. I kept my expression stiff. He'd not struck me. That was a good thing.

Mugs of ale and bowls of glistening stew with hunks of boar meat in it arrived. I sipped a little ale to stop my mouth drying up and lifted a small spoon of stew, but I could not put it in my mouth. My hand would not do it. All I could think about was what was coming for me. I could not even look at the stew. It turned my stomach.

Minstrels started singing in the main hall and then a roar came from beyond the hall and chants in Norman rolled like thunder, as if the saviour had arrived. Everyone scrambled to the two wide doors in the wicker wall. A crowd gathered around each, peering over each other for a glimpse beyond. I went to the back of one of them, the man set to watch me a little behind.

I didn't see the duke coming into the hall, but I did glimpse a corner of a golden crown for a moment, while cheers and chants in the Norman tongue rang out so loud my ears hurt.

I stepped back, went to the table, sat down again. The thumping of booted feet on the floor in the hall made the packed earth beneath me tremble. Some of the lighter rushes on the floor even drifted into the air, as if a spell had been chanted to rouse them.

Then the shouting stopped and a single voice cried out, and then trumpets blared, two or more, and then another voice, louder, more commanding, began speaking in their stupid tongue. From the reverential hush and the sighs and cheers as he spoke, I guessed the duke was speaking.

The speech did not last long. It was followed by more jubilant cheers and the sound of lyres and then a sweet boy's voice singing some strange, chanting song. From the laughter that accompanied it, the song was probably a bawdy homage to their new king.

The women I'd arrived with were all preening, adjusting each other's tunics, exposing a little more flesh, dabbing at lips or eyes. I was offered some of their paints and potions, but I declined. This was not a time for flirting.

"Synne." My name made me swing my head.

Odo was walking towards me wearing a long black tunic with a grotesque gold cross around his neck on a thick gold chain. Where had that come from? Plunder, most likely.

"You look pale, Synne," he said as he came near.

I didn't reply.

"You English have lost this land, Synne. It is time you accepted the truth. We are the future. Listen!" He pointed at the hall beyond the wicker fence. "We've been gifted this entire goldsmith's hall for our first royal celebration in this city and it is alive with joy!"

He leaned down towards me, wide-eyed, gloating. "If the Godwins had only accepted the true heir for the kingship sooner, many lives would have been saved. Perhaps even yours too." He was drunk.

He nodded at a guard watching me, then went to grab my arm. I moved it out of his reach.

"You do not need to lead me," I said.

He pointed at the door in the wicker wall. "Go through it yourself, then."

After I went through the door, a hush spread through the hall, followed by lone shouts. Even the pages moving about stopped and stared at me. I held myself firm, determined not to show fear. The main table, to my left, was filled with Normans now, all in high spirits as if they'd just finished appreciating some joke. Their faces were ugly, each man drunk and capable of turning on anyone in a moment and gutting you if you said the wrong thing or looked at him the wrong way. I kept my chin up.

A dagger landed with a deep thud on the table at the end nearest me. The man beside it grabbed it and spun it into the air again as he studied me with a slight smile, as if a game he'd been waiting for had just begun. Without looking down, he put his hand where the blade had dropped before. The knife tip landed with a thud between his fingers. A ragged cheer went up. The man stuck his tongue out at me, waggled it. The air was hot and thick with the odour of men, meat, and ale.

I looked along the top table. It was strewn with gold goblets and plates. It looked as if a treasury had recently been broken open and spilt onto it.

From behind the table, near the centre, the new king glared at me while a man bent down beside him, whispering in his ear. Behind them, two guards in red mail coats stood with their hands by the pommels of their swords, ready to defend the new king.

The king said something I was too far away to catch. His words were repeated, shouted by others at the top table. They spread around the room until the whole crowd took them up in a drunken, wild chant. I had no idea what they were shouting about, but I suspected it was about me. A twitch of fear ran through me.

Be iron-strong, my mother's words came back to me. I whispered them.

Odo went in front of the main table. He motioned to me, flapping with his fingers for me to approach him.

I did.

He put a hand on my shoulder and turned me to the new king. Everything was happening too fast.

"What are they saying about me?" I asked, my voice stronger than I'd expected.

"They say the games must begin." He pointed at a spot near the front table, just a few steps from it, directly in front of the king. "Kneel, there."

Time slowed as I went forward. I remembered blood, faces, my dreams. I heard a distant caw. The bird that flies too high disappears; isn't that what they say?

My toe hit something. I looked down. A broken shield lay on the floor in front of me. Beside it lay a torn banner and parts of another shield. The shields had been hacked apart. The remnants showed white martlets, the bird that never stops flying, the symbol of Saxon and English kings. If anyone had predicted this a year ago in London, they could have been hanged for sedition.

The line of English and Saxon kings we'd all believed in was broken, its emblems scorned.

I stared at the new king, willing my gaze to harm him, but all he did was laugh and turn to his companions. Odo went to the table, leaned over it, spoke to his brother, then came back to me, unsteadily. He stood in front of me.

"Kneel," he said, growling with disdain.

I glared at him.

He grabbed my shoulder, pushed me down. I resisted. He pushed me harder. My knees buckled and struck the packed rushes, but I kept my chin up. Be iron-strong.

Odo was behind me. The crowd had hushed. Everyone was expecting some entertainment. I took a deep breath, held it, no longer trembling, just waiting, breathing loud.

Soon it would be over.

Something dripped onto my head and slowly down my face. I touched my cheek, looked at my wet fingers. They were wet with oil.

"Stay still, healer," he said, then he murmured something in Latin. The words felt like a threat.

His hands pressed hard into my shoulders and more oil dripped onto my hair. I shook my head. He spoke again in his chirping Latin.

Then he whispered in my ear, "You may wish to pray."

My neck muscles tightened, as if a spell had been cast on me. What would bring an end to all this?

I stuck my chin forward.

"Traiteresse," he shouted. Other voices echoed the word.

It'll be over soon. I'll be with you, Mother, and with you, Stefan, too. The people I love and miss most. My breath rasped.

"Synne," a familiar voice shouted from behind. I half turned. At a table not far away sat Magnus.

My heart thumped, not once, but repeatedly, and hard against my ribs. He was leaning forward, his face straining, pale. He said my name again, narrowed his eyes, frowned. He was trying to tell me something.

Odo whispered in my ear, "Your liege, Magnus, son of Harold, is here."

I could feel many eyes on me and hear shouts and laughter. A chorus of female voices shouted, "Traiteresse." The women I'd come with were making their allegiance known. A wave of hatred poured over me.

From somewhere, I heard my mother's voice. "You must fulfil the prophecy."

Odo bent down, put his face near me. "Stand up."

I came to my feet. Magnus was by his table. Two guards were blocking him. A deep surge of longing rose inside me. I wanted to go to him. He was so near, so close.

Odo took my arm. "Now you will learn your fate."

I had an urge to grab a knife, stab him. I glanced along the top table. No knife was within easy reach.

The noise in the hall grew rowdier. The women I'd arrived with were dancing wildly, tunics half off their shoulders, breasts visible, bawdy shouts and lustful jeering following every move.

The new king pounded his table with a gold goblet, laughing at it all. His eyes glittered, reflecting light from the beeswax candles on the tables. He looked me up and down, assessing me as if I was a swan ready to be plucked. He said something dismissive I didn't catch, raised a hand, pointed down the room and waved, signalling someone to come forward. The smell of sweet and honeyed ale and old sweat filled my nostrils.

Under my breath, I spoke the fate-twisting charm I'd learned from my mother, hoping that something immediate could happen to him, though I knew charms don't work that way.

Odo had a wild look in his eyes I did not like. Beer residue had gathered around his mouth. I blinked. I'd spotted Catheryn coming towards us in the passage between the tables. Why was she here?

For a stupid moment, I thought she'd come forward to help me, that she'd set aside our differences. She carried a wicker basket in front of her. What was she carrying?

Odo held my arm.

The king shouted something. The room hushed, except for a creaking noise as men stood to see what Catheryn would do.

Her gaze met mine. Her mouth twisted into a half-smile. She put the wicker basket down about ten paces from us, undid the straps holding it together, and pushed the sides of the basket apart so that all could see what was inside.

I'd guessed already what was in it. But the sight still made me gasp. A head, the Dane's head, his eyes oozing bloody sockets.

"Traiteresse, traiteresse, traiteresse." The crowd took up the call.

Odo's hand gripped me as I stared at the Dane's head, a mixture of disgust and fear making my breathing falter.

"See what happens to traitors," he whispered in an excited tone.

"Give your witness now, Catheryn," Odo shouted.

Catheryn nodded. Her gaze, wide-eyed, enraptured, was on the new king. I looked at her, wondering what bile was going to come out of her mouth.

"I speak true witness. This healer, Synne, who I see with you, is involved with the traitors who set the fires today that disturbed your coronation. I speak the truth. She is a traitor."

"Liar," I shouted at the top of my voice, my neck straining. I put my free hand up in front of me, made a shaking fist of it.

Catheryn screamed back, her face contorting with her words. "I am no liar. This Dane told us all about you before he met his end. There are other witnesses too, traitor Synne." She laughed madly, as if she'd told the best joke ever. Others laughed with her as if it was clear to all that she spoke the truth.

I shook at Odo's hand holding me. "Let me go to her." I looked up into his face. He released me.

She cocked her head as I approached, an odd smile on her face, as if she'd been waiting for this.

A dagger had appeared in her hand.

An angry-icy feeling rose inside me. So, this was her plan.

"I claim the right of holmgang," Catheryn shouted, turning so that all in the hall could see her, her dagger high, its blade bright.

Men cheered wildly, welcoming this, as if they'd expected it. People crowded forward. Smoke from the hearths swirled in the air above us all, tongues of it reaching down to us. My breathing sped up. All sounds seemed too loud. I could taste blood on my lips. I knew not where it came from.

Holmgang, the ancient law of challenge, used to be a right at Yule time under the old Dane laws. I'd only heard about it being used once by women, to settle a dispute over a lover a long time ago.

Dane law had stopped years before too. But what laws applied now? The new king could make the laws whatever he wanted. And if I refused, my guilt would be assumed and my punishment for being a traitor dealt out, without any chance to give my side. But if I won, my innocence would be proved by God's decision to save me.

Shouts rolled over us. "Holmgang, holmgang, holmgang."

A dagger landed with a shuddering thud point down in the rushes in front of me – the dagger the man at the king's table had been playing with. It glistened, its point embedded deep in the hard-packed earth.

Picking up the dagger would signal I'd accepted the challenge.

Mocking laughter rolled around at my hesitation. It grew.

I had to pick it up.

I yanked the blade from the dirt. A great cheer followed. A ring of soot had been thrown on the ground already, I noticed. An area a little more than the width of our combined arms outstretched was where my fate would be decided.

More wild cheers went up as four men in dull chain mail shirts took their places around us, to push us back into the fight, should we be tempted to run.

Catheryn was up on her toes already, delighted, revelling in all the cheers. A deep, long shiver ran all the way through me. My last moments might well be coming.

But there was hope. We'd been jumped by thieves many times, Stefan and I, and I'd had to fight back with

The Rise of Synne

my knife. Every fight had ended with grappling and bleeding and the thought afterwards that I'd been lucky. Stefan had taught me well. We'd practised many times.

I would not be afraid. My mother's power was in me. And I wanted vengeance. Catheryn deserved to be cut down.

"Look," Catheryn shouted. "The traitor will not fight." She turned her back on me, then spun around, as if she'd expected me to run at her.

I stood, unmoving, my dagger down by my side.

"Fight, fight, fight." The fighting chant rolled over us, loud and insistent, making me blink as sweat bloomed on my forehead.

All this excitement had pulled many spectators around us, faces wide-eyed with expectation, excitement, and bloodlust.

A Woden drum began a steady beat, timed to our hearts, picking up as each moment passed.

We circled.

I followed her. She followed me. The king and Odo were whispering to each other, their faces animated. I saw Magnus, both his fists up, willing me on.

Catheryn came at me.

Her knife was high, swinging. On me in a heartbeat.

I raised an arm to take her blow, so I could swing my knife inside, wound or disable her, even if it meant a cut to my arm.

The moment slowed, then sped up.

Catheryn had stepped to the side.

I stepped to the other side, held my knife pointed down towards the earth in a gesture of appeasement, giving her an opportunity to do the same.

Groans went up as people saw my gesture. They wanted blood.

Catheryn's eyes, which had blazed with hate, softened. Her hand also dropped.

She sprang at me.

A gasp and laughter came from the crowd.

I leaned back, fast. She missed me, stuck her tongue out at me and waggled it; or was that for the new king behind me?

"You want him," I hissed. Her eyes were on me. She smiled, glanced over my shoulder, then swung again.

I slouched to the side, her glittering blade slicing death through the air near me. I remembered my brother's words: go under.

I dropped, risked everything, rolled awkwardly towards her feet, swinging my arms and legs. I felt the air move around my cheek as her blade passed whisker-close to me. Then I banged into her legs.

She staggered.

I took my chance, grabbed at her knee. She fell back, her knife swinging. I pushed at her again with both hands. She twisted and fell. I scrabbled forward like a spider, placed my blade near her swan-like throat, my body pinning down her knife hand. She could not move it.

Her skin glowed with sweat no more than a hand's breadth from my eyes, fury blazing from her eyes.

Veins moved in her neck. I had one chance.

That was the way of things.

"You'll not escape your fate," she hissed.

She shifted fast, desperate, her free hand grabbing at my knife hand. We turned. She came up over me.

"I'll walk from here with two heads."

The shouting ceased. Her knife hung above me. Each of our knife hands was held by the other's hand. Wind howled across the roof like a Valkyrie's shriek.

She twisted her arm. Her knife came free, plunged. I shifted, but felt the cold bite of metal in my side. Pain swept through me. I did not care. I heard Stefan's voice, *"When they think they have won, their guard goes down."*

I shook my hand free like a snake writhing and slashed my blade across her gleaming, beating neck above me. It went too easily into her creamy skin, blooming a line of red behind it, as the iron-thick smell of blood came and I twisted away from her as her blood fell in a red shower.

Relief blossomed inside me. I pulled my blade back, and watched, engrossed as she fell, gasping, an accusing, terrified look in her eyes as she stared into me.

The room erupted.

A new red mouth was gaping wide across her throat. Her hand went to it, as if she might stop the blood pumping thick and flowing shiny through her fingers. Her other hand flayed, trying to cut me, but I was on her other side. Then her hand flopped, her eyes dimmed, and her head fell back onto the packed dirt floor.

Hands pulled me straight up.

I'd won. My innocence was proved.

My body stiffened, every muscle taut, my heart beating wildly, my mouth ashy, my breathing fast, a wild trembling coming and going as they put me onto my feet. Shouts filled the air, an exultation of bloodlust.

Drums beat. My head spun.

It felt as if I'd drunk too much from the wrong wine sack. I revelled in the giddy pleasure of victory, the killing of someone who had wanted to kill you. It felt good.

Hands pushed me towards the top table. Servants were moving about already, carrying platters, as if they'd been waiting for us to finish. Grizzled boars' heads steamed, roast swans glowed strangely, and sweating pots of buttered leeks, beans, and onions moved around.

The stink of it all made me want to vomit.

Something warm and wet touched my leg. Blood. My blood. Someone pushed at my tunic to see the wound. I slapped at the hand.

Magnus's face was in mine. I gripped his hand so tight he winced.

"I pray leave, Your Majesty, to take the victor where her wound can be bound," Magnus shouted, his eyes on me. "Her truthfulness has been proven by combat."

The king looked away. A minstrel had started singing. The dancers were dancing again. It felt wrong that a fight and a death had come and gone as if it was all just a song for their entertainment. I sighed. But I was alive.

Odo came towards us and pointed at me. "The woman you defeated, healer, was going to recite a Saxon blessing for the new king. I did not want this." He sounded angry as he waved towards where the fight had taken place. "As the winner of the challenge, you must do it instead."

Was this another of his tricks?

He frowned. "You know such a blessing, don't you? All healers in this country get taught such blessings. That is what I've been told. You have won your freedom by your victory," he said. "We will keep to your old Dane laws. But Magnus is not free." He waved at some guards nearby to come closer.

He had more tricks.

He looked around, as if looking for someone. "I hear there's a hog farm near here where we can dispose of traitor's bodies. It is where they will take Magnus if you refuse." He said the last part slowly.

I kept my face still. Had someone told him that having the winner of a holmgang either bless or curse you gave the words power, as you'd been favoured by God?

Magnus looked as if he was about to start a fight, his face red, almost exploding. He would not get out of here alive if he did try something.

"You will let us both go if I do this?"

Odo put his hands up. "Yes, yes, we will, but if we ever hear of either of you taking part in any sedition against your new king, you will be dealt with harshly as traitors."

Magnus shook his head. "You don't have to do this," he said looking at me.

"You're a brave man," said Odo. "I'll enjoy seeing you broken."

"I'll do it," I said. "Come, let's do it now."

Odo put his hands up and walked to the top table. He banged a gold plate hard against the wood until people stopped talking and the minstrels stopped playing. Then he

The Rise of Synne

shouted in their Norman tongue and even the new king sat up straighter.

He motioned me forward. Shouts echoed as I stood in front of King William. I wanted this all over quickly. I wanted away from this place.

Odo banged the plate again on the table and slowly quiet descended until all I could hear was cawing. It sounded as if a blackbird was with us in the hall.

Odo made a bowing gesture for me to start. I paused. This was definitely more than what my mother had meant when she'd said I might find this spell useful. I hummed, then said the words, loud and clear in our English tongue. As I spoke, it felt as if a giant had entered the room silently and was breathing over me.

"Through earth and stars, hearts and souls,
Through the bonds of the eternal and all that is holy,
Bless this celebration."

I paused, closed my eyes, added loudly,
"Bless this King,
In the name of God, and of his Kingdom."

Odo clapped and in a moment the rest of the hall was clapping too.

I felt guilty that they'd persuaded me to do this, but hopeful too that we'd be both free, at last. Magnus stepped forward, looked at Odo, who nodded, briefly, and Magnus put his arms under me and picked me up.

"I can walk," I said as loud as I could manage. I was still shaking inside, the reality of what I'd done, all that had happened, memories of the fight coming back to me, each moment vivid in my mind and then the strange feeling of a giant entering as I'd recited the blessing.

Magnus put me down. We walked down the centre of the hall. I felt something moving, realised the amulets around my neck were now outside my tunic. They must have come free in the fight. I pushed them away. The men at every table were banging the butt ends of their daggers and stamping their feet so that a rolling noise followed as we passed down the hall, shaking into my bones. Many of the men had froths of beer on their faces. Others swayed, their eyes drunk and glistening. Some had their fists up, recognising my victory. One man smiled at me, showing his broken teeth, then made a licking gesture with a giant tongue. The men around him laughed and pointed at me.

I held my hand tight to my cut to slow the bleeding, then glanced back up the hall for the last time. The women I'd come with were at the front, dancing wildly. I put my other hand out to steady myself against a table. Magnus put an arm around me. I pushed his arm away.

"Don't be stupid, Synne. You're wounded. You need help."

I let him put his arm around me and hold me. I could feel my blood slipping down my side.

That is how I left the Yule feast of the new King of England, after blessing him on the night he was crowned. I'd arrived in fear, but I had survived. I'd dealt death and almost died, and my fate still lay before me, its thread stronger now than ever.

23

We walked slowly towards wolf skull hall. I didn't want Magnus to think I'd be a burden, so I pushed his arm away soon after we left the hall behind. I winced at each step but tried not to show it. He stopped me, looked at the cut, and assured me I'd be unlikely to die from it. He tied a strip from my tunic tight around my belly to slow the bleeding. It felt as if there was danger in the air, so we kept moving. Young men were running about drunk. Looking weak would not be a good idea. We passed houses that had been ransacked. Some were burning fiercely, warming us as we passed them. Magnus asked me how I'd ended up at the feast. I explained everything. He told me he'd heard Danes were looking for me. After all that had happened, I did not care. What we should do next was the problem.

After crossing a bridge at an overflowing stream, we saw a cart heading downriver. After some discussion, the woman driving it agreed to take us in her empty cart. It was a relief to lie in the back and press a cloth she gave me

The Rise of Synne

onto my wound, the bite of it painful still. When we finally reached wolf skull hall, the old woman who minded the kitchens wrapped a new bandage tight around me with a honey salve over the wound. The pain eased slowly.

"You're lucky," she said. "'Tis only a graze." Then she leaned close. "Be careful with Magnus," she whispered, then shook her head and went back to her kitchen.

I knew what she meant; orphan healers and the sons of kings are not meant for each other.

***

I slept for half of the following day on a thick bed of rushes beside Magnus's bed, dreams of the fight recurring as I slept, sometimes ending with Catheryn winning. Every single moment repeated inside me, every cut and thrust and knowing how close to winning she came until it all dulled, as if thinking about it forced the memories away. My victory tasted like dust when I thought about the blessing I'd given the new king, and how it would be spoken about. Guilt came too as I remembered my craving for vengeance. I had to walk around inside the hall to loosen these thoughts and to remember that I'd be cold already if I'd not cut Catheryn's throat when I did.

What of Magnus? He went missing all the next day, though the old kitchen woman fussed around me as if she knew I would be let down by him. But he returned late that night. I'd eaten only a little. The first thing he did was get a large bowl of stew from the kitchen woman for himself. I shook inside with relief that he'd not abandoned me, but I breathed deep to calm myself. I could not show him my fears.

He sat at the table in the hall and pushed the food into himself. I sat opposite him, my side bound tight, my body stiff to avoid pain. I wanted to know what he'd been up to. The hall was empty. No guard stood at the barred door, and no one had knocked that day. My wound prickled with a burning cut sensation.

"We leave tonight," said Magnus between spoons of stew, his eyes darting around as if he thought spies hid in the shadows.

"Tonight?"

"The new king has decided what parts of this city will be his, and this whole place" – he pointed around angrily with his spoon – "he has claimed as the spoils of war. He wants to build a tower here. He claims this is part of my father's estates, which are all forfeit to him."

"Where will you go?"

He put his spoon down. "Where will we go." He gave me a hard look. "You will come with me."

"I don't have to." I shook my head.

The Rise of Synne

"You do. There is a story going around that you used witchcraft to win the fight because you're the daughter of a seer. That's why they asked you to do the blessing. Everyone knows this."

"So what!"

He laughed. "They say you're possessed by seven demons. Is that true?"

I growled at him and made a demon face. He looked good, strong, his eyes on me, staring.

"You'll be torn apart by a mob if you stay here, Synne. Everyone will be against you. You'll be the scapegoat. We cannot stay here." He said the last part with his hands up and shaking in the air.

"You're not bound to help me," I said. I had to know where all this was going. I could not stand to have him close, to go with him and lose him. This was the moment my dreams must come true or shatter.

"I'll go south, find Stefan's resting place, and pray for his soul, as I should have done two moons ago. They won't have heard of me there." I'd assumed that Magnus not pressing me to sleep in his bed meant he had no plans for me except as his healer or someone to save and discard.

He put his hands up. "Synne, it's too dangerous to go south. The Normans control all the roads from here to the coast. They kill anyone they wish to. As a son of Harold, I'd end up as sport for them."

"You don't have to come with me." I stuck my chin out. "Tell me where I can find Stefan's resting place, as was promised to me, and I'll find my own way."

One part of me wanted him to press on with his talk of going with me, but another part told me not to be so stupid, that someone like Magnus could not want me. He'd done his duty bringing me here, helping me recover from my wound.

He took a swig from his ale cup, then fumbled in the purse on his belt. My heart clenched. He was going to give me a few coins and wish me well. I would not take his charity. I would take no coin from him. I would throw any on the floor. Anger rose like a flame inside me.

He held his fist out towards me.

I could not even look at whatever coin he wanted to give. I could not look him in the face. Something soft, all hope, was being crushed inside me. I would miss him, sorely, but it was better to get this over with quickly. I shook my head, stood, pushed down hard on a burst of emotion.

"Synne," he shouted.

I shook my head. I would not take any of his coins.

"Listen, this is my grandmother's ring. I am offering it to you as a token of my…" He hesitated, then his words came in a hoarse rush. "My prayers to God, that you will be my woman, forever, that we will marry." He smiled.

My chest filled up. I blinked. Something prickled at my eyes. A heavy gold ring with an emblem on it lay glowing in his palm. The emblem had the wavy lines of the fire rune on it. My mouth opened. Fire connected us. This was meant to be. I blinked fast, warmth spreading all through me. I pressed my lips together to keep my strength. Don't let this be a dream.

I opened my mouth. No words came out. He walked around the table and went down on one knee.

"Be mine, Synne." It was almost a command.

I shook my head. This was impossible. "No, no, I am an orphan, without family or land. You cannot want me. Stop." This could not happen. Why was he playing with me?

He moved closer.

His presence felt like a hot breath over my skin. A slow pounding began in my chest. A tingle followed and spread through me. I turned my head, tried to push thoughts of him away, how much I was drawn to him, my body to his. How I wanted him, completely.

"I'll be a dangerous outlaw soon," he said with a half laugh. "I'm probably in an even worse position than you, Synne."

He pushed his hand close to me with the ring staring up at me. It felt as if I was about to be caught in his web.

But I could not stop myself.

I picked up the ring, examined it. It had a carving at the front.

"What is that symbol?" I tried to sound normal, but my voice had a crack in it.

"It's the mark of my grandmother's family."

"The bead the seer gave me has almost the same dragon on it." The bead connected us. "My mother said the dragon symbol was used for healing, that it brings good things."

"For my family it's a symbol of protection," he said. "The dragons sleep underground until they are needed."

"How do we rouse them?"

His body was too close.

A hand's width separated our faces.

I could smell him, warm and sweet like hot honeyed wine. Was this really happening? I waited, the moment dragging on, sweet torture, our faces close, closer, our breathing loud. His lips too near. Every part of me wanted him. We must not pull away.

He kissed me, fast, hard, his tongue alive.

I responded strongly. I was untouched for so long. His lips sent waves through my body, straight to my groin.

I dropped his ring on the table. Our bodies locked together, his mouth pressing, urgent. The hall was dark, empty, thank the gods. The pain from my cut dulled in that moment, but I knew I had to be careful. I pointed at my side. He nodded.

But I needed him. I'd been strong for so long.

He pushed his fingers through my hair, reached under my tunic, ran his hands up my bare legs, a silky tremble on my skin following his fingers. He growled, pressed against me, warm, hard. A surge of want rose inside me. Soon we were on the floor among the rushes, his hands all over me, soft, firm, touching every part of me.

***

Afterwards, I asked him what his plan was now he'd got what he'd wanted.

"Do not doubt me," he said angrily. "My promise is real. We leave at dawn." He coughed. "But there is something I haven't told you."

"What?" This was it. This was the moment he'd tell me about someone else. An icy pit opened inside me. I stared at him, waiting for the bad news.

"Catheryn has family here in this city. They've sworn revenge on you." He stopped.

I was concerned, but relieved too, that the news was not worse.

He gripped my wrist. "We must go soon. Are you ready to come with me?"

He was angry; perhaps he'd expected me to plead for protection. I wouldn't. He let my wrist go, shook his head. "You're a strange one, Synne, you're not like any other woman I've known."

I was not sure if that was a good thing or bad. We looked at each other in silence, listening to the seagulls.

"Where will we go?"

"To a land where there are no Normans, somewhere we can rebuild our lives and make plans to return some day."

"We'll need a full purse for that." I had to say it. Our plans would have to be very different if we were beggars.

He beckoned me to follow him. We went to the back of the hall and into the kitchen hut. The old woman was sleeping in a corner. He woke her with a gentle nudge, then pointed at the hearth, made a digging motion.

"Aye, so you're leaving us, my lord. Leaving the land of your father," said the woman.

"We'll be back," he said, pride in his voice. Then he hugged her. "This hall will be taken by the bastard soon. Ask the woman in the hog farm behind for work," he said. "She'll help you. And I have something for you."

He took a big iron ladle from where it hung on the wall and began moving the still-hot ashes from the hearth. I knew what this meant. So did the woman.

The Rise of Synne

"I'll watch for visitors," she said. Then she bowed slightly to me. "I wish you well, healer." Her voice softened to a whisper. "You have my prayers. You may need them."

She went out, leaving us. I still wasn't sure about Magnus, and her words made me wary.

"You have Hilda's blessing, Synne. She helped raise me, so that makes me happy." He raised his fist. He was oblivious to the note of caution in Hilda's voice.

"Your mother and the rest of your family will not bless us so easy." This was a problem he hadn't considered.

"They'll be happy to see me free and alive. Everything is changing here, Synne. They cannot stop us." He looked serious now. "What about the amulets around your neck. Where did you get them?"

What had my amulets got to do with anything? "My father gave them to use. He gave each of his children one. I kept Stefan's, after he was cut down."

Magnus smiled, nodded. "I thought as much. Amulets like yours are given to the offspring of kings in Zeeland and Scania and the other north kingdoms, Synne. They are meant to protect offspring of royal blood."

My hand touched the amulets through my tunic. Was he right? Had our bloodline been hidden from us?

"My grandmother knew all about such things. She was royal blood and had a similar amulet. She would have liked you, your spirit," he said.

My mouth hung open. This would explain a lot. I felt strange, as if something had moved above us, as if a great bird had passed over us. Was my father more than what we'd been told? Was there a reason we hadn't been told this? Was this why Danes were searching for me? No. It couldn't be.

Laughter burst out of me. "My mother would have told us if my father had such a bloodline." Then something came to me. Was this why she'd not allowed any of us to marry a local boy from the village, always telling us we were meant for better, no matter how any of us pleaded?

"They wanted to keep you all secret, Synne. That has to be the reason." He grinned. "Perhaps your father had a brother or uncle who wanted his father's throne."

Our mother had also warned us not to talk about our father when we met people. I'd always wondered why, but she'd firmly hushed any of us who asked. That was when it dawned on me why Magnus felt able to marry me, and why I could accept.

As I stared at him, taking all this in, Magnus began moving the ashes fast until only the hearthstone remained. He cut into the earth around it with a blade, then put water on everything to make sure it was cool, and finally, after

The Rise of Synne

the hissing was over, he pushed one end of the ladle under the stone at a corner and tried to lift it with one hand, his other still not fully able to lift such weight. The stone didn't budge. I helped him. Slowly, with plenty of grunting, we got that end up a hand's width.

"Look, see the bag," he said. "Pull it out."

I peered into the gloom under the hearthstone, saw a dirt-encrusted leather bag, scorched black. It looked empty. Had someone else been here? I pulled it out. Under it was another bag. It was heavy. He balanced the hearthstone on its end, and we dragged the bag free. We lowered the hearthstone back with a scattering of dust and went to the hall with the bag held between us. It was that heavy.

"We'll have enough for a new life," he said as we sat at the nearest table. "We can find your brother's resting place in the future, when there's no hue and cry for us."

I would have preferred to visit Stefan's grave sooner, but I knew what he would have said: *"Enjoy your dreams, while you can."*

I had other things to think about, too. Not just what happened to me, but about my sisters. I had to find them, help them, tell them what Magnus had said about our bloodline. Now I knew where they probably were, I could find them. My mother had wanted us to live free, always. Magnus could help us. He had to.

"Where did all this gold come from?" I asked, looking inside the bag.

"My father buried it when he became king. We cannot leave it for the Normans to find."

"I have to find my sisters," I said. He had to know. I was beside him on the bench, the bag on the table between us.

"Will you help?" If he refused, it would tell me a lot about him.

"I will. I swear." He put his hands up in submission. "And I'll buy their freedom if we find them."

He smiled, put a hand out towards me. This was what I wanted to hear. His words felt real. I took his hand. We stayed like that for a long moment. This was good, right, all that I'd longed for. The dream I'd wished for, the prophecy fulfilled.

Hilda appeared behind him, coughing. Magnus gave her three gold coins. She hugged him, then went away.

I peered into the bag again. There were enough gold coins in it to start many new lives. There was also a golden hunting horn in it with deep carvings all around it.

"The Normans will want all this." I nodded towards the bag.

"We'll be long gone before they get here," he said. He went to the front door of the hall, unbarred it, and looked out. I went with him. A sliver of moon gave the only light.

The Rise of Synne

The river glistened, broad and shiny, like a giant black snake. No boats passed along it.

He barred the door again. "Let's get some sleep. We'll move quick once we get the signal."

I was excited more than exhausted, so I could not sleep with so many thoughts about all that had happened, his promises, my bloodline, all of it spinning inside me. I also wondered, with a sinking feeling, if all this would be taken from me. I prayed with my eyes tight shut that it wouldn't. I held the amulets, as I did every night now. Magnus kept getting up, pacing back and forth, and going to the front door again and again to listen and look through a crack in the edge of the door.

I woke to the sound of urgent banging. I rose fast, my heart thumping in my mouth, put on my shoes. If the Normans had come, we had no hope of hiding the gold. I put my hand on the bag, tried to lift it. I would not get far with it.

"Synne, where are you?" a voice called. A familiar voice.

I ran to the curtain. It was only half-closed. I looked down the gloomy hall. Someone in a monk's habit was coming towards me.

Ulf. I could have kissed him.

"Be quick," he shouted. "The slave trader's ship has docked. It'll not wait when they see I've been followed." He screamed those last words.

Magnus was behind him. "Ulf, help me, come." They ran to the back to get the gold.

I grabbed my cloak, pushed on the ring he'd given me – it fitted my finger tightly – grabbed my purse and was ready to go in a few moments. I followed them to the door. Magnus and Ulf ran with the leather bag between them. I spotted movement down the road far in the distance, men walking towards us, axes in their hands. They were not Normans. Shouts rang out as they spotted us. They began running.

They looked like Danes, like the men I'd seen take my mother's life.

But how? I raced after Magnus and Ulf.

Docked at the short wooden quay on the far side of the road was a longboat with a high curled prow. Its sail was furled, but it bobbed in the flow of the river. Its gangplank had two men with cudgels at it. They waved at us to come quick.

We ran up the gangplank. It bounced under us. Magnus half slipped. I pushed him forward. We all fell into the bottom of the ship together and the gangplank landed on top of us a moment later. I was panting. The ship rolled as the ropes holding it were cut and we pushed away and

The Rise of Synne

swung viciously to the point I was sure the ship would turn over and we were heading for the dark cold water. Then the river took us.

Thuds sounded. We rocked.

More thuds. Shields were being held up by the crew members. Magnus held one up over the two of us. I looked over him and then over myself. No arrow had hit us. We were alive and the ship was away from the dock and rocking and twisting so much I thought I'd vomit now. Dirty water slid up the inside of the vessel and it creaked loudly as if it would break.

I heard arrows hissing into the water behind us.

"Can you help him?" Magnus shouted a few moments later, after no more arrows came. He pointed behind me.

One of the crew was lying with his head back and an arrow in his neck, the arrow twitching as he breathed.

I scrambled towards him, going from side to side. When I reached him, I could see that he would die soon. Deep red blood was spurting out from around the arrow, which had gone almost through his neck. I could see its point bulging inside his skin. His gurgles were slow too and his eyelids flickering. My fists shook with rage at the Danes. We'd escaped, Magnus with me, but they'd murdered this man. A surge of guilt that he'd died for us, because of us, made me bend my head as I held his hand in his last moments. There was a final twitch, then his hand went limp.

The Danes had been looking for me. It all made more sense now, but what Magnus had said made me wonder if they'd ever give up, and what they really wanted from me.

I looked back at the shore, relieved we'd escaped. The dock was well behind us. The men on it walking away.

Two of the crew picked up the body of the dead sailor. A loud splash and grunted prayers followed.

No one asked what was in the bag we'd carried aboard. Soon after, we sat in the stern, under a leather tent-like cover. The sun was well up and crimson clouds drifted on the horizon out to sea as we followed the wide bends of the river. On the far side, smoke was already rising from the few low houses along the shore. Seagulls wheeled in packs, cawing. Exhilaration filled me like powerful ale. We'd survived. Our escape would be reported, but we had a chance to get away, and not as paupers either, and I was with Magnus, and we could marry. I had hope of rescuing my sisters. It had all been hard won, but it was real.

Magnus put his hand on my thigh as we headed downriver. "The Normans will be glad I've made an outlaw of myself. It'll allow them to put a price on my head."

"Someone has a price on my head, too."

He nodded. "Perhaps they'll make a song about you that'll keep the tavern bards busy."

"They don't make songs about seers winning fights." I stopped. Catheryn's death was not something I would ever be proud of.

He stroked my thigh.

"Do not blame yourself for Catheryn's death," he said.

Was he a mind reader?

"She was going to kill you. You were lucky to defeat her."

"I had help," I said slowly.

"What help?"

I took the bead I'd been given out of my purse and showed it to him. "The dragon helped me." I held the bead to the sun. It sparkled crimson inside if you held it the right way. Otherwise, it just looked like a dull stone.

He smiled. "What else can this dragon do?"

"It can help me find my sisters."

Before You Go!

Please do **write a reader review on Amazon for this book.**

Reader reviews are more important than ever.

Thank you very much if you can.

https://www.amazon.com/Rise-Synne-LP-OBryan-ebook/dp/B0CVQJDZ13

And look out for the three novels in this series!

Thank you!

Book Two in this Series is Now Available...

Read the first few pages here now.

The Power of

Synne

LP O'Bryan

1

"I'm off to see the king," Magnus shouted. He was at the door already.

"I'll join you," I replied from the other side of the hall, where I'd been checking some herbs hanging from the roof.

"I won't be long, stay here. You need to get on with your preparations," he shouted back.

I should have gone with him, but he blew me a kiss and gave me a big smile and I fell for it.

I was also in no mood for dealing with the King of Dublin. He enjoyed keeping visitors waiting and always answered questions with another question.

I thought little more about him until that afternoon, when I found myself listening to the sounds from the street, wondering what was taking Magnus so long. Was the king showing even more disrespect than usual?

That was when I heard a street urchin shout something about me I couldn't quite make out as he passed

The Rise of Synne

by. Some of them called me the-seer-that-blessed-the-Normans, but his words, except my name, were lost in the shouts of the hawkers along our street, so I went back to the list of preparations I'd been obsessing over.

I loved one gift I'd been given, a blue silk ribbon I'd wear in my hair on the big day. The way it slipped through my fingers reminded me of water and how everything was changing, flowing fast. We didn't have ribbons like this when I was growing up, but I'd heard about them, and I'd always hoped that on my wedding day I'd have one. And now, my dream was coming true.

Or was it? I had a lot of doubts, because we going ahead without either of our families present.

But perhaps I was worrying too much? Perhaps I should just be happy. What I'd known was impossible, was happening to me. That should be enough. Right?

It had been a long year since we'd escaped from London. The good part was that the hall we were living in was one of the best in Dublin. We had servants, and guards, and a well for water just outside our front door. Some other parts we'd get to.

Our wedding would be the best thing ever, though I half expected it would be delayed, again, because of Magnus and his dithering or something the king would say. Was why he late?

The never-ending rain that April day meant, I hoped, that there'd be few visitors to the king to delay Magnus and few interruptions when we ate, which should be soon.

I walked around the darkening hall lighting candles as I went, my thoughts mostly on the celebrations we'd been planning for in two days' time, after a small ceremony at the tiny church nearby.

These thoughts circling inside me all that day were my best excuse for not being aware of what should have been blindingly obvious.

But I'd never felt like this before. Being in love was about lying to yourself, wasn't it?

A hammering on the door broke my blissful chain of thoughts. The hall guard, Bjorn, went quickly to see who it was.

"Mistress," he called to me from the door. "Someone needs your help."

I went to see who was there. Women in this city had been coming to me since soon after we'd arrived, ahead of a big mid-winter storm. They said our safe arrival, when others had perished at sea the same day, meant I was favoured by the Queen of Heaven. People here also liked that I'd escaped a battle-torn England and was with the man I loved, the son of a king. Everyone soon knew what had happened in London, the fighting we'd been involved in. I was fortunate that lots of people here needed healing.

The Rise of Synne

Getting paid for healing turned out to be lucrative.

At the half-open door stood a child of about ten summers, shivering. A long well-patched cloak reached down to his bare muddy feet. The cloak was splattered all the way to his elbows.

"Healer, please, please come, please," he said, holding his hands out, speaking the tongue of the city, that mix of words from near and far, which I'd come to understand, barely.

I looked along the muddy, stinking street. There appeared to be no one with him. Only a few distant figures could be seen, all hurrying away from us.

"What happened?" I asked, leaning down, putting a hand on his shoulder to steady him. I was wary. It wasn't unheard of for people to try a trick to lure you out of your house, but the gates of the city would be closing soon, and the sun was about to go down, so escape would not be easy for an outlaw.

"It's me ma," said the boy, in a frightened voice. "You helped her a few months ago. She needs you. The baby is gonna come."

I hesitated for only another moment. There was something familiar about him. I grabbed my cloak, wrapped it around myself, gave the boy one of our old cloaks to keep him warm and went with him. Magnus would likely get angry at me for giving another cloak away, but I didn't care. Bjorn followed us. Magnus had insisted I always bring a guard with me. I didn't bother arguing with that. There were plenty of other things for us to argue about.

We ended up at a long hovel near the river wall, where many families lived in what had once been a fish market.

The boy's mother was inside, lying flat out on a mound of skins near the hearth at the centre of the low-roofed hall. Thankfully, a fire was going. A pot of water and another of stew were bubbling over it. Around the woman a crowd had gathered, all of them other women. They parted as I approached.

I went down on my one knee beside the woman and spoke a prayer as I went down, a hymn I'd learnt from Ulf: *Humbly we honour heaven's guardian, humbly we honour the great maker, humbly Queen of Heaven we pray to you.* The words were for those watching as much as for the woman, but also to still my racing mind, for the task ahead.

The woman was on her back with her legs wide, breathing fast, puffing. I turned to the women around us, tried to speak as calmly as I could. "Bring hot water," I said, my words coming fast.

The Power of Synne is available now on Amazon at this link:
https://www.amazon.com/dp/B0CXMMFRFK

Printed in Great Britain
by Amazon